WORST CASE SCENARIO

by

CHENELL PARKER

WOR$T CA$E $CENARIO

Prologue

ears came to Stori's eyes, but she refused to let them fall. Her mother, Latoya or Lady, as she was known to most people, was one of the most selfish bitches that she'd ever had to encounter. Nothing that she said or did should have surprised Stori, but she always seemed to amaze her. Stori had been taking care of herself since she was tall enough to reach the stove. When Lady gave birth to Toi when Stori was eleven years old, she stepped in and started taking care of her too. Lady was always there financially, but that was about the only good thing that Stori could say about her. She was all out for self and she never tried to hide that fact.

"I know you love to cook, so maybe you can open up a restaurant or something. You already got your culinary certificate," Lady said.

"I'm only eighteen years old. I can't open up my own business. Besides, I just started cosmetology school two months ago," Stori reminded her.

"Okay, well, maybe Richard and I can buy you a hair salon," Lady said, speaking of her older, rich, white husband.

"How the fuck can I do anything while trying to raise a seven year old child?" Stori yelled angrily. She didn't care about being respectful at this point. Lady would never scold her on her use of language anyway. She never did.

She didn't even know how to feel about what her mother had just told her. Only two weeks after being married, Lady was telling her that she was leaving her seven year old sister in her care while she traveled from state to state with her husband. Richard was an entertainment lawyer, but he was nothing more than a fixer for most people. He was who rappers, producers and other famous people called on to fix the messes that they'd gotten themselves into. He made millions traveling all over the world to assist his wealthy clients. Lady met him at a concert in New York when he was there on business. He flew her out to wherever he was for months, while Stori stayed home and took care of her little sister. After a year of dating, Richard flew Lady out to Paris and married her in an intimate ceremony that her kids weren't even there to witness. She had just come back home after being on a two week long honeymoon and hit Stori with some more bullshit.

"You know that I don't trust her with just anybody Stori. Lorraine would be happy to do it, but the bitch already hates me," Lady noted.

"I wonder why," Stori said while rolling her eyes.

Lorraine was Stori and Toi's paternal grandmother, but she was more of a mother to them than Lady ever was. Lady and Stori's father, Shawn, were together for years until he got killed when Stori was nine years old. He was a dope boy and Lady was his kept bitch. She never had a job in her entire life that Stori could remember, but they always had the best of everything. Lady was beautiful with her honey colored skin and slanted eyes. Her lips were full and she had the cutest button nose. Her teeth were perfectly straight and she had her hair cut low and chic. Her beauty was only a small part of why she was desired by so many. Lady's shape was to die for and her body was all natural. She didn't have huge breasts but they were enough to grab at least a handful. Her waist was small and her ass stuck out just enough to complete the package. She hated Nicki Minaj but that's who a lot of people compared her looks to. Both of her girls looked exactly like her but their personalities weren't the same. Stori even had Lady's shape but that's where the similarities ended. She remembered how her father doted on her and Lady and always saying how beautiful they were. When he got killed, Lady was devastated but not more than Stori was. She was a daddy's girl and a part of her died with him.

About a year after he died, Lady started messing with Shawn's younger brother, Troy and that's when Toi came along. Stori always assumed that her uncle was coming around to make sure that they were okay after her father's death. He used to spoil her and Lady and they never had to ask for anything more than once. When Stori first saw them kissing, she was confused and they never tried to explain things to her. She just knew that her mother went from one brother to the next and she now had a baby sister. Her grandmother was livid as were the other members of the family. Troy got killed when Toi was only two years old and Lorraine has hated Lady ever since. She had two babies by her only two sons and that was the only good thing to ever come from her. Lorraine always said that she was happy that she didn't have any more sons left for Lady to sink her claws into. She only had her three daughters left and they hated Lady just as much as their mother did. Because their mother wanted to be a hoe, Stori and Toi were not only sisters, they were first cousins too.

Lady stayed on the arm of a dope boy and she was as hood as they came. When she met her suit wearing white husband, she became an entirely different person who Stori no longer knew. The hood still came out of her when she was upset, but she was prim and proper any other time. Lady's mother was a twin, but she was an only child. She had always been spoiled and selfish and not much had changed. Her two girls were really the only family that she had besides a few aunts and uncles that she rarely saw. Stori and Toi were close with their fathers' side of the family and they were all that they knew. Lady's mother died when Stori was five, so she didn't really remember her. From what she'd heard about her, Lady got her attitude the honest way.

"Richard travels too much and we can't do that with a small child," Lady said, pulling Stori away from her thoughts.

"Why can't he travel by himself while you stay home and raise your own child?" Stori asked.

She loved Toi more than anything in the world, but she was too young to take care of her all by herself. It was different when Lady was out of town because Stori knew that she would eventually be coming back. Now, Lady was talking about giving her full custody and she was scared to death. Richard didn't have any kids and he made it clear that he didn't want any. He treated Stori and Toi very well, but they weren't his kids. Throwing money at them was the only way that he knew how to show them love.

After only six months of dating, Richard had purchased Lady a beautiful five bedroom home with a huge finished basement. He was over sixty years old and he never stayed in one place for more than a few months at a time. Richard had never even owned a home because he traveled too much. The home that he got for Lady was where he stayed whenever he was in town. Since they were never there, Stori basically ran the house however she saw fit. She helped Toi with homework and made sure that she got to and from school every day. She cooked her breakfast and dinner each day and tucked her into bed every night. If she were being honest with herself, she'd been having full custody of her sister for years. The only difference was that now she would have the paperwork to back it up.

"We're married now Stori. He wants me with him when he travels and I want to be there for my husband," Lady said.

"Your husband? What about your children? We need you here more than he needs you on the road," Stori replied.

"I'll still be here for you, Stori. All you have to do is pick up the phone and let me know whatever you need. Haven't I always given you whatever you wanted? You were still in high school when you begged me to let you take culinary classes at night and I did. When you decided that you wanted to do hair, who was it that wrote the twelve thousand dollar check to make that happen? I'll never leave you hanging and you know that," Lady noted.

Lady had unlimited access to her husband's money and she had no problem spending it. Richard was borderline obsessed with her and he always let Lady have her way. Money didn't fix every problem, but Lady thought it did. She was speaking on material things, but Stori needed her to be there physically and emotionally. Still, no matter how she felt about it, she knew that she didn't really have a choice. They had a big family on their father's side, but she would never trust any of them to keep her baby sister. Toi was spoiled and Stori was the one who spoiled her. She couldn't imagine her baby sister being mistreated in any way. The thought alone made her physically sick. Toi used to cry every time Stori left the house and that broke her heart. She didn't even like to be left alone with their mother. It was crazy, but she barely even knew her.

"I don't know about this ma. I already have enough on my plate as it is. I just need more time to think about everything," Stori sighed after being quiet for a while.

Stori had always been fascinated with doing hair. Her grandmother used to let her practice on her hair and she had at least fifteen mannequin heads in her closet. Aside from that, cooking was something that she loved to do as well. Stori loved to create new recipes and put her own spin on older ones. Toi loved when she made her heart shaped pancakes with sprinkles on top. Everything that she did was to put a smile on her sister's face. It wasn't fair that Toi was being robbed of having her mother there to care for her like most girls her age.

"We need to finalize this within the next week Stori. Richard has a very important case coming up and we'll be in between California and New York for the next three or four months. One of his friends is a family attorney and he's agreed to do all the paperwork for us. The house is yours and we'll have the paperwork changed over to reflect that. Richard and I will still take care of the bills and cover whatever other expenses you and Toi have. I want to set up a bank account in your name, so we can deposit funds in there every month. I'll get Toi during her summer breaks and holidays to give you a break," Lady said, speaking as if Stori was Toi's mother.

There was no need for her to even reply. Lady's mind was made up and Stori really had no say so in the matter. She'd put a lot of thought into her decision and Stori had no choice but to go along with it. Her little sister was her heart, so the thought of someone else raising her wasn't an idea that she wanted to entertain.

"Just let me know when we have to meet up with the lawyer," Stori replied as she stood up from the sofa.

"How about we take Toi out to lunch and then we can do some shopping?" Lady said, happy that Stori was on board with her plan. She knew that she would be because she was so overprotective of Toi.

"How about you show yourself out and let me process the bullshit that you just dropped on me?" Stori said as she walked away and headed downstairs to the basement.

Stori put a sofa set, tv and radio in the basement for whenever she had company over. The space was huge and looked like a small studio apartment with a bathroom attached. She heard the front door when it opened and closed, letting her know that Lady had left. She never even bothered to say goodbye to Toi.

When Stori got to the basement, her boyfriend, Corey, was down there watching tv while her best friend, Kalani, helped Toi put a puzzle together. They were both already there when Lady came home and told her that they needed to talk. Kalani kept Toi occupied while Corey did nothing, just like always. Over a year of being with him and Stori was over it. Corey was a corner hustler who added nothing to her life or their relationship. He always wanted to stay the night at her house, but he never even offered to contribute anything. Stori didn't need his money, but it was just the principle. He always joked about her mother marrying a rich man, so maybe he didn't feel like he had to. He used to be very attentive in the beginning, but the nigga got too comfortable. Once Stori gave him her virginity, he stopped doing the things that he used to do before. Like now, Stori was standing there with tears in her eyes and he didn't even bother to ask if she was okay. Kalani noticed immediately. She jumped up from her place on the floor to make sure her girl was okay.

"What's wrong Stori?" Kalani asked as she looked into her best friend's eyes.

Instead of replying, Stori burst out in tears as realization set in. She didn't have any kids, but she was about to be a full time guardian to a seven year old. She should have been out there enjoying life, but her mother had other plans. Lady was thirty-eight years old and trying to live life as if she didn't have any responsibilities at home.

"What happened boo?" Kalani asked as she led her friend to the sofa and sat down right next to her. Toi stopped doing her puzzle and sat on her big sister's lap.

"Don't cry Stori. It's okay," Toi said as she wiped her eyes. When her baby sister kissed her cheek, it seemed as if everything really was okay. Toi was so sweet and innocent and she loved Stori just as much as she loved her. She was so smart and wise beyond her seven years.

"As long as you're around, it's always okay." Stori smiled as she hugged her.

"Yep, because I'm your best friend, huh?" Toi asked.

"Excuse me," Kalani said as she looked at Toi like she was offended.

"Yes, you and Kalani are my two best friends," Stori said as she laughed.

When Toi got up to finish her puzzle, Stori took a few minutes to whisper to her friend about what was going on. Kalani was just as upset as she was, but she would always be there for her girl.

"We got this friend. You know I'll do whatever I can to help. I'll babysit whenever you need me to and you know that my mama will too. We love Toi just as much as you do," Kalani assured her.

"Thanks friend. You know I appreciate you more than anything," Stori said as she wiped a few stray tears from her eyes.

After a while, she felt better about the entire situation. As she watched Toi on the floor putting her puzzle together, she realized that things weren't all that bad. Not only did she have help from Kalani, but she had her grandmother, aunties and a few cousins who loved her baby sister too. She might not have given birth to her, but Toi was still her baby.

"What you cooking today?" Corey asked as he finally tore his gaze away from the tv screen.

Stori looked over at him with disgust written all over her pretty face. She was a mess just a few minutes ago and he never even bothered to see what was wrong. Even her seven year old sister tried to comfort her and her own boyfriend didn't give a damn. Stori saw the direction that their relationship was heading and she had to put a stop to it now. If Lady showed her nothing else, she showed her how a man was supposed to take care of his woman. Stori could just see Corey trying to lay up on her while he did whatever he wanted to do with his money. She didn't care if Richard did pay all the bills, he wasn't going to reap the benefits. He had her fucked up and she was over it. She didn't even love him, so there was nothing to hold on to anymore. The idea of having a boyfriend excited her more than actually having one.

"You need to leave," Stori said, shocking Kalani and Corey with her words.

"For what? I didn't even do shit," Corey replied.

"That's the whole problem nigga. You never do shit. Buying me shoes and something to eat every now and then ain't gon' cut it. I got a baby and bills now and I don't need no dead weight," Stori snapped angrily.

"Come on Toi. Let's go upstairs and get something to snack on," Kalani said as she grabbed Toi's hand and led her upstairs to the kitchen so that Stori could talk freely.

"Why would you even come at me like that in front of your friend? I ain't no bum ass nigga. If you needed money, all you had to do was ask," Corey fumed. He didn't have it like that, but he would make something shake for Stori.

"I shouldn't have to ask you for shit. You're here more than you're at your own house. Common sense would tell you to offer your assistance. As of today, my mama no longer lives here. This house belongs to me and Toi now and I refuse to have a nigga laying up on me," Stori pointed out.

Hearing her say that had Corey both happy and scared. Stori's house was nice as hell and he'd basically moved in without asking. Lady and her husband paid all the bills, so he got comfortable. They were never home and Lady didn't care who Stori let in there. Corey sold a little weed, but it wasn't enough for him to be paying bills. Shoes, clothes and a nice dinner every now and again was about all that he could afford to do for her. He didn't want his financial status to be the deciding factor in their relationship though. Stori was a hot commodity and all of his friends wanted her. He felt privileged to be the one that she chose and he wasn't trying to end things. Stori was beautiful and had a shape that was even better than her mother's. Niggas used to line up trying to get at Lady and Stori had them feeling the same way.

"Just give me a chance to get my finances straight Stori. You act like I'm pushing some serious weight. I got you just as soon as my money gets right," Corey promised.

"Nah nigga, I'm good on you. You had a whole year if you really wanted to do anything. I can't even get mad because I let you get too comfortable. I'm up in here fucking you and making sure you got a hot meal like that's my responsibility. I gave you husband privileges when you barely act like my boyfriend. Come get your stuff and be on your way," Stori said as she stood up and headed for the stairs.

Corey was in panic mode, but he tried to play it cool. He'd had lots of girlfriends in his twenty years, but none of them were like Stori. She was the complete package. Besides her looks and shape, she dressed nice and could cook her ass off. She was young, but she was about her business. Sex with her was amazing and he wasn't ready to give that up. Even though he was her first, Stori was a fast learner. She had him hooked and he wasn't opposed to begging if he had to.

"Don't be like that Stori. Nigga not asking you to wait for another year. Just give me a few months to get straight," Corey begged. He grabbed her arm and pulled her closer to him. He didn't foresee her breaking up with him, but he was willing to fight for what he wanted.

"Let me go Corey. I have a lot going on right now and I don't need the added stress. I was bawling my eyes out a minute ago and you never even cared enough to ask why. All you cared about was what I was cooking. You're selfish and inconsiderate. Those are two traits that I despise because my mother is the exact same way. I let shit slide for too long, but I'm at end of my rope now. I don't have it in me to try and save a dead relationship," Stori said.

"Dead? Since when? Shit was all good before your moms got here," Corey argued.

"Open your eyes Corey. Shit hasn't been all good with us in months. When is the last time you saw me genuinely smile if Toi wasn't around? I've been avoiding this conversation for months, hoping that things would get better. I tried throwing you hints that went completely over your head. I have enough to deal with already and I don't need any added stress. Just get your stuff and leave," Stori said with finality.

"I'm not a mind reader Stori. How do you expect me to know when something is wrong with you?" Corey questioned.

"It wouldn't have hurt you to ask," Stori pointed out.

"Okay, I'm asking. What happened?" Corey questioned.

"Bye Corey," Stori said with a sarcastic chuckle.

"Man, fuck! What else do you want me to say? You're having a bad day and you want a nigga to kiss your ass. I don't have time for this dumb shit!" Corey yelled.

"Neither do I. That's why I want you to go," Stori replied while walking away.

"Fuck you, Stori. Straight like that," Corey snapped angrily.

14

"Thanks for letting me know that I made the right decision," Stori said as she walked up the stairs.

Before she got too far, Corey pulled her by her hair and threw her to the floor. He was hurt, angry and a mixture of other emotions that he couldn't identify. Stori was treating him like a lame and that bruised his ego. Before he had a chance to walk up to her, she was up on her feet in a flash. Stori ran to the sofa and reached underneath it. When she pulled out a silver gun and pointed it at him, Corey's eyes nearly popped out of his head.

"I dare you to put your hands on me again muthafucker," Stori sneered.

Lady taught her a few bad habits and keeping guns stashed around the house was one of them. Being with so many dope boys had Lady paranoid and she had Stori the same way.

"Chill out Stori. My bad for doing that. I was acting off of emotions," Corey said as he raised his hands in surrender.

"Yeah and so am I," Stori replied with a murderous gleam in her eyes.

Corey was no fool. He'd robbed a few niggas with his cousins, but he wasn't as hood as he pretended to be. Stori looked like she was about that life and he didn't want her to make an example out of him. She was Lady's daughter, so there was no telling what she'd do. He walked up the stairs to the house and Stori followed right behind him. She kept the gun at her side as he packed up all of his belongings and left her house. She was happy that Kalani had Toi occupied in the kitchen because she didn't want her little sister to see what was going on.

"Look Stori, we made popcorn balls," Toi said excitedly when her sister came back into the kitchen.

"Really Kalani," Stori laughed as she discreetly slipped the gun into an empty drawer.

"What? She wanted popcorn balls and this was the only thing that I could think of." Kalani shrugged. Toi was making a mess with the microwaved popcorn, candy and syrup that Kalani had given her.

"She's gonna be jumping around all night with all that sugar in her system," Stori replied.

"Well, I'm staying over tonight, so I'll be up with her. I can tell that my best friend needs me." Kalani smiled as she bumped hips with Stori.

"Girl, you must be trying to knock me down with those child bearing hips," Stori laughed.

Kalani was a thick size ten with sharp, wide hips. Her chocolate skin was flawless and her smile could light up the darkest room. She and Stori had been best friends since seventh grade. Some girls were trying to jump Kalani in the bathroom of their private school, but Stori wasn't having it. It was just the two of them, but they took down four girls like it was nothing. They exchanged numbers after they were suspended for fighting and had been inseparable ever since. Kalani still lived at home with her mother, but she was always at Stori's house. She was an only child and Stori was like the sister that she never had. She and Stori graduated together, but they both bypassed going to college. Stori got her certification for culinary arts, but she didn't want to be a cook. Doing hair was really her passion so that's what she wanted to do. Kalani was trying to find a job, but she hadn't had any luck yet. She was thinking about going to a trade school to become a dental assistant. If she didn't find a job soon, that's exactly what she planned to do.

"Girl, these hips open a lot of doors," Kalani laughed as she bumped her again.

"I know they do. What's for dinner tonight Toi?" Stori asked her baby sister.

"Um, let's eat chicken and fries!" Toi yelled excitedly.

"Okay, chicken and fries it is." Stori smiled.

Toi had been picking out their daily meals ever since she got old enough to talk. Sometimes Stori had to improvise, but she let her have her way most times. After getting Toi washed up, Stori turned on a movie for her to watch as she prepped their dinner. She and Kalani enjoyed a bottle of Lady's expensive wine as they talked and tried to come up with a solid game plan.

When the alarm beeped, Stori groaned inwardly but she didn't make a move to get up. She hit the snooze button and laid there a little while longer. She always set her alarm for a few minutes earlier than she actually needed to be up. She hated having to jump right out of bed and she wanted to lay there and relax first. As usual, she had a busy day ahead of her. It was Saturday and she had a lot of heads to do. Toi was fourteen years old now and she helped Stori out a lot. Toi shampooed hair, washed towels and kept the fridge filled with drinks for the customers. She didn't need the money, but Stori paid her for helping out on Friday nights and all day Saturday. Lady sent them a nice bit of cash every month, but they were good. Stori had made a name for herself and she had steady clientele. She had to turn people away sometimes because she was too busy. She didn't like to have her customers in the shop all day and she liked to be done early. Although she worked from home, she still liked to be professional and on time. A few months after she got custody of Toi, Richard and Lady had the huge garage remodeled and turned into a hair salon. It was beautiful and Richard spared no expense. He even had a door put up so that her clients didn't have to come into her house. They could enter and exit right from the shop. He had another bathroom added on and it looked better than most commercial businesses. Richard always joked and called them Toy Story like the movie and that's exactly what Stori named her shop. The only difference was that she spelled it like their names instead. It had been seven years since Lady left Toi in her care and they were doing great. Toi was an honor student and she never gave Stori any trouble. She was a cheerleader at school and Stori let her be a teenager. Toi had sleepovers and she did what most girls her age did. Lady came to visit every now and then, but she made sure to call them almost every day.

"I'm too damn tired," Stori said as she sat up and yawned.

When a pair of strong arms pulled her back, she looked behind her and locked eyes with her husband of two years, Gavin. Stori met Gavin three years ago when she went to a hair show in Atlanta. Gavin was a barber and he was there with some of his friends. As handsome as he was, Stori wasn't interested at first. He wouldn't take no for an answer and he damn near followed Stori around the entire day until she agreed to go out with him. The one date turned into several others and they became a couple after two months. When Stori introduced him to Toi, they hit it off immediately and she felt good about being with him. When he asked her to marry him, she was skeptical because she wasn't in love with him. She told him how she felt and he was okay with it. He told her that it would happen over time and she foolishly took his hand in marriage.

Sadly, after being married for two years, Stori still wasn't in love with her husband. Gavin was good to her and Toi and that's what helped to make the decision for her. She didn't need his money, but he paid all the bills and gave her and Toi whatever they wanted. Gavin had smooth cocoa colored skin with a nice toned body. He had dreads when they first met, but he rocked a curly mohawk now. He catered to her and Toi and her baby sister adored him. Most of their chemistry was in the bedroom and Gavin seemed to never get enough.

"You on your period?" Gavin asked as he pulled her body closer to his and kissed her neck.

"Yep. You know that's the only time I wear clothes to bed," Stori replied.

"I kind of figured that," Gavin replied solemnly.

Gavin wanted kids more than anything in the world. He and Stori had been trying for the past six months, but they hadn't had any luck yet. They even went to a fertility specialist, but they were both healthy. Maybe it just wasn't their time, but Gavin wasn't trying to hear that.

"Don't start stressing about that Gavin. It'll happen when it happens," Stori said as she sat up and scooted to the edge of the bed.

Gavin licked his lips in appreciation when his wife got up and stretched. Stori was beautiful and sexy as fuck. Gavin still couldn't believe that he was married to someone like her. He was confident in the eyes of others, but he used to suffer with self-esteem issues when he was growing up. Gavin's parents always told him that he tried too hard to be liked, but he couldn't help it. Growing up as an only child was lonely and he started clinging to his friends. He wasn't street smart, but he was good at pretending. He always wanted to hang out with the popular kids in hopes that he would one day be popular too. Even now, the barber shop where he worked was the place to be. The place was huge and there were fifteen barbers on staff. They used to have a hair salon in the rear, but the owner said that it was too much work to keep up. Cuttin' Up was one of the hottest barber shops in New Orleans and it was almost impossible to get hired. Gavin's boy got him on over there and that wasn't easy to do. You had to be the best of the best for the owner to even consider you. At thirty years old, Gavin finally felt like he was a part of the in crowd. He had a beautiful wife that turned heads everywhere she went and life couldn't get any better than that. Well, unless Stori gave him a baby.

"Put some clothes on. Nas is here," Gavin said.

"Again? The hell did he do this time?" Stori asked.

"Same shit as always. Nigga be out there playing with them hoes, knowing that he got a wife at home. Milan put his ass out again and I had to pick him up. He was too damn drunk to even drive," Gavin laughed.

Naseem was Gavin's best friend. He was also a barber who Gavin met in cosmetology school. He and his identical twin brother, Kareem, owned a strip club and they were always into some shit. Nas and Gavin worked at the same barber shop, but Nas was into all kinds of illegal activities too. His brother mostly ran the strip club because Nas' wife hated for him to be there. Milan used to be a stripper, but she didn't dance anymore. She knew all too well how thirsty the dancers were because she was just as bad at one time. Her sister, Misty, still stripped at the club and Toi sometimes watched her six month old daughter, Summer. Stori lost count of how many times she woke up to see her husband's friend camped out in one of their spare bedrooms. He even had Toi's number and she opened the door for him sometimes if they weren't home. Nas was cool though and so was his brother.

"Him and Remo just need to get another apartment together," Stori said, calling Kareem by his nickname.

Remo had dreads that Stori kept maintained. He was always coming to get his hair retwisted and styled, which was how he met Kalani two years ago. For a while, Kalani brushed him off, but Remo was persistent. She had a boyfriend at the time, but Remo didn't seem to care. The two of them ended up dating exclusively and buying a house together. Since he had a record that was a mile long, Kalani had to get the house in her name. She even quit her job as a dental assistant and started working as a bartender at their club. She made more in tips and pay every week than she made at the dental office for the entire month. Her money was flowing nicely, but the same couldn't be said about her relationship. Since Remo couldn't keep his dick in his pants, Kalani broke up with him but he wasn't having it. He moved out of the house, but he still paid all the bills. He swore that Kalani was his future wife and he refused to let her move on. He had a different bitch every month, but he was out for blood if she tried to be with someone else. He wanted Kalani to wait on him to settle down, but he didn't give her the same respect. Remo wanted to fight any man who even looked at her too hard and that drove Kalani crazy.

"Them niggas can't get nothing in their names. I don't even know how they got that strip club," Gavin replied.

Nas was his boy, but Remo didn't really fuck with Gavin for some reason. They all started out in cosmetology school together, but Remo got locked up after only being there for two months. Nas and Gavin got close during that time and Remo didn't seem to like that very much. He let Gavin know that he didn't like him, so he never even bothered to be in his company.

"I'm going to get breakfast started," Stori said once she did her morning hygiene and put on some decent clothes.

Gavin got up and headed into the bathroom to get ready for work. Stori went downstairs to the kitchen and started getting things out of the fridge. She was used to making breakfast for four because Nas' visits were becoming more frequent. He was at their house at least three times a week, but Stori didn't mind.

Once she got everything started, Gavin came downstairs dressed in jeans and his barber's smock. He stood behind Stori and wrapped his arms around her waist as she cooked. Gavin didn't refer to many things as perfect, but that's exactly what he considered his wife to be. She boosted up his self-esteem in a major way and Gavin was borderline arrogant now. He was never that way at home, but he was an entirely different person when he wasn't in Stori's presence.

"Good morning," Toi said as she came waltzing into the kitchen.

"Hey, my Stanka. How did you sleep?" Stori asked as she moved away from Gavin and kissed her sister on the cheek.

"I slept good. Mommy just called me," Toi announced.

"What did she want?" Stori asked.

"She asked if we needed anything and I told her no. She keeps asking when I'm coming to spend the summer with her but I don't want to," Toi said.

"And you don't have to," Stori replied.

"I told her that she had to ask you, so tell her no when she calls," Toi begged.

"You already know I will," Stori assured her, making Toi smile.

"Why don't you want to go spend some time with your mama?" Gavin asked as he looked at Toi.

"Because she doesn't have to. Lady don't even stay in the same place for too long. She knows not to play with me when it comes to Toi," Stori answered on her sister's behalf.

"Calm down baby. I was just asking," Gavin laughed.

"I'll go visit her for a few days, but I don't think I can do the whole summer," Toi said.

"Depending on where she is, you might actually like it," Gavin replied.

"I don't know, maybe." Toi shrugged.

"What's for dinner tonight Toi?" Stori asked her.

"Can we do stuffed shrimp and pasta again? We haven't had that in a while," Toi said.

"You got it my love." Stori smiled, as Gavin tried not to show his annoyance.

After three years of being together and being married for two, Stori had yet to ask him what he wanted for dinner. Even when he confronted her with his feelings, nothing ever changed. She claimed that she and Toi had been doing that for years, but he didn't care. He was in the picture now and that should have changed. He was her husband and the only time he got a say was when Toi wasn't home. The shit annoyed the fuck out of him, but he would never say that to Stori. She would go to war with her own mother behind Toi, so he didn't stand a chance. Toi was a sweet little girl, but Stori had her too damn spoiled. Gavin hated to feel like he was in competition for his wife's affection, but that's exactly what it seemed like.

"I washed and folded all the towels that we used last night. I made you a list too because you need some more supplies," Toi spoke up.

"Aww, thank you, Stanka. My baby is too sweet," Stori cooed as she repeatedly kissed Toi's face, making her blush.

"Stop treating that damn girl like a baby. She's fourteen years old," Gavin fussed.

"I don't give a damn if she was twenty-four. She's my baby and she always will be," Stori said, right as Nas walked into the kitchen.

"Good morning," he spoke in his deep, raspy voice. He looked like he was hungover and he was still wearing his clothes from the day before.

"Hey Nas. I didn't know that you were here." Toi smiled brightly.

She liked Nas and Remo because they kept her laughing. They were clowns when they got together and it was comical to see them in action. Remo always came to the shop to get his hair washed and Toi looked forward to it.

"What's up pretty girl?" Nas said as he pinched Toi's cheek.

"Boy, I don't know how you plan to cut nobody's hair today. You look a hot ass mess," Stori laughed.

"I feel like a hot ass mess too. You got some coffee Stori?" he asked with a yawn.

"Yeah, I'll make you a cup. Do you want breakfast too?" Stori asked.

"I want it all. I'm hungry and tired as fuck," Nas replied.

Stori brewed him a cup of coffee before she finished cooking their breakfast. Once she was done, she fixed everybody a plate and cleaned up her kitchen. Nas smirked when he saw Gavin following her around like a little puppy. That nigga was obsessed with his wife and Stori couldn't even breathe without him sharing her oxygen. Gavin was lame as fuck, but Nas tolerated him. Gavin was the one who used to take all of his tests when they were in cosmetology school. Nas was a natural at cutting hair, but school was never his thing. He knew that he couldn't get his license without passing, so that's where Gavin came in. Nas had a gift of pointing out the weakest link amongst the bunch. As soon as Gavin walked into class and introduced himself, Nas knew that he'd hit the jackpot. Remo wanted no parts of him, but Nas was always the friendlier of the two. When Remo went to jail, Nas finished the program and got his cosmetology license

Unfortunately, he couldn't get rid of Gavin after that. He was like a groupie and wanted to do everything that Nas did. It was annoying as fuck and Nas tried to distance himself as much as he could. He showed his appreciation by getting Gavin a job at one of the hottest barber shops in New Orleans, but that obviously wasn't enough. Gavin considered Nas to be his best friend and that didn't go over too well with Remo. It was weird to Nas how a grown ass man always copied another man. Gavin had dreads for a long time until he saw Nas start to grow his hair out for a mohawk. Nas and Remo had a nice grain of hair like their mother. When Nas got his curly mohawk colored blonde at the top, Gavin was trying to mimic him. He probably would have if Stori wouldn't have stopped him. She was the one who colored Nas' hair and she refused to do her husband's. He wanted his hair curly too, but he had to use chemicals to make it happen.

Besides bragging about his wife and money, Gavin wasn't all that bad though. Nas was a closed book to most people, so Gavin didn't know a damn thing about him. Besides going to school and working together, he didn't need to know anything else. Nas only trusted one person and that was the nigga who he came into the world with. Remo hated Gavin, but Nas knew that it was just a little jealously. Since day one, it had always been the two of them. The thought of having someone trying to come in between their bond angered him. Nas assured his twin that Gavin was nothing more than an associate. The only real friend he'd ever had was his brother.

"You ready to get to work Toi? We got a busy day ahead of us," Stori said once her kitchen was nice and clean.

"I'm always ready to have fun," Toi replied, right as her phone rang. She loved to interact with the clients in the shop and their gossip and friendly banter kept her entertained.

"Who is that calling you this early?" Stori asked.

"Hey Misty," Toi said when she answered for Nas' sister-in-law.

"Tell her to unlock the door, so I can come take a shower and get ready for work," Nas said when he heard Toi call Misty's name. His sister-in-law and her baby lived with him and his wife and he needed her to let him inside.

"Misty wants to know if I can babysit tonight. She said that she'll pick me up and bring me back home in the morning," Toi said while looking at Stori.

"Yeah, that's fine," Stori replied, right before Toi repeated what she and Nas said to Misty.

"Okay, I have to check Stori's appointment book," Toi said as she got up and headed downstairs to the shop. Stori did Misty and Milan's hair too and Toi kept up with most of the appointments.

"You ready to get up out of here bruh?" Gavin asked while looking at Nas. They were over an hour early for work, but he needed to drop Nas off home.

"Yeah, I'm ready," Nas replied as he stood up and stretched.

"Make sure you keep your phone close by. I hate it when I call and you don't answer," Gavin said as he wrapped his arms around Stori's waist.

"It don't matter if the phone is close by or not. If I'm busy, I can't answer it. You know I don't like to keep my clients in the shop too long," Stori replied.

"Put your ear plugs in or something. I be needing to hear your voice sometimes. I love you, baby, and make sure you come lock the door. You be all the way in the basement and the door be unlocked," Gavin said as he kissed her lips and walked away.

"Pussy whipped ass nigga," Nas joked once they walked out of the house.

"Man, you just don't know. I wish I could put that shit in a bottle and sell it. Pussy so good I be wanting to cry sometimes. I'm mad as fuck that she's on her period right now," Gavin replied.

Nas never understood niggas like him. There was no way in hell that he would tell another nigga about how good his wife's pussy was. Niggas were grimy as fuck and that was a rookie mistake. Gavin was always bragging on Stori and niggas were listening. Some of the same dudes who sat in his barber chair were lusting after his wife. They knew he was lame and some of them had even tried to get at her. He should have been happy that Stori wasn't a hoe. A lot of men wanted her just because of the shit that her husband said about her. Milan was an ex-stripper, but Nas still wouldn't put her on blast like that. Stori was bad as fuck, but she wasn't out there being a hoe like some other woman probably would have been. The way Gavin talked about her all the time had a lot of niggas curious though.

"I think it's real fucked up that y'all still got Toi babysitting Summer," Nas spoke up as Gavin neared his house.

"Who is y'all? I don't have shit to do with that," Gavin replied.

"You need to man the fuck up and say something nigga. I know I do some fucked up shit, but that's foul on a whole new level," Nas said while shaking his head.

Gavin didn't even have a reply, but he knew that his boy was right. Shit was too far gone for him to intervene now though. Toi had been babysitting Misty's daughter, Summer, for three months now, if she couldn't find anyone else to do it. Milan was supposed to be helping out, but she was too busy chasing behind Nas.

When they pulled up to the house, Gavin got out of the car and followed Nas inside. Milan was sitting on the sofa with her legs tucked underneath her. She frowned when Nas walked in, but he didn't bother saying anything to her. He went straight down the hall to their bedroom and she jumped up and followed right behind him. Gavin kept going until he came to the second room at the end of the hall. When he opened the door, Misty was standing there trying to comfort Summer, who was crying.

"Hey baby." She smiled as she walked up to Gavin and gave him a kiss. Gavin loved when she called him baby because Stori never did. She wasn't into all the pet names unless she was talking to Toi.

"What's up? Why is my baby crying?" Gavin asked as he took Summer out of her arms.

"She's hungry. I need to go make her a bottle. She needs more diapers and wipes too," Misty replied.

"I'll get her some later today or tomorrow," Gavin said as he rubbed Summer's back lovingly.

Stori would die if she ever found out about his little secret and he'd die before he let her. Shit was crazy, but having a baby on his wife was not something that he was proud of. He didn't even know that he was the father until the baby was born. Granted, he did have sex with Misty a few times before she got pregnant, but he wasn't the only one. Misty had fucked with Remo and another nigga around the same time. When she said that she was pregnant, Remo wanted her to get rid of it. Misty wanted to keep her baby, but she couldn't dance while she was pregnant. She ended up disappearing for a while until the baby was born. Since their mother lived in Beaumont, she stayed with her for a while and had her daughter in Texas. She came back when the baby was two weeks old and asked all three men for a blood test. Gavin was the unlucky one and he now had a six month old daughter.

Nas let Misty come back to the club, but Gavin still helped out with their daughter. Misty hated that her baby was a secret, but she just went with the flow. Gavin was an only child but not even his parents knew about Summer. He would have done anything in his power to keep from Stori knowing the truth. It was bad enough that Milan and Misty went to his wife to get their hair done, but Toi had taken a liking to the baby. Every time Misty would come to the salon, she would take Summer to her room and keep her the entire time. After a while, Misty started asking Toi to babysit. Sometimes, Summer would come to their house or Toi would go to theirs. Nas always told him that he was foul for letting it happen and Gavin couldn't even disagree.

"We need to be looking for another babysitter too. Shit is too close to home for Toi to keep doing it," Gavin said when Misty handed him a warm bottle to feed their daughter.

"I've been looking Gavin, but I don't trust just anybody with my baby. She loves Toi and Toi loves her too. She takes better care of Summer than Milan does. That bitch is home every day and I don't trust her with her own niece," Misty replied.

Misty and Milan had a love/hate relationship. They were originally from Texas, but the two sisters visited New Orleans one year for Mardi Gras and fell in love. They decided to move there temporarily to see if they liked it and they did. They both ended up working at the club until Misty got pregnant. She went back home and used her savings to survive. She was broke after she had her baby, but it was worth it.

Once she decided to move back to New Orleans, Milan promised to help out with Summer since she no longer had a job. She even agreed to let her sister and niece move in with her. Misty left her daughter with Milan once and she never made that mistake again. Summer's diaper looked like it hadn't been changed in hours and she was screaming to the top of her lungs when Misty got home. Milan was knocked out and never even bothered to wake up and see about her. It was sad that Misty trusted a fourteen year old with her daughter more than her own sister. Milan wanted a baby so bad, but she wasn't ready. She only wanted a child to keep Nas around, but she wasn't mother material.

"Well, look harder. I can't have this shit blow up in my face and my wife find out about it," Gavin said.

"Maybe if your parents knew about her, I wouldn't have to look so hard. You know that I don't have any family here. Everything ain't always about your wife. I didn't lay down and fuck myself. Where was your loyalty to her when you got me pregnant?" Misty inquired.

"Fuck all that dumb shit Misty. Stop acting like I wasn't one of three possible fathers. My luck just wasn't as good as the other two," Gavin said.

"Wow. So, being her father is bad luck?" Misty questioned.

"Don't act like I'm some deadbeat ass nigga that's out here doing my daughter dirty. I take care of my responsibility. When the test proved that she was mine, we agreed to keep everything under wraps. I fucked up, but you and everybody else know how I feel about my wife. Don't even try to start getting in your feelings," Gavin said as he laid his now sleeping daughter down in her bed.

"I'm not getting in my feelings about nothing. I'm just telling you that it's not easy to find a reliable babysitter." Misty shrugged.

"Maybe you should think about getting a day job and I can pay for her to go to nursery," Gavin suggested.

"Where am I gonna find a day job that pays as much as the club? I can't use my real estate license here. It's only good in Texas. I'm just starting to build my savings up again. I don't want to stay with Milan forever. I'm used to having my own place. You take care of Summer, but you don't do shit for me," Misty reminded him.

"You're not my responsibility. Now, if you're trying to make some extra cash before you go to the club, I got you," Gavin said as he slipped his hand underneath her dress.

"Stori must be on her period. That's the only time you come over here trying to fuck me," Misty replied while rolling her eyes.

"Stop acting like you don't want it," Gavin said as he dropped his jeans and got a condom from her drawer.

He'd learned his lesson from before and he'd never hit Misty raw again. Sex with her was okay, but it would have to do until Stori got right. Misty wasn't nearly as tight as Stori and she was never as wet. Still, he put the condom on and slid inside of her. He only had a few minutes to spare before he had to get to work, so he was leaving as soon as he was done.

Misty held on to the dresser as Gavin pumped into her from behind. Although she cared for Gavin, he wasn't who she really wanted. Remo was that nigga and Misty spent nine months praying that he was Summer's father. It was crazy because she even named her daughter after his deceased mother. Remo was furious when she got pregnant and he wanted her to get rid of it. Misty had been with him way more than she was with Gavin and the other man and she just knew in her heart that she was having his baby. Instead of getting rid of it, she hid out by her mother until she had her baby. There was no way in hell that Remo would have let her have it had she stayed in New Orleans. When she came back to town, Misty got right to work and demanded a blood test from all three men that she was with. She was pissed when she found out that Remo wasn't the father, but Gavin was her second choice. Besides being borderline obsessed with his wife, he wasn't so bad.

Gavin was handsome in his own right, but Remo was a fucking god. He stood well over six feet tall with a body that seemed to be hand crafted by the most high. His warm beige skin tone, kissable lips and exotic bedroom eyes made up the perfect face. He resembled a thugged out version of Odell Beckham with dreads. Misty was sometimes salty that her baby sister was walking around with an identical version of him. Nas was every bit of Remo, minus the hair. He actually wore his mohawk similar to the football player that he and his brother resembled. He was more laid back than his twin but he was a piece of work too. Misty wasn't a grimy bitch, at least not to her family. If she was, she would have fucked her sister's husband a long time ago. The way Milan talked made it seem like Nas was the shit in the bedroom. His twin brother was too, so she knew what had her sister so hooked.

Once he found out that Misty's baby wasn't his, Remo refused to even touch her again. He really didn't want her to come back to the club but Nas intervened on her behalf. It was all about business with him and she was one of their top money makers. She hated to see how gone Remo was over Kalani, but he was crazy in love with that bitch. Misty often wondered what she had done to make him feel that way but she would probably never know. She was thankful that Gavin wasn't a deadbeat but she still hated how things played out. No one knew that he was the father of her child and he was determined to keep it that way.

30

Misty always thought that she would be in a relationship with the father of her child and, sometimes, she really wanted to be. Unfortunately, all she got was Gavin's body because Stori already had his heart.

"At least hear a nigga out before you say no." Nas frowned as he looked at his older brother, Jarvis.

At forty-four years old, Jarvis was the closest thing that Nas and Remo had to a father. Their parents were killed when they were ten and Jarvis was twenty-six. Jarvis was married with a baby on the way at the time, but he and his wife didn't even think twice before they took the twins in and raised them.

"I heard everything that y'all said, but I can't do it bruh. I already got y'all strip club and rental properties in my name. I don't even make that much money for all that shit. Y'all gon' have the feds looking at me like I'm doing something illegal," Jarvis argued.

He was a local truck driver for Budweiser and his wife was a paralegal. Together, they made a pretty decent living and they had three teenage daughters. It was like he had five kids because he had been raising his two younger brothers since they were ten and they were now twenty-eight. Jarvis was devastated when their parents were gunned down in their home. His grandparents offered to take the twins in, but he couldn't even do that to them. Nas and Remo were bad as fuck and nobody could handle them like their parents could. They were identical and it was hard for anyone to tell them apart. Even Jarvis had trouble figuring out which one he was talking to most times. The twins both had a birthmark on the inside of their thigh on opposite sides. They used to swear that Jarvis was trying to look at their dicks but that was the only way that he knew how to tell them apart. He was happy as hell when they got older and Remo started growing his dreads. That made his life and the lives of others so much easier.

Their parents left them a nice lump sum of money in the bank and with their life insurance policies. Jarvis was fair and he divided everything up three ways. He set it up so that the twins would be able to have access to their money when they turned twenty-one. He wanted them to invest their money and do something positive with it. Knowing how they were, Jarvis knew that he was expecting too much. He wasn't even surprised when the twins put their money together and got some dope instead. That was the beginning of the end from there. They stayed in some shit and they both had a rap sheet that was longer than Chinese arithmetic.

When they finally got their money up the way they wanted it, they decided to open up a strip club, but that didn't stop them from selling dope. Nas got the hookup with a pharmacy and they sold prescription drugs and anything else that they could get their hands on. They had people selling the shit right out of their club and they made a killing. With more money came more problems and the twins had lots of them. Everything they did was extreme and they fed off each other's bad habits.

Unfortunately, they couldn't get anything in their own names. Everything that they owned was in Jarvis and his wife's names. Not only did they have a lengthy criminal record, but Remo didn't have any legal income besides the club and rental property. Nas finished cosmetology school, but Remo never went back. Nas wanted to open up his own barber shop but he didn't even have credit. He ended up working in a shop that belonged to one of their grandfather's old acquaintances. Mr. Herbert had been their grandfather's best friend up until the day he died seven years ago. They suspected that he was messing with their grandmother now, but they always denied it.

"Your scary ass." Remo frowned, pulling Jarvis away from his thoughts. He needed more legal income and Jarvis was acting like a bitch.

"Nigga, fuck what you saying. Y'all need to stop chasing hoes and handle y'all business. Get your records expunged and build up your credit. I'm not putting nothing else in my name for y'all and neither is Latrice," Jarvis said, speaking of his wife.

The twins had been to jail several times but they were never convicted of anything. Most times they were locked up, waiting to go to court. None of the charges ever stuck and they never did any real time. They both had been arrested on murder charges, but the witnesses always mysteriously disappeared. Jarvis had been telling them to hire a lawyer to get their records cleaned but they never took his advice. His wife worked with lawyers every day and all she had to do was say the word. Both their cars and their motorcycles were in his wife's name and Jarvis was fed up.

"I told you not to ask this nigga," Nas replied.

"Yeah and you told him right. You got a wife, nigga. Ask her to do the shit for you," Jarvis said while pointing to Nas. They were trying to open a hookah bar, but Jarvis wasn't bending. He already had their strip club and four rental properties in his name for them. He had to draw the line somewhere.

"Fuck no. I don't want that bitch name on nothing that belongs to me," Remo fussed.

"Shit, me either. I don't trust her ass," Nas said, agreeing with his brother.

"The fuck you married her for then?" Jarvis asked.

"Because the bitch asked me to. Nigga, I was in jail. It ain't like I had shit else to do." Nas shrugged.

He had only been married to Milan for a little over a year, but there was nothing blissful about it. He went to jail on a drug charge and ended up doing six months before the charges were dropped. He only stayed in there that long because he was going back and forth to court. He and Milan were kicking it before he got locked up and she used to come visit him every week. Nas spit the usual bullshit and promised to be with only her when he got released. Milan foolishly believed him and suggested they get married. Nas laughed her off, but she was dead ass serious. She called the prison to arrange it and even purchased the rings. He married her and went to the infirmary and fucked a female prison guard less than an hour later. The shit was a joke to him but Milan took their marriage seriously. She stopped dancing and was begging him to give her a baby.

Nas tried to do right but the shit was just too hard. He was still kicking it with the prison guard and another chick that he'd recently met. Milan always complained, but she wasn't giving him a reason to be faithful. She was spoiled and she wanted Nas to cater to her. He paid all the bills and barely had a hot meal when he got home. The only time he didn't eat fast food was when he went to Gavin and Stori's house.

"Let's just say y'all do open up a hookah bar. Who's gonna run the shit? Y'all niggas don't even trust nobody," Jarvis noted, as Remo and Nas looked at each other. That part was indeed true. Besides each other, they didn't trust a soul. They often reminded Jarvis that they didn't trust him either. Their cousin, Bee, helped out at the club sometimes but he was just as nutty as they were.

It was always eerie to Jarvis how much his little brothers looked and acted just alike. Remo and Nas had a bond that even he didn't understand. They knew shit about each other without even being told. Their mother had a condition called Manière disease which affected her hearing over time. She was partially deaf and she made sure that all of her kids learned sign language at an early age. Over the years, Jarvis had forgotten most of what he learned but not the twins. They mastered the art of sign language and it was often their source of communicating with each other. They were smart as hell but they made some of the dumbest decisions. They didn't think rationally and Jarvis was tired of thinking for them.

"What about Kalani?" Nas asked while looking at his brother.

"Nope. She's good working at the club. I need my eyes on her at all times," Remo replied.

"For fucking what? Kalani is not your girl no more," Jarvis reminded him.

"Keep thinking that if you want to," Remo replied.

"I swear I don't understand you niggas. Remo, you bought Kalani a house and you don't even have a steady place to stay. Nas gets put out every other day but he's the one who pays all the bills. I don't understand why y'all gave up y'all apartment to stay with people who you can't even be faithful to. Y'all are the dumbest, smart muthafuckers that I've ever met," Jarvis fussed.

"First off, fuck what you think. I have a place to stay. I just don't stay there every night. And my heart is very faithful to Kalani. My dick might be disrespectful as fuck, but this is a part of me that another bitch can never say that she's ever had," Remo said while pointing to his heart.

"Man, I'm good. If I could get a place in my name, I would have done it a long time ago. Milan needs me more than I need her. I'm ready to settle down and start a family," Nas said like he made sense.

"The fuck you mean? You're already settled. You got a wife nigga," Jarvis pointed out.

"I'm not trying to settle down with no damn Milan. I'm probably about to divorce her ass anyway. Tell Latrice to call me so I can talk to a lawyer," Nas replied.

"Man, I don't know where I went wrong with y'all bruh. I know mama and daddy are probably rolling over in their graves by now," Jarvis sighed stressfully.

He was surprised that he didn't have a head full of gray hair by now. Remo and Nas drove him to the brink of insanity most times. Them being in the dope game was nothing new because their parents were deep in it too. Sadly, that was how they lost their lives. Instead of his brothers doing things differently, they followed right in the footsteps of their parents. Jarvis didn't pray for much but he sent up a special prayer for his brothers every day. He was ready for them to calm down and relax.

"Let's go bruh. I'm trying to get on my bike and ride to the lake. Ole girl said they gon' pass through. I told you that this was a waste of time," Nas said as he stood to his feet.

"Come run me home to get mine too. I need to take a shower and change," Remo said as he too stood up.

"Home? Exactly where is that these days? You be here and by grandma more than anything," Jarvis noted.

"Shut your fake ass up. Me and my brother are good as long as we got each other. We don't even know you like that anyway," Nas spoke up on Remo's behalf.

"Stupid ass nigga. Who do you think raised your crazy ass? I'm your brother too," Jarvis pointed out as he often had to.

"I don't trust no nigga that I didn't climb out of the pussy with. Fuck outta here," Remo said, making Jarvis laugh.

They had no problem letting him know that he was an outsider too. He knew that it was all bullshit though. The twins had a funny way of showing it, but they loved their big brother. They were the ones who paid off his house as well as the cars that he and his wife drove. They appreciated their big brother and his wife more than they would ever know. Jarvis fussed but he was the first one at the courthouse whenever they got locked up. Although he said no, they knew that they would have their hookah bar soon too. Jarvis did make a good point though. They would still need somebody to run it.

"Don't call your fake ass friend either. I want to be fuck boy free today. Leave that lame ass nigga right where he's at," Remo said when he and Nas got into the car.

"Besides you, I don't have no friends. Gavin is my associate," Nas said as he pulled off and headed towards Kalani's house where Remo's bike was parked.

"Yeah nigga, I hear you. The nigga letting you crash up in his house and shit. It sounds like he's more than an associate if you ask me." Remo frowned.

"Stop acting all jealous and shit nigga. You're my only bitch. Stop worrying about the next nigga. I only love you," Nas said, making his brother laugh.

"That bitch ass nigga better be happy that I love Kalani the way I do. I would have been went at Stori and had his punk ass sick," Remo replied.

"Loving Kalani never stopped you from cheating before," Nas pointed out.

"I know man but Stori is her best friend. I would never do my wife dirty like that. Besides, Stori is my girl. I would never go at her on no disrespectful shit. I got a nigga who I know be watching her on the low though," Remo smirked.

"Chill out with that shit bruh. Mad niggas be trying to get at shorty but she's faithful as fuck to his lame ass. I told him that it's fucked up how he got his lil sister-in-law babysitting his baby. That nigga foul for that shit. He dropped me off home yesterday and went fucked Misty's ole dusty ass before he went to the shop," Nas said.

"How the fuck you cheat on a broad like Stori for a bitch like Misty? Bum bitch better be happy that it wasn't my baby that she snuck off and had. Me and Kalani would have been raising it after I killed her hoe ass. Dumb bitch named her baby after mama like I was really the daddy. Gavin is a real fuck boy for that shit. That nigga ain't even on Stori's level." Remo frowned, as Nas pulled up to the house.

"We all know that but she obviously doesn't," Nas said.

"Don't get soft on me out here bro. My heart can't take that shit. I remember at one time you didn't give a fuck about nothing and nobody. It used to be fuck a nigga and his feelings," Remo replied.

"Nigga, you of all people know that ain't nothing soft about me. I still don't give a fuck about a nigga and his feelings, but I already told you what it was," Nas replied.

"I gave you a way in though bro," Remo pointed out.

"I know but I can't fuck with it like that." Nas shrugged.

"Alright man. You know I got you if you need me to do anything," Remo said.

"I already know. Meet me uptown on Josephine St. so we can ride out together," Nas requested.

"You coming to the club tonight or is your wife still on her bullshit? I can get Bee to come through if you can't make it," Remo said.

"Man, fuck what she be talking about. That's my business too. I'll be there," Nas assured him before he got out of the car.

Remo knew that Kalani was home because the BMW that he got for her two months ago was parked in the driveway. He was hoping that his key still worked because Kalani was always changing the locks on him. Remo always managed to get inside anyway and she never knew how.

When he walked into the house, her music was the first thing that greeted him. He was quiet as he searched the first floor, but she wasn't down there. Remo silently made his way up the stairs and found Kalani in the master bedroom. She was standing in the mirror messing with her hair while talking on the phone. There was nothing strange about that, but the huge smile that was on her face had him looking at her sideways. Remo was no saint but he wanted Kalani to be. She was sneaky as fuck, but he always gave her enough rope to hang herself. He stayed two steps ahead of her, but she still tried him.

"Warn him about me, Kalani. That nigga better be prepared to die if he's trying to fuck with you," Remo threatened when he walked into the room.

Kalani jumped at the sound of his voice and the phone fell from her hand. Remo could have easily snatched it up to see who she was talking to but he didn't move like that. He had his ways of finding out what he needed to know and Kalani was well aware of that. She picked the phone up and ended the call without even saying anything. Remo smirked as he watched her discreetly mute the volume on her ringer. She was playing with him but he loved games, and she knew that better than anyone.

"What nigga? I was talking to Stori," Kalani said.

"Yeah, okay. What you got going on today?" Remo asked as he admired her sexy body in her boy shorts and tank top.

"Me and Stori might get some seafood and go to the lake," Kalani replied.

"Nah, I don't want you on the lake. Too many niggas be out there," Remo said.

The chick that Nas fucked with was bringing her girl to the lake for him. They were supposed to be getting a room later that night before they went to the strip club. Although Kalani knew that he did his thing, he never disrespected her. He would never flaunt what he did in her face and she'd never seen him with anybody else. Hoes just talked too much and that was how he always got caught.

"Your dog ass must be going out there, but so am I. We already made these plans last week and we're not changing them. You're not my man, so your hoes shouldn't feel threatened," Kalani fussed.

"You always trying to fuss with a nigga. Fuck it. Go to the lake if that's what you wanna do, but you can be prepared to post up right with me and Nas. You got me fucked up if you think you bout to smile in another nigga face," Remo replied as he walked into the bathroom and closed the door.

He had to send Nas a text to tell him to abort their previous mission. Unbeknownst to him, Kalani was texting her boo, telling him the exact same thing. She was going to the lake with Stori but that was just to throw shit off. Her boo was supposed to meet her there but she had to cancel. She almost got busted on the phone and she was happy that she didn't say anything to incriminate herself. Remo was a different kind of crazy and she didn't need those problems.

"Fuck that! You must be trying to meet up with a bitch. That's the only time you be wanting me to stay home," Milan argued as she followed Nas around their bedroom.

He was getting dressed to meet his brother at the lake and she wanted to go with him. Nas had cheated on her so much and her insecurities ran deep. Everybody told her not to get involved with him, but she didn't listen. Not only had Milan got involved, but she fell in love too. Her and Misty were only supposed to be dancing at the club. Falling in love with the owners was not supposed to be a part of the plan. At least Milan got a husband out of the deal. Remo wanted nothing to do with Misty outside of her making his business some money. Although Milan and Nas didn't get married the traditional way, she still honored her vows. Sadly, she took their marriage more seriously than her husband did. Nas was still the same as he was when they first met. He never fulfilled any of the promises that he made when he was locked up. Milan was still living in her three bedroom apartment because he had yet to buy her a house. Even starting a family seemed to be farfetched because he was never home. They still had sex quite often, but it was always a quickie because he was always in and out of the house.

"I'm not in the mood to argue with you, man. A nigga can't even enjoy his off days in peace," Nas said as he continued to get dressed.

"Yes, you can, but you're gonna enjoy them with your wife. It's fucked up that I have to make you spend time with me, but it is what it is," Milan said as she started applying her makeup. Nas thought it was a game, but she was dead ass serious. They were about to be joined at the hip for the entire day.

"I'm riding my bike today Milan. Damn man, this insecure shit is for the birds," Nas fussed.

"But, why am I insecure though, Naseem? How many bitches have I caught you with? Huh? Let's not forget that I walked down on you and Remo fucking a bitch in your office. And you wonder why I have a problem with you being at the strip club," Milan reminded him.

"Why get in your feelings when I met you the exact same way though?" Nas inquired.

"I don't give a fuck. The fact remains that I'm your wife, not them other hoes. You put a ring on my finger!" Milan yelled as she held up her hand.

"Nah, you put that ring on your own finger. I was locked up," Nas laughed.

"Everything is a fucking joke to you. You and Remo have had enough hoes to last y'all a lifetime. Y'all are too old to still be on the same bullshit," Milan argued.

"Stop speaking on my brother. My dude got who he want and it ain't your hoe ass sister," Nas said.

"He got who he want, but he's still fucking with other hoes. Kalani dumb as fuck if she wait for that nigga to get it right," Milan spat.

"You sound salty though. That's all on them. That man gon' settle down when he gets ready and so will I," Nas replied.

"The fuck you mean so will you? You're a married man Naseem. You should already be settled. You don't even know what it's like to be faithful. All you do is cheat!" Milan yelled.

"Give me a muthafucking reason not to then! Nigga pay all the bills and can barely get a hot meal up in this bitch. Another nigga's wife feeds me more than my own. You want me to buy you a house but you don't even keep the apartment clean. The fuck I look like trying to put a baby up in you when you still act like one," Nas said. His honesty always hurt her feelings, but she was used to it by now.

"I'm trying Nas, but you don't even try to meet me halfway. I can't even go nowhere without a bitch confronting me about my husband. I'm getting too old to still be fighting hoes over a nigga. A nigga that's supposed to mine at that," Milan ranted.

Nas was over it and he was done talking. It would have been different if they didn't have the same conversation at least three times a week. Remo told him not to do it but he married Milan anyway. Now, he needed to get with his sister-in-law to see how he could get out of it. He needed to take Jarvis' advice and get his record cleaned. Then, he would be able to have more legal income and get a place of his own. Crazy as it may have sounded, Nas was really ready to settle down. Milan was right and he'd had his share of being with multiple women. She just wasn't the woman that he could see himself settling down with.

"You ready to go?" Milan asked, shaking him from his thoughts. Nas thought it was a game, but she was done playing with him.

"I'm riding my bike like I just told you," Nas replied in disgust.

"Okay, well I'll meet you there," Milan said as she walked away.

"Man fuck!" Nas hissed when he heard the front door open and close.

He wasn't in the mood for the drama, so he was about to cancel the plans that he and Remo had made. As soon as he pulled his phone from his pocket, a text from Remo was coming through. Nas couldn't do nothing but laugh because it seemed as if he and Remo were on the same page once again. He was telling Nas to cancel their plans because Kalani was going to the lake as well. It was all good to him. Milan could try to be on his back as much as she wanted to. She wasn't going to stop him from doing whatever he wanted to do. Truth be told, she never could.

S tori woke up with the worst cramps ever. She was happy that she didn't work on Sundays and Mondays because she didn't know how she would have survived. She didn't want to get out of bed but she had to bring Toi to school. She never let Toi stay out on school nights, but Misty begged her to let her little sister babysit after Milan backed out on her without notice. Toi assured her that she would be okay and Stori conceded. She made sure that Toi had her uniform and everything else that she needed for school.

"You can relax baby. I know you don't feel good. I'll go get Toi and bring her to school," Gavin offered as he sat up in the bed.

"Thanks Gavin. Make sure you stop her somewhere to get breakfast too. She hates the breakfast at the school,"

Stori said as she laid back down.

Gavin frowned slightly but he would do whatever his wife wanted him to do. Stori usually got up early enough to fix breakfast, but Gavin knew that she wasn't in the mood. As much as Lady and her husband paid for Toi to attend school, she should have had three meals and a snack. Stori catered to her too much and it was annoying as fuck. Gavin was already in a foul mood because she was still on her period. Having sex with Misty was okay but nothing and nobody compared to his wife.

After completing his morning hygiene, Gavin grabbed his keys and headed to Misty's house. Nas' Range Rover was parked out front but Milan's car wasn't. Gavin remembered seeing him on his bike at the lake the day before, so maybe he was still on it. Instead of ringing the doorbell, he called Misty and told her to open the door. As soon as she did, Gavin walked in and followed her to her bedroom.

"Where's Summer?" he asked when he didn't see his daughter in her bed.

"In the room with Toi. Give me the money so I can pay her for babysitting," Misty answered angrily as she held out her hand.

"You can kill that attitude. It's too damn early for the bullshit," Gavin replied as he pulled out some money from his pocket.

Misty was in her feelings because everybody was at the lake the day before but her. It was too hot and she didn't want to bring Summer out there. She tried hard as hell to find a babysitter but she didn't have any luck. She hated that her family lived in Texas because she didn't have any help. Milan was supposed to be watching her daughter while she went to the club, but she never even answered her phone when Misty called her. Misty was already skeptical about leaving her daughter in her sister's care, but she was desperate. Milan was too busy running behind Nas to give a damn about anybody else. Misty had to beg Stori to let Toi stay the night with Summer because she couldn't afford to miss out on any money. She was pissed when she got to the club and saw Milan there following Nas like a shadow. He looked annoyed with her sister and Misty knew the feeling.

"It's mighty funny how you and your wife were at the lake having a grand old time while I was stuck in here with your daughter. So yeah, you fucking right I have an attitude," Misty replied.

"What's up with you finding another babysitter? I'm surprised my wife even agreed to let Toi stay here on a school night. She don't play those kinds of games," Gavin said, ignoring everything else that she said previously.

"I've been looking. One of the girls at the club is trying to put me down with her niece. She's in college and she's trying to make some extra money. But, why is it just on me to find a babysitter? She's your daughter too," Misty snapped.

"The fuck is up with you and this attitude? You need some dick or something? I got some time. Come up out of them clothes so I can get you right before I leave," Gavin said as he dropped his sweats.

He reached into the drawer that was next to her bed and grabbed a condom. He pulled down his boxers and rolled it on right as Misty walked over to him. She only had on a t-shirt with a pair of thongs. Gavin didn't even try to be gentle and Misty didn't want him to. He pulled her thong to the side and rammed his dick into her with force.

"Ah, shit! Fuck me, baby!" Misty moaned as she held on to the dresser.

Gavin wrapped his hands around her neck to hold her in place while he pounded into her from behind. Misty was throwing it back at him, but he couldn't help but compare her to his wife. Misty had a nice shape but Stori's was better. Gavin was the poster child for wanting his cake and eating it too. His wife could run circles around Misty and he didn't have a reason to be unfaithful. He did it only because he knew that he could. Nas was married and had more side bitches than the average single man. Gavin didn't want to feel lame, so he joined in on the fun.

"You need to kill that attitude," Gavin growled as he stroked her harder and faster.

"Yes baby! Umm. Do it harder," Misty moaned in pleasure. She threw her leg up on the dresser to give him better access to her goods.

Toi was dressed for school and ready to go. Stori called and told her that Gavin was on his way to pick her up. Summer had just woken up and Toi changed her diaper and gave her a bottle. She was on her way to bring her to Misty's room, but she stopped before she got to her door. Misty was moaning and screaming, making Toi hurriedly turn around and go back to the spare bedroom. Although she was a virgin, Toi was far from naïve. She had watched pornos with her cousins at their grandmother's house a few times before. She knew how it sounded when someone was having sex and Misty was getting it in at the moment. Toi was over an hour early for school, so she played with Summer until it was time for her to go. Summer was the best baby ever and watching her was easy money. After twenty more minutes passed, Toi heard talking coming from the living room.

"Toi, Gavin is here to get you!" Misty yelled. A few seconds later, Misty opened the door and walked into the room.

"I just changed her diaper and gave her a bottle," Toi said.

"Thank you, sweetie. Here you go. I put a little extra in there since you came through for me at the last minute," Misty said while handing her some money. She gave Toi forty extra dollars from her own money just for looking out.

"Thanks Misty. Bye Summer," Toi said as she kissed the baby on the cheek. When she got into the living room, Gavin was standing by the front door waiting for her.

"Let's go get you some breakfast so you can get to school," Gavin said as he grabbed her overnight bag from her.

When Toi walked out of the house, he winked at Misty and walked out behind her. After getting himself, Stori and Toi some breakfast, he dropped his sister-in-law off to school and headed back home to his wife.

"Hey baby. How was school?" Stori asked when Toi got into the car.

Stori had laid around all day and got some much needed rest. She felt much better and she was no longer cramping. She didn't even cook anything and she was happy when her mother-in-law invited her and Toi out to an early dinner. Gavin was helping his father paint his shed and his mother promised to bring them some food back from the restaurant.

"It was good. I made an A on the test that I took Friday," Toi replied as she smiled brightly.

"Good job. I'm so proud of you Stanka," Stori beamed.

Since she'd been in school, Toi had gotten nothing less than a B on her tests. Her GPA was always higher than a 4.0 and Stori couldn't have been more proud. As nervous as she was when Lady left them, she had to admit that she'd done a great job raising Toi. She was smart, respectable and beautiful inside and out.

"What did you cook? I forgot to call and tell you what to fix," Toi said.

"I didn't even cook anything baby. We're meeting Karen at Olive Garden. She knows that's one of your favorite restaurants," Stori replied while referring to Gavin's mother.

"Yessss," Toi cheered. "I'm starving."

"So am I. I stayed in bed all day until it was time to come and get you. How did you make out with Summer last night? I hope she didn't keep you up on a school night. I really don't like you staying away from home, but Misty was damn near in tears when she called," Stori replied.

"I never have any problems with Summer. Misty gave her a bath and she went right to sleep after that. She didn't wake up until this morning. But, guess what?" Toi quizzed.

"What?" Stori countered.

"I heard Misty having sex this morning," Toi giggled.

"What! With who?" Stori yelled.

"I don't know Stori. It wasn't like I was in the room. I was about to bring Sumner to her, but I heard her when I was walking down the hall. I just went back to the room and waited until she was done." Toi shrugged.

"Yeah? And she just lost a babysitter," Stori fumed.

"Stori, no. Don't say nothing to her. She really didn't do anything wrong. I don't want to stop babysitting Summer," Toi pouted.

"Well, she might have to start bringing her to our house. I'm not dumb enough to think that you don't know what sex is because we've talked about it several times before. I just don't want nobody exposing you to something that I've never exposed you to. You're there to watch her baby while she works. It's not your job to babysit while she gets fucked. She must have been loud as hell for you to hear her in the hallway," Stori noted.

"She was," Toi laughed as they pulled up to the restaurant.

"We'll finish discussing this later," Stori said as they got out of the car. Her mother-in-law had just gotten there and was already seated.

"Hey, my girls," Karen said as she stood up to greet them.

Stori and Toi hugged her before they took their seats and waited for the server to take their orders. Karen loved Stori like a daughter and her son couldn't have found a better wife. The way Stori raised her sister was commendable and Karen always complimented her. She was thrilled to know that they were trying to start a family. Gavin was an only child and she was ready for some grandkids. Karen was well aware of her son's shortcomings, but meeting Stori seemed to be just what he needed.

Growing up without siblings had a negative effect on Gavin. He tended to be a follower and he latched on to his friends. Right or wrong, whatever his friends did, Gavin tended to do as well. She was hoping that he grew out of it after his teen years but not much had changed.

Karen was a short, thick woman with flawless cocoa colored skin. She was feisty and outspoken, just like Stori was. She didn't sugarcoat anything, especially when it came down to her son. She had a heart of pure gold, but she didn't take shit from nobody. She didn't pacify Gavin and neither did her husband.

"I see you're keeping up with your new cut," Stori said as she admired the pixie cut that she had given her.

"Girl yes and Gordon loves it," Karen said, speaking of her husband.

"So do I," Toi chimed in.

"Thank you, baby. And I know that this is one of your favorite restaurants so order as much as you like. You can get something to take home for later too." Karen smiled.

"Thanks Mrs. Karen," Toi said.

"You're welcome sweetheart. You're doing such a great job with her, Stori. I just know that my grandkids are going to be in good hands. That makes me feel good," Karen said, right as the waitress came to the table.

The three of them ordered enough food to feed an army. Karen also ordered her husband and son some food to go. They enjoyed themselves as they ate and talked about everything that they could think of. Once they parted ways, Stori and Toi left to go home.

"Do you have homework Toi?" Stori asked.

"No, I just have to look over some stuff for another test on Friday," Toi replied.

"Okay, well, let me know if you need any help," Stori said when they walked into the house.

"Hey Gavin," Toi said when she passed him up on the sofa.

"What's up baby girl?" he spoke before she disappeared up the stairs.

"I got your food Gavin. Let me see if it needs to be warmed up," Stori said as she walked into the kitchen.

Stori was such a nurturer. Gavin never had to worry about lifting a finger as long as she was around. She would cook, bring the food to him, get the dishes when he was done and wash them too. She nursed him back to health when he was sick and she went above and beyond her wifely duties.

"Thanks love," Gavin said when Stori handed him a plate of piping hot pasta and breadsticks a few minutes later.

"You're welcome. What do you want to drink? You got Coronas, tea or water," Stori said.

"Bring me some tea," he requested.

Stori came back into the living room with a bottle of tea and some napkins. She sat down next to him while he ate his food.

"Toi said that she heard Misty fucking this morning," Stori blurted out, making him choke on his food. Gavin's eyes watered as he grabbed his tea and took a huge gulp. Stori was asking him if he was okay, but it took him a while before he found his voice to answer.

"Yeah, I'm good. Who did she see her having sex with?" Gavin asked nervously.

"She didn't see anything. She only heard it. Toi doesn't want to stop babysitting Summer but I think it's for the best. I'll let her help out until Misty can find somebody else, but she has to bring Summer over here from now on," Stori replied.

"I'll tell Nas to let her know," Gavin said.

"I don't need Nas to speak for me. Her and Milan have an appointment Thursday. I'll tell her myself," Stori said.

"I don't know if that's a good idea Stori. I don't want her to take shit the wrong way and y'all get into it," Gavin replied.

"Ain't nothing scary about me and you already know that. I know how to approach the subject with class," Stori assured him.

"Just let me handle it baby. I know that you can take care of yourself but let your man fix it," Gavin said as he leaned over and kissed her lips.

"Okay, but she can consider this Toi's official two week notice. She'll need to find herself another babysitter," Stori replied.

Gavin's appetite was gone but he forced himself to finish eating. He didn't want to seem too suspicious and have Stori thinking that something was wrong. He was so thankful that Toi wasn't standing in the hallway when he walked out of the bedroom. That was too damn close and Gavin wasn't willing to take any more chances. He swore to himself that he was done sexing Misty. He didn't give a damn if Stori was on her period or not. He would just have to please himself until she got him right. He wasn't willing to lose his wife behind being stupid and careless. Fuck a two-week notice, Misty needed to find another babysitter now.

WOR$T CA$E $CENARIO

"That nasty, trifling, no grip pussy having hoe. I wonder who her nasty ass was in there fucking," Kalani fumed after Stori told her what Toi had said about Misty.

Thankfully, things worked out better than she thought they would. When Misty came to get her hair done the day before, she told Stori that she'd found another sitter for her daughter. She wanted to thank Toi for helping out when she needed her but she was at school.

"Girl, I don't know and I don't care. I just don't want Toi witnessing all that bullshit. The last time she was there, Milan and Nas were in there fighting. I should have put a stop to it then. She don't see shit like that at home and I don't want her to see it nowhere else either. I know I can't shield her from the real world but I can damn sure prolong it," Stori said.

"Toi know what's up. She's smart as hell and you keep it real when you talk to her. She can handle herself in any situation. I probably wouldn't have even been pissed if it was anybody else. You know how I feel about that nasty bitch Misty though." Kalani frowned.

"Bitch, everybody in New Orleans know how you feel about her. Remo don't want that hoe and you know that," Stori said as she curled the sew-in that she'd just put in Kalani's hair.

"Fuck him too! I can't wait to go out on my date tomorrow," Kalani replied.

"Don't do it friend. You know what happened the last time you invited somebody to your house. Nigga ended up getting his jaw wired shut," Stori laughed.

"That was dumb on my part to even bring somebody over there. I don't know what the fuck that nigga be doing to get in my house. I'm tired of changing locks and I'm tired of tiptoeing around Remo. He fucks every bitch that come through the club, but he expects me to be faithful. I already got the other bartender to cover my shift and I didn't even tell his ass nothing. I almost got busted on the phone with my boo but Remo didn't say nothing about it," Kalani giggled.

"Where are you and ole boy going?" Stori asked.

"He's taking me to a concert at the casino in Biloxi and then we're going chill at his house. I told him all about how crazy Remo is and he suggested ordering in. We can't take the chance on being seen in public too close to home. He lives in a nice subdivision, so we don't have anything to worry about. That's the kind of area where nothing ever happens. They probably don't even lock their doors at night," Kalani said confidently.

"I don't know friend. Remo seems to find out about everything that you do," Stori pointed out.

"I know and I really don't know how," Kalani replied.

"Bitch, I think Remo and Nas work for the FBI. How the fuck do they be into so much shit? Nas got like ten different driver's licenses and they all have his picture on them. I wasn't trying to be nosey but he pulled them out of

56

his pocket when he was trying to get to his phone. I just turned my head like I didn't even see shit," Stori said.

"I wonder what the hell that's all about," Kalani sighed, as Stori handed her a mirror to see her hair.

"I don't know but you need to be careful. Remo is crazy as fuck and nobody knows that better than you," Stori said.

"I don't know what made me even go there with his ass," Kalani fussed.

"Play dumb if you want to. I'm married but even I can see that Remo is fine as fuck. It's rare that you get a nigga that got the full package. That nigga is cute, fine and got money," Stori pointed out.

"And let's not forget that he's also a dog," Kalani said as she rolled her eyes.

"A dog who loves your dirty thong," Stori laughed.

"Don't even remind me. If only I hadn't been in your shop that day when he came. That's what I get for walking in without an appointment. I keep thinking back to what I did to make the nigga love me so much. I'm trying to make sure that I never do no shit like that again. That's my karma though," Kalani said seriously.

"Don't feel like that bestie. He'll get it together eventually," Stori assured her.

"Maybe so but I'm not sitting around waiting until he does. You got a good one so you don't understand my pain," Kalani said.

"I guess," Stori said while waving her off.

"Aww boo. Still no changes with you and Gavin?" Kalani questioned.

"Nope and I feel guilty as fuck. Like, how do you tell a nigga that has never done you wrong that you're just not in love with him? Truthfully, I don't think I love him at all and I shouldn't have gone through with marrying him. I just feel like we're roommates who have sex and sleep in the same bed. I can't even bring myself to call him baby or none of those other cute names that couples have for each other. He's just plain ole Gavin." Stori shrugged.

"Damn friend. I'm sorry that you have to go through that. I just feel like life is too short to be unhappy though. You need to sit him down and tell him how you really feel," Kalani suggested.

"I really don't want to hurt his feelings though. He's good to me and Toi and I know I would feel like shit if I did. I also don't want to keep bringing different niggas around my sister. I want to be a good lead for her to follow," Stori noted.

"Bitch, you are a great role model for Toi. Corey's stupid ass was a long time ago but he's the only other man besides Gavin that she's ever seen you with. The other two niggas were just for sex and she didn't need to meet them," Kalani pointed out.

Once she was done with Corey, Stori had two brief flings. They had never come to her house and they always got a room when they wanted to chill. Most times, Toi would be with Kalani or one of their family members when that happened. Corey was still around but he was even more of a scrub now than he was seven years ago. He had five kids with three different women and he didn't do shit for any of them. He was still a petty hustler who stayed in and out of jail. His cousin worked in the shop with Gavin and he went there all the time to get his free haircuts.

"I just hate that I don't have the kind of husband that I want to fuck on sight. Nigga shouldn't have to play in my pussy with his hands or mouth to get me wet. I want a nigga to make me drip just by looking at me," Stori said.

"Yeah, like how I feel about Remo's dog ass. I get what you're saying friend but I don't agree. Staying with him for any other reason besides love is crazy. You deserve a nigga that will have you leaking like a faucet when he walks into the room. If a nigga gotta spit start the pussy, something is definitely wrong," Kalani replied.

"Don't get me wrong, our sex life is straight. I just don't get those butterflies in my stomach when I see him. I don't count down the hours until he's home from work. I don't feel the need to talk on the phone with him all day and I don't miss him when he's not in my presence. He won me over with his love for Toi but that shouldn't have been enough. I feel like I'm an actress and I'm putting on an

Oscar worthy performance. The shit is draining," Stori huffed.

"He knew that getting in good with Toi was the way to your heart. I know you love baby girl, but you have to think about yourself sometimes too. Above all else, I just want you to be happy. You deserve that more than anything. You basically became a single parent at eighteen years old at no fault of your own. Ain't no way in hell should you be walking around here settling for no nigga who doesn't keep a smile on your face. You know I got you, though. Just say the word and Remo is on that shit. He's been dying to hook something up," Kalani noted.

"I'm a lot of things but a cheater and a hoe are not on the list. I'll pass on the hookup," Stori replied.

"Bitch, this is me that you're talking to right now. How many times have we discussed this before?" Kalani asked.

"Too many to count but my feelings remain the same. I'm good on the marital affair," Stori laughed.

"Okay, but we'll talk about it some more later on. I gotta get to the mall before they close. I need me some cute lingerie for my boo to rip off," Kalani said.

"Keep fucking with Remo if you want to," Stori warned.

"Fuck Remo! That nigga do what he wants and I'm about to start following his lead. Besides, my boo is the brother of the dentist that I used to work for. I doubt if him and Remo will ever cross paths. He's never been to jail so they don't run in the same circle," Kalani laughed.

"Call me later boo. Love you friend," Stori said as she hugged her.

"Love you too bestie and I need some more candy. My stash is running low," Kalani said, right before she hurried out of the house to get ready for her date the following day.

"The fuck are they doing up in there?" Remo yelled to his cousin Bee.

They had a huge crowd of niggas that just walked into the club and a few of the girls were still in the dressing room. Time was money and he didn't have time to play. He was happy that Nas was there to keep shit flowing smoothly. Their cousin Bee was cool, but it wasn't his business and he wasn't as invested in it as they were. Bee was the nigga who did everything around their club. He was the bouncer, security guard and dope boy if they needed him to be. He wore many hats but he never complained. He was getting paid very well to do it all. Besides, Bee was ugly as fuck but he got pussy thrown at him left and right when he was there. He was the first cousin of the bosses. It didn't matter that he looked like the long lost twin of Biz Markie. He was the man at Twin Tails Strip Club.

"I told them hoes to come on up out of there but they feel like playing," Bee replied.

"Yeah, and I'm with all the bullshit tonight!" Remo barked as he headed downstairs to the dressing room.

Before he made it there, he saw Nas walking out with a scowl on his face. All the dancers who he'd just sent Bee to get came rushing out of there soon after. As usual, Remo and Nas were on the same tip. They didn't play when it came down to making their money.

"They must think it's a muthafucking game. I don't give a fuck about how their makeup look. They better get out here and make the club some money," Nas snapped angrily.

He followed Remo back upstairs where their joint office was located. From there, they could look down and see what was going on in the entire club. The crowd was thick and the girls were working. That's exactly what they loved to see. They made it their business to hire some of the baddest females in New Orleans and their club was known for that. Niggas didn't mind spending money on a bitch when a pretty face and a fat ass was attached to her.

"Bro, did you see that new bottle girl? That hoe is fine as fuck," Remo said as he hit Nas on the arm.

"Yeah, I saw her but I'm good on that. I already fucked up and wifed a stripper. I'll never do that shit again." Nas frowned.

"I tried to tell your stupid ass not to do it but you don't listen. Besides, I already got a wife. Once I hit it a few times, she can keep it pushing," Remo replied.

Both men continued to stare down at the club for a while. When someone knocked on the door a few minutes later, Nas opened it to find one of the youngsters who they had selling pills in the club.

"What's up Nas? I'm out of product. A few people have been asking for candy so you might want to get some more of that too. Here, I got all your money," Eno said as he handed him a wad of cash.

Of all the dudes that they put on, Eno was the best. He was hungry and his ambition showed it. Eno was twenty-one years old but he was very responsible and mature for his age. He and his little brother, Eric, lived with their grandmother because their mother was strung out on dope. She stole everything that wasn't nailed down and her kids were usually her victims. Eric hung around the barber shop a lot, running errands and keeping things clean. All the barbers loved him and they kept money in his pockets. He was only fifteen and that was their way of keeping him out of the streets. Eric was still in school and they wanted him to stay there.

"Good looking Eno. Go grab a drink and relax. I'll come find you when I got something else for you to sell," Nas said as he slapped him on the back.

He and Remo never let anyone see where they kept their dope and money. As soon as Eno left, Nas locked the door behind him. He and Remo moved the huge oak desk and the rug that was underneath it. Once Nas punched in the code, the safe that was built into the floor popped open. Nas put the money inside and grabbed a bag of pills out of it. Once they had everything back in place, they went back to people watching until somebody else knocked on the door a short time later. Nas opened the door once again and it was their cousin Bee that time.

"Aye cuzzo, the bar needs some change," Bee said as he handed Nas a slip of paper with the five hundred dollar bills that one of the bartenders had given to him. Nas and Remo made sure to have a paper trail on everything. They didn't want to hear no bullshit when it came down to their money.

"I'll be down there in a minute," Nas replied. Bee was their first cousin but they didn't trust his ass either. He was cool and had never given them a bad vibe, but that's just the way they were.

"Aye, put this in my wife's tip jar. And I'm watching your fat ass too," Remo said as he pulled out two crisp hundred dollar bills from his pocket. The bartenders had their own personal tip jar and Remo made sure that Kalani's stayed full.

"Don't even try to play me like that nigga. You can put your lil money back in your pocket anyway. Kalani ain't even here," Bee noted.

There were always three bartenders on duty and Kalani was always one of them. She didn't have any off days and Remo made sure of that. She took breaks on the clock all the time, but he didn't care as long as she was at work. He wanted his eyes on her at all times and he didn't even notice that she wasn't at work. He was so busy trying to make sure that shit was running smoothly, he never even paid attention.

"The fuck you mean she's not here?" Remo asked as he looked out towards the oval shaped bar area. Sure enough, three bartenders were busy knocking the crowd down but Kalani wasn't one of them. Remo pulled his phone from his pocket and tried to call her. After three attempts, Kalani never answered for him once.

"Shit, as much as you keep tabs on her, I thought you already knew." Bee shrugged.

Nas looked at his brother and he could see the anger flashing in his eyes. Kalani hadn't told Remo that she wasn't going to be there and he was pissed.

"What's good lil brother?" Nas asked, as if they weren't the same age. He came out two minutes before Remo, which made him the oldest.

"Aww shit, here y'all go with this hand talking and shit," Bee said when Nas and Remo started talking in sign language. It was always so weird to him how two niggas as hood as they were even knew that kind of shit. He stood there mesmerized for about ten minutes until they were done. They had a whole conversation in front of him and he didn't know one word of what they said.

"You know I got you, bro," Nas said with a head nod. They sent Bee on his way and moved the desk to get some change for the bar. Once everything was back in place, Nas was about to head out of the office.

"Aye bruh, send Tameka up here," Remo requested, referring to the new bottle girl that they'd hired.

When she came in inquiring about a job a week ago, she was dressed down in jeans and boots. She was petite with a cute face, so they told her that they would give her a shot. When she showed up for her first day of work, Remo was shocked to see the body that she was hiding underneath her clothes. The corset, fishnets and heels had her looking like a playboy centerfold.

"Think with your head and not with your dick for once. I know you're pissed with Kalani but I told you I got you," Nas replied.

"I know you got me. You always do. Now, do what I just asked you to do and send that bitch up here," Remo replied with a look of pure anger on his face. He didn't think straight when it came to Kalani and Nas knew that. Remo made irrational decisions that only made matters worse. Nas had never been in love before, so he didn't know exactly how his brother was feeling. He came close with his ex, Alissa, but creeping around with Milan put an end to that relationship. Alissa was a traveling nurse, so she stayed out of town a lot. That made it way too easy for Nas to fuck up all the time.

"And her name is Lexus, not Tameka," Nas smirked. Remo never even tried to remember any of the employees' names. He called them whatever he thought their names was and he was never even close. Nas made it a point to know everything that he needed to know and more. Not only did he know their first names, but he'd memorized their last names too. He and his brother were alike but different in so many ways. They balanced each other out whenever they needed to.

"As long as the bitch can suck dick, I don't give a fuck what her name is," Remo replied. Nas wasn't in the mood to talk some sense into his brother, so he just walked away.

"Hey Nas," one of the bottle girls, Tammy, spoke with a flirtatious smile.

She, along with every other woman in the club, wanted a shot with one of the bosses. They knew that Remo fucked a few strippers in the club and Nas had married one. In their eyes, they could be chosen next. Remo and Nas were like walking, talking orgasms. There was no need to compare who looked the best because their features were identical. Although Nas was married, they knew that he still messed around. Unlike Remo, he didn't really fuck with nobody at the club anymore. Everybody knew that Remo loved the hell out of Kalani but that didn't stop him from doing his thing. A few girls got lucky and were with both brothers at the same time. Her luck was never that good but she was always hoping.

"What's good?" Nas spoke back as he scanned the club for the new bottle girl. He felt sorry for her already and he was hoping that she didn't catch feelings easily.

"Would you like something to drink?" Tammy asked him.

"I'm working sweetheart. I don't drink on the clock. Don't worry about me. They got mad niggas in here ready to spend some money. Go do your job and get that shit," Nas snapped as he looked at her in frustration.

Everybody said that Remo was the mean one but she begged to differ. Nas never smiled and there was nothing friendly about him. Tammy hurriedly moved to the other side of the room but she kept her eyes on her boss. He seemed to be looking for someone and she wanted to know who. When he walked up to the new bottle girl, Tammy scrunched up her face. She watched as Nas whispered something to the other woman and a smile covered her heart shaped face.

"Damn. Lucky bitch," Tammy hissed when she saw her walking up the stairs towards Nas and Remo's office. Since Nas was on the floor, she already knew who the other girl was going upstairs for. Tammy was salty and she couldn't even lie about it. She had been working there for six months and she didn't even know how the inside of their office looked. She was cute with a nice shape, just like all the other girls who danced and worked there. She didn't know what she was doing wrong but she was going to switch shit up until she got it right.

WOR$T CASE $CENARIO

"Fuck! I'm not ready to come yet baby," Gavin hissed as he pulled out of Stori.

He couldn't seem to get enough of her since she got off of her cycle and they got it in all day. They had already moved from the bed to the dresser, so he picked her up and sat her in the chair. Stori couldn't even get comfortable before Gavin dove into the pussy face first.

"Shit Gavin," Stori moaned as she grabbed his head and pushed it in deeper.

Gavin's tongue swiped up and down rapidly, making Stori's eyes retreat to the back of her head. Gavin's tongue game was official and Stori was releasing all over his face a few minutes later. In one swift motion, Gavin flipped her over and entered her from behind.

"Damn Stori. I swear this shit gets tighter and wetter every time I hit it," Gavin said before kissing the back of her neck.

He started out giving Stori long, deep strokes. When she started pushing back, he already knew what she wanted. Gavin grabbed a handful of Stori's hair as he hammered into her. Stori's moans bounced off the walls, but Gavin was even louder than her. He had been with a few women in his thirty years but none of them compared to Stori. Gavin knew that he had to marry her after his first taste. He couldn't imagine another man getting it after him. It didn't even matter when Stori confessed to not being in love with him. His goal was to make her fall head over heels and it seemed to have worked. He catered to his wife and she never had to ask for anything more than once. Even though Toi was a spoiled lil bitch, he knew that making her happy made his wife happy. Truthfully, Toi was the sweetest little girl that he'd ever met. It was his own jealously that had him annoyed with her at times. Stori was so accustomed to it being just the two of them that she forgot to include Gavin sometimes. Being an only child, he was used to all the focus being on him and he hated competition. It might have sounded selfish but that's just how it was.

"Don't stop Gavin. I'm 'bout to cum!" Stori yelled as she looked back at him.

She looked so sexy with her lip caught in between her teeth. Gavin pulled her back into him and stuck his tongue in her ear. He knew that was Stori's spot and he felt her walls contracting around him as she came. She felt so good to him and it wasn't long before he was releasing inside of her. Gavin was hoping that she would get pregnant soon and that would make their union complete.

"You got a nigga not wanting to go back to work," Gavin panted while pulling out of her. Being a barber gave him the freedom to come and go as he pleased. He didn't like missing out on money, so he tried to be there every chance he got.

"Well, I really don't have a choice," Stori said as she jumped up and rushed to the bathroom. She had a client coming in less than an hour and she didn't like to keep anyone waiting. When Gavin found out that Stori had a little break in between appointments, he rushed home to get in a quickie.

"Yeah, I guess I'll go make some more money too," Gavin replied as he walked into the bathroom behind her.

"We might have to order out again tonight. I need to finish helping Toi with her project. I thought we would have finished last night but it's almost done," Stori said when they stepped under the steaming hot shower water.

"That's cool. I'll grab something before I come home," Gavin replied as he walked up on her.

Stori was so perfect to him and he couldn't resist. He pushed her back up against the tiled shower wall and lifted her off her feet. Stori instinctively wrapped her legs around his waist before he entered her again. After another quickie, they cleaned themselves up and got dressed.

"Basement door," the alarm announced, stopping Stori and Gavin in their tracks.

Stori grabbed her phone to look at the camera to see who had entered her shop. She saw Remo sitting down in her chair right before her phone rang, displaying his number.

"Hey, I'm coming down now," Stori said when she answered for him.

"I don't know why you don't ever lock the door. That shit is dangerous," Remo scolded.

"Shit, I thought I did. I'm coming down right now," Stori said before she hung up.

"Who was that?" Gavin asked.

"That was Remo. I'm about to shampoo and re-twist his hair," Stori replied.

"You gotta be more careful with locking up Stori. That could have been anybody just walking up in here. I lost count of how many times I came home to find the front door unlocked and you were all the way in the basement. That nigga should have called before he just walked in anyway," Gavin fussed. As paranoid as Stori sometimes was, he was surprised that she wasn't more careful. Maybe it was because she had guns hidden all over the place.

"I thought I did lock up but it's cool. Remo is like family," she replied before walking away.

Gavin frowned as he put his barber's smock on and headed downstairs to her shop. He didn't trust Remo for some reason and he hated when he came around. He knew that Remo had a thing for Kalani, but he hated for Stori to be around him when Kalani wasn't there. Remo had no boundaries and Gavin would take a chance going to war with him before he let him have his wife. He considered Nas to be his best friend but his brother could get it. Gavin had never been the violent type but he would shoot it out with a nigga over Stori.

"What's good Remo?" Gavin spoke when he walked into the room. Remo looked at him and frowned before turning his attention back to Stori. He didn't know how many times he had to tell Gavin that he didn't fuck with him before he got the picture.

"Man, you better talk to your girl, Stori. She's been on some sneaky bullshit lately. She already know what's up if I find out. The next nigga I catch in my house gon' leave up out that bitch in a body bag. The other one was lucky that all he got was a wired jaw," Remo said, as Stori turned on the water to shampoo his dreads.

Kalani had missed work again the following Friday and Remo was on one. Nas assured him that he had shit under control but he was losing his patience. She claimed that she wasn't feeling well both days that she missed but she seemed to be fine whenever he saw her. Kalani didn't care about missing out on money because Remo paid all her bills.

"You know I don't get in you and Kalani's business like that," Stori replied as she started to wash his hair. She was puzzled as to why Gavin was still there, but he took a seat and watched her work.

"Yeah, okay. If you love your friend like I know you do, you better sit down and have a come to Jesus moment with her ass. She better start acting like she got a man," Remo fussed.

"Do you act like you got a woman?" Stori asked as she massaged his scalp.

"Hell yeah and everybody know who she is. Everything that Kalani hears about me is hearsay. She ain't never see me do shit because I don't disrespect her. I was supposed to bust her shit wide open when she invited another nigga into the home that I paid for. Shit don't get no more disrespectful than that," Remo noted.

"I thought you and Kalani broke up though," Stori said as she turned the water off and wrapped a towel around his head. Remo moved over to her chair, preparing for her to condition and style his dreads.

"She can miss me with that breakup shit. I agreed to give her some space and that was it. I ain't never agree to her being with no other nigga. I told her to wait on me and that's what the fuck I expect for her to do," Remo snapped.

"How is that fair though, Remo? I don't like to get into the middle of you and Kalani's relationship but you are selfish. My friend was heartbroken when she thought you had a baby on the way with another woman. She was happy that it wasn't yours but you were still a prospect," Stori pointed out.

"Man, Misty ole hoe ass knew that wasn't my baby. Besides Kalani, I make sure I strap up every time. She was fucking two other niggas besides me. Her baby is for one of them other bitch ass lames," Remo said while looking directly at Gavin.

The scowl on his face had Gavin shifting uncomfortably in his seat. Remo was on another level of crazy and Gavin really didn't want no problems with him. Everybody swore that Nas was just like his twin brother but Gavin didn't see it. He felt like he was under a microscope, so he got up and walked over to Stori.

"I'm about to head back to the shop beautiful. I'll call you later to see what you and Toi want to eat," Gavin said as he kissed Stori's lips and headed back upstairs to get his keys.

"How the fuck did you end up with a nigga like that?" Remo said as soon as Gavin was gone.

"What do you have against my husband? He's your twin brother's best friend," Stori laughed.

"Keep believing that shit if you want to. Besides me, Nas don't have no friends," Remo said.

"Aww, Remo is jealous," Stori teased.

"Baby girl, trust me, your husband ain't nobody to get me in my feelings. I just think you can do a whole lot better. You're more gutta than the nigga you married. Now, that's one for the books," Remo laughed.

"Shut up Remo. You're not supposed to tell nobody nothing like that about the person they're married to," Stori said as she popped him in the head with her comb.

"Stop fronting Stori. You don't even love that nigga. Pillow talk is a muthafucka, so don't even ask me how I know," Remo smirked as he looked at a text message that he received on his phone.

"I'm gonna kill Kalani," Stori fussed

"Not if I kill the bitch first." Remo frowned.

"Don't call my friend a bitch," Stori said as she popped him with the comb again.

"Aye, Nas wants to know if you got some candy," Remo inquired as he read his brother's text message.

"Yeah, depending on how much he wants. Kalani came got most of the last batch that I made," Stori replied.

"Let me get whatever you have left and stop selling that shit to my wife," Remo said as he replied to his brother's message.

"That's my best friend, nigga. I don't sell her nothing. You know Kalani can get whatever she wants from me," Stori noted.

"We need to link up and go into business together Stori. I'm telling you, sis, you can make a killing without even leaving the comfort of your home. You got the kind of skills that'll keep your pockets full," Remo said.

Stori made all kinds of edibles and she was a fool with it. She knew how to make them all flavors, shapes and sizes. She also made lean but only when someone asked for it. Nas usually got some candy from her and doubled the price when he sold it at the club. Niggas went crazy over it and they always wanted more.

"I don't have that kind of time on my hands Remo. I be booked up all week and I'm only off on Sunday and Monday," Stori noted.

Making lean and edibles was yet another bad habit that Lady had taught her. One of her mother's boyfriends sold anything that would get a person high. He taught Lady how to cook dope and everything else that she needed to know about the game. Instead of shielding her daughter from that life, Lady taught Stori how to perfect it. She always told her that it was a for sure money maker and she wasn't lying about that.

"Ain't no off days when it comes to making money. All you have to do is make the shit and me and bro can sell it at the club. Them niggas be going crazy over that shit and they don't mind paying a higher price for it. We can split the profits down the middle and go in half on the reup supplies," Remo offered.

Stori didn't understand how valuable her services were to a lot of people. Gavin had a fucking boss bitch on his arm and didn't even know it. Ain't no way in hell should he and Stori have been working at separate locations. They were supposed to be on their power couple shit and open up a shop together. With the skills that Stori possessed, they could have been rich in no time. His lame ass wasn't seeing no real money just by cutting hair. He made enough to pay Stori's bills and take her shopping but that was about it.

"How much money are we talking about?" Stori asked.

"Thousands more than what you're making now. I don't talk money with too many people but I can keep it real with you. Me and Nas see at least ten extra grand a week just off of dope sales alone. Niggas like to get high and we like to make sure they stay that way. The good thing is, we never have to leave out of the club to make it happen. And we don't even push no real weight like we used to. This is light work compared to how it was a few years ago. You need to get on board with us and we can all eat good as fuck," Remo replied.

"Shit, you ain't said nothing that I didn't want to hear. Let's talk numbers," Stori said.

"First, we need to talk about you dropping your dead weight and getting on the winning team. I'm telling you, Stori, I can make the call right now and get shit poppin'. That shit would be epic," Remo said as he rubbed his hands together excitedly.

"I can't believe you and Kalani. I don't cheat and y'all shouldn't be encouraging me to. That shit is just grimy and I don't want no parts of it," Stori replied.

"We live in a grimy ass world my baby. My wife loves you like a sister and I just want what's best for you," Remo said.

"I appreciate that Remo but hooking me up with somebody else is not the answer. Besides, what makes you think that Gavin isn't what's best for me?" Stori questioned.

"You need to be asking yourself that question. You're the one who married his bitch ass knowing that you didn't love him. Why would you even do some shit like that? You're almost as bad as Nas," Remo said, shaking his head.

"I can't speak for your brother but I was honest with Gavin. He knew that I wasn't in love with him because I told him," Stori said as she continued to twist his hair.

"Why did you marry him then? I couldn't see myself marrying a broad who told me some shit like that," Remo replied.

Stori had just unknowingly let him know just how much of a fuck boy Gavin was. Stori was bad and a blind man could see that. She had most of the dancers at their club beat with looks and body. He was sure that Gavin wanted to marry her because of that. She was definitely eye candy but she was a hustler too. Stori was smart and she didn't move like a lot of other woman. Kalani was the same way. They didn't mind being taken care of but they could do it on their own if they had to.

"Besides me getting comfortable and him being familiar, I really don't know. I just want stability for Toi more than anything," Stori noted.

"I understand Stori. I respect the way you look out for your sister but who's looking out for you? Toi is smart as fuck. She know that you wouldn't make a decision that wasn't best for her. Don't ever compromise your happiness for the sake of someone's else's," Remo said.

"Look at you trying to fix my life and shit," Stori laughed.

"I know I joke a lot but I meant what I just said. Life is too short to spend a minute of it being unhappy. And I'm about to show your friend just how short it is when I choke the life out of her sneaky ass," Remo said, returning to the person that Stori knew.

"My friend is not sneaky," Stori replied.

"Keep playing like you don't know what's going on. You gon' be the first one standing over her hospital bed crying when she flatline," Remo fumed.

Stori was laughing, but he was dead ass serious. Kalani was on some bullshit, but he wasn't ready to call her out on it just yet. He was going to let her have her fun while he put a plan in motion. Kalani was unlike any other woman that he'd ever come in contact with. She wasn't trying to fuck him on the first day and she was skeptical about going anywhere with him. Before her, Remo have never even been on a real date. Kalani made him chase her and that was the sexiest shit in the world to him. She wasn't afraid to pop off and she didn't let him get away with anything. Remo gave her the world but that wasn't enough for Kalani. Being faithful was all that she asked him for and he had a hard time doing that. His heart belonged to her and that should have been enough. Obviously, it wasn't though because she was on some bullshit. It was all good and he was ready for whatever. Kalani was going to regret the day that she made Remo fall in love with her ass. She was the first woman to ever accomplish such a hard task. Unfortunately for her, she was stuck with him for the rest of her life.

"My friend is an angel," Stori said, snapping him out of his thoughts of love.

"That bitch gon' be a guardian angel when I kill her ass," Remo replied, making Stori laugh again.

She finished up his hair, but he didn't leave right away. He called Nas on FaceTime to talk business with him and Stori. Nas was able to get most of what Stori needed from his pharmacy connect and she had a few connects of her own. Stori was able to make her edibles in large quantities and Remo was going to get Kalani to help her package it. Gavin was too dumb to see what he had but Remo knew a money maker when he saw one. Stori was a hustler's dream come true. All she needed in her life now was a real hustler.

WOR$T CA$E $CENARIO

6

66 Damn girl. You must be trying to suck the skin off my shit," Nas hissed as he pulled Danni's hair for her to ease up.

Danni was on her knees looking up at him like an obedient dog. For some reason, she was always doing too much and trying to prove a point. Danni was a corrections officers at the last prison where Nas was locked up at. He had been off and on with her for a while but she always came when he called. Danni wanted to be chosen but that would never happen. She was too thin for him and Nas preferred his women thick with a lot of ass. Remo was more into sharp hips and thick thighs but Nas lived for a big donk. Danni had a cute face, but Nas wasn't interested in her like that. She thought she was special because he chose her out of all the other women in the prison, but he had his reasons. Danni was the weakest link and he saw that the first time he laid eyes on her. Nas had her sneaking in all kinds of contraband for him. He had a cell phone and he still sold pills while he was in there. He didn't see any of the other women doing that for him, so the choice was easy. Danni took it to be more than what it actually was though.

Thanks to her, Milan found out that they were fucking since Danni so happened to mention it to another guard while in her presence. She made sure to always be in the visitation room when she knew that Milan was coming. It was comical to Nas because Milan used to do the same thing with his ex-girlfriend Alissa. Milan used to take pictures of him while he was sleeping and send them to his girlfriend. Nas never even knew until he saw Alissa and she went off and showed it to him. Now that the tables had turned, Milan was in her feelings and trying to play like the victim. Danni called his phone while he was in the shower and Milan went ballistic. She told Nas to get out like she always did and he wasted no time doing so. Danni rented them a suite and he had been there with her since the night before. Since they ran out of condoms that morning, Nas refused to even touch her. When Danni saw that he was about to leave, she wanted to give him something to keep her in mind.

"Ease the fuck up and stop trying to do too much," Nas snapped angrily.

He was ready to slap the piss out of her but she got the hint. Danni followed his command and he was spilling his seeds down her throat a few minutes later. She swallowed every drop like she was dying of thirst.

"You want to go grab something to eat before you go home?" Danni asked as she fixed herself up.

"Do I ever?" Nas countered.

"You don't have to be so mean about it." Danni frowned as she walked into the bathroom to brush her teeth.

"I got shit to take care of. I don't really have no time for all that. I'm already dreading going home to hear Milan with all that bitching," Nas sighed.

"Fuck Milan!" Danni barked angrily.

"If I loved the bitch, I would have slapped fire from your ass for being disrespectful," Nas said as he grabbed his keys and prepared to leave.

"When am I gonna see you again?" Danni asked as she walked up to him.

She looked like she wanted to kiss him, but she knew better. Nas wasn't big on kissing and Alissa was the only female that he had ever really been affectionate with. The first time he kissed Milan was the day they got married at the prison.

"Don't get comfortable my baby. I've been seeing you two and three times a week and now you're starting to look forward to it," Nas replied.

"What's wrong with that?" Danni asked, not seeing what the problem was.

Nas was sexy as fuck and every female employee at the prison wanted him. He looked over all of them and chose Danni. That act alone spoke volumes to her. Nas was like a hood celebrity when he was locked up and everybody knew him and Remo. Danni had heard about the handsome Donaldson twins before but it was a dream come true for her to actually be dealing with one of them.

"Don't get too attached sweetheart. That's the quickest way to get your feelings hurt," Nas warned as he walked out the door and to his truck.

Milan had called and messaged him too many times to count. She was crazy as fuck and he was tired of going through the motions. She was always telling him to get out, then she would blow his phone up begging him to come back. The shit was just draining. Nas was ready to find one solid female to settle down and start a family with. The way things were going in his life, that didn't seem like it would happen any time soon. Remo hadn't settled down yet but at least he found the person that he wanted to settle down with. Nas hadn't been so lucky.

When he pulled up to the house, Nas frowned when he saw Gavin's car parked out front. He wasn't in the mood to play follow the leader with a grown ass man. Gavin was like a love struck bitch when in his presence and the shit was annoying. Maybe he didn't have friends growing up but Nas couldn't do nothing for him. Gavin wanted to do everything that Nas did, which was why he'd started fucking Misty. He wanted to be down so bad but it always came off as desperation.

"Where have you been all night Naseem?" Milan asked as soon as he walked into the house.

Nas heard arguing coming from Misty's room as he walked down the hall. She and Gavin appeared to in a heated argument that he wasn't in the mood to hear.

"Why do you care where I've been? You told me to get out and that's exactly what the fuck I did," Nas replied as he walked into their bedroom.

"I'm really getting sick of this shit Nas. We're still newlyweds and we don't even act like it. You're never here and all we do is argue when you are!" Milan yelled.

"That's all on you, Milan. Every time you get mad, you want a nigga to leave. I'm only doing what you ask me to do," Nas said nonchalantly.

"You don't even try to stay and work it out though," Milan replied.

"I wish the fuck I would stay somewhere that I'm not wanted," Nas said.

"I do want you here but I won't be disrespected. It was bad enough that I had to share you with the bitch when you were locked up. I'm not doing the shit now that you're home. That bitch is disrespectful and you don't ever try to put her in her place. Where were you last night?" Milan asked.

"At a hotel," Nas answered.

"Were you with Danni?" Milan asked, even though she was dreading the answer.

"Yep," Nas answered truthfully.

Sometimes, Milan wanted him to be on his Jody and Baby Boy shit. She wanted him to lie to her because he loved her. Tell his hoes the truth but spare her feelings as much as possible. Nas wasn't on it like that, so everything that he told her was real.

"Wow. You should have just stayed gone. The fuck did you come back here for? You obviously don't want to be here," Milan snapped.

"You're right. I don't want to be here," Nas said as he opened the closet and started grabbing his clothes.

"What are you doing Naseem?" Milan asked in a panic.

"Getting the fuck up out of your house for good," he replied.

"I'm sorry Nas. I know that I have to control my emotions but I can't help it. I just love you so much and sometimes I go too far. Please don't leave baby," Milan begged.

Marrying Naseem was the equivalent of being the first runner to cross the finish line. It was like having cold water in the desert or opening gifts on Christmas morning. He was a prize that every woman wanted to win, but Milan walked away with the gold. Losing him would not only be hurtful, it would be embarrassing too. She hated to lose. That was a part of life that she hadn't fully grasped yet.

"Nah, I'm good on you, Milan. Let's just get a divorce and be done with this shit. We shouldn't have gotten married in the first place," Nas said as he continued to grab his stuff.

"Divorce!" Milan yelled. "I said I'm sorry but you're taking it too far now."

Nas ignored her and walked out of the room. He went to the kitchen to grab some garbage bags with Milan hot on his heels. When she saw Nas start to put his items in the bags, Milan started hyperventilating.

"Naseem, please don't do this. I'll do better, I promise. I know that I haven't been the best wife, but I promise to do better. I'll get a job or go back to school. I'll do whatever you want me to do," Milan swore.

"Oh, so now you're ready to get it right since you see that a nigga is serious about leaving. I really don't give a fuck what you do. It's too late to try to save a marriage that should have never happened. I should have listened to my brother," Nas replied.

"Fuck Remo!" Milan yelled angrily.

"I know that you're hurt and shit, so you got that one for free," Nas said as he grabbed his shoe boxes and stuffed them in a garbage bag.

"I understand that Remo is your twin but I'm supposed to be your better half. You act like you love him more than me!" Milan yelled as tears spilled from her eyes.

"I do. The fuck you thought," Nas replied.

"That's not right Naseem. I'm your wife," Milan sobbed.

Nas ignored her as he picked up two bags and started carrying them outside. Milan was screaming and acting a pure fool as she chased after him. Gavin and Misty heard all the commotion and came rushing out of the room. Misty looked like she'd been crying too, but Nas didn't really care why.

"You good bruh?" Gavin asked as he walked outside after Nas. Milan stayed behind and talked to Misty and he was happy for that.

"I'm straight," Nas replied, not really in the mood for conversation.

"Are you moving out?" Gavin asked.

"The fuck do it look like nigga? Come on man. I'm really not in the mood for the twenty-one questions right now," Nas snapped angrily.

"My fault bruh. Forgive me for trying to make sure that my best friend is good," Gavin said sarcastically.

"Nigga, we're not sixteen year old girls at a sleepover. You can miss me with that bestie shit. My brother is my best and only friend," Nas replied angrily.

Gavin hadn't done anything wrong and he wasn't mad with him. He was just in the wrong place at a fucked up time. Nas was mad with himself but that was his own fault. He and Remo were hardheaded and they never listened. All the money that he had didn't matter because he still felt like he was homeless. Having money was no good if he couldn't even put anything in his own name. He didn't even trust anybody enough to let them sign for him a place to stay. Going to his grandmother's house wasn't happening because she was too old school. Lucille had been locking her doors at ten o'clock since they were kids and nothing had changed since then. She didn't believe in handing out keys because she expected everybody to be inside before she locked up. The only time Remo slept there was when he was dog tired and wanted a peaceful night's sleep.

"I know you're heated right now fam but I'm not the enemy. You know we got more than enough room to accommodate you for as long as you like. Stori won't mind and you know that," Gavin noted.

"I'm in a fucked up mood right now but I appreciate it," Nas replied.

"Yeah, Misty got me fucked up too. Bitch mad because she had to miss two days at the club. It ain't my fault that the babysitter she hired is not reliable." Gavin frowned.

"I see you finally got your mind right and stopped letting Toi do it," Nas said.

"That wasn't my doing. Stori put a stop to it. Toi heard me and Misty fucking and told her about it. I'm happy as fuck that she didn't see me coming out of the room. Shit scared me all the way straight. I'm not fucking with her like that no more. If it ain't about my daughter, I don't want no parts of it," Gavin replied with a smirk as if something was funny.

"I hear you," Nas said as he walked away to finish gathering his stuff. In his opinion, it was dumb as fuck for Gavin to cut Misty off now, especially since she'd already had his baby. Misty and Milan were emotional as fuck and Nas already knew that shit was going to turn out bad.

"Can we talk Naseem?" Milan asked with tears steadily cascading down her cheeks.

"Don't beg that nigga to stay. Let him go if he wants to," Misty said with a frown.

Milan didn't know it but Misty was happy that she and Nas were separating. If she couldn't have who she truly wanted, she didn't want her sister to have his twin. Nas reminded her too much of Remo and she was happy that she wouldn't have to see his face every day.

"Listen to your sister for once. She's a hoe but she's on point with what she's saying," Nas replied.

"Fuck you, Naseem!" Misty snapped angrily.

"I'll pass but did you tell your sister that you tried," Nas smirked.

"That's a lie! Don't listen to him, Milan. He's just trying to start confusion between us!" Misty yelled as she jumped up from her place on the sofa. Gavin and Misty looked at her sideways and her guilt was shining through.

"Yeah, okay," Nas chuckled as he walked away with Milan following close behind home.

"When did my sister try to sleep with you and why didn't you tell me?" Milan asked.

"Stop trying to prolong my stay. Ask your hoe ass sister whatever you want to know," Nas replied.

It was true. Misty tried to fuck him more than once, but he always brushed her off. Nas knew that it was Remo who she really wanted and he was a replica of the man that she desired but couldn't have. He never even mentioned it to anyone other than his brother and he would never go there with her.

"Naseem, please don't leave. We can work it out. Just give me a chance," Milan begged.

"Milan, listen, and pay close attention because this is some real shit that I'm about to say. When you came at me about getting married, I laughed the shit off at first. I was in prison fighting a case that I didn't even know I would win. When you made it all happen, I foolishly went along with it when I shouldn't have. We were just fucking and I didn't even love you. Hell, I didn't think that you loved me either. I'm getting older and the streets are wearing me down. I do want to settle down and have a family but I'm not trying to do that with you. This relationship is toxic and I can't deal," Nas announced.

"How can you say that Nas? I do love you and I always have," Milan cried.

"I don't doubt that Milan but the feelings were never mutual. I'm not saying this shit to hurt you. I'm just keeping it real. Ain't no hard feelings my baby. If you want to come back to the club to make some fast money, just say the word," Nas said, making her look at him like he was crazy.

There was no way in hell that she was going back to their club. She had some money saved up but she would go broke before she did something so embarrassing. She had bagged a boss. There was no way that she was going to start stripping at his club again. They had other clubs but she wasn't trying to go back to that lifestyle at all.

"I'm not giving up on us, Naseem. I know you better than you think I do. You want the freedom to do you without answering to anybody. I'll give you as much time as you need but what I won't give you is a divorce," Milan replied.

Nas wasn't in the mood to go back and forth with her, so he grabbed the rest of his things and left. Gavin walked out right behind him.

"Here you go brother. Use it whenever you need to and I'll let Stori know what's up," Gavin said as he handed him a spare to key to his house and a card with the code to the alarm. If Remo had heard him call Nas brother, he would have gone ballistic.

"Good looking," Nas said before he got into his car and pulled off.

As soon as he did, Mr. Herbert, the owner of the barber shop where he worked, called him. The older man took a liking to Nas when he was a young boy, so it wasn't out of the ordinary that he was calling. Mr. Herbert had been a licensed barber for over forty years but he didn't cut hair anymore. He was the one who encouraged Nas to go to school to get his license to cut. Nas got Remo to enroll with him but that didn't work out quite like he wanted it to. A dude who Jarvis was cool with put Nas down with his brother, who was also a barber. He let Nas work with him as an apprentice for a while and showed him everything that he needed to know. As a result, Nas was nice with the clippers long before he graduated and he had a long list of clients. Nas and Remo ended up getting tight with the other man and he became their weed connect until he got out of the game.

"I know it's your off day but I need to rap to you about a few things," Mr. Herbert said as soon as Nas answered the phone.

"Okay," Nas replied.

"I'm over here by Lucille's house," Mr. Herbert said, referring to his grandmother.

"I'm on my way," Nas assured him before he hung up.

That was even better because he was about to unload all of his belongings in one of his grandmother's spare bedrooms. As he drove, Nas called his sister-in-law to see if she could get him and Remo an appointment with a lawyer. Not only was he serious about getting a divorce, he was serious about getting his criminal record cleaned up too. It was time for him and Remo to do things differently. Latrice was so happy that she told them to come in early the following morning.

When Nas pulled up to his grandmother's house, he laughed when he saw Mr. Herbert's Lincoln parked behind her Cadillac. They were too old for the bullshit. Everybody in the family knew they messed around but they swore that it wasn't true.

"Look at my handsome baby," Lucille said when Nas walked into her house.

Nas was young when his mother died but he vividly remembered how she looked. Jarvis still had lots of pictures of their parents that Nas and Remo always looked through. His grandmother reminded him so much of his mother with her light caramel complexion and slanted eyes. She also had the same curly hair that he and his brother possessed.

"Hey grandma. Where is Mr. Herbert?" Nas asked after he kissed her cheek.

"He sitting in the dining room eating. I cooked some red beans and chicken. I'll fix you a plate," Lucille said, making his stomach growl at the thought of a home cooked meal. Nas walked down the hall to the dining room and sat down at the table.

"What's up old man?" he asked while looking at Mr. Herbert.

"I would usually cuss you out for that comment but the shit is true. I am old and that's what I wanted to talk to you about," Mr. Herbert replied before wiping his mouth with a napkin.

"What's up? You good?" Nas asked him.

"I'm fine but I decided that it's time for me to retire. I'm seventy years old and it's starting to be too much. That's why I shut down the hair salon part of the shop. I can't deal with all that mess no more. I'm selling my house and the shop," Mr. Herbert announced.

"Man, you can just consider this my official two-week notice. You know I don't do too well with new people. I'll fuck around and be back in jail for shooting my new boss." Nas frowned.

"Shut up and let me finish talking boy," Mr. Herbert fussed.

"I'm listening," Nas said.

"I haven't even told this to nobody else yet. I wanted you to be the first to know. I also wanted you to be the first one in line to buy the shop if you're interested," Mr. Herbert replied.

"Real shit?" Nas asked excitedly.

"Very real shit," Mr. Herbert chuckled, right as Lucille walked in with Nas a plate of food. Nas waited until she left before he started talking again.

"What would I have to do? I don't have no credit and you already know what my rap sheet looks like," Nas pointed out.

"None of that matters Naseem. You'll be buying it from me, not the bank. It's only gonna be transferred from my name to yours," the older man said.

"Ours, you know I can't leave my bro out. But, let's talk numbers. What are we looking at in terms of prices?" Nas inquired.

"Trust me, it'll be a deal that you can't pass up. I just need to get a few of my other affairs in order and we'll make it happen," Mr. Herbert answered.

"What about the salon in the back? That's a for sure money maker. Is it able to be back up and running?" Nas inquired.

"Definitely. I just didn't want to deal with it no more. It was easier for me to deal with the barber shop but people are always asking me about renting a booth. You're young, so you can handle it. I just put my house on the market last month and I got a few offers already. Once I get that squared away, we can focus on the shop," Mr. Herbert noted.

"That's what's up. Where you moving to?" Nas asked as he finished off the last of his food.

"Here," Mr. Herbert replied, making him laugh.

"I knew it! I knew you and my grandma were creepin' around!" Nas yelled.

"Boy, hush up. I'm too damn old to be creepin' anywhere," Lucille said when she walked into the room.

"Grandma, please tell me you ain't having sex. That's really gone kill me," Nas said with a frown as Mr. Herbert laughed.

"Get out of my house Naseem. You should be good and full by now," his grandmother replied.

"Aye, since I'm homeless and shit, can I leave my clothes and stuff in one of your empty rooms?" Nas asked.

"Watch your mouth lil boy. And what do you mean you're homeless? You can come stay right here with me. I don't know why Jarvis didn't let me have you and Kareem when Summer and your daddy first died. Y'all wouldn't have gotten into half as much trouble if y'all were here with me," Lucille argued.

"He loved you, that's why. You couldn't handle us and everybody knew it. Jarvis did alright with us. Me and Remo just always had a mind of our own." Nas shrugged.

"Y'all had a mind for sin. That's why y'all went out there and opened up that naked women's club. And you went even further and married one of them lil nasty gals. Kareem got a good woman and he still won't settle down. Jarvis ain't did a damn thing right if you ask me," Lucille fused.

"I'm going get my stuff grandma," Nas said as he walked away laughing.

"You can come stay right here with me!" Lucille yelled after him.

Nas loved his grandmother but living with her wasn't happening. He also didn't want to overstay his welcome at Gavin and Stori's house. He was going to figure it out eventually but he had something else on his mind at the moment. He grabbed his phone from his pocket and called his twin.

"What's good bro? I was just about to call you. I'm stressing and Kalani is about to get fucked up for real. She's all out of chances and I'm done waiting," Remo fumed as soon as he answered the phone.

"You know I got you bro, but I got some news that'll make you feel better. It's on now, my nigga. Mr. Herbert just offered us another stream of legal income that we can't pass up. Where you at?" Nas asked.

"I'm at home," Remo said, referring to Kalani's house.

"Bet, I'm on my way. We got a few things to discuss," Nas replied before he hung up.

He took everything out of his truck and took it to one of his grandmother's spare bedrooms. She continued to fuss about everything under the sun, but Nas just ignored her. Once he was done, he grabbed him and Remo something to drink before he headed over to his house to talk business.

"Kalani, bitch, shut the fuck up!" Stori yelled as she laughed hysterically.

"Bitch, I'm serious. I don't even know why I listened to you. I'm happy that I used my first mind and put an extra pair in my purse. Me wearing edible underwear is not what's up," Kalani fussed as she used the wipes from her purse to clean herself up.

"That's because you don't listen. I told you to put them on no longer than thirty minutes before you handle business. It's candy Kalani. The heat from your body will cause the sugar to melt," Stori noted.

"Yeah, and I had to learn the hard way. Shit looked like a big ass fruit roll up smeared across my cookie," Kalani said, making Stori laugh again.

She was in the bathroom at a fancy restaurant giving herself a hoe bath. She couldn't believe that her edible underwear had melted and made a mess underneath her dress

"Well, besides that little mishap, how is the date going?" Stori asked.

"Everything is perfect. I wanted to have something for him to lick off of me, but I'll just have to improvise. Maybe I can grab a can of whipped cream or something," Kalani replied as she slipped on a fresh pair of underwear. She was happy that the restroom was single occupancy only because she damn near had to take a bath below her waist.

"Okay boo, well call me when you make it home," Stori said.

"I will," Kalani replied before she hung up.

She checked her hair and makeup before going back out to join her date. Omar wasn't someone that she would usually go for but maybe she needed a change. He was an investment banker and he had been asking Kalani out for a while. He used to always come to his brother's dental office but she always turned him down when he asked. It wasn't until a few months ago when she ran into him again that she decided to give him a chance. Omar would be considered a nerd to most people but he was a sweetheart. He was a gentleman and he treated Kalani with respect. He was nothing like Remo and that wasn't a bad thing in her opinion. He was shy, but Kalani was going to make the first move when they got back to his house. She and Omar had only kissed once and she had to initiate that too.

"Is everything okay?" Omar asked when Kalani came back to the table.

"It is now." Kalani smiled.

"Do you want some dessert or another glass of wine?" Omar offered.

"No thanks, I'm stuffed," Kalani replied.

"So am I. Let me call for the check so we can go," Omar said as he raised his hand and called the waiter over.

Once he paid the bill and left the tip, he and Kalani were on their way back to his place. They made small talk until they pulled up to his house and parked in the garage.

Omar and his family weren't wealthy but they all had good jobs. He came from a two-parent home and the street life was foreign to him. Remo was the first hood nigga that Kalani ever dated and she wanted him to be the last.

"Do you wanna watch a movie?" Omar asked when they entered the house through a side door.

"Sure." Kalani smiled.

"Give me your hand. It's dark in here. I don't want you to trip over anything and fall," Omar said as he grabbed her hand in his. Kalani followed him into the living room and watched as he turned on the light.

"Ahh!" Kalani screamed as she let go of Omar's hand and held her chest. Her heart felt like it was beating way faster than it should have.

"What's up my love?" Remo asked as he sat on Omar's leather chair like he belonged there.

Kalani felt like she was about to lose her bladder right there on the hardwood floors. Her luck couldn't have possibly been that bad but obviously it was. She didn't know what she had done in life to deserve a man like Remo. He had a good heart but he wasn't all together mentally. No one in their right mind would have done half the shit he did. Kalani was baffled as to how he even knew where she was. She had too many questions and not enough answers. Meeting Remo was her karma. That was the only way she could describe it.

"Kareem! What the hell are you doing here? Are you trying to go to jail?" Kalani yelled.

"I'm calling the police," Omar said as he grabbed his phone from his front pocket.

Kalani had already warned him about her crazy ex, but he didn't know he was that kind of crazy. Omar really liked her, but not enough to lose his life. He had just unlocked his phone but he never got a chance to make the call. The barrel of a gun being placed to his head stopped him from moving altogether.

"Is that how you treat company? I'm kind of offended. Go have a seat my man. My brother wants to rap with you for a minute," Nas said as he motioned towards the sofa with his gun.

Kalani wasn't even surprised that he was there. Wherever one brother was, the other was never too far behind. She had to do a double take when she saw that Nas had a sandwich in his other hand that he took a huge bite out of. They were really nuts. Not only did they break into someone's house, but they made themselves at home. Kalani felt so bad for Omar. He looked terrified as he took a seat on his leather sectional. He usually lived a normal, ordinary life and she felt like shit for bringing her drama to his front door.

Omar looked over at the two men and had to take a second glance. Besides one of them having dreads, everything else about them was identical. They looked so much alike that it was almost eerie. Even their deep, raspy voices sounded the same.

"Sit down baby. Let's talk," Remo said as he looked at Kalani.

"No Remo. We can talk when we leave. This feels weird. Let's go," Kalani replied.

"Calm down sweetheart. I'm not on no bullshit, I promise," Remo swore while flashing his panty dropping smile.

"Yeah right. Bullshit is all you're ever on," she fussed as she walked over to the sofa.

"I wish the fuck you would sit next to that nigga," Remo dared with a frown on his handsome face.

Kalani hurriedly made her way over to him and he pulled her down to sit on his lap. He wrapped his arm around her waist possessively as he looked over at Omar.

"Why are you here Kareem?" Kalani asked him.

"Nah, the question is, why the fuck are you here? Who is this nigga, Kalani?" Remo asked.

"He's just my friend," Kalani replied.

"Your friend, huh?" Remo repeated as he looked over at the other man.

"Yes, we're only friends and nothing more," Kalani assured him.

"What's your name, friend?" Remo asked sarcastically.

"Omar," the other man replied in a shaky but proper voice.

"Man, I should knock you the fuck out Kalani. Look at that nigga with them tight ass pants on. Nigga hairline is receding and everything," Remo fumed as he pushed her off of his lap and stood up. Kalani sat back in the chair that he'd just gotten up from and shook her head.

"Aye Omar, what kind of sandwich meat is this? That shit good as fuck. I'm going make me another one," Nas said as he turned and headed back to the kitchen.

"Did you know about me, Omar?" Remo asked as he looked over at him.

"Yes," Omar admitted truthfully.

"I respect your honesty, but I need to know why you thought it was a good idea to touch something that belongs to me," Remo gritted.

"I'm not a piece of property Kareem. I don't belong to you," Kalani corrected.

"Don't fuck with me right now Kalani. I already feel some type of way about you being here!" Remo barked.

"I'm so sorry Omar," Kalani said as she turned to the other man. He didn't deserve what was happening to him and it was all her fault.

Hearing her apologize to the other man angered Remo. He pulled the gun from his waistband and pointed it at Omar's head. Kalani gasped as Omar held his hands up like he was being robbed. His entire body trembled and he didn't know if he was going to live or die. He tried to hold them in, but the tears cascaded down his cheeks rapidly. He was embarrassed but he was too scared to care at the moment. He didn't have an alarm but his home was fairly secure. He was wondering how the men got into his house and how they knew where he lived.

"You gon' sit up in my muthafucking face and apologize to another nigga Kalani. You must want me to blow this nigga's head off!" Remo barked angrily.

"Baby, no, please don't do this. I won't talk to him anymore, I promise," Kalani swore.

"Don't tell it to me. Let this nigga know what's up," Remo demanded.

"Omar, please don't call me anymore and I won't call you either. We can no longer be friends and we can never see each other again," Kalani said as she turned her body to face Omar.

"Is this nigga crying? Come on sis. You could have done better than this," Nas said when he walked into the room and looked at Omar.

"Can we please not do this right now Remo? We need to leave. You and Nas are trespassing," Kalani replied nervously.

"As if I give a fuck. The worst case scenario is that we'll get locked up and probably be home in a day or two. I'll find Omar, because I know he'll try to hide, and put a bullet in his head. Since the star witness will be maggot food, the case will be dropped and me and bro can go on with our lives. It's simple." Nas shrugged, making Omar cry even harder.

"I... I swear I won't call the police. I won't even mention this to anybody. You got my word. This never happened," Omar stuttered and sobbed.

"Nigga, man the fuck up! Even if my bro wanted to kill you, crying wouldn't have stopped him. At least go out with some dignity," Nas fussed as he looked at Omar's wet face.

"Let's go," Remo said as he looked at Kalani. She jumped up and stood next to him.

"No, we can't leave out of the front door Remo," Kalani panicked when she saw where he was headed.

"Why not? We came in this bitch through the front door," Remo replied while grabbing her hand.

Omar sat there stoically as Nas followed them out. Remo led Kalani to the end of the block where his car and Nas' bike was parked. Remo watched as Nas drove away before he and Kalani did the same. The car ride was quiet for a while until he turned and looked over at her.

"Stop playing with me, Kalani. That's your last warning," Remo said sternly.

"Exactly how am I playing with you, Kareem? I'm tired of doing this all the time. How is it fair that you can move on but I can't?" Kalani asked.

"Who the fuck did I move on with Kalani? I'm not even doing shit. I run the club with my brother and stack money for the both of us. You need to stop believing everything that these hoes tell you. Most of the bitches who bring the bullshit to you be begging for the dick behind your back," Remo noted.

"Why should they have to beg for something that you give so freely? I'm tired of doing this same old song and dance with you. Just leave me the fuck alone and be free to do what you want to do," Kalani said as tears fell from her eyes.

"If leaving you alone was that easy, I would have been done that shit. You think I like playing Inspector Gadget trying to find clues to see what the fuck you be doing? This shit is draining me too," Remo argued.

"Well, let me go!" Kalani cried.

"I tried but I can't," Remo sighed as he ran his hand down his face in exhaustion.

The street life was wearing him down and he was exhausted. It seemed that he was sleeping less and running the streets more. When he had to run behind Kalani, that only stressed him out more. Thanks to Nas, he didn't have to chase her for long. His brother had his back just like always. Nas had followed Kalani a few times in Danni's car and she didn't even know it. Kalani always parked her car in the mall's parking lot and Omar would pick her up. Remo had known where he lived for weeks but he had to put a plan in motion. Nas had a connect at the DMV who made bogus driver's licenses and he and Remo had lots of them for different reasons. All Remo had to do was get one made with Omar's address on it and it was smooth sailing from there.

He called Pop-A-Lock and told them that he was locked out of his home. When they came out and saw that his identification had the correct address, they wasted no time letting him in. Remo was a criminal but he was the worst kind. He was smart with his moves and he was always two steps ahead of Kalani. She always wondered how he managed to get into her house when she changed the locks, but he would never tell.

"That's what I get though. Karma came back and got my ass real quick," Kalani said, pulling him away from his thoughts.

"I wish you stop saying that dumb shit." Remo frowned.

"It's true though. I cheated on Jamar to be with you and look at what happened. I left a faithful nigga to lay up with some community dick," Kalani said angrily.

Kalani had been with her ex-boyfriend Jamar for almost three years before she met Remo. Jamar was in the military and he was always in and out of town. Kalani traveled with him sometimes but she wasn't always able to. She told Remo that she had a man when they met, but he didn't care. He pursued her relentlessly until she gave in. Kalani was lonely, so it wasn't that hard for him to do. Remo was heaven sent in the beginning and it was easy for her to fall in love with him.

By the time Jamar came home, Kalani had moved out of their apartment and into the house that Remo had purchased for them. Jamar was heartbroken and he tried his best to get her back. Remo wasn't having it though and he made that very clear. He went to Jamar's job to let him know what was up and he hadn't called Kalani since then.

"Man, fuck that nigga. I told you to stop bringing that old shit up. I'm not perfect but stop talking like a nigga is all bad. You can say what you want, but I guarantee you'll never find another nigga that loves you as much as I do," Remo noted.

"That's the whole problem," Kalani said as she started crying again. Remo stopped at a red light and put the car in park. He reached over and pulled Kalani onto his lap. He knew that she was getting fed up with his actions and he always promised to do better. Kalani deserved much more than he was giving her and he had to get it right. She was his weakness and he hated to see her cry.

"Stop crying baby. That shit breaks my heart," Remo said as he wiped her tears. He could be a menace in the streets but he was always putty in Kalani's hands. She was the only female that he'd ever dealt with who saw the softer side of him.

"Obviously not since you keep doing the same shit," Kalani argued.

"Just tell me what you want Kalani," Remo begged.

"You already know what I want Kareem. We've been having this same conversation for months," Kalani replied.

"I'm trying to do better but you don't cut a nigga no slack. How the fuck you put me out of a house that I paid for? I pay all the bills in that bitch and I can't even live there," Remo fussed.

"You already know why I put you out though. Put the game on two players nigga. If I have to share you, then you better be prepared to share me too," Kalani noted.

"You never had to share me and I'll make a nigga bleed before I share you," Remo swore.

"Whatever," Kalani said as she rolled her eyes.

"You trying to let a nigga come back home or what?" Remo asked her.

"Are you trying to keep your dick in your pants?" Kalani countered.

"Always," Remo said as he pulled her in for a kiss.

"We'll see," Kalani said once they came up for air.

She thought she loved Jamar when they were together but it was nothing compared to how she felt about Remo. He was a lot to deal with but he was kindhearted once you got past his rough exterior. Kalani remembered when everything was good between them and she wanted that again.

"I love you, baby, but you gotta be more understanding. I don't have a regular day job and my hours are mostly at night," Remo said as she climbed back over to her seat.

"Don't even try to come at me like that Kareem. I know the kind of hours you work. Hell, I work there too. Time was never an issue and you know that. My only problem with you is your infidelity. If you were really good at what you were doing, I would have never found out about it. You just fuck with gutter rats who can't seem to keep the shit to themselves. They want everybody to know that they fucked one of the bosses," Kalani replied.

"I'm done with all that shit baby, I promise," Remo said as he grabbed her hand.

"I'll trust you until you give me a reason not to," Kalani replied, right as someone blew their horn behind them. Remo was at a red light that had changed multiple times. Every other car went around but some asshole just had to blow.

"Go the fuck around!" Remo yelled as he tried to get out of the car.

"Relax baby, he's going around," Kalani said as she laughed at the frown on his face. Remo and Nas popped off at the drop of a dime and always have. Remo had terrible road rage and Kalani always had to calm him down.

"I should shoot his stupid ass," Remo fumed as he looked at the driver who drove on the side of them.

"I need to go get my car," Kalani said once he started driving again.

"Your car is already at home with your sneaky ass," Remo said while looking over at her.

"How did you know where my car was?" Kalani asked. She knew that Remo had a spare key but he couldn't have known where she parked.

"The same way I knew where you were. Don't ever make the mistake of underestimating me. You should know better than that by now," Remo smirked as he continued to their destination.

Kalani didn't even bother asking him any questions. She knew the kind of man that she was dealing with and he wouldn't answer anyway. Remo was cut from a different cloth. It scared her to know that there was an exact replica of him roaming the streets somewhere.

"I don't know what you want me to tell you. I got her enough diapers, wipes, milk and clothes to last for a few months. I'm handling my business and I always have," Gavin said as he cradled Summer in his arms.

"Okay, Summer is straight but I have bills too. I missed work two Saturdays in a row and my pockets are feeling it. You and your wife are straight financially but I won't be if I keep missing on the busiest days. Today will make Saturday number three!" Misty yelled with tears in her eyes.

She was frustrated and she didn't know what to do. The babysitter that she had lined up turned out to be a disaster. She was a college student and all she wanted to do was party. Misty came home twice to find Summer crying with a soiled diaper on. She was no better than Milan and she just couldn't deal. One of the bottle girls at the club got her mother to babysit a few times but that didn't work out either. Tammy had three kids of her own and her mother was already having a hard enough time with them. Watching Summer was just too much on the older lady.

"What do you want me to tell you, Misty? It ain't like I can do the shit myself. I come over here on my off days to spend time with her but I can't babysit all night for you to shake your ass in the club. I have a wife at home," Gavin pointed out.

It was Saturday, but he still made time to go to the store and stock up on everything that his daughter needed. He had been cutting hair since six that morning and he was tired. Hearing Misty bitch about the same thing was not something that he was in the mood for.

"You had a wife at home when you used to come over here and fuck me too," Misty spat angrily.

"I think that's what the problem is. You must be feeling some type of way because a nigga ain't fucking you no more. I already told you that shit was a wrap when Toi heard us. All she needed to see was me coming out of your room and I would have been busted," Gavin said.

"Are you fucking serious right now? I don't give a fuck about you not sleeping with me anymore. Dick comes a dime a dozen and I've never had a problem getting it. This is about me needing a reliable babysitter so I can work when I need to. You're always saying how your mother wants grandkids. Why can't you tell her about Summer?" Misty inquired.

"Yeah, she does want grandkids, from my wife. In her eyes, Stori's baby will be my first child and her first grandchild. I know you don't like it but that's just the way it is." Gavin shrugged.

"Wow. So, you really don't have any intentions on telling your family that you have a daughter? Stori can push out ten babies but they'll never be your first," Misty pointed out.

"You were the one who was so adamant about having a baby. You were so desperate for Remo to be the daddy and look at how that turned out. Don't get mad at me for how this shit went down. You played yourself," Gavin said as he laid Summer down in her playpen.

Misty wanted to claw his eyes out but she kept her composure. She didn't regret her daughter but she knew that life would be a whole lot easier if she didn't have her. It was crazy to her how a fourteen year old could do a better job of taking care of her child than grown ass women. Misty missed the hell out of Toi and she even swallowed her pride and called Stori. Gavin already told her what his wife had said, but she took a chance anyway. Just like she'd told her husband, Stori told her the exact same thing. She didn't appreciate Toi keeping her baby while she was sexing a nigga right down the hall. Misty wondered how she would feel if she knew that the nigga in question was her husband.

"Fuck you, Gavin. Get the fuck out of my face with your lame ass. I bet if Nas told you to do something, it would have already been done by now. You be so far up his ass and all him and Remo do is sit back and laugh at you. They don't even like you going nowhere with them because they know your ass is a fraud. You can't even dress yourself without asking Naseem where he gets his shit from. You're too damn grown to still be a follower," Misty snapped.

"I guess you saying that is supposed to make me feel some type of way," Gavin laughed.

Truthfully, her words did make him feel some type of way. He was well aware that Remo didn't fuck with him but Nas was his boy. He liked the way Nas dressed so, yeah, he did like to know where he shopped at. Nas was popular and Gavin got clout just for being his friend. Misty was in her feelings and she was trying to hurt his.

"No, I'm saying it because it's true. Every crew has that one stupid looking friend who tries to be down but does too much. That one friend who they laugh at for trying to be hard knowing that they're really a fuck boy. I hate to be the bearer of bad news, but that friend is you," Misty said as she laughed hysterically.

"Laugh at the fact that you still don't have a babysitter. Stupid ass bitch," Gavin smirked as he walked out of the room and out the front door.

Misty hated to admit it, but he was right. Saturday nights at the club were always lit and she never walked away with less than eight hundred dollars. Unfortunately, she would never know because she had no one reliable to watch her baby. After grabbing the baby monitor, Misty walked out of the room and headed to the kitchen. She poured herself a glass of wine before taking a seat on the sofa. She aimlessly flipped through the channels on the tv until her phone started to ring. She blew out a breath of frustration when she saw that one of the dancers from the club was calling.

"What's up girl?" Misty greeted when she answered the phone.

"Where have you been stranger? A few of your regulars have been asking for you," Pinky said.

"Girl, shit is just all fucked up. I can't find a reliable babysitter nowhere. Remo and Nas will probably fire my ass if I don't get it together soon," Misty replied.

"You know them crazy ass niggas don't care. As long as the club is making money, they don't care about nothing else. But, bitch, you need to make it your business to get over here tomorrow night. A local rapper and his crew are having a record release party and it's supposed to be lit. Remo and Nas already hired extra security and everything. They're expecting at least one hundred niggas to arrive with their entourage. I'm going get me some new gear and get ready to make that money!" Pinky yelled.

"Damn bitch! My pockets been hurting too. I have to find somebody reliable to watch Summer. I'm not missing out on all that money," Misty replied eagerly.

"Why can't your sister watch her? All she do is hang around the club following Nas all day. He handled her ass bad last night and she still didn't want to leave," Pinky noted.

"Milan is dumb as fuck. A nigga only have to tell me it's over one time for me to get it." Misty frowned.

"Stop lying hoe. You used to be the same way behind Remo. And speaking of his ass, I heard that he was fucking the new bottle girl," Pinky said.

"Which one?" Misty asked.

104

"I think her name is Lexus or Lexie. Bitch, I don't know. She be looking at his ass just like you used to. Remo hit her with that dope dick and she's in love. Kalani is still that bitch so she's wasting her time," Pinky replied.

"Girl, fuck Kalani. That bitch be in her feelings every time she see me. I never let that hoe fix my drinks. She might spit in my shit," Misty laughed.

"Well, I just wanted to call and tell you what was up. I know none of them other hoes would have. You know they hate a little competition but I welcome it," Pinky said.

"Thanks for the heads up boo. I'll be there tomorrow, even I have to dance with Summer on my hip," Misty laughed before she hung up.

As soon as she did, she heard yelling coming from the front porch. She jumped up and discreetly peeped out of the window. When she saw Milan standing there going off on an older white man, she opened the door to see what was up.

"This is against the law! It's almost nine o'clock on a Saturday night! This shit is bogus!" Milan yelled to the uncaring man.

He got back into his car without uttering a word before he pulled off. Milan was hysterical as she continued to scream and curse at him.

"What's going on?" Misty asked as Milan dialed a number on her phone.

"That high yellow, dog ass nigga had me served with divorce papers! I'm not signing shit!" Milan yelled as tears cascaded down her rosy cheeks.

"I know the fuck he didn't." Misty frowned in anger.

"We didn't have irreconcilable differences. He should have kept it real and said that he couldn't keep his dick in his pants. I'm not signing shit," Milan fumed as she read over the divorce decree.

"Nas is wrong for that bullshit. Fuck him, sis. If he wants out of the marriage, let his ass go," Misty replied.

"Yeah, I bet you would like to see that," Milan said while looking at her sideways.

"What the hell does that mean?" Misty questioned.

"Don't act like you weren't salty about me and Naseem being together. You couldn't have Remo and you didn't want me to have Nas. You probably did try to fuck him like he said," Milan argued.

She wasn't dumb. She saw the looks that Misty used to give her husband. It was the same look that all the hoes in the club gave him. Milan and her sister were close and, in her heart, she didn't believe that Misty really wanted her husband. It was Remo who she was head over heels in love with. Truthfully, Milan had to stop herself from lusting over her brother-in-law a few times too. He was just so much like her husband and she couldn't help it.

"I know you don't believe that dumb bullshit. I might not be a saint but fucking over you is something that I would never do. No man walking this earth can make me cross my only sister. I'm offended that you would even come at me like that," Misty replied.

"I'm sorry Misty. I'm in my feelings about this divorce shit but I know you wouldn't do me like that," Milan said as she hugged her.

"It's okay girl. Let me pour you a glass of wine," Misty offered.

"Fuck a glass. Bring me the whole damn bottle. I'm stressed the fuck out," Milan said.

"Looks like we're both having a bad day," Misty sighed as he sat down on the sofa and handed her sister the half full bottle of wine.

Misty laughed when Milan turned the bottle up to her mouth and drank until it was empty. She got up and grabbed another bottle and filled her glass up again.

"What's going on with you?" Milan asked.

"Same shit as always. I'm tired of doing everything on my own. Gavin gets to live his life like he wants to while I'm stuck inside with a baby. Pinky told me that the club is gonna be lit tomorrow night but I doubt if I'll even be able to go. Not unless my baby sister wants to watch her only niece," Misty said while looking over at Milan.

Milan was twenty-seven and only a year younger than Misty. She was the worst babysitter ever but Misty was desperate to make some quick cash. She would even

106

compromise with her sister and try to make it back earlier than her usual time. She just needed to keep her bank account right and she couldn't do that without the club.

"I'm sorry girl but me and kids just don't mix," Milan replied.

"Why were you trying to have a baby with Nas if you feel that way?" Misty questioned.

"The same reason you were trying to have one with Remo. I want to keep my man around just like you wanted to keep yours." Milan shrugged.

"Sometimes I wish I would have just stayed in Texas. At least we have family there and lots of help. I'm not sure if moving here was the best decision. I should have just visited every year for Mardi Gras and stayed my ass at home," Misty sighed.

"That's all on you, but New Orleans is home for me now. I just have to get my stupid ass husband to get his mind right," Milan said as she started drinking from the new bottle of wine.

"Fuck these niggas. They're even worse here than in Texas. Especially Gavin, with his weak ass. You talking about me but he's the one who acts like he wants to fuck your husband," Misty replied.

"Girl, Nas don't give a fuck about nobody but Remo. Gavin is a damn fool if he thinks Nas is his friend. Naseem only tolerates him because he gives him a place to stay sometimes. He probably would have been cut him off if it wasn't for that," Milan said.

"I wouldn't even be having all these problems if he would just tell his family that Summer exist. He's an only child and I'm sure his parents would be happy to help out since they're both retired," Misty noted.

"You're better than me, sis. I wouldn't wait for his ass to do shit. You need to look them up and tell them yourself," Milan said.

"I don't know nothing about them except their last name is Mitchell. They got a bunch of people with that common ass name," Misty pointed out.

"Okay, and we're about to get online and find the right ones. Go get the laptop. I got time today bitch. Nas pissed me off and everybody can get it," Milan said as Misty laughed.

She tried to remember any and every thing that Gavin had told her about his parents. It was mostly sex with them but they did talk occasionally. Milan was grilling her but she didn't have many answers to her questions. All Misty needed was a number or address and she would take it from there. Mr. and Mrs. Mitchell were about to be introduced to their very first granddaughter.

"Bitch, wait, that nigga was crying real tears?" Stori asked once Kalani finished telling her about her final date with Omar.

They had just finished bagging up a bunch of candy for Nas and Remo. Stori hadn't been in business with them long but the money was already lovely. They were now in the basement where Stori tightened up Kalani's sew-in. Her shop was closed on Sundays but she usually did Kalani, Toi and her grandmother's hair on that day. Toi and her grandmother got their hair done the night before since they were going to church that morning. Toi stayed by their grandmother for a little while afterwards and Gavin was on his way to pick her up.

"Girl, real newborn baby tears. I felt so bad about everything. I tried to call him to apologize but he changed his number," Kalani said.

"I would have changed my shit and probably moved

too. I wonder how the fuck they got in that man's house though. Them niggas should have been evaluated when they were younger," Stori laughed.

"Bitch, they were sitting in there like they pay bills. Nas was fixing sandwiches and everything. I don't know how they got in there and I don't know how they knew exactly where my car was parked. Remo keeps telling me not to underestimate him and I never will again," Kalani replied.

"That's some crazy shit right there. If it didn't happen to you, I probably wouldn't have believed it," Stori said.

"I feel the same way. Remo is on some good nigga shit right now. He moved all his stuff back in the house and he's been the perfect man. I know it won't last long but we'll see. He better not let me find out about nothing that he's doing wrong. I told that nigga that if I have to share him, he better be prepared to share me too," Kalani replied.

"Let it go Kalani. You gon' fuck around and get somebody killed. You know your nigga ain't wrapped too tight. Stop involving other people in your bullshit," Stori fussed.

"I'm not trying to involve nobody else but Kareem got me fucked up. He can't do whatever he wants and expect me to take it. He got options and so do I," Kalani huffed.

"Gavin is in his feelings about me working with Remo. He claims that he don't trust him like that," Stori said while changing the subject.

"Why not? Remo loves you like a sister. He would never try to do you dirty. Fucking over you is the equivalent of fucking over me. That nigga ain't stupid. Tell Gavin that you're working with his best friend too. Does he trust Nas?" Kalani questioned.

"Truthfully, I think he's just scared of Remo," Stori chuckled.

"Seriously? How can he be afraid of Remo and not Nas? They're both the same kind of crazy," Kalani noted.

"I don't know. I guess he considers Nas as more of a friend. And let's just be honest, Remo makes it very clear that he don't fuck with Gavin on no level," Stori laughed.

"Remo don't fuck with nobody who he thinks is trying to get close to Nas. He's like a possessive bitch. He barked on a dude at the bar for calling Nas brother," Kalani said while shaking her head.

"Front door," the alarm chimed, letting Stori know that Gavin and Toi were home.

"We'll continue this conversation later," Stori said, right as Toi came bouncing down the steps.

"Good evening," Toi spoke politely. She gave Kalani a hug before wrapping her arms around Stori's waist.

"Hey, my Stanka. How was church?" Stori asked before kissing her cheek.

"It was good. Can I go by Maddie and Hannah for a little while?" Toi asked.

Maddie and Hannah were two sisters who lived across the street from them. Their mother was a single parent and she took good care of Toi when she visited. They were always inviting her somewhere and Stori felt comfortable letting her go. They had been staying over there for three years now and Toi clicked with them instantly.

"Yeah, go change out of your dress first," Stori replied.

"Can we eat pizza tonight since you didn't cook anything?" Toi asked.

Stori had spent the majority of her off day cooking up candy for Remo and Nas. The shit was selling faster than she could make it, so she doubled up on her ingredients to make more. Toi was used to seeing pots on the stove but there were none that day.

"Pizza it is." Stori smiled before Toi walked away.

"Toi is so sweet. Lady better not try to take credit for nothing when she becomes something special. You know the deadbeat parents always come out of the shadows for shit like that," Kalani said.

"Lady better keep that same energy that she got now. A phone call a day and a visit four or five times a year will suffice. My baby said she's gonna be a pediatric nurse and I'm gonna make sure of it," Stori said, right as Gavin came walking down the steps.

"What's for dinner baby?" Gavin asked as he walked up and hugged her from behind. Stori was almost done curling Kalani's hair. She had to work the bar and she was already dressed in the club's shirt with some leggings.

"Toi wants pizza," Stori replied.

"What about what Gavin wants?" he asked while kissing her neck.

Stori wanted to feel something, anything, but it just didn't happen. Her neck was one of her hot spots and Gavin couldn't even make her wet by kissing it. He stuck his tongue in her ear and all Stori felt was a little tickle.

"I hope Gavin wants pizza too because that's what we're eating. I can get you some wings or something else off the menu if you don't want that," Stori offered.

Gavin was happy that her back was turned because the frown on his face couldn't be contained. Stori always disregarded his feelings and that shit drove him crazy.

"I don't want nothing from the pizza spot. It'll be nice if I get to pick the meal every once in a while," Gavin noted.

He sounded like a jealous bitch to Kalani but she stayed out of their business. Kalani liked her best friend's husband but she had never seen that side of him before. For as long as she'd known Stori, she and Toi had been doing the exact same thing. She understood that Gavin was her husband now but he had that only child syndrome bad. Stori did all that she could to make Toi feel loved and wanted. She never wanted her sister to feel like she was thrown away by her, the same way she often felt about Lady. She was fourteen years old and Gavin's overgrown ass should have understood that. He was acting as if he and Toi were rivals fighting for Stori's affection.

"It's not even that serious Gavin. If you wanted something else, that's all you had to do was say that. Toi is not hard to please at all," Stori replied.

"Okay, well let's eat Chinese," he replied.

"That's cool." Stori shrugged like it was no big deal.

"Thanks baby," Gavin replied with a satisfied smile on his face.

Kalani couldn't believe her ears. Remo always called him a fuck boy and she was starting to see it for herself. He seemed pleased that Stori was letting him choose the meal. He was acting like he'd accomplished something serious. Kalani never thought she'd dislike Gavin for any reason but she couldn't stand him at the moment.

"I'm leaving Stori. I have my phone and my house key," Toi said when she came back downstairs.

"Okay baby. Do you mind if we eat Chinese tonight instead of pizza?" Stori asked.

"No, I don't mind," Toi said sweetly, right as someone knocked on the shop's door.

"I know damn well they see that big ass closed sign out front," Stori said as she finished Kalani's hair.

Toi looked out of the windows and squealed in delight before she opened the door.

"Summer! I missed you so much." Toi smiled as she grabbed the baby's car seat and took her out of it. Summer was eight months old now and a little bigger than when Toi last saw her.

"What's good Misty? I'm closed today and I already told you that Toi can't babysit anymore," Stori spoke up.

Misty sat two huge duffle bags on the floor, along with Summer's diaper bag. Gavin's heart was beating out of his chest and he was praying that Misty wasn't on no bullshit.

"That's cool, her daddy can watch her," Misty smirked while looking at Gavin.

She was fed up and at the end of her rope. After searching online all night, she and Milan ran into a brick wall while trying to find something on Gavin's parents. She was looking for people who she knew nothing about and it did nothing but frustrate her. Misty was tired of missing work while Gavin got to live a carefree life. She didn't give a fuck about his feelings and she cared even less about Stori's. She was going to the club and make some money.

"Bitch, who is her daddy? Inquiring minds want to know. That pussy got more miles on it than a triathlon!" Kalani yelled as she jumped up.

"You shut the fuck up and mind your business. Gavin, get your daughter. I have to work," Misty said as she hurriedly rushed out the door and into Milan's awaiting car.

"Did that bitch just say your daughter? Did I hear that right Gavin? Summer is your baby? The same fucking baby that you had my little sister babysitting. Is that what I just heard?" Stori asked as she pulled her long sew-in into a knot at the top of her head.

"Stori, baby, just let me explain," Gavin pleaded with a shaky voice.

"Nah nigga, explain this ass whipping that you're about to get!" Stori yelled as she punched him in the face.

Gavin grabbed his nose as the blood gushed in between his fingers. Stori didn't mind swinging on anybody, so he wasn't even surprised. When Kalani saw that her friend wasn't done, she kicked off her slides and got ready to put in work with her. As soon as Gavin tried to come at her, Stori and Kalani charged at him. They punched, scratched and kicked every part of his body that they could. Toi was screaming for them to stop and Summer was wailing to the top of her little lungs. When Gavin fell to the floor, Stori grabbed her hot flat irons and started hitting him with them until they fell apart.

"Ahhh! Fuck!" Gavin screamed as the hot tools connected with his skin.

"Stori! Stop, please!" Toi cried as she pulled her sister's shirt.

She had strapped Summer back in her car seat as she attempted to break up the fight. Hearing her baby sister sound so broken snapped Stori back to reality. She was breathing hard and so was Kalani. Stori felt bad when Toi buried her face in her chest and cried.

"I'm sorry Stori. I didn't know that she was Gavin's baby, I swear," Toi sobbed, breaking Stori's heart.

"Don't cry baby. I know you didn't know and I'm not mad at you. Go upstairs and wait for me, okay?" Stori said, trying her best to sound like her normal self.

"Will you be okay?" Toi asked worriedly.

"I'll be fine baby. I'm coming up in a minute," Stori promised her with a forced smile.

Toi nodded and reluctantly went upstairs. Gavin's pathetic ass struggled but he was finally able to stand. Stori grabbed his keys that had fallen on the floor and removed her house and car keys before throwing them at him.

"Get your baby and get the fuck out of my house. You can come back and get your shit whenever I'm available," Stori fumed as she looked at him in disgust.

"Baby, please, just hear me out," Gavin begged.

"Just leave Gavin. If you know what's best for you, you'll walk out that door and don't look back," Stori gritted.

"Is it that easy for you, Stori? The least you can do is talk to me. I fucked up and I was wrong, but I swear that was my first and last time stepping outside of our marriage," Gavin said through his swollen, bloody lips.

Stori opened her drawer and grabbed her gun. She pointed it directly at his head without an ounce of fear in her eyes. If she did love him, Gavin couldn't tell. Stori was emotionless as she threatened his life like it was nothing.

"I'm giving you a choice. You can either walk out on your own or get carried out in a body bag. What's up?" Stori asked him.

Gavin wanted to continue pleading his case but he was no fool. Stori had her own little arsenal of weapons hidden throughout the house. Even Gavin didn't know where all of them were. Misty was a dirty bitch but she would get hers soon enough. Gavin had never been alone with Summer and he didn't know what to do. She was sitting in her car seat looking around like she was just as confused. Although he was in pain, he limped over to the car seat and managed to pick it up. Once he had the bags secured in his hand, Stori pushed him out and slammed the door behind him.

"Aww friend. I'm so sorry about all of this. It's okay to cry. You know I got you," Kalani said as she pulled Stori in for a hug. She rubbed her friend's back, trying her best to comfort her. Kalani was waiting for her shirt to be saturated with tears, but that never happened. When she pulled back and looked at Stori, her eyes were as dry as cotton.

"Are you okay boo?" Kalani asked her.

"I'm fine," Stori replied nonchalantly.

"You don't have to be strong in front of me, Stori. You can cry if you want to. I know it hurts," Kalani said.

"Bitch please. I'm not hurt and I'm not about to cry. I'm pissed the fuck off." Stori frowned.

"Okay, I'm lost," Kalani said with her face twisted in confusion. Stori didn't look like she even cared about what had just happened.

"I'm pissed that my sister was put in the middle of Gavin's bullshit. I'm pissed that I had that bitch Misty sitting in my shop and didn't know what was up. I'm pissed that I fucked his ass like a porn star for two hours this morning. And most of all, I'm pissed that I stayed with a muthafucker that I didn't even love for so long. I wanted a way out and he gave me a damn good one," Stori rambled.

"Well, look on the bright side. At least you didn't have no babies for his ass," Kalani said.

"Thank God for that. I just want to make sure that Toi is okay. She really loved Summer," Stori sighed in frustration.

"Go see about her while I clean up this mess," Kalani offered.

"I thought you had to bartend tonight," Stori reminded her.

"Girl, fuck that bar. You and Toi are way more important. I'll let Remo know what's up. I should tell him that Gavin hit me." Kalani frowned.

"Gavin is a bitch but he doesn't deserve to die," Stori laughed as she headed up the stairs.

She found Toi lying in her bed facing the wall. When Stori laid next to her, she turned around to look at her.

"Is he gone?" Toi asked.

"Yes and he's never coming back," Stori promised.

"Good. I hate him for what he did to you. I can't believe that he Summer's father." Toi frowned.

"That makes two of us. But, listen Toi, I don't want you to feel bad about this. You didn't know and neither did I. You know I would have never agreed to let you babysit if I did. None of this is your fault and I'm not mad at you. You're my baby and I love you," Stori said as she kissed her forehead.

116

"I love you, too." Toi smiled.

"It was just me and you long before Gavin entered the picture and it'll just be the two of us again," Stori noted.

"If I ask you something, will you promise not to get mad?" Toi inquired.

"Do I ever? You can talk to me about anything. You know that, don't you?" Stori asked.

"Yes, I do." Toi nodded.

"Okay, so what's up?" Stori questioned.

"Was it Gavin who I heard in the room with Misty that day?" Toi inquired.

That entire situation had slipped Stori's mind but she now wondered the same thing. That nigga was doing his thing right up under her nose and she never suspected a thing. She couldn't wait to talk to Kalani about what Toi had just said. She had forgotten all about that situation.

"I don't know baby. Maybe it was." Stori shrugged.

"Do you love Gavin?" Toi asked, taking Stori by surprise.

"Do you think I love him?" Stori countered.

"Sometimes I do and sometimes I don't. I think he annoys you a lot." Toi shrugged.

Her baby sister was very smart and observant. Stori didn't even think Toi picked up on how she felt about her husband but she obviously did.

"I told you that I would never lie to you and I meant that. No, I don't love Gavin but I really tried to. I got comfortable with him but that shouldn't have been enough. Never settle for anything less than what you deserve. When you grow up and decide to date or get married, make sure it's for love and nothing else," Stori said.

"Okay." Toi nodded with a smile.

"Are you okay Stanka?" Stori asked.

"Yeah, I'm okay. Are you sad Stori?" Toi asked her.

"Not at all. If you're good, then so am I," Stori said as she got up from the bed.

"Remo said that I can always call him or Nas if I need anything," Toi said as she followed Stori out of her bedroom.

"I'm sure you can but what do you need?" Stori asked.

"Nothing but maybe I can ask him to beat Gavin up," Toi said seriously, as Stori doubled over with laughter.

"No baby, I don't want you to do that. Call Maddie and Hannah to see if they can come over for a while. We can order pizza and pig out on junk food," Stori said.

"Yay!" Toi yelled excitedly as she ran back to her room to get her phone.

Stori smiled when she heard her on the phone talking and laughing with her friends. Kalani came upstairs a little while later and they ordered some food. Toi's friends came over and they had a good time. Once everyone ate, Stori and Kalani enjoyed a bottle of wine while the girls danced and sang karaoke. The smile on Toi's face was genuine and that was all that Stori wanted. If her baby sister was happy, then so was she. Finally being rid of Gavin was also something to make her smile. She was good on money, so his finances wouldn't be missed either.

"So, about that hookup," Kalani leaned over and whispered in Stori's ear.

"Bitch, Gavin is gone but I'm still a married woman. It's only been a few hours. And don't tell Remo about what happened. I know he'll be trying to find me a new man tomorrow," Stori laughed.

"Fuck tomorrow. He'll be trying tonight. The nerve of Misty to be all up in your shop getting her hair done knowing that she was fucking your husband." Kalani frowned.

"That doesn't bother me as much as them having my little sister babysit her. That was a line that they should have never crossed. It's all good though," Stori said as she nodded her head, deep in thought.

"So, it's a no on the hookup?" Kalani asked.

"It's a hell no," Stori laughed.

She enjoyed the company of men but she wasn't pressed or desperate to get one. Not every man could be trusted and she had Toi to think about. She was good on a hookup. She had to officially get rid of Gavin before she did anything else. Once that was done, she would probably think about dating again. Until then, it was just her and Toi and she was good with that.

After driving around looking for Misty all night, Gavin finally pulled up to his parents' house. He knew that her pathetic ass was in the club because he saw her car parked out front. He couldn't go inside with a baby and he couldn't leave Summer in the car alone. He tried calling Nas a few times but he didn't answer. Gavin ended up parking in front of Misty's house waiting for her to return, but she never did. When he went back to the club, her car was gone and so were most of the others. Nas was still there but he had turned his phone off.

It was now a little after seven that morning and Gavin was exhausted. He stopped at Walmart to pick up a few things since Stori didn't let him take anything from the house. He wanted a shower and a bed more than anything but he knew that would have to wait. Gavin dreaded having to go into his parents' house but he really had no other choice. He didn't know the first thing about taking care of a baby. Misty had packed Summer more than enough stuff, so he didn't know when she planned to come back for her.

"Fuck it," Gavin said as he eased his aching body out of the car.

Stori and Kalani had really done a number on him but he couldn't even be mad. He had done the unthinkable and his wife had a right to be upset. He was scared about what the future held for him and Stori. He loved his wife more than anything and he couldn't see himself with anyone else. Gavin was a fool for cheating on her and he had lots of regrets. He prayed that once she calmed down, they could have a talk and try to repair what he had broken.

"Come on pretty girl. Time to go meet your grandparents," Gavin said as he got Summer's car seat out of the car.

He walked up the steps to his parents' home and rang the bell. The fresh aroma of coffee could be smelled, even though the door hadn't been opened yet.

"Who is it?" Gavin's mother, Karen, sang from the other side of the door.

"It's me ma," Gavin replied. He heard her fumbling with the locks before the door was finally opened.

"Gavin! Oh, my God! What happened to your face?" Karen screeched.

Gavin had cleaned up the dry blood from his face with some of Summer's wipes. He still looked a hot ass mess even without it. His nose was swollen and his lip looked almost twice it's normal size. He had scratches everywhere and his eye had a black ring forming underneath it. No one would have ever believed that two women as small as Kalani and Stori would have done so much damage.

"Me and Stori had a fight," Gavin said.

"What! I know damn well you didn't hit your wife," Karen fumed.

"Look at my face ma. Does it look like I got a lick in?" Gavin asked sarcastically.

"Don't get smart with me, boy. I'll leave your ass on this front porch, black eye and all," Karen fussed.

122

"I wasn't getting smart ma. I apologize for how that came out," Gavin said.

Karen moved aside to let him in. She was so busy focusing on his face that she never did see the car seat until he walked into the house.

"Whose baby?" Karen asked, right as her husband walked into the living room.

"Hey son. What in the world happened to your face and whose baby is that?" Gordon, his father asked.

"Stori beat his ass, so that explains the face. But, I wanna know who this baby belongs to," Karen said.

"She's mine," Gavin admitted.

"Excuse me? I don't recall ever seeing your wife pregnant," Karen said as she put her hand on her ample hips.

"I think we need to sit down," Gordon suggested. He grabbed his wife's hand and pulled her down on the sofa next him.

Gavin blew out a breath of nervousness as he ran the entire story down to his parents. His mother was so hurt and upset that she started crying. She loved Stori and she hated that her son had done something so stupid. As much as she loved her son, she sometimes wanted to be done with him. A mother's love was unconditional and she had to take the good with the bad. She didn't have to ask how Stori took the news. His bruised face showed just how pissed she obviously was.

"How do you even know if you're really the father Gavin? She's a beautiful baby but she looks nothing like you," his father said as he held his wife's trembling hand.

"We had a DNA test done. We actually had two because I wanted to be sure. She looks like her mom," Gavin replied.

"How fucking stupid can you be Gavin? It was bad enough that you cheated on your wife and got a stripper pregnant. Why the hell would you involve Toi in the bullshit?" Karen fussed.

"That wasn't my doing. Misty was the one who asked her to babysit," Gavin said, sounding as dumb as he looked.

"And you let it fly?" his father questioned, as Gavin lowered his head in shame.

"I want to see this Misty bitch. I don't even know her and I don't like her ass already. What kind of mother drops their child off and doesn't even call to see how they're doing?" Karen fussed.

"An unfit one obviously," Gordon chimed in.

Gavin didn't say anything but he didn't agree with what they were saying. Misty was wrong for leaving Summer the way she did but she wasn't unfit. She took great care of their daughter and she didn't leave her with just anybody. She was fed up and her actions showed it.

"I feel so bad for Stori. She didn't deserve this," Karen said as she wiped her teary eyes.

"And neither did we. Because of your selfishness, we missed out on almost a year of our first grandchild's life. What's her name?" his father asked.

"Summer," Gavin replied.

"How did you meet her mother?" Karen asked.

"Nas is married to her sister, Milan," Gavin replied, making his father shake his head.

"That figures. You always did follow everybody else's lead," Karen said in disgust.

"I didn't follow nobody's lead. I made a mistake," Gavin replied angrily.

He hated when his parents ganged up on him like that. He hated it even more when they insinuated that he didn't have a mind of his own.

"Yeah, just like you made a mistake when you got caught selling weed. You let your so called friend sucker you into some shit that cost us almost ten grand to get you out of. You swore that you wanted to be an electrician until one of your friends said something about cosmetology school. You never even knew how to cut hair before then. You were in love with your Audi until you saw one of your friends with a Camaro that you just had to have. When is this going to end Gavin? You're thirty years old son. It's time for you to lead and stop following. Now, you've gone and ruined your marriage following behind Naseem," his father argued.

124

He told his son from day one that Nas wasn't the kind of friend that he needed in his life. Gordon could tell that Nas had lots of street smarts and that was something that his son lacked. Still, Gavin looked up to the younger man, almost to the point that he idolized him. Gordon had met Nas a few times and he could see that he ran circles around his son. Nas was well known and popular with the ladies. That was all it took to make Gavin worship the ground he walked on.

"I didn't ruin my marriage. Me and Stori haven't even discussed it yet," Gavin replied.

"You're a damn fool if you think Stori's gonna take you back after this. You might as well get comfortable in your old room. I'm sure that's where you'll be staying at from now on," Karen said as she got up to get Summer out of her car seat.

"We need to talk to her mother. This is our grandchild and we don't mind helping out sometimes, but we're done raising kids. We had one child for a reason," Gordon said.

"You got that shit right. Get that bitch on the line and let me talk to her," Karen fumed.

"She's not gonna answer," Gavin said.

"When's the last time you changed her diaper? She's drenched. Where is her bag? This is ridiculous. This poor baby is not even being cared for properly," Karen fussed as she walked to the back of the house to clean Summer up.

Gavin went out to his car and got his and Summer's bags. Staying with his parents was the last thing that he wanted to do but he was praying that it was temporary. As much as he didn't want to, he knew that he had to take a few days off from work. There was no way in hell he was going to the shop looking like a monster. He wouldn't be able to convince anybody that his wife and her best friend did it and he wasn't going to try. All of that was irrelevant to him anyway. Getting his wife back was his main focus. Stori wasted no time blocking his number, but Gavin wasn't giving up on his marriage. He made a stupid mistake and he needed Stori to forgive him. His wife was his world and he was willing to do anything to make her see that.

"Man, I'm tired as fuck," Remo said as he and Nas put the rest of their money away.

"Me too but it was worth it. We made a killing up in this bitch. Misty showed the fuck out," Nas replied with a yawn.

Misty hadn't been to the club in a few weeks but she made up for it when she returned. She had them niggas going crazy and she secured a nice bag at the end of her shift. As many times as Remo wanted to fire her, he was happy that he didn't. She was good at what she did and she kept the customers coming back for more.

They had a huge crowd in there the night before since some local rappers came through. Nas and Remo had never worked so hard before and they ended up staying at the club overnight. They made almost a month's profit in one night, so they weren't complaining. They took turns resting in their office but that wasn't enough. They both wanted a shower and a bed.

Remo was happy that Kalani didn't work that night because it would have been too hard for him to keep up with her. Something was up with Stori, so she ended up staying the night at her house. It was now after ten and he and Nas were drained. Nas had to be up early the following morning to go to work.

"I hope Kalani ass ain't sleep. I'm hungry as fuck and I don't feel like stopping nowhere," Remo said as they headed out together.

Mondays were always slow and they were letting Bee close up for them. They only needed one bartender and a few girls to work.

"Kalani been having that ass on lock," Nas laughed.

"Yeah man, I gotta get my shit together before she really try to leave my ass," Remo laughed.

"That bitch Milan been on some fatal attraction shit lately. She got them divorce papers and went crazy," Nas replied.

"Fuck her. I told you not to even marry that bitch." Remo frowned.

"Alright bro. Be safe and let me know when you get in," Nas said as he gave his brother a one-armed hug.

"Fuck work tomorrow nigga. Rest up," Remo said before they both got into their cars and pulled off.

"Fuck!" Nas hissed when he realized what time it was. He planned to crash at his grandmother's house again but he was past her deadline. Going to Milan's house was out and Danni was starting to annoy him. She was getting too comfortable and she wanted Nas to be up in her face every day. The thought of getting her to rent him a room crossed his mind briefly, but he decided against it. Knowing her disgusting ass, she would have been trying to stay there with him. Just then, Nas thought about something. Gavin had given him the key to his house and the code to the alarm. He'd only used it once but Stori didn't mind. Gavin had been blowing his phone up for the past two days, but Nas was too busy to answer. Whatever he had to say probably wasn't important anyway.

When he pulled up to the house, Nas noticed that Gavin's car wasn't there but that was nothing new. Stori's car was usually parked in her garage so he figured they both went somewhere in Gavin's. Sometimes they had date nights and he figured that's where they were. Nas grabbed his duffle bag from the trunk and let himself into the house. He rushed to shut the alarm off before locking the door behind him. Nas didn't want to turn on any lights, just in case someone was home. He used the flashlight on his phone to maneuver his way up the stairs. The door was closed to Stori and Gavin's bedroom, so he kept going down the hall to the room that he usually occupied. Before he got there, Stori's voice startled him.

"I guess asking if you already knew is a stupid question," Stori said as she turned on the lamp to reveal her beautiful face.

She was in the room right next to the one that Nas always slept in. Stori had been sitting in the dark drinking wine when she heard the alarm go off. Although she'd taken Gavin's keys, she still didn't underestimate him. She relaxed when she looked at the camera on her phone and saw that it was Nas instead.

"What's good Stori? Did I already know what?" Nas asked.

"Did you know that Summer was Gavin's baby?" Stori asked, catching Nas by surprise.

Now he knew why Gavin's car wasn't out front. Nas felt like he had walked into the middle of some bullshit that he was too tired to entertain. He really had to get his shit together now because that was probably his last night at Stori's house. Had he known that they were into it, he would have gone to Remo and Kalani's house for the night.

"Man, shit was mad crazy but, yeah, I knew. That was Gavin's shit and it wasn't my place to interfere," Nas replied honestly.

"You're good Nas, I was just asking. You didn't owe me anything and I don't have no hard feelings towards you. Gavin owed me loyalty, not you. Good night," Stori concluded.

She didn't sound upset and he was happy for that much. Nas kept going to the bedroom and she heard the shower water turn on a few minutes later. Stori had been deep in thought all day about her situation with Gavin. It was over and there was no doubt in her mind about that. She had already made an appointment to speak with a divorce lawyer, so that was a wrap. She knew that she had to talk to him eventually but she was too upset to do it now. Stori didn't want or need him to explain anything. He just needed to get all of his belongings from her house and nothing more.

When the shower water turned off about twenty minutes later, Stori was downing the last bit of her wine. She wasn't drunk or tipsy but the wine made her feel relaxed. Stori got up from her spot by the window and prepared to go to bed. She had to get up early to fix breakfast for Toi and make sure she got to school on time. Gavin usually helped out with that, but Stori had it covered. None of her appointments were that early anyway.

"You good?" Nas asked when Stori passed by the room.

She peeked inside and saw Nas standing there shirtless with a pair of Nike joggers on. His arms, chest and back were covered in a variety of colorful tattoos. Nas looked like he had on a long sleeve graffiti shirt that stopped at his wrist. The colors looks vivid against his light colored skin and the art work was remarkable.

"Yeah, I'm good." Stori smiled.

"You gon' be straight love. Hurt don't last forever," Nas encouraged.

"Who said I was hurt? Angry, yes, but that's the only emotion that I feel," Stori said honestly as she walked into the room.

Something happened and she felt like she was no longer in control of her own body. Maybe it was the scent of the masculine soap that he used or the way his chiseled chest was on full display. Stori didn't know and she really didn't care. She walked up to Nas and ran her hand along his tattoos. His eyes grew dark as he lowered them to meet her gaze. He didn't move as Stori's hands went up and down his chest and abs. When she pulled at the waistband of his joggers, Nas grabbed her small hands and held them in his.

"How much wine did you drink Stori?" Nas asked.

"Just one bottle. Why?" she countered.

"I need you to really be aware of what you're doing right now. Ain't no turning back if we go there. I don't need you waking up in the morning with regrets," Nas replied.

"The only regret I have is marrying your fake ass friend and not doing this sooner," Stori said as she stood on the tips of her toes and kissed him.

As rugged as Nas was, his kisses were soft and sweet. He picked Stori's small frame up and she instinctively wrapped her legs around his body. He walked her over to the door and closed it to give them some privacy. Stori's tongue tangoed with his as he palmed her round ass. When he stopped the kiss, Stori looked at him in confusion.

"What's wrong?" Stori asked him.

"You know the kind of nigga that I am Stori. I need you to really be sure about this before we go too far," Nas replied.

"Are we talking or fucking?" Stori inquired, making Nas smirk. She didn't need a pep talk. She needed him to break her back in the right way.

"You ain't said nothing but a word," Nas said as he tossed her on the bed.

When he dropped his joggers, Stori swallowed hard and scooted up to the headboard. Kalani told her that Remo was working with a monster and Nas was definitely his twin. Unlike when she was with Gavin, Stori was dripping wet just from his kisses. He grabbed her ankles and pulled her to the edge of the bed. Once her clothes had been discarded, Nas took a minute to admire what he considered perfection. Stori was beautiful and her body was nothing short of amazing. He knew that Stori had a tattoo that started from her ankle and wrapped around her leg. He had no idea that it started at her ankle and went all the way up her body and stopped at her shoulder blade. The tattoo looked like a tropical oasis with colorful flowers and butterflies. Nas licked his lips and leaned in closer to her. He placed Stori's legs over his shoulders and dove right in to her honeypot head first.

"Umm," Stori moaned as she arched her back.

Nas used his mouth expertly to make love to her lower lips. He wasn't big on giving oral sex and Stori was only the second woman to receive it. His ex, Alissa, was the first and she had to beg him for over a year. It was different with Stori and Nas wanted to get freaky with it. She made him want to do things that he swore he'd never do. Stori's eyes popped open when she felt his tongue near her anal hole. Nas used his tongue to make circles around the area before he pushed it deep inside of her. He fucked her with his tongue for a while before slipping two fingers into her vaginal opening. His fingers moved at the speed of lighting as his tongue continued to dart in and out of her.

"Nas, fuck!" Stori screamed as her body bucked and twitched.

Nas removed his fingers and replaced them with his mouth. Stori got scared for a minute when he stood up with her in his arms. He still had his mouth connected to her as she held on to the back of his head. Stori looked at their reflection in the mirror and couldn't believe what was happening between them. She'd thought about it more times than she cared to admit but she didn't know if it would ever happen. She lost count of how many times she'd fantasized about it.

Nas was the hookup that Kalani and Remo were always talking about. Stori was very attracted to him but she just couldn't see herself doing Gavin dirty like that. She often wondered why she couldn't have met him first. Since Gavin didn't seem to give a fuck about her, all bets were off. Nas was giving her back to back orgasms and she didn't care about anything else at the moment. When he finally came up for air, he laid Stori down on the bed. Before she could say anything, he flipped her over onto her stomach and positioned himself behind her.

"I hope you got condoms," Stori said as she turned around and looked behind her.

"Girl, I'm clean as fuck but I got you," Nas said as he grabbed a condom from his wallet.

Nas got around so he didn't blame Stori for wanting to be safe. He couldn't lie and say that he'd always used protection because he had a wife who was trying to get pregnant. One thing he and Remo did do regularly was get checkups though. They had never contracted anything and they wanted it to stay that way. Nas rolled the condom on and gave Stori's ass cheeks a hard slap before he penetrated her.

"Oh shit Nas, go slow," Stori begged when he started to enter her. She was nowhere near being a virgin but he wasn't the size of an average man.

"Put this big muthafucker up in the air," Nas demanded as he slapped her ass again.

Stori smirked as she put the perfect arch in her back. She gripped the sheets tightly as Nas started giving her long, deep strokes.

"Damn Nas," Stori moaned when he picked up the pace.

He got down closer, making sure that she felt every inch of him. Even with the condom on, Stori was tight and wet. Nas tried to be gentle but the shit was too good. He grabbed Stori by the neck and started fucking her just like he'd always wanted to.

Years ago when he first got Gavin on at the shop, Nas had gone into work late one day. When he pulled up to the shop, he had to do a double take when he saw the woman who was standing out front. She was beautiful and had a body like a video vixen. Nas was about to get out and talk to her but Gavin came out of the shop before he could. When he saw him and the woman kissing, he was in awe. Gavin was always bragging about one thing or another and Nas usually ignored him. When he used to talk about his girlfriend, Nas never paid him much attention. Even when he said that he was getting married, Nas cared even less. He was shocked when he found out that Stori was his wife. She didn't belong on the arm of a nigga like Gavin. She needed a thug in her life and Nas wanted to be the one.

When he told Remo about it, his brother started asking around about her. Remo found out that Stori was a stylist, so he made an appointment to get his dreads re-twisted. He only wanted to feel Stori out but he ended up liking her work. When Remo met Kalani there, that was even more of a reason for him to always go around. Kalani told them about Stori making candy and they became one of her faithful customers. Remo wanted Nas to be on some savage shit and take Stori from Gavin but he couldn't do it. Remo thought that he was getting soft but that wasn't the case. Stori wasn't like most chicks and she was faithful to her husband. Nas didn't give a fuck about Gavin but he didn't want to disrespect Stori.

She confessed to Kalani that she was attracted to Nas and that was all that Remo needed to hear. He was relentless in trying to hook them up and Kalani was no better. Nas tried to fight his attraction to her but it was almost impossible. Now that he had her, he was willing to do whatever needed to be done to keep her. It was his fantasy come true and he didn't care how fucked up the situation may have seemed to anyone else. Stori was his now.

"You feel good as fuck," Nas whispered as he stretched her walls with his girth.

"Shit Nas, you feel good too," Stori moaned.

She was supposed to feel guilty. She should have been ashamed of herself. She was fucking her husband's friend and she felt nothing outside of pleasure. He fucked her the way that Gavin should have. He talked dirty to her like she wanted her husband to do. He wasn't afraid to get freaky and there was no position that he didn't put her in. Her sex life with Gavin was good but her first time with Nas was amazing. Stori was hooked and she knew that she would crave him once it was over with. She knew that they couldn't be together for more reasons than one. They were both still married and that was a disaster within itself. Instead of dwelling on what was wrong, Stori enjoyed everything that was right. Nas was a fucking beast in the bedroom and he didn't seem to get tired. Stori couldn't hang and she was barely holding on. Four condoms later and they finally collapsed from exhaustion.

S tori heard her alarm going off from her bedroom and she wanted to scream. It felt like she had just gone to sleep and she was still exhausted. She tried to sit up but her entire body was weighed down by a pair of strong tattooed arms.

"Where you going?" Nas asked while pulling her back.

"I need to take a shower and get Toi up for school," Stori giggled as he nibbled on her ear.

As wrong as it was, she couldn't lie and say that it didn't feel right. She knew that her and Nas were wrong for what they did but at least she fulfilled her fantasy.

"Cancel all your appointments and chill with me," Nas said as he pulled her on top of him. He didn't do appointments and he didn't care about missing a day. His money was good and he would make sure that hers was too.

"I can't do that Nas. That's too unprofessional. I

only have three clients today and your brother is one of them," Stori replied as she tried to get up again. Nas held her in place and pulled her closer to him for a kiss.

"Put it in," Nas said as he positioned her over his erection.

"I can't Nas. I have to get Toi up and fix her some breakfast," Stori whined.

He looked so sexy that she had to stop herself from doing what he asked her to do. Stori had to be responsible and make sure that her sister got up and ready for school on time though. Fucking with Nas would have her acting recklessly and she couldn't have that.

"You can stop and get her something to eat," Nas replied as he slipped a finger inside of her. Stori moaned but she had to stay strong.

"I need to take a shower," she said as she removed his hand.

"Stop playing girl," Nas fussed. She didn't want to leave him hanging but she didn't have a lot of time on her hands.

"Lay back," Stori said as she pushed him down by his chest.

She started at his neck and kissed down his perfectly sculpted body until she got to his erection. When Stori wrapped her lips around his dick, Nas hissed and grabbed a fistful of her hair. Nas knew that he was working with something, but Stori was swallowing his shit up like it was effortless. Nas was shocked and he had to look down to see her in action. He was amazed by her skills and he now had yet another reason why he had to have her. It was fucked up that he would now have beef with her husband but he was ready for whatever. Gavin wasn't going to give Stori up without a fight and neither was he.

"Shit girl! Fuck!" Nas yelled as he gripped her hair tighter.

He thrusted his pelvis upwards, as Stori sucked him up like a vacuum. When she started massaging his balls as she sucked, Nas lost it. He erupted like a volcano and Stori swallowed every drop. Fuck Gavin and Milan. Stori was his wife and she didn't even know it.

"I gotta go," Stori said as she jumped up and headed for the door.

Nas just laid there, too weak to even protest. Stori peeked out into the hallway before she quickly rushed to her bedroom. She threw on a silk robe and woke Toi up before going to her master bath to shower. She started the water and brushed her teeth as it heated up. She still had enough time to fix Toi some breakfast but she had to make it quick. When she stepped into the shower, she grabbed her sponge and quickly cleaned herself up. She didn't know if Nas was going to work or not but she felt weird about him being there when Gavin wasn't home.

"Ahh!" Stori screamed when she was pulled back by her waist.

She was so deep in thought that she didn't even hear when Nas walked into the bathroom. She had to have a talk with him about boundaries because he didn't seem to have any. She didn't want her sister to see him creeping in and out of her room because it wasn't a good look. Stori was about to fuss at him but he never gave her the chance. Stori held on to the shower wall as Nas kneeled down behind her. He spread her ass cheeks wide and stuck his tongue inside. Stori held in her moans because she didn't want Toi to hear her. She bit down on her bottom lip hard as his tongue made her dizzy with pleasure. She wanted to tell Nas to hurry up but she didn't want to rush perfection. When Nas finally came up for air, Stori was ready to get out.

"You ain't going nowhere," he said as he picked her up and pinned her up against the shower wall. Stori wanted to say no but she just couldn't get the word to come out of her mouth. She was under his spell and she knew that things would never be the same again.

Thankfully, Nas didn't keep her in the bathroom as long as she thought he would. Toi had fixed herself a bowl of cereal and Stori was thankful for that too. She had about ten minutes to spare before they had to leave and she was happy that they didn't have to rush. She and Nas had a quickie in the shower before they washed off and went their separate ways.

"What's for dinner tonight Stanka?" Stori asked.

"Ummm... can we have spaghetti?" Toi quizzed.

"We sure can," Stori replied, right as Nas walked into the kitchen. He was dressed in his barber's smock with some jeans and Air Max. Stori tried not to blush when she looked at him but it was too hard.

"Hey Nas," Toi said excitedly.

"Hey beautiful. Did you eat breakfast?" Nas asked as he tried to wrap his arms around Stori. She moved out of his grasp and he looked at her like she was crazy.

"Yeah, I ate cereal," Toi replied.

"Go get your backpack and let's get ready to go," Stori told her. Once Toi was out of sight, Nas turned his attention back to her.

"Don't play these childish ass games with me, Stori. The fuck was that about?" Nas gritted angrily.

"I'm not playing games with you, Nas, but us being together so soon is not a good look. Me and Gavin just split up Sunday. I don't need people whispering and I don't need Toi thinking that her big sister is a hoe," Stori whispered.

"I don't give a fuck about the court of public opinion. This is your life and you should live that bitch the way you want to. I blaze my own trails and I'm unapologetically me. They can take it or leave me fuck alone. And stop referring to yourself as a hoe. I've met plenty of them in my lifetime and you don't fit the bill. You raised Toi better than to even think something like that about you," Nas replied. Stori was like forbidden fruit. He couldn't get a piece of her when he wanted to but there was no going back now that he did.

"I know Nas but it's not like we made anything official," Stori replied.

"The fuck you mean? I gave you your disclaimer last night before anything ever happened. That was your chance to back out then. Shit became official the minute I slid up in you," Nas replied.

"I just think we're moving way too fast," Stori said.

"See, I really don't think we're on the same page right now. I'm not asking if I can have you. I'm telling you that I want you and I don't do too well with rejection," Nas said, making her wet just by his words.

138

"Can we discuss this later Naseem? I don't want to talk in front of Toi," Stori said when she heard her sister coming back into the kitchen. Nas frowned, hating to be dismissed. Stori was gon' learn a few things about him and he was about to give her lesson number one.

"I'm ready," Toi announced.

"Toi, Stori is my girlfriend now. Are you okay with that?" Nas asked her as he pulled Stori closer to him.

"Naseem!" Stori yelled out in embarrassment.

"Really?" Toi beamed excitedly. "Yeah, I'm okay with it."

"Cool, then we're all good since your opinion is the only one that matters. I'll see y'all later," Nas said as he kissed Stori on the lips and walked out of the house.

"What the fuck did I get myself into?" Stori mumbled to herself.

"That is so cool Stori. You and Naseem and Remo and Kalani. Two brothers and two best friends. Gavin is never coming back now," Toi said happily.

"Let's go baby. We need to talk," Stori said as she ushered her out the front door.

Thanks to Nas, she now had to explain to her little sister why she was supposedly dating her husband's friend only two days after they separated.

"I'm so fucking happy right now," Kalani said as she dug her spoon into the gallon of ice cream that she and Stori were sharing.

Stori was done doing hair for the day and she had about two hours before she had to get Toi from school. Since she had some free time, she decided to go chill with Kalani and fill her in on what was going on.

"This is so fucked up. Toi is happy and I feel like shit. I shouldn't have even approached him on no fucking tip. I don't want to be that girl who jumps from one relationship to another. And besides all that, he's my husband's best friend," Stori said as she dropped her head in shame.

"Bitch, you can kill all that noise. That nigga has been wanting you for years and he finally got you. I promise that your life will never be the same as long as Naseem is in it," Kalani replied.

"It doesn't help that the sex was good as fuck. That's gonna make it even harder for me to walk away," Stori said.

"Stori, Nas wanted you even before he married Milan. He used to talk to me and Remo about you every single day. He would always tell us how unhappy you looked being with Gavin and how he had to force himself not to stare at you when he was at the house. The nigga was in love with you before he even had you. There is no walking away. Welcome to my life." Kalani shrugged.

"I don't want no parts of your life. Remo is crazy as fuck," Stori fussed.

"And so is his identical twin brother. Remo gave me the same disclaimer that Nas gave you before we had sex. I should have taken heed to his warnings but I didn't listen. Now I'm dick dizzy behind a nigga who can't even keep the dick to himself," Kalani said while shaking her head.

"Don't tell Remo nothing Kalani. I don't need him getting excited about something that will probably never happen," Stori said.

"Stop being in denial Stori. The shit already happened. Besides, Nas and Remo got some kind of sixth sense when it comes to each other. He'll eventually figure the shit out on his own if Nas don't tell him first." Kalani shrugged.

"How have things been going with y'all?" Stori asked.

"Too good to be true. It's sad that I'm holding my breath waiting for some bullshit to pop off," Kalani said while shaking her head.

"Don't feel like that friend. Maybe he really is trying to do better. Just give him some credit for that much," Stori replied.

"We'll see." Kalani shrugged.

"Remo is on his grown man shit," Stori laughed.

She and Kalani continued to pig out on ice cream as they talked about everything that had been going on. When Kalani heard the front door open, she knew that it had to be Remo. She heard him talking to someone and she just assumed that it was Nas.

"What's good baby?" Remo greeted Kalani before he kissed her lips. He spoke to Stori too, right before Nas and their brother Jarvis walked into the room.

"Good evening ladies," Jarvis spoke politely.

He was just as handsome as the twins but their personalities were nothing alike. Jarvis was the calm, level headed brother who the twins looked up to. They always gave him a hard time but they knew that everything he told them was right.

"Hey Jarvis," Kalani said, as Stori smiled and waved.

Stori had met Jarvis and his wife before when they came to Kalani and Remo's house. Nas just stood there staring at her and Stori felt the tension between the two of them. It was almost time for her to get Toi from school and she was ready to go.

"Y'all niggas are rude as fuck," Jarvis fussed when Nas started saying something to Remo in sign language. It always amazed Stori and Kalani when they saw them do that and they both swore that they were going to learn how to communicate in silence.

"Get the fuck outta here!" Remo bellowed as he looked over at Stori. He had a huge smile on his face and Stori's cheeks burned with embarrassment.

"I'll call you later friend. I have to go get Toi from school," Stori said as she got up from the bar stool that she was sitting on. She grabbed her purse from the counter and was about to go. Before she could walk away, Nas pulled her to him by her arm and she collided with his chest. He picked her up and kissed her as he walked her to the front of the house.

"Get out your feelings love. Shit happened exactly the way it was supposed to happen," Nas said as he carried her to her car.

"Exactly how was it supposed to happen Naseem? We're both still married," Stori pointed out.

"Nah, I already filed for divorce," Nas informed her.

"When?" Stori questioned.

"Not too long ago. Shit, I don't remember the exact date but I know they served Milan with the papers Saturday. My sister-in-law handled it for me." Nas shrugged.

"I'm meeting with a divorce lawyer Friday," Stori confessed.

"Cool, then we're all good." Nas smiled as he put her down to stand on her own.

"I just think we're moving too fast Nas," Stori said worriedly.

"Again, last night was the time for you to voice your concerns. Stop stressing over what the next muthafucker might think. I've waited too long for this shit to happen and I don't feel bad about it. If I was anybody else, you wouldn't even be as concerned," Nas replied.

"Maybe not but you're Gavin's best friend Nas," Stori noted.

"Why the fuck does everybody keep saying that shit? Gavin is not my friend and he never was. The nigga was weak as fuck and he served his purpose with me when we were in school. Me and that nigga can never run in the same circle because he can't keep up." Nas frowned.

"Just do me a favor and don't tell him anything. It's only been two days, but I should be the one to tell him what's up," Stori remarked.

"Go get Toi from school and go straight home. I'm coming through once I handle this business with my brothers," Nas said as he kissed her lips and opened her car door.

He couldn't make Stori any promises that he wasn't sure that he could keep. He didn't give a fuck about Gavin or anybody else knowing about them. But, he would try his best to respect her wishes.

"Bruh, please tell me that you ain't fucking with Gavin's wife," Jarvis said as soon as Nas walked back into the house. Kalani had gone to her room and left the men in the kitchen.

"Okay, I won't tell you then." Nas shrugged.

"Man, listen, that shit just made my muthafucking day. Let's have a drink nigga," Remo said excitedly. He grabbed his bottle of Hennessey from the cabinet and poured him and Nas a shot.

"Don't encourage that shit Kareem. That's real fucked up Naseem. I thought Gavin was your friend," Jarvis fussed.

"My brother is my friend," Nas maintained.

"And that's big fucking facts," Remo said as he gave Nas dap.

"Y'all do some shady shit. How the fuck you sleep with that man's wife behind his back?" Jarvis questioned.

"Nigga, that's my wife," Nas said.

"Does Gavin know that?" Jarvis asked.

"He will just as soon as I see his bitch ass." Remo smiled deviously.

"Chill out on that bro. She's not trying to have the nigga hear it from nobody else but her," Nas replied.

"Damn man. I been waiting for this shit for a long ass time. Now that it finally happened, I can't even rub it in the nigga's face," Remo argued.

"That's fucked up bruh. That man opened his door and invited you to stay up in his house and everything," Jarvis said while shaking his head in shame.

"Fuck that nigga! I already live there," Nas argued.

"Since fucking when!?" Jarvis yelled in frustration.

"Since she dropped her thong for a real nigga," Nas replied as he and Remo fell out laughing and slapped hands.

"Man, you niggas are giving me a headache. Let's just get this business handled, so I can get the fuck away from y'all. Grandma was right. Y'all seem to be getting worse by the day. I should have known that y'all would grow up to be this way when y'all got suspended in kindergarten. I ain't never even heard of no shit like that happening before you niggas came along," Jarvis said while rubbing his temples.

Jarvis always swore that he wouldn't let his brothers get him riled up but they always did. He never had to deal with high blood pressure before he started raising them. He tried his best with the twins but there was only so much that he could do. They fed off of each other's negative energy and he didn't understand their logic. Nas was always the leader of the duo and Remo followed wherever his twin led him. Jarvis only went over there to discuss the finances on their club and rental properties; he didn't ask for the added drama. But, just like always, the twins had him with a damn migraine. Jarvis needed a vacation. Not from anything else, just his two younger brothers.

"What's good bro?" Remo asked when he walked into their office at the club.

Nas was in the window staring out at everyone else in the club. The windows looked tinted to everyone else but they had a clear view of everything that they needed to see. The crowd was thick but there was only one person that he was trying to see.

"That's what the fuck I'm trying to see," Nas said as he eyed Stori sitting at the bar sipping on a glass of wine. She had never been to their club before and he was wondering why she wanted to come there now.

"Kalani said that she was bored so she told her to pass through," Remo replied.

"And you believed that bullshit?" Nas asked as he looked over at him.

"Shit, I don't know what to believe. Toi is staying

by their grandmother for the weekend, so it's not impossible. It's Friday nigga. Let that girl live a little," Remo laughed.

Nas knew exactly where Toi was but he was wondering what was really up with Stori. She had been doing hair since earlier that morning and she claimed to be so tired. He planned to dip out earlier than usual to go lay up with her. He wasn't expecting to see her in their club.

"Fuck outta here with that dumb shit. The only reason you be so calm is because Kalani works here and you can see what she's up to," Nas replied.

"Man, you know Stori ain't on no bullshit like that. It ain't even been a week yet and you trippin' already," Remo said as he went and stood next to him.

Remo knew that Nas had been wanting Stori for a long ass time. Besides his ex, Alissa, he couldn't remember his brother being so interested in another woman. He thought that Alissa was the one, but she couldn't take all the late nights and other women. Remo had a feeling that it was even deeper with Stori than it was with Alissa. She was like the forbidden fruit that he wasn't supposed to touch. Now that he'd had a taste of her, he was hooked.

"I'm not trippin'. I'm just trying to see what's up," Nas said as he continued to stare.

Stori was dressed down in a pair of PINK leggings with the matching shirt. She had Nikes on her feet and her hair was pulled up in a ponytail. Still, in his eyes, she was the most beautiful woman in the club. Nas made Bee sit at the bar not too far from her, just in case one of the niggas in there had a death wish. Nas hadn't gone down there by her yet but he did let her know that he was there. He had been by her house every day and he didn't have any plans to leave. He was discreetly sneaking his clothes inside and Toi was helping him. Stori didn't even pay attention or at least she pretended not to.

"What's up with her bitch ass husband?" Remo asked.

"Man, I don't even know. That nigga ain't been to work in a minute and it's been peaceful as fuck. I know I promised Stori that I wouldn't say nothing but I don't know.

That nigga say the wrong thing and I might fuck around and lay his stupid ass out," Nas replied.

"Has he tried coming back to the house yet?" Remo asked.

"Nah, but he be calling all the time getting on my fucking nerves. His mama came over there to get some of his clothes the other day. Toi and Stori packed up some of his shit for her to give to him. I told her to give him all of it," Nas answered.

"Did his mama see you there?" Remo inquired.

"Nah, I was sleep when she came through and my car be in the garage with Stori's," Nas replied.

"Man fuck! That nigga ain't gon' never find out about y'all." Remo frowned as Nas laughed.

Remo couldn't wait for the day when Gavin found out about Stori and his brother. Gavin was scary as fuck but Remo was hoping that he tried to bring some smoke his brother's way. He was gonna make sure that his mama and daddy said their final goodbyes to his bitch ass. Stori was all that Gavin had going for himself. Besides her, he really didn't have anything else to brag about.

"Between him, Danni and Milan, I don't know who calls me the most. Milan act like she's losing her fucking mind out here," Nas said, shaking his head.

Milan had really been on some other shit lately. He had to make the bouncers stop her at the door when she came to the club because she was always trying to cause a scene. Nas posted on Instagram a lot for the club and the barber shop. Milan started going under every post leaving all kinds of crazy messages. She did the same thing to his voicemail and he was sick of her crazy ass.

"I can't wait for that bitch to find out too. Her and Gavin can lose their minds together. I'm happy that you're divorcing her stupid ass. Stori is the one though bro, I'm telling you," Remo replied.

"You ain't telling me shit that I don't already know." Nas smiled, right as someone knocked on the door.

Since he was closer, Nas opened the door and found Lexus standing there looking scared. As soon as Remo saw her, he frowned and rushed over to the door and pulled her inside.

"The fuck you doing up here Lisa?" Remo barked.

"My name is Lexus," she replied with a roll of her eyes.

"I don't give a fuck what your mama named you. Didn't I tell you not to come near this office when my wife is here?" Remo snapped.

"Yes, but I needed to talk to you in private," Lexus said as he looked over at Nas.

"You can say whatever you have to say in front of my brother. Ain't gon' be no private meetings as long as my wife is in the building!" Remo barked.

"It's personal," Lexus said nervously.

"You got two seconds to say what the fuck you need to say," Remo spat.

"I missed my period," Lexus blurted out as she lowered her head.

"Aww shit! You pregnant?" Nas asked as if he was the one who did it.

"Bitch! Pregnant by who?" Remo barked as he pulled out his gun and put it up to her head.

"Oh, my God!" Lexus screamed as she dropped down to her knees in fear. Her entire body was trembling and she regretted approaching him.

She knew that she shouldn't have listened to the dancer who told her to do it. Lexus only approached her about possibly stripping to make more money and she foolishly confided in her about her dealings with Remo. When Lexus mentioned that she thought she was pregnant, she confessed to not knowing if Remo or her boyfriend was the father. Remo didn't even know that she had a man. Lexus was so excited about him wanting to be with her, she never even mentioned it.

Her boyfriend was in the same predicament that she was in. He still lived at home with his middle class parents while working to help pay for school. When the dancer told Lexus to pin the baby on Remo, it seemed like a good idea at the time. If she was pregnant, Lexus didn't have any intentions on keeping it. She couldn't afford it even if she wanted to. Since Remo had lots of money, she thought it was a great idea to get him to pay for the abortion. Now, she wasn't so sure about that anymore.

"Nigga, put that shit up and stop trippin'," Nas laughed as he helped Lexus up from the floor.

"This bitch is trying to ruin my life and make my wife leave me," Remo fumed as he nervously paced the floor.

"That's not what I'm trying to do, I swear," Lexus cried.

"Did you take a test?" Nas asked her.

"No, but I've never missed a period before." Lexus sniffled.

"Bitch, I used rubbers every time I went up in you," Remo fussed as he snarled at their newest bottle girl.

"No, you didn't, not every time," Lexus countered in a timid voice.

"Fuck!" Remo yelled out angrily, making Lexus jump in fear.

"So, what's up ma? You in college and shit. I know you ain't trying to have no baby," Nas reasoned.

"No, I don't want a baby. I'm hoping that I'm not even pregnant. But, if I am, I have to get an abortion. I can't afford a kid right now. I also don't want to lose this job. This is helping me pay for school," Lexus said.

"Your job is good but you need to go take a test. If you are, we need to see some proof before we talk about abortion money. No offense, but females play all kinds of games just to get a few dollars," Nas replied.

"I would never do that," Lexus swore.

"Yeah, right. Shady ass bitch," Remo fumed as he continued to pace.

"Look, come see me when you find out what's up and I got you," Nas assured her.

"Okay, thank you," Lexus said as she hurriedly left the office.

"Calm down bro. You know I got you," Nas said as he put a comforting hand on Remo's shoulder.

"As soon as that bitch is no longer a problem, I want her ass fired. Fuck college and fuck her too," Remo snapped angrily.

"You need to chill out with that shit bro. This is the second chick that tried to pin a baby on you. Kalani ain't gon' stay around forever. As much as you want to blame these other women, you have to take some of the blame too," Nas scolded.

"You're right but I'm done bro. You hear me? Fucking done. On mama and daddy's grave, I'm done with all these hoes. I'm about to drag Kalani to the court house and make her marry my ass," Remo swore.

"It's about time nigga," Nas said while giving him dap.

They both went back to the window and looked down at the crowd below. Stori was holding a conversation with Kalani and Nas kept his eyes on her the entire time. When the DJ turned down the music, the lights went low as he announced one of the featured dancers. That usually meant that one of the more popular girls was about to hit the stage.

"I hope everybody is having a good time with our lovely ladies here at Twin Tails. We got a special treat for y'all tonight. Get your money right and show some love for Misty Rain!" the DJ yelled as the beat dropped on Rihanna's hit song "Work".

When the lights came back on, Misty was on the stage twerking to the beat in some kind of army fatigue outfit. The crowd went crazy and the men started making it rain on her just like they always did. Nas and Remo were watching but it was nothing that they had never seen before. Misty was all into her act when she was suddenly snatched off the stage. Her arms were flailing, as Stori rained blows on her like a heavyweight champ. Everything happened so fast that a few people didn't even see what was going on. Nas and Remo looked on in shock for a second before they took action.

"The fuck!" Nas yelled as he ran out of the office with Remo hot on his heels.

Bee was supposed to be keeping an eye on Stori but he was smiling all up in some woman's face when they made it downstairs. Nas saw the bouncers headed towards the fight and he was praying that he got there first. He was bound to start shooting up in his own club if they tried to manhandle Stori like they did everyone else. He knew that her and Kalani were on some bullshit talking about Stori was bored and wanted to get out. Her ass had a motive for coming there and Nas was heated.

"Whoa, calm down fam," Remo said as he approached one of the bouncers. He was about to grab Stori and he knew that Nas would have lost it if he did.

"Get your wild ass up," Nas fussed as he picked Stori up and threw her over his shoulder like she weighed nothing.

She had fucked Misty up something serious and the barely there outfit wasn't there anymore. Misty was butt ass naked on the floor with a bloody face as some of the men recorded. Stori had ripped some of the tracks from her hair and people were throwing them up in the air laughing. Remo, Bee and the bouncers were regaining control of the club as Nas carried Stori away. He took her up the stairs to their office and threw her on the sofa.

"Don't be trying to manhandle me, nigga," Stori fussed as she jumped up and got in his face.

Nas towered over her, so her little tantrum didn't even bother him. He pushed her back down and caged her in with his muscular arms. Her feisty attitude was turning him on but he was too pissed to think about sex.

"I know you ain't in my muthafucking club fighting over another nigga," Nas gritted as he got into her face. They were so close that his lips brushed up against hers as he spoke.

"Fuck him and fuck her too. This ain't even about no Gavin," Stori fumed.

"What the fuck is it about then Stori?" Nas questioned angrily.

"What kind of stupid ass question is that? That bitch sat up in my shop like it was all good, knowing that she was on some shady shit. I've been doing that hoe hair for months. That's just why I ripped them tracks right the fuck out. Hoe had my sister watching a baby that she knew was for my husband. Nah, that bitch wasn't getting away with that shit," Stori said angrily.

"Okay, you got the shit off your chest, so it's dead now. You damn near shut the whole damn club down with that bullshit," Nas fussed

"I really don't give a fuck. I wasn't done with the bitch and you shouldn't have stopped me," Stori snapped in anger as she mushed his head.

If anyone else had done that, Nas would have been ready to shoot. Everything that Stori did was sexy to him, so he licked his lips and smirked at her. Nah, that nigga Gavin wasn't hitting it right. Stori was wild and she needed a nigga like Nas to tame her the right way.

"You sexy as fuck to me right now," Nas said, right before he parted her lips with his tongue.

Stori kissed him back aggressively and they were pulling each other's clothes off soon after that. Stori squealed when Nas lifted her up in the air and sat her on his face. She held on tight as he feasted on her like a buffet. She was hoping that nobody walked in on them but, then again, she really didn't care. Stori's body shuddered with every flick of his tongue and vibration of his moans. She felt an orgasm building and tightened her legs around his head. Her thighs were almost smothering him but Nas didn't seem to mind.

"Shit Nas. I'm cumming baby!" Stori yelled, shocked at herself for calling him baby. That was new for her but it felt so natural.

Nas stroked her middle with his tongue until she begged him to stop. Once he did, he lowered Stori onto his erection and put her back up against the window. Stori licked her juices from around his lips before she stuck her tongue in his mouth.

"Fuck girl," Nas hissed as he placed his hands up on the glass.

Stori was bouncing up and down his length as her tongue glided from his ear to his neck. Nas looked down on the crowded club, as Stori fucked him like a porn star in his office. Gavin was right about one thing. Stori really did have the best pussy in the world. Unlike him, Nas was willing to kill a nigga behind it.

"Did you handle that for me, Misty?" Milan asked her preoccupied sister.

"Huh?" Misty asked, not paying attention to what her sister was saying.

"I asked if you handled that business for me with ole girl," Milan repeated.

"Not yet but I will," Misty assured her as she continue to stare at the computer.

"Stop stressing over that shit and disable your page for a while," Milan said as she looked over at her sister.

Misty was holding an ice pack up to her swollen eye and lip. Stori had done her dirty but that was to be expected. Milan didn't agree with what had happened but she wasn't surprised by it either. Neither Milan nor Misty had boundaries when it came to the men they wanted. Although Gavin approached Misty first, him being married never mattered to her much. Now, she was suffering the consequences of her actions. Stori had tagged that ass and it was all over social media. People kept sharing and reposting and Misty was losing her mind.

"That bitch gon' see me again. I hope she don't think this shit is over," Misty fumed.

"Let that shit go girl. Y'all are even now. You had a baby for her husband and she beat that ass like a drum," Milan laughed like what she said was funny.

"I'm not letting shit go. I'm missing out on money because of her stupid ass," Misty argued.

"How is that her fault though?" Milan asked.

"Bitch, look at my face. I get paid to shake my ass and look cute. Niggas ain't paying to see no black eyes and busted lips," Misty replied.

"Well, I guess we better start searching for another stylist," Milan snickered.

"You laughing now but Pinky told me that Stori and Nas stayed up in that office for almost a whole hour after he broke up the fight," Misty noted.

"And? What that mean to me?" Milan questioned.

"Bitch, you know just as well as I do how Nas and Remo get down. Business is not the only thing that's conducted in that office. Bitches don't step foot in there unless some fucking is going on. I got fucked up in there plenty of times and so did you," Misty replied.

"Girl bye. Nas might be fucking somebody but it damn sure ain't Stori. The bitch is hood as fuck sometimes but she's not a hoe. Naseem and Gavin are still cool. He was probably just looking out for his wife," Milan said, praying that she was right.

"You're a damn fool if you think Stori is still with Gavin after finding out about Summer. That bitch is probably fucking Nas on some catch back shit," Misty said, giving Milan a lot to think about.

"Bitch, I would put a hit out on him and that hoe if I even thought that was true," Milan fumed.

"With what money boo? Maybe you need to think about coming back to the club. I'm sure your money is running low and, without Nas, it's only gonna get lower," Misty said.

"I'd sell my ass on the nearest corner before I give them hoes the satisfaction of seeing me dance at Twin Tails again. Nas is just acting stupid but he'll be back," Milan assured her.

"Don't be too sure boo. Pinky said that him and Stori came out of the office together and left soon after," Misty said, repeating what she'd heard.

"Pinky needs to go sit her lopsided ass down somewhere. That bitch is always gossiping." Milan frowned.

"Say what you want but that bitch be on point," Misty replied, right as someone rang the doorbell.

Her and Milan looked at each other to see who was going to move first. Misty was nursing her wounds, so she really didn't care who it was. Summer was with Gavin's parents and she was free to do nothing. She wasn't even going to tell them that she wasn't going to work that night. She loved her daughter but she needed a break.

"Your lazy ass," Milan fussed as she got up to go see who was at the door. She smirked when she saw Gavin standing there holding Summer and her diaper bag. Misty thought she had a free weekend but her day was about to be ruined.

"What's up?" Gavin spoke as he walked inside.

He went into the living room and didn't even bother saying anything to Misty. He hated her hoe ass after the stunt she pulled with Stori. He still took care of his daughter but he wasn't fucking with Misty unless it had to do with Summer.

"What are you doing here? I have to work," Misty lied.

"That's not my problem. My mama made plans and she can't babysit," Gavin said as he kissed Summer and sat her bag down.

"She told me that she was keeping her for the whole weekend." Misty replied.

"Shit happens and things change. Besides, I saw that video just like everybody else. You ain't going to no club looking like that," Gavin snickered as he pointed to her bruised face.

"It's all good. Tell your bitch she gon' see me again," Misty said.

"My wife got them hands but I'm sure you know that already," Gavin laughed.

"Boy, fuck you! I see I can't depend on y'all to babysit either," Misty snapped as she took Summer out of her car seat.

"Well, stop being a hoe and get a day job. I'll be happy to pay for daycare," Gavin replied as he walked out of the house.

"Stupid ass bitch is worthless, just like her son." Misty frowned while speaking of Gavin's mother. They hadn't even known each other long and shit was going left already.

From day one, Karen let her know that she didn't like her and nothing about her. Misty wasn't allowed at their house and Gavin was the one who picked Summer up and dropped her off. She had to call Gavin if she wanted to check on her daughter because Karen didn't want Misty with her number. She was a disrespectful old bitch but she was Misty's only help. She thought she was reliable but she was obviously mistaken. Gavin must have told his mother something because she had never sent Summer home early. It had only been a short time since she found out about Summer but she was crazy about her already.

"You better be happy that she's even helping at all. Summer is not her responsibility," Milan said, interrupting her thoughts.

"Fuck them. She better be happy that her hoe ass son ain't on child support," Misty replied.

"That's fucked up Misty. That man takes care of his baby. You're mad because he ain't dropping dick off in you no more." Milan smiled, enjoying getting under Misty's skin.

"Sex is very easy to get boo. Mad niggas be begging to dig up in these walls. You just worry about who your husband is dropping dick off in. If what Pinky said is true, you and Gavin will be crying on each other's shoulders soon," Misty said as she walked away with her daughter.

The smile on Milan's face dropped when she said that. Nas was a dog and there was no disputing that. She just didn't see Stori in the same light. Stori was about her business. The only thing that mattered to her was Toi and her shop. Her and Nas weren't even on the same level. Still, Milan went to Nas' Instagram page just to see what he had been up to.

It took two whole weeks before Gavin finally went back to work. The bruises on his face had healed but the ones on his heart remained. He begged and pleaded with Stori to talk to him but she had no words. And if that wasn't bad enough, she'd had him served with divorce papers at his parents' house the day before. Gavin was sick, both mentally and physically. He'd just finished eating when he read over the documents and threw everything right back up. He was heartbroken that Stori wasn't even trying to hear him out. She answered for his mother and talked to her for a while. She'd even let Karen come to the house to get some of his stuff. She made it clear to her that she was done with Gavin and Karen didn't blame her. As much as she loved Stori, she knew that she deserved more than what her son had given her. Gavin wasn't giving up though. While on his way to work, he dialed Stori's number again using an app and, to his surprise, she answered.

"Yes Gavin," Stori said when she picked up. She knew that it was him because he had been calling from all kinds of weird numbers since she had him blocked. Gavin was almost at a loss for words because he wasn't expecting her to answer at all.

"Can we talk Stori? Baby please, I just need you to hear me out," Gavin begged.

"I'm listening," Stori noted.

"No, not over the phone. I want us to talk face to face," Gavin said.

"Sorry, but that's not happening. It was childish of me not to talk to you before now but I can't run from this conversation forever. You really don't even need to waste your time trying to explain anything. Truthfully, I'm more angry than I am hurt. All those months you spent begging me to give you a baby, knowing that you already had one. Then, to involve Toi the way you did is just unforgivable," Stori rambled.

"I wish everybody would stop saying that. I wasn't the one who asked you if Toi could babysit. That was all on Misty," Gavin replied.

"But, you could have intervened Gavin. You could have been a man for once and put a stop to it. It broke my heart to see my sister crying over some bullshit that you created. Everything that I do is to make her smile and you temporarily took that away from her. It's all good though. Just sign them papers and we won't have no problems," Stori said.

"Just like that Stori? You act like you don't even care. I don't even know why I'm surprised by your nonchalant attitude. It's not like you ever gave a fuck about a nigga anyway. Toi got shown more love than I did. You're right, everything you did was to make her smile because you damn sure didn't care if I was happy or not. She was your baby and your Stanka, but I was just plain ole Gavin. All those years we were together and nothing changed. At least Misty made me feel wanted," Gavin argued.

"Don't even go there with me, Gavin. You knew how I felt from day one because I kept it real and told you. If the bitch made you feel so much better than I did, you should have let me go and married her ass. Trust me, I would have been fine either way. There is no excuse that you can give that will justify you fathering a child with another woman. As my husband, any problems that you had

160

with our marriage should have been discussed with me, your wife," Stori pointed out.

"I tried to tell you how I felt more than once. You never even tried to take my feelings into consideration. I couldn't even pick out a damn meal for my wife to cook," Gavin argued.

"You sound like a spoiled lil bitch Gavin. What grown ass man tries to compete with a fourteen year old? Toi and I have a special bond and you knew that from day one. You had me fucked up if you thought you were gonna come in between that. You do right to be back under your mama's roof since you act like a fucking thirty year old baby. We've both said what we needed to say so make this your last time calling me," Stori said, right as he pulled up to the shop.

"Stori! Hello! Fuck!" Gavin yelled when he realized that she'd hung up.

He felt like crying. The conversation with Stori didn't go anything like he wanted it to. He could admit that he was wrong but he wasn't giving up on his wife or his marriage. With a heavy heart, Gavin got out of his car and prepared to work for a little while.

Tuesdays at the barber shop were usually slow. Gavin wasn't surprised when he saw most of the barbers standing out front talking. He spoke to everyone as he made his way into the shop to look for Nas. He spotted him sitting in his chair with his feet propped up on his work station. Nas was talking to a customer, but the other man gave him dap and started walking away when he saw Gavin approaching.

"Damn bruh. You're a hard ass nigga to catch up with," Gavin said as he walked up and gave Nas dap.

"Been busy," Nas said uncaringly as he scrolled on his phone.

"For two whole weeks nigga?" Gavin asked.

"Basically." Nas shrugged.

"Damn boy, them bitches look nice as fuck. That must be some new shit," Gavin said as he admired the black spiked red bottom tennis shoes that Nas had on.

"Yeah, something like that," Nas replied nonchalantly.

"I gotta go snatch me a pair of them bitches," Gavin said, sounding like a groupie.

"What's good Gavin? You been blowing me up for two whole weeks," Nas noted.

"Man, so much shit has been happening lately bruh. I was really trying to tell you to chill out from going to the house for a minute," Gavin replied.

"Why is that?" Nas asked as if he didn't already know.

"Stori ain't been fucking with a nigga like that lately. That bitch Misty came over there and dropped Summer off. Bitch told Stori that she was my daughter and everything. I ended up having to bring her by my people and that was even more bullshit that I had to deal with. I saw the video of Stori tagging that ass Friday night. That's good for that bitch," Gavin ranted.

He was shocked as hell to see Stori posted up in the strip club. When he saw her beating the dog shit out of Misty, he understood why she went. He saw that Misty had responded to one of Pinky's messages under the post telling her that she was taking a few days off. Gavin wasted no time packing Summer up and bringing her right back home. His mother didn't mind babysitting because she was getting to know her granddaughter. Misty had him fucked up if she thought she was going to use her though. Karen already hated her and they had never even met.

"When's the last time you talked to Stori?" Nas asked after a long pause. Stori told him that she was going to answer for him the next time he called from one of those bogus numbers. Nas wanted to see if that had happened yet. He also wanted to know if Stori had told him that she had moved on. Just by Gavin's conversation, Nas knew that she hadn't.

"I just hung up with her a few minutes ago. Before that, I hadn't talked to her since all that shit happened. The conversation went all the way left too. I told her ass how I felt and we ended up arguing. I'm her husband but her sister gets treated like she's paying all the bills," Gavin said, sounding like a whining lil bitch to Nas.

"How the fuck are you jealous of a fourteen year old lil girl bruh?" Nas asked with a disgusted frown.

"I'm not jealous of nobody. Toi is alright but I just had to voice my opinion. I'm going crazy though, bruh. Stori won't even let a nigga come see her," Gavin sighed.

Stori had blocked his number the day she put him out. Gavin tried calling from his parents' house phone and his father's cell phone. The minute she heard his voice, she would hang up on him. He tried messaging her on Instagram and he even called Toi's phone. Nothing worked and he was stressing. He knew that Stori would never change her number because that was how she made her money. She didn't do walk-ins, so her clients had to call for appointments. When he found out about the app, he tried it out and was pleased to know that it really worked. Each time he called, it seemed as if a different number showed up to the person that he was calling.

"I hear you," Nas said, not really giving him much conversation.

"I'm trying to give her some time but this shit is frustrating," Gavin replied.

"Give her some time for what?" Nas asked as he put his feet on the floor and stood up.

He was praying that Gavin didn't let something stupid come out of his mouth. Nas was about to lay him the fuck out if it did. He wasn't into keeping secrets and shit but he promised Stori that he would. He felt lame as fuck looking in Gavin's face like everything was all good. He didn't know why Stori didn't want him to know yet, but he was following her lead.

"I'm trying not to just pop up over there and make her ass talk to me. She sent me some divorce papers but I threw that shit in the trash. I'm not signing shit," Gavin fumed.

"Yeah, you might want to reconsider that. You need to go ahead and sign that shit fam," Nas replied.

"Hell no bruh. I'm having withdrawals already. It'll be over my dead body before another nigga hit that good pussy," Gavin joked, making Nas turned red with anger.

"Nigga, check it, Stori is my-," Nas started before he was abruptly cut off.

"Aye bro, when you finish talking to your bitch, I need you to line me up right quick. I'm taking my wife shopping and out to lunch," Remo said when he came busting through the door.

He bumped into Gavin as he made his way over to his brother's chair and sat down. As usual, Remo came in at just the right time. Nas was about two seconds away from hurting Gavin's feelings. Stori would have been pissed with him, so he was happy that things played out the way that they did.

"Say Remo, you got a problem with me or something?" Gavin asked, sounding like he was really about that life. He was fed up with Remo treating him like a bitch. He had never done anything to him and he didn't know why he hated him so much. Remo was always coming at him sideways and that was the first time that Nas ever saw Gavin defend himself.

"Nigga what?" Remo frowned as he tried to get up from the chair. That was the day he had been waiting for. He was ready to put Gavin to sleep right there in the barber shop.

"Chill bro," Nas said as he pushed him back down by his shoulder and whispered something in his ear. He needed Remo to remain calm for Stori's sake if nothing else.

"You're right bro, you're so right." Remo nodded with a devious smile on his face. The time was coming for Gavin to get what was coming to him and Remo couldn't wait.

"Where Kalani at?" Nas asked, trying to change the subject.

"She's getting her hair curled. I just left from by my sis getting my dreads hooked up," Remo said as he smirked at Gavin.

"I'll talk to you later brother. I'm going make a run right quick," Gavin said as he looked at Nas and walked out of the shop.

"Brother? Did that bitch ass nigga just call you brother?" Remo asked angrily.

"Relax bro, it's just a word," Nas replied.

"Nah, not to me it ain't. And you're good with him calling you that shit?" Remo asked as he turned around to face his twin.

"The fuck you want me to say bruh? I know who my brother is," Nas replied.

"Yeah, well, you better act like it," Remo said as a frown marred his face.

"What's up with you, dog? You must be having a bad day. You need a hug or something nigga?" Nas asked him.

"You fucking right I do," Remo replied.

Nas shook his head as he pulled him up from the chair and gave him a brotherly hug. Remo was possessive like a bitch sometimes, but Nas was used to it. He had been that way since they were kids and he didn't want anybody to get too close to his twin brother. He wasn't like that with females but he wasn't letting another nigga step in and take his place in Nas' life. Nas barely had friends when they were in school because Remo was always beating them up. Their father used to stress to them how important it was for them to stay close. He always told them that they were two bodies with one heartbeat and Remo took that shit seriously. It was so real to him that he convinced Nas to get a tattoo with that quote on his back to match his.

"You feel better now?" Nas asked once they pulled away.

"I'm straight," Remo smirked as he sat back in his brother's barber chair.

"Stop acting like a lil bitch all the time. You know a nigga love your stupid ass," Nas said.

"I love you too bro," Remo replied while smiling like a big ass kid.

Kalani sat in the stall and listened to two of the dancers as they talked. She had just walked into the bathroom when Misty and Pinky walked in right behind her. Kalani usually used the private bathroom that was next to Nas and Remo's office, but she was too pushed to make it up the stairs.

"Girl yes, she was in here crying and looking like she was about to lose it," Misty said to Pinky as they touched up their makeup.

"That's fucked up. Them niggas look good as fuck but they're identical twin man whores," Pinky replied.

"Especially Remo," Misty said loudly.

She saw when Kalani walked into the bathroom and she pulled Pinky inside to talk soon after. Pinky was oblivious to the game that Misty was playing but she was playing her part well.

"He needs to just stop with the foolishness.

Everybody can see that Kalani got him wrapped around her finger. I don't even know why he's wasting time on other women when he's clearly in love with her." Pinky said as Misty frowned. That was not something that Misty wanted her to say.

"He can't love her too much if he got one of his bottle girls pregnant," Misty replied.

"That's fucked up. Lexus is a sweet girl but this is not the job for her. She's too shy and timid," Pinky said as she puckered her lips to make sure her lipstick was on point.

"I agree. She was asking about becoming a dancer and I had to stop myself from laughing," Misty giggled.

She just so happened to walk in on Lexus crying in the bathroom one day. Misty tried to offer her comfort while getting in her business at the same time. When Lexus inquired about dancing, Misty almost laughed in her face. Lexus was cute with a nice body but it took more than that to be a stripper. You had to have tough skin and be prepared for whatever. Twin Tails was the most popular club in New Orleans and the crowd was always thick. Lexus was barely able to handle being a bottle girl. Dancing was ten times worse. Misty had seen niggas beat their dicks while she was on stage and a few of them shot their loads right on her. She didn't mind if they were big tippers. She got the bouncers to deal with the ones who weren't.

When Lexus told her that she thought she was pregnant, Misty really didn't care. It wasn't until Lexus told her about messing with Remo did she become interested. Misty told her how to handle the situation and Lexus did everything that she said. Lexus found out that she was indeed pregnant and she showed Misty the paperwork to prove it. Misty tried telling her how to finesse some cash out of Remo, but she was too afraid. Remo had her shook after their first encounter and she steered clear of him as much as she could. She still confided in Misty for a while but Lexus started acting weird after that. She didn't really talk to Misty anymore and she was very vague with her whenever she did. Misty didn't really care because she already knew enough.

"Hell no. She's not even a good bottle girl. Niggas grab her ass and she be about to cry," Pinky said, pulling Misty out of her thoughts.

"Exactly and that's probably why Remo approached her. She's gullible and he knew it," Misty replied.

"Girl, we better get back out there before them crazy ass twins be trying to fire us," Pinky laughed as she ran her fingers through her long hot pink hair.

When they left, Kalani walked out of the stall and washed her hands. She was fuming as she made her way out of the bathroom. Misty watched her with an amused smirk as she made her way upstairs to Nas and Remo's office. Her job was done and she'd accomplished what she set out to do.

"What's up baby?" Remo smiled when Kalani walked into his office. He was sitting behind the desk but he got up to hug her.

"Nah nigga, don't put your dirty ass hands on me," Kalani fumed as she pushed him away.

"The fuck did I do this time?" Remo questioned as he held his hands out in confusion.

"I'm so sick of this shit Kareem, I swear I am. I'm just ready to find me an apartment and a new job too. I'm ready to give you all your shit back and move the fuck on," Kalani fumed.

"What are you talking about Kalani? I didn't even do shit," Remo replied with an angry frown.

"So, getting another bitch pregnant is considered nothing to you?" Kalani wanted to know.

"Man, I don't know who the fuck told you that but they got me wrong. I'm not fucking nobody but you. I've been doing good baby. You even said so yourself. I don't even be talking to nobody," Remo swore as his heart started to beat a little faster.

He knew that Kalani had to be talking about the bottle girl but that was a done deal. Remo hadn't been on no bullshit since he stopped dealing with her. It had been all about Kalani and it always would be. He was done with entertaining anybody else. He was running out of chances with her and he knew it. Remo was nervous as hell and he needed Nas there to help him out.

"Don't lie to me, Kareem. You already know that the truth will come out eventually. I'm done with your ass if I find out anything," Kalani promised.

"Baby, I'm not lying. I don't know why you be listening to those birds. All the fuck they do is chirp," Remo fussed, right as his phone started vibrating in his pocket. Nas was calling just like he always did whenever his brother needed him. Too bad Remo couldn't answer.

"Call her up here. I want to hear the shit from her mouth," Kalani said. She also wanted to see how Lexus and Remo would react while in each other's presence.

"Are you serious right now?" Remo asked.

"Do you see me smiling nigga?" Kalani countered angrily. "Do what the fuck I said!"

She watched as Remo picked up his phone and called Bee. "What's up cuz?" Bee asked when he answered.

"Aye bruh, send Lauren up here right quick," Remo requested.

"Who?" Bee questioned.

"The new bottle girl nigga! I don't know the bitch name," Remo yelled.

"Oh, you mean Lexus. Alright, I'm on it cuz," Bee said before he hung up.

Kalani paced the floor as she waited for the other woman to come up. Remo was a nervous wreck but he prayed that Lexus didn't say anything to incriminate him. He would kill her stupid ass if she did. When he heard soft knocks at the door, Remo jumped up to go answer it. He wanted to threatened Lexus with his eyes but he never got the chance.

"Sit your dog ass down. I got it," Kalani said as she walked over to the door. When she opened it, she saw the look of shock on Lexus' face when she saw her.

"Um, hey. Bee said that Remo wanted to see me," Lexus said nervously.

"No, I wanted to see you," Kalani corrected

"Okay. What's up?" Lexus questioned as she tried to appear as calm as possible. She saw the look of anger and nervousness on Remo's face and she already knew what was up.

"I'm not one to beat around the bush, so I'm coming straight out with the shit. Are you fucking Remo and are you pregnant with his baby?" Kalani questioned.

"Wow. I was not expecting that at all," Lexus said, seemingly offended by Kalani's questions. There was no way that she was going to be honest and risk getting killed by Remo. She was ready to put on her big girl thongs and give the best performance of her life.

"Yeah, well that makes two of us. It's fucked up that it has to even come to this," Kalani flippantly replied as she frowned at Remo.

"But to answer your question, no, I'm not nor have I ever slept with Remo. And no, I'm not pregnant either. I have a boyfriend. If I was pregnant, he would be the father. I can't believe that somebody threw me in some mess like that. I barely even talk to anybody. I come here to make money and nothing more," Lexus said, as Remo visibly relaxed.

Some of what she said was true though. She was no longer pregnant because she'd had an abortion two weeks before. She showed Nas proof that she was pregnant and he gave her the money to terminate it. Lexus made sure to get the birth control shot the following week and she went on with her life.

"I'm sorry for having to come at you like this but Kareem is known for fucking the help. He's also known to lie about doing it," Kalani said, interrupting her thoughts.

"Man, I told you that I was telling the truth," Remo spoke up.

"Shut the fuck up Kareem! I shouldn't even have to go through all this bullshit behind your sad ass," Kalani fussed. Lexus was shocked when Remo closed his mouth like an obedient child. Everybody always said that he didn't play with Kalani and she was seeing it with her own eyes.

"I understand Kalani but whoever told you that is lying. Remo has never even looked at me in an inappropriate way. It's always been business and nothing more," Lexus swore. She enjoyed the money and tips that she made at the club but maybe it was time for her to find another job. She had never been in so much mess before in her life and she was over it.

"Okay, thanks Lexus," Kalani replied as she opened the door to let her out.

"You need to stop believing everything that you hear," Remo said as he walked up to Kalani and wrapped his arms around her waist.

"Nigga please. I hope you don't think I believed nothing that hoe just said. I don't know if you threatened her or what but I can spot a liar from a mile away. That bitch was scared to death up in here," Kalani replied.

"I love you, baby," Remo said as he kissed her and hugged her tighter. Kalani wasn't stupid, so he didn't even respond to the comment that she had just made. She had no proof, so he was innocent until she could prove that he was guilty.

"I love you too, baby. Oh, and I want Misty gone by the end of the week. Her time is up," Kalani said as she gave his lips one final kiss before walking out of the office.

She didn't give a damn how much money Misty made for the club. It was time for that bitch to go. Kalani didn't object to her working there after she had her baby because that was mostly on Nas. He was married to her sister, so he felt somewhat obligated. Since he and Milan were no longer together, all of Misty's passes had run out. When Kalani walked out of the office, Misty's eyes were right on her. She smiled as she looked at her and Kalani smiled right back. She was sure that they were smiling for different reasons, but Kalani was going to have the last laugh.

"Don't go over there on no bullshit Naseem. I'm not worried about a damn thing that Milan is saying on Instagram," Stori said as she talked on the phone with Nas.

"I'm not worried about that shit either. I already know that the bitch is lying. I'm just tired of playing these childish ass games with her stupid ass," Nas replied.

"Okay, well I'll see you later," Stori said before she hung up the phone.

Stori was on her grown woman shit, so Milan didn't really bother her with the childish games that she played. Milan was posting a positive pregnancy test all over Instagram, claiming to be pregnant. She was tagging Nas in everything, saying that he was already being a deadbeat. Although she was trying to get pregnant while they were together, Nas knew in his heart that she was lying. Milan hadn't called him once before she started posting all over social media. He wasn't in the mood to deal with the foolishness but he was over the dramatics.

Stori was everything that he thought she would be and more. Nobody was going to get in the way of them being together and he put his life on that. She was helping Nas build his credit and he had already received two credit cards in his name. It might not have seemed like much to some, but that was a huge accomplishment to him. Stori made him want to do better and no other woman had ever made him feel that way. The lawyer that Latrice hooked them up with was on his job and he and Remo were a few steps closer to having a blemish free criminal record. Things were looking up and he wasn't going to let anyone ruin it. Milan needed to know her place and he had to get at Danni too. She had been blowing his phone up like crazy and he was over her ass too.

Sighing heavily, Nas got out of his car and headed up the stairs and knocked on Milan's front door. He didn't even tell her that he was coming but he knew that she would welcome him in. Everything that she did was to get his attention and he was finally giving her some. Milan claimed to be pregnant, but he smelled the weed as soon as he stepped on the porch.

"Who is it?" Milan yelled.

"It's me, Milan. Open the door," Nas replied. Although she was right there, it took her about three minutes before Milan finally opened the door. When Nas looked at what she had on, he knew exactly why. Milan must have hurriedly changed into some black boy cut underwear with a black crop top to match. Nas couldn't even lie, she was fine as fuck but she still didn't have nothing on Stori. She tried to mask the potent weed smell with air freshener but it was a waste of her time.

"What are you doing here Naseem?" Milan asked. She was happy as hell to see him but she didn't want her excitement to show.

"The fuck you mean? This is obviously what you wanted since you keep posting all that dumb shit on Instagram. You wanted some attention, so what's up?" Nas asked as he folded his arms and looked down at her.

"How is me announcing my pregnancy wanting some attention?" Milan asked.

"That's bullshit Milan. If you were really pregnant, I should have been the first one that you called," Nas pointed out.

"You never even answer the phone for me!" Milan yelled.

"That's because you're always calling with some bullshit. I don't have time to play games with you," Nas said.

"Well, me having your baby is not bullshit," Milan replied as she turned and walked away.

Nas was a man before he was anything else, so he looked at her ass as soon as she did. He smirked as Milan flopped down on the sofa.

"Am I supposed to take your word Milan? I know you don't think I'm that dumb. You can buy a positive pregnancy test online. Get up and meet me in the bathroom," Nas said as he pulled out the test that he got from the store from his front pocket.

"Seriously Nas? I have the paperwork to prove it," Milan said as he jumped up and grabbed her purse.

She pulled out some papers and shoved them into his hand. He took one look at the paperwork and laughed before throwing it back at her.

"That shit is bogus. It's a copy Milan. Stop trying to insult my intelligence," Nas argued.

"What are you talking about Naseem? It is a copy that I got from the doctor's office," Milan swore.

"Man, I got shit to do Milan. Are you coming to piss on the stick or not? My girl is cooking and I'm hungry as fuck," Nas said while rubbing his rock hard stomach.

"Your girl?" Milan yelled as he cocked her head to the side and glared at him.

"That's what I said," Nas replied.

"Fuck you and that bitch. Tell that hoe that she got seven more months until she's a step mama," Milan said.

"I'm gone. I don't have time for the games," Nas said as he headed for the door right as Misty opened it.

She was carrying Summer and her diaper bag when she walked into the house. She mean mugged Nas but he laughed at her facial expression. Kalani made Remo fire her two weeks ago and she had been in her feelings ever since. They weren't even going to lose any money because she had already been replaced. Two chicks messaged Nas on Instagram inquiring about a job. They were bad as fuck and Nas hired them on the spot. They used to dance at another club and some of their regulars became regulars at Twin Tails. Money was lovely and Misty would not be missed.

"You good Milan?" Misty asked her sister.

"Yeah, I'm straight. Fuck Naseem. Me and my baby will be good without him," Milan argued.

"Fuck you too, bitch. And by the way, your tampon string is hanging out," Nas laughed as he walked out of the house.

Milan felt stupid but she refused to let him have the last word. She jumped up from the sofa and ran outside after him.

"That's because I've been having complications. Thanks to you, I'm stressed the fuck out and bleeding!" Milan yelled.

"Stop making a fool of yourself Milan. Faking a pregnancy is played the fuck out. High school girls don't even do that kind of shit no more. I guess you'll be posting that you had a miscarriage next. Who raised you hoes to act like this?" Nas laughed as he got into his car.

"Fuck you, Naseem! Me and my baby don't need shit from you. I hate your bitch ass," Milan cried as he pulled away from her house.

"Crazy ass bitch," Nas said as he shook his head and drove away.

He was sitting back waiting for Milan to pull some dumb shit and he didn't have to wait very long. When Lexus quit the club two weeks ago, she told him everything that Misty had done. Misty got a pregnancy test for Lexus to take but she never told her why she wanted her to do it. She even asked Lexus for a copy of her papers from the doctor and Lexus foolishly complied. Misty knew that the younger woman was naïve and it worked in her favor. Not even a week later, Milan started posting all that dumb shit about being pregnant online. Nas had already peeped game and he was two steps ahead of them.

Just like he'd assumed, a week later, Milan was posting that she'd suffered a miscarriage. Nas laughed as he read all the messages of condolences that people were sending her. Milan was an attention seeker and they were giving her just what she was looking for. Nas was done with her. The only thing he was waiting on was their divorce to be finalized. He didn't have any paperwork to prove it but he already had a new wife.

It had been two whole months since Gavin and Stori separated and he felt like he was losing his mind. He and Stori had slept in the same bed for over two years and he was having a hard time letting go. Gavin had never had a relationship longer than six months. He had never come close to loving a woman enough to even think about marrying her. Stori came along and changed all that. She was Gavin's dream woman in more ways than one. He did everything to make her see that he was the one for her.

He saw how much she loved Toi, so he used that knowledge to his advantage. He started buying Toi gifts and doing little things that he knew she liked. Once he had her wrapped around his finger, he started working on Stori. Things took longer than expected but he finally got the girl of his dreams. It didn't matter that Stori confessed to not being in love with him. He was confident that it would happen eventually. Cheating on her was the dumbest thing that he'd ever done and he regretted it. He just needed to see her and plead his case one last time. He was sure that seeing the sincerity in his eyes would at least make her think twice. He missed her and it seemed as if he was more in love with her now than he was before.

When Gavin pulled up to her house, he didn't see her car but that wasn't unusual. Stori usually parked in her garage while he always parked out front. The lights were on in the shop and two other cars were parked out front. Gavin took a deep breath to calm himself down before he got out of his car. He didn't know what Stori's reaction would be but he just needed to see her.

When he walked into the shop, two ladies were sitting under the dryers. They both looked up and spoke when Gavin walked in. Stori wasn't down there, so Gavin made his way upstairs to find her. He looked in the kitchen first before going upstairs to the bedrooms. He heard water running in the master bath and he made his way towards the sound. As soon as he got into the bathroom, he paused at the sight before him. Stori had the water running in the sink as she kneeled in front of the toilet, throwing up. That alone was a sight in itself. But, it was nothing compared to the positive pregnancy test that was still sitting on the counter.

"You're pregnant?" Gavin asked, startling Stori.

She jumped at the sound of his voice but she felt too bad to even acknowledge him. Gavin grabbed a towel from the cabinet and ran some cold water on it. He placed it on Stori's forehead and she felt better almost instantly.

"What the hell are you doing in my house Gavin?" Stori managed to ask in between dry heaving.

"I'm so fucking happy right now! We're having a baby," Gavin said excitedly.

"I wish the fuck I would," Stori said as she flushed the toilet and stood up. She grabbed her toothbrush and brushed her teeth to get the taste of vomit out of her mouth.

"What is that supposed to mean?" Gavin asked.

"You must be out of your fucking mind if you think I'm having a baby for you." Stori frowned.

"Please don't do this Stori. I fucked up, but what does an innocent child have to do with that?" Gavin asked as he looked at her with pitiful eyes.

"I don't want no parts of you, Gavin. I don't even want to see you. Why would I want to bring a baby into the world with your blood flowing through its veins?" Stori questioned.

That was only a small part of the reason. Truthfully, she didn't even know if Gavin was the father or not. She'd slept with him on Sunday morning and was fucking Nas Monday night. She couldn't call Lady a hoe anymore because she was her mother's child. Stori had been feeling sick a lot lately but she wasn't ready to face reality. When she woke up that morning, Stori felt like the room was spinning. She was happy that Nas offered to take Toi to school because she was able to sleep in a little longer. Stori knew her body and the changes weren't hard to see. After she put her two clients under the dryer, she grabbed the test that Nas tried to get Milan to take. Stori already knew what it would say but she took it anyway just to be sure. She didn't expect Gavin to find out and she was sorry that he had. He couldn't keep shit to himself, so Nas would know soon too. Stori had already planned to get rid of it and nothing that he said was going to change her mind.

"Baby, please, I'll do whatever I have to do. Please don't kill my baby. It's not fair for you to punish my unborn child for the mistakes that I made," Gavin noted.

"There is no unborn child. I'm getting rid of it the first chance I get. Trust me, it's for the best," Stori said.

"That's fucked up Stori. I swear I never took you as that type of female. You can raise your sister, but my baby is not good enough for you to keep," Gavin snapped angrily.

"You must be trying to get shot. Is that what you really want Gavin? You know I stay ready nigga. I suggest you get the fuck up out of my house and don't come back. And stop talking to me about a baby that'll be a distant memory by next week," Stori replied, just as heated as he was.

She grabbed her phone and started searching for abortion clinics right in his face. Gavin was livid but there was only so much that he could do. Stori was good for pulling guns out on people and there was no telling where she had them hidden.

"Stupid ass bitch," Gavin fumed as he hurriedly walked away.

"Your baby mama is a bitch nigga!" Stori yelled after him.

Gavin wanted to knock some shit over in her shop as he walked through it, but he wasn't crazy. Stori had cousins that he did not want to deal with. She was kind of crazy at times too and he wasn't in the mood to be in no bullshit. It seemed as if he and Stori were drifting further apart and he didn't know what to do. As much as it pained him to admit it, he had to start looking for another place to stay. It didn't look like he was getting back with his wife no time soon and he was already over living with his parents. Gavin was so depressed that he didn't even want to go to work. Things there seemed just as tense. He didn't know what he had done but Nas had distanced himself. Gavin tried talking to him but he always gave him a dry, one word reply. He was starting to act just like Remo and Gavin didn't like that. He was tempted to look for another shop to work in but that would have been a stupid move. Mr. Herbert's shop was popular and they had a steady flow of customers, even on slow days. Besides that, Gavin had a hard enough time trying to find a shop before Nas got him on there.

Since he needed to make some money, Gavin decided to go to work. When he got there, the shop was packed and he got right to work on a few of the walk-in customers. Nas was busy too and they hadn't said anything to each other. Gavin felt like he was losing his best friend and he hated that feeling.

"You went to school today boy? And don't lie," Nas said when Eric walked into the shop.

Eric always came in after school and on the weekends to help out around the shop. He made good grades but he was known to cut class sometimes. Nas took a liking to him and he made sure that he was straight. He was the one who got Eric's uniforms and everything else that he needed for school. Eric had all kinds of shoes and clothes that Nas kept locked up at the barber shop. He came in every morning to change out of his Nike slides into a pair of the shoes that he had there. On weekends, he would shower at home and come into the shop to change into his good clothes. Eric's mother was on drugs and she stole everything. Although he and his brother lived with their grandmother, their mother was always there. To keep from having to kill her, Nas didn't let Eric bring anything of value to his house. Eric kept a fresh cut, courtesy of Nas and he was forever grateful to the man that he looked up to.

"Yeah, I got my report card too," Eric said as he showed it to him.

"That's what's up bruh." Nas smiled proudly as he looked over Eric's grades.

Eric went straight to his locker and took off his new Jordon's and put them back in the box. He put his Nike slides back on and grabbed the broom. He knew what he had to do and no one ever had to tell him. He kept the two bathrooms clean and made sure that they were always stocked with soap and tissue. Nas did the most for him, but the other barbers kept money in his pockets too.

"Are you ready to eat?" Nas asked Eric after a while.

"Yeah," Eric replied. Nas handed him some money to go get them both something to eat from the corner store across the street. When he came back with the food, Nas took a break and went into the employee lounge in the back. Gavin waited a few minutes before he went back there to join him.

"Man, you'll never guess what the fuck happened today?" Gavin said as soon as he took a seat. Nas was eating his chicken plate but he looked up at him as he talked.

"What's good?" he questioned.

"I was kind of in my feelings earlier so I popped up on Stori," Gavin replied.

Nas paused midair with a piece of chicken in his hand. Gavin didn't miss the look of anger that flashed across his face but he didn't really think anything of it.

"The fuck you go over there for?" Nas asked angrily. Again, Gavin thought nothing of it because Nas did have a mean side to him.

"Man, I was missing the fuck out of her and I just wanted to see her. But picture when I went there, she was upstairs in the bathroom sick as a dog. She was throwing up and I didn't know what the fuck was wrong with her. Then, I look on the counter and see a positive pregnancy test," Gavin announced.

"She's pregnant!" Nas yelled a little louder than he needed to.

"Yeah man. Pregnant with my baby and she's trying to abort it. I'm so fucked up behind that shit. I started not to even come to work," Gavin replied.

"How do you know that she's having an abortion?" Nas inquired.

"Because she told me so. All that time we spent trying to have a baby. Now that it finally happened, we're separated. I just feel like this might be a sign from God. Maybe this is just what we need for us to get back together," Gavin replied.

"I doubt it," Nas said with a big smile on his face.

"The fuck you smiling so hard for nigga?" Gavin laughed.

"Because I'm happy as fuck right now," Nas replied as he stood to his feet. He threw the rest of his food away and washed his hands. Gavin didn't know why he was so happy but it had been a while since he'd seen Nas genuinely smile.

"Where you rushing off to nigga?" Gavin asked.

"Home," Nas said as he walked out of the break room and back to the front of the shop. Gavin didn't know exactly where his home was since he wasn't with Milan anymore.

Unfortunately, Nas couldn't leave as soon as he wanted to. Three of his regulars came in and he had to service them before he left. Once that was done, Mr. Herbert came in and wanted to talk about him and Remo buying the shop. He had finally sold his house and he was ready to move forward with selling the shop too. Nas was half listening to everything that the other man was saying. He was too busy thinking about Stori and her possibly being pregnant with his baby.

Nas didn't leave from the shop until after seven that night. As soon as he walked into the house, the aroma of a home cooked meal was the first thing to greet him. Even after working all day, Stori still made time to have a hot meal on the stove every night. Milan was lazy as fuck. She didn't work at all and she still refused to cook. Nas didn't miss a damn thing about being with her.

"What's up baby?" Nas greeted as he wrapped his arms around Stori's waist. She was standing in front of the stove finishing up their meal.

"Hey boo. How was your day?" Stori asked, making him smile. Little shit like that was what had Nas falling more and more for her every day. No one had ever asked him about his day and that meant a lot to him.

"It was straight. What about yours?" he asked her.

"Let's just say that I'm happy it's over," Stori replied.

She froze when Nas placed his hands on her belly. She didn't have to ask if he knew because she was almost sure that he did. Gavin never did know how to keep his mouth closed but he was confiding in the wrong nigga.

"I want it. I don't care who the father is," Nas whispered in her ear.

"Naseem, please don't. I've already made the appointment to terminate it," Stori replied.

"What if it's mine?" Nas questioned.

"What if it's not?" Stori countered.

"I really don't care Stori. I want it either way. Besides, I really don't believe in abortions," Nas replied.

"I'm sorry Nas but I just can't do it. The thought of this possibly being Gavin's baby just makes me sick to my stomach," Stori said.

"Just fuck what I want, huh?" Nas questioned.

"I would never say that baby but I need you to understand how I feel. I want kids, just not with Gavin. We can start a family as soon as I get this problem taken care of," Stori promised.

"Let me make sure I got this straight. You want to kill a baby, just to turn around and have another one. The way karma is set up, you'll fuck around and can't even have no more kids. For all we know, that could me my baby that you're trying to get rid of," Nas argued as he looked down at her.

"Yeah but there's also a chance that it's not," Stori replied.

"Alright baby. I don't want to argue with you. What's the plan? When is this supposed to happen?" Nas asked as he tried to suppress his anger.

"Hopefully next week. I have a consultation and hopefully the procedure can be done soon after," Stori replied.

"Cool. Where is Toi?" Nas asked while changing the subject. Stori could tell that he was upset but he tried his best to remain calm.

"She's upstairs doing homework," Stori replied.

Nas nodded his head and walked away. Stori felt bad for what she was about to do, but her hands were tied. She honestly had no clue as to who the father of her child was and that was driving her crazy. Still, she didn't want her decision to affect her relationship with Nas. They knew each other through Gavin but they were still getting to know each other as a couple. Nas was an open book but he was unlike anybody else that she'd ever dealt with. He didn't really get angry and he did some crazy shit when things didn't go his way.

Once the food was done, Stori called Toi down to eat right before she fixed Nas a plate. She put his food and drink on a tray and took it upstairs to her bedroom. Nas was on the phone when she walked in and she could tell that he was talking to Remo. He smiled when he saw her walk in with his food and sat up in the bed.

"Fuck off my line nigga. The queen just walked in," Nas said as he hung up the phone.

"You didn't have to get off the phone," Stori said when she sat the tray in his lap.

"Don't start doing shit like this for me now and try to switch up on me later. You can't spoil a nigga like me and then try to stop," Nas said when Stori grabbed the fork and started feeding him the steak, loaded potato and shrimp that she fixed.

"I never start something that I don't plan to finish," Stori assured him.

"That fuck boy told me that he came through earlier today," Nas said as he looked at her.

"I figured that he would," Stori said as she rolled her eyes.

"Would you have told me if he didn't?" Nas questioned.

"I don't hide anything from you, Naseem," Stori replied as she continued to feed him.

"You don't have a reason to," Nas said.

"Are you mad at me?" Stori asked as she looked up at him.

"Nah, I'm not mad. I'm pissed. But, it's all good. I'll let you handle it how you see fit." Nas shrugged.

"I'm sorry Nas but I just need you to understand how I feel," Stori replied.

"I already know how you feel baby. I'll be okay. And like you said, we can always try again," he replied.

"Do you really mean that Naseem?" Stori asked.

"Fuck no," he answered honestly.

"Why did you say it then?" Stori laughed.

"Because I'm not trying to argue with you, love. You're stubborn and so am I. See, Gavin was your bitch and he let you call all the shots. I can see that you don't really like to compromise and neither do I. You like to have your way," Nas observed.

"Is that a problem?" Stori inquired.

"Not at all. I'm all for spoiling you but I don't want you to ever get shit twisted. I'm a born leader baby. All you have to do is follow me. I'll never lead you wrong and you got my word on that," Nas replied.

"Are we good though Nas?" Stori asked him.

"Always baby. I don't ever want you to doubt that," he replied.

Stori smiled and he smiled back at her. Having his support meant a lot to her and that was all that she needed. She wouldn't make matters worse by asking him to go with her to terminate her pregnancy. She knew that Kalani would take her and that's who she was going to ask. Truthfully, Stori wasn't going to try for another baby any time soon. As soon as she got rid of the one that she was carrying, she was going to get on some type of birth control. She wasn't ready to take that step with Nas just yet. They still had a lot to learn about each other before they tried to start a family. If things kept going as good as they were, Stori could see it happening in the future though.

"You okay boo?" Kalani asked as soon as Stori got into her car.

"Yeah, I'm okay." Stori smiled nervously.

A week after finding out that she was pregnant, Kalani was bringing Stori to get an abortion. Stori had already done her consultation and paid her deposit. She was nine weeks in and she had no idea as to which man had fathered her child. It was embarrassing and she didn't even want to think about it. Nas hadn't said anything else about it and it was as if Stori wasn't even pregnant. He didn't treat her any differently and he didn't appear to be upset anymore.

"Remo said that I'm an accessory to murder," Kalani said.

"Bitch! Why the hell did you tell him anything? I

need to find a new best friend." Stori frowned.

"Do it and I'll make Kareem kill her," Kalani threatened.

"You pillow talk too damn much. I haven't even talked to Nas about it anymore since the first day," Stori noted.

"Nas was the one who told him first anyway. I just filled in a few of the blanks." Kalani shrugged.

"I just want this to be over with. Morning sickness is kicking my ass," Stori said.

"I just wish we knew for sure. I hate that you could possibly be terminating a baby that might actually belong to Nas," Kalani replied.

"I know but there's no way for me to know that before the baby gets here," Stori assumed.

"Yes there is. Remo said him and Nas looked into it. You can do an amniocentesis or noninvasive prenatal test. Most of them can be done when you're only ten weeks in. Just think, if you wait one more week you can find out who the baby's father is," Kalani pointed out.

"Well, too bad that I'm having the abortion today," Stori snapped.

"Okay boo. It was just a thought." Kalani shrugged.

"I'm sorry about my attitude friend. Everything just seems to have changed overnight. Gavin and I were trying to have a baby, so I hadn't been on birth control for a while. Nas and I started out using protection but it didn't take long for us to get careless. I just hate that Toi has to witness all this bullshit. She saw me go from being married to Gavin one day to being in a relationship with his friend a day later. I can only imagine what she's thinking," Stori rambled.

"Toi loves Nas and you know that. She's happy just as long as you are. You worry too much about nothing," Kalani said as she grabbed Stori's hand to comfort her.

"Don't forget that I need you to get my Stanka from school today. I'm not sure how I'll feel after the procedure. I'll just probably be in bed for the rest of the day," Stori replied.

"I got you, friend. I'll get her from school and make sure she gets something to eat," Kalani assured her as she continued to drive.

When they turned on the street where the clinic was located, they were stopped right at the corner. The entire block was pure chaos and they didn't know what was going on. They had police cars and SWAT trucks all over the area. Men in white hazmat suits were walking around looking like astronauts.

"What the hell?" Stori asked out loud as she looked around.

The clinic that she had to go to seemed to be the focus of whatever was going on. When someone knocked on the window, she and Kalani jumped in fear. Kalani hurriedly let her window down when she saw a police officer standing there.

"You can't come this way ma'am. The entire area is off limits until further notice. I'll stop traffic so you can back up," the officer said.

"What's going on?" Kalani asked.

"Bomb threat made to the women's clinic," he replied before he walked into the street to stop the cars from coming. He assisted Kalani with backing up and they were on their way once again.

"Oh, my God. They are really crazy," Stori said as she looked over at her friend in shock.

"Who's really crazy?" Kalani asked.

"Remo and Nas. I'm sure you know that they did this," Stori replied.

"What! Are you serious Stori? You really think they would do something extreme like this?" Kalani asked.

"Everything that they do is extreme Kalani. Did you expect them to be sitting up in Omar's house when you got there?" Stori countered, giving her friend something to think about.

"Those retarded bastards," Kalani fumed as she dialed Remo's number.

"I'm at Stori's house baby. Come fuck with me," Remo said when he answered the phone and then hung up. Kalani already knew what that was about. Remo never liked to discuss certain things over the phone and that's why he dismissed her before she could say anything.

"Who raised these niggas?" Stori questioned as Kalani drove to her house in stunned silence.

"Jarvis did but it ain't his fault. I'm sure he tried his best. I seriously doubt if anybody can tame those two wild animals," Kalani said as she shook her head.

She knew that Remo and Nas were crazy but something else was obviously wrong. Kalani would have loved to meet their parents because there had to be some kind of explanation. Jarvis was nothing like them and she needed answers. Maybe it was a chemical imbalance or something that caused them to behave the way they did. When she pulled up to Stori's house, they both jumped out of the car, hoping to get to the bottom of everything.

"What's up sweetheart?" Nas asked when Stori walked into the house. Him and Remo were sitting on the sofa watching tv like they had done nothing wrong.

"Please tell me you didn't do what I think you did," Stori said as she looked at Nas expectantly.

"Okay, I won't." Nas shrugged like it was no big deal.

"Naseem! Oh, my God! That is a federal offense. I can't believe you did that," Stori said in a panic.

"Calm down sis. They can't trace that shit back to us. Bee stole the phone from one of them drunk niggas at the club. Once we made the call, we threw that shit in the lake," Remo replied.

"Why are you sitting here acting all calm and shit. This is not normal Naseem. What is wrong with y'all? I can't live like this," Stori argued. She was beginning to look at Kalani sideways for being with Remo so long. She didn't know if she could do it with Nas.

"Stop trying me, Stori. How many times do I have to tell you that? I'm not like none of them other niggas that you were with before me. Stop dismissing my feelings. I told you not to do it and that's what the fuck I meant," Nas replied.

"Why are you doing this to me, Naseem? I don't want this baby," Stori said as she dropped her head and cried.

Stori wasn't an overly emotional person. Kalani hadn't seen her cry since the day Lady gave her full custody of Toi and that was seven years ago. She didn't even shed a tear when she learned that Gavin had fathered Misty's child. Maybe it was the pregnancy hormones that was doing it to her. Kalani jumped up to go comfort her girl, but Nas wasn't having it.

"Get your wife Remo," Nas ordered as he looked at his brother.

Remo grabbed Kalani by the arm before she had a chance to get to her friend. He ushered her out of the front door to give his brother some privacy. Once they were alone, Nas pulled Stori onto his lap and wiped her tears. He knew that he was a lot to handle at times and he went to the extreme to get his point across.

"I'm not forcing you to have this baby Stori," Nas said.

"Yes, you are and you don't even know if it's yours," Stori sobbed.

"No but there is a way for us to find out before you abort it," Nas pointed out.

"How?" Stori questioned.

"Me and Remo looked at a few places online that can do a DNA test before the baby is born. We can look to see which one of them is the best and make the appointment. If I'm not the father and you still want to get an abortion, I'll take you to do it myself," Nas swore.

"Why didn't you just tell me that before Naseem?" Stori asked him.

"You never gave me a chance. You just up and made the decision without even asking how I felt about it. Me and Remo looked into it last night but you never asked for my input," Nas replied.

"I'm sorry boo," Stori said as she laid her head on his chest.

"We're good baby and we always will be," Nas promised as he rubbed her back.

"Do you ever feel guilty Nas?" Stori asked him.

"About what?" Nas questioned.

"I'm talking about us being together. Do you ever feel guilty about it?" Stori asked again.

"No, why? Do you?" he inquired.

"I feel guilty about not feeling guilty. It's like, I know I should feel bad but I don't," Stori answered honestly.

"This shit was meant to be baby. I should have listened to Remo and took you from that nigga a long time ago," Nas said.

"What makes you think I would have left him for you?" Stori asked.

"I don't know. Would you?" Nas questioned.

"In a fucking heartbeat," Stori said, making him laugh.

"Damn man. Now I'm mad that I didn't do it sooner," Nas replied.

"So, who made the call?" Stori asked as she lifted her head up to look at him.

"What call?" Nas asked.

"Stop playing dumb Naseem. The call that shut down the entire block where the clinic is located," Stori replied.

"Oh, I did. That shit made the news and everything. I feel like a hood celebrity," Nas laughed as she shook her head.

"I can't believe you. A bomb threat though, Nas. That was a bit much," Stori said.

"Yeah but it got the job done. Let's go see about making an appointment at one of these clinics. We can go grab something to eat once we get Toi from school," Nas replied as he and Stori headed upstairs to the bedroom.

Stori didn't know much about the procedures, so she took a few minutes to read up on everything. She did notice that the accuracy rating was extremely high and that made her feel good about doing it. She also noticed that the procedure carried a slight chance for miscarriage. Stori hated to feel the way she did but she wouldn't have even felt bad if she was among the small percentage of women who it happened to. In her mind, God didn't make mistakes. Whatever was meant to be was going to happen, regardless of how she felt about it.

"Man, fuck!" Remo cursed as he looked at all the big bills that was in his and Nas' safe. He was supposed to stop at the bank earlier that morning but he forgot. Now, the bar needed change and he didn't even have any. It was almost seven at night and all of the banks were closed. He was hoping that Bee could run to a corner store and at least get a few small bills to hold them over.

"What's good bro?" Nas asked when he walked into the office. He threw a leather bank bag to his brother that Remo caught midair.

"Boy, I love the fuck out of you, nigga. I was just in here stressing about this shit." Remo smiled as he thumbed through the bag of money that Nas had just given him. They must have had some kind of twin super powers because he and Nas were always in sync with one another.

"Yeah, I saw that we were running low when I was in here last night," Nas replied as he took a seat on the leather sofa.

"I wasn't expecting to see you in here today. How is Stori feeling?" Remo asked.

"She's good. She's just relaxing like they told her to. I was just passing through to drop that money off to you. I'm going grab her and Toi something to eat and head back home," Nas replied.

Two weeks had passed since Stori was supposed to terminate her pregnancy. She was now eleven weeks in and starting to show already. She had the amniocentesis done that morning and they now had about another week or two to wait before they got the results. Stori was still in her first trimester but she hated the small pouch that was forming in her belly. That meant that the baby was growing and she was feeling guilty about getting rid of it. Nas was adamant about her having it, even if Gavin was the father. She knew that things would only get worse if she did. There was no way that Nas was going to want Gavin to come around and she wasn't in the mood for the drama that she knew would come as a result.

"Man, I hope we get some good news. I got nieces but I need me a nephew to spoil." Remo smiled.

"Stori don't want a boy but I need one. A lil girl gon' make me too soft," Nas replied as he stood to his feet.

"Go take care of your wife and call me later," Remo said as he gave his brother a hug.

"Later bro," Nas replied as he walked out of the office.

He sent a head nod to a few of their regulars as he made his way to the front door. He was almost to the exit when Danni stepped in his path and put her hand on his chest.

"Well, hello there stranger." Danni smiled up at him.

"What's good Danni?" Nas said as he removed her hand. He didn't need Kalani to see anything that she would feel compelled to report back to Stori.

"Damn. I can't touch you no more or something?" Danni asked in an offended tone.

"Nah, I'm already spoken for," Nas replied as he sidestepped her and made his way outside.

"Spoken for by who? I hope you're not talking about Milan because that ain't nothing new. I was there when she was your girlfriend and I was still around once you made her your wife," Danni noted as she followed him out.

Nas had been avoiding her more than usual and she was not happy about that. She never went to his club without being invited, but she really wanted to see him. She missed being with him and she needed a fix that only sex with Naseem could satisfy.

"I'm not with Milan no more Danni. I got a girl and I'm not on that dumb shit no more," Nas said.

"Since when?" Danni said as she tried to touch his chest again.

"Chill out Danni. I'm good on you and whatever we had. I love my girl and I'm happy," Nas replied.

"How the fuck do you love a bitch that you probably just met? Just keep shit real Naseem," Danni argued. She'd been dealing with Nas for a minute and had yet to hear him say that he loved Milan. She was supposed to be next in line once he and Milan separated. She wasn't about to let some new bitch take a spot that she'd waited so long to get.

"See, I was trying to be civilized with your stupid ass but fuck it. Since you don't seem to like it when I'm a gentleman, I'll talk to you in a language that you might understand. Your pussy is trash and your head is even worse. I only needed you when I was locked up and you served your purpose a long time ago. Stop calling my phone and stay the fuck away from my club. Is that clear enough for you?" Nas asked menacingly.

He was trying to spare her feelings and that was something that he rarely did. Since she wanted to act stupid, he had to show her that he could be just as dumb. She was no better than Milan. They wanted him to be honest and he had no problem doing that.

"Fuck you, Naseem!" Danni fumed as she backed away from him and rushed off to her car. She sped away, making her tires screech as she did.

"Who the fuck is raising these hoes?" Nas asked himself out loud. That was a question that he never seemed to have an answer to. He wasn't in the mood to entertain none of the foolishness. He pulled off from the club and headed to the restaurant to get Stori and Toi something to eat.

"I wanna see exactly who this new bitch is," Danni fumed as she followed behind Nas.

She pulled away from the club but she didn't go very far. Once she saw Nas drive away, she kept her distance and followed right behind him. When he pulled up to a Chinese restaurant, Danni parked at the end of the parking lot and turned off her lights. It took Nas about twenty minutes before he got back into the car and drove away. He seemed to be preoccupied with his phone call and she was happy for that. She couldn't risk being seen by Nas. He would probably kill her if he knew what she was up to. He was usually on point but whoever he was talking to had all of his attention at the moment. Danni followed him until he pulled up to a nice house and opened the garage door. Once the door closed and he was no longer in sight, she jumped out of the car to read the business sign that was out front.

"Toi Stori Hair Salon. The fuck kind of name is that?" Danni questioned out loud.

She took a picture of the sign with the phone number and Instagram information on it. Danni had braids in her hair but they weren't going to be in there forever. She had a feeling that once she took them out, she was going to be paying a visit to the new hair salon that she had just discovered.

"**M**an, Stori, I'm not calling you with no bullshit. I need to get my important documents that I left over there," Gavin said as he left Stori yet another message.

He hadn't spoken to her since learning of her pregnancy and he was sure that she'd had the abortion by now. Gavin was hurt but there really was nothing that he could do about it. After searching for two weeks, he'd finally found and been approved for a two bedroom apartment. He had gotten all of his belongings from Stori's house but his folder of important documents that he kept at the top of the closet was still there. His social security card, birth certificate and lots of other important information was there and he really needed it. Stori was on some bullshit and he didn't have time for it.

"You and wifey having problems?" Carlton, one of

the other barbers, asked.

"Man, she's on some bullshit right now," Gavin fumed. He was happy that the barber shop was fairly empty because he really needed to vent. Nas wasn't there and Carlton was always cool.

"Shit, the way you used to be talking, I thought shit was all good," Carlton noted.

He knew Stori very well but he wasn't going to elaborate for Gavin. His first cousin, Corey, was Stori's first love but that had been a long time ago. In Carlton's opinion, Corey was never Stori's type and neither was Gavin. He loved his cousin but Corey was as grimy as they came. Carlton's younger brothers and cousins hung out with him a lot but he was good on him. Besides cutting his hair, Carlton didn't really deal with Corey like that. He got weed from him occasionally but that didn't happen too often either.

"It was all good with us until I fucked up," Gavin said, bringing Carlton back to the present.

"How so?" Carlton asked.

"I made a baby on her and shit kind of went left. I don't think we're over for good but she's pissed with a nigga right now," Gavin said.

"Damn boy. Who the fuck did you find that was better than Stori? She's good people," Carlton noted. He used to have a crush on Stori back in the day but his cousin beat him to her. He was happily married with kids now, so another woman was nowhere on his mind.

"That bitch ain't better than my wife. I just got caught up. Fucking with Nas and got his sister-in-law pregnant." Gavin frowned.

"The stripper!" Carlton yelled.

He didn't know Nas all that well but he did know who his wife was. Milan used to always come to the shop and she sometimes got her weed from his cousin. Corey tried to get with her but she shut him down real quick. Corey didn't have enough money for her to even entertain him.

"Don't even remind me. That bitch ruined my life." Gavin frowned.

"It sounds like you did that all on your own," Carlton replied.

He wasn't knocking Gavin because he was no saint back in the day. It took his wife leaving him and threatening to divorce him before he got his shit together. He realized that none of the women that he was cheating with were better than what he had at home. They weren't even worth it and that made his decision to be faithful a lot easier. Gavin, on the other hand, didn't seem to be as smart. Carlton didn't indulge in gossip but it appeared that not many of the barbers were very fond of him. Gavin bragged a lot and that rubbed people the wrong way. Carlton had never met a man who talked outside of his bedroom like Gavin did. It was whack as fuck but he didn't see anything wrong with it. He and Nas seemed to be worlds apart, but Gavin all but worshipped the ground that Nas walked on.

"Yeah and I'm paying for that shit too," Gavin sighed right as the front door opened.

"What's up cuz? I need to get lined up right quick," Corey said as he walked into the shop and sat in Carlton's chair.

"Where my stupid ass lil brothers at?" Carlton asked as he fixed the cape around Corey's neck.

"Making my money," Corey laughed, as Carlton frowned at his statement.

Corey was almost thirty years old and still didn't have anything going for himself. He'd been selling weed for years and still had to rob niggas just to get ahead. Carlton didn't know why his little brothers followed his lead because he always led them into some bullshit. They stayed in jail and so did Corey.

"Stori, I know you see me calling you. Answer the fucking phone!" Gavin bellowed, as Corey looked over at him.

"Calm down fam. Raising your pressure won't make her pick up the phone," Carlton noted.

"I'm going make a food run right quick. You good?" Gavin asked him.

"Yeah, I'm straight," Carlton replied. As soon as Gavin walked out of the shop, Corey started up with the questions.

"What Stori is that nigga talking about?" Corey asked.

"What other Stori do you know?" Carlton countered.

"She fuck with that fake ass nigga?" Corey wanted to know.

He always saw Gavin when he came into the shop and he rubbed him the wrong way from day one. Corey always saw him with Nas and that's who he had his eyes on. Corey made it his business to know everybody who had money and Nas was one of them. He knew that Nas and his brother owned a strip club but he knew that they were into more than just that. They were known to be crazy and unpredictable, which was the only reason why he never tried them. Not yet at least.

"That's her husband," Carlton noted.

"The fuck do she even see in his stupid looking ass? She couldn't handle a thug like me." Corey frowned.

All those years later and he was still salty about Stori breaking up with him. Stori was even more beautiful now than she was before but she barely acknowledged him. She spoke when she saw him but she wasn't giving up no conversation.

"Not every woman wants a thug. Some of them actually want a real man," Carlton said.

"I'm as real as they get nigga. Fuck you mean," Corey snapped.

Carlton just shook his head and ignored him. Corey would never change and, sadly, neither would his two younger brothers.

200

Nas smiled when he pulled up to the house and saw Toi and her two friends outside dancing. They had their speaker on the sidewalk but it wasn't up too loud. He pulled his car into the garage and headed inside soon after. It was six that evening and he had been out handling business all day. He didn't even go to the barber shop because he didn't have time.

"Hey boo. How did everything go?" Stori asked as soon as he walked into the living room. She was stretched out on the sofa watching tv wearing nothing but a t-shirt.

"Everything is taken care of. Me and Remo are officially the new owners of the barber shop." Nas smiled as he kicked off his shoes and laid down on the sofa next to her. Mr. Herbert showed mad love with the price that he sold the shop for. Nas and Remo paid him in full and he was happy about that. The money didn't even put a dent in their bank account and it would take no time to replace it.

"Congrats boo. I'm so happy for y'all," Stori replied with a genuine smile.

"I told you baby, you're my good luck charm. Shit has been looking up for me since we got together. My credit score is going up and my record is about to be clean. All I'm waiting for now is the results from the DNA test. Did the mail come yet?" Nas asked as Stori's smile faded.

"I don't want you to get your hopes up too high Naseem. We already talked about that and you know that the results can go either way. My gut is telling me that we won't receive any good news," Stori replied.

"Your gut ain't telling you shit. You had that fucked up ass dream and you've been having negative thoughts since then," Nas said, calling her out.

An entire week had passed and they still hadn't heard anything from the lab regarding their test results. The technician told Stori that they would either receive something by mail or a phone call from the lab. Stori had a dream three days after the procedure was done that had her shook up and afraid. She dreamt that they'd received a call from the lab saying that Nas was not the baby's father. She broke down crying in her dream and she woke up sweating with tears falling from her eyes. She'd been paranoid ever since then and not knowing for sure only made it worse. She was officially three months now and the guilt of aborting her baby was starting to eat at her. The longer she waited, the harder it became. Nas had her taking prenatal vitamins and that only added to her stress. She was giving nourishment to a baby that she wasn't even sure that she was going to keep. It didn't help that she was beginning to show. It just seemed so wrong and cruel to even go through with terminating the pregnancy now.

"I know but it seemed so real. I wonder what's taking them so long with the results," Stori sighed.

"Why can't you just have the baby Stori? I don't give a fuck who the daddy is," Nas replied.

"But, I do. You promised Naseem. Don't try to go back on your word now," Stori said.

"I'll never do that. My word is law," Nas assured her right as her phone rang.

"So fucking disgusting," Stori huffed as she silenced her ringer.

"Who is that?" Nas asked.

"That's Gavin's annoying ass," Stori replied.

"The fuck is he still calling you for? I thought you gave him all his shit," Nas said.

"I did but he said that he left his folder with his birth certificate and stuff at the top of the closet," Stori replied. She didn't answer for Gavin but she did listen to his messages.

"Fuck him. He should have told his mama to get it when she came to get the rest of his shit." Nas frowned.

"I really don't care about nothing that has to do with Gavin. I'm so damn lazy now. I didn't even cook anything. As soon as my last client left, I laid down and haven't gotten up since," Stori yawned.

"I don't know how it's even possible but that ass is getting fatter. Shit is just ridiculously big and I'm in love like a muthafucker," Nas said as he smacked her ass.

"Naseem stop!" Stori laughed when he bit down on her ass cheeks.

"Stop trying to fight me when you know you want it," he said as he pulled off her underwear.

202

"Naseem nooo! Toi is right outside," Stori said as she stopped him from burying his face between her legs.

Nas was nasty as hell. He spread her ass cheeks wide and ran his tongue along her crack. He didn't listen to her protest and he dove in between her legs head first anyway. Stori grabbed the back of his head and moaned as he sucked her clit up into his mouth. She kept watching the door to make sure Toi didn't bust up in there and catch them in the act. She was having a hard time enjoying her man because she was on edge.

"Let me bring your scary ass upstairs," Nas laughed when he saw how nervous she was.

Stori held on tight as he carried her upstairs with his face still nestled in between her legs. Once he laid her on the bed, he undressed himself and she pulled her t-shirt over her head. When Nas got in the bed and sat her on his face, she flipped her body upside down so that they were in the position to please each other. Stori took him into her mouth and had him sounding like a soprano a short time later.

"Who's scary nigga?" Stori bragged, as Nas yelled her name.

"Not you baby. You ain't never scared," Nas said as he gripped the sheets tighter.

He alternated between singing her praises and trying to please her as much as she was pleasing him. His dick stroked the inside of Stori's mouth as she attempted to swallow him whole.

"Fuuuuck!" Nas hissed as his dick hit the back of Stori's throat.

He was gone and there was no coming back. He was picturing what kind of ring he was going to put on Stori's finger. It didn't matter that they were both still married. He was ready to break the law and make her his wife. She was too perfect and he couldn't imagine his life without her in it. When he felt himself about to cum, he pulled Stori up and turned her around. Stori got in the squatting position and lowered herself onto his erection. Nas grabbed her breasts as she threw her head back and started riding him like a cowgirl.

"Damn baby," he groaned while his teeth gritted in pleasure.

"You like that boo?" Stori asked as she bounced up and down.

"Hell yeah," Nas moaned as he smacked her ass repeatedly.

Stori's hands were on his chest as she hopped up and down faster. Their moans bounced off the walls, along with the sound of their skin slapping. Nas was begging her not to stop and Stori didn't plan on it.

"Ahh!" Stori screamed when her hair was pulled from behind.

"The fuck!" Nas yelled when their connection was broken.

"Bitch! You're fucking my friend!" Gavin yelled as he stood there with wide eyes and a shattered heart.

Death had to feel better than how he was feeling. He was already in hell after seeing his wife fucking his best friend in a bed that they once shared. Gavin left the shop with the intentions of going to get food. When he tried calling Stori again and didn't get an answer, he decided to just pop up on her like he did before. He saw Toi walking across the street with her friends as soon as he turned on their block. He intended to enter the house through Stori's shop but it was already closed. When he walked up on the porch, he knocked on the door and waited for someone to answer. Since that never happened, he turned the knob and walked right in. The tv was on in the front room but that wasn't what got his attention. Gavin noticed a pair of men's shoes sitting right there in the middle of the floor. It wasn't just any kind of shoes though. It was the same shoes that he'd admired on Nas' feet not too long ago. The shoes were popular, so he didn't want to overthink it. They could have belonged to anyone, he reasoned with himself.

Gavin felt weak as he headed up the stairs to look for Stori. He heard the moaning clearly but he didn't want to believe it. His best friend and the love of his life being intimate was not something that he even wanted to think about. When he opened the door, his worst fears had been confirmed and he couldn't think rationally. He grabbed

Stori by her hair and pulled her away from Nas. Seeing her with no clothes on confirmed something else for him too. Stori was still pregnant. Having sex with another man while pregnant with his baby infuriated him even more. Gavin was out of it but a hard punch to the face snapped him back to reality. Nas hit him so hard that he went falling to the tiled floor. He didn't stop there though. He hit Gavin three more times before Stori intervened. Gavin was too distraught to even fight back. He knew that he wouldn't have won anyway.

"Bitch ass nigga! You must be trying to die in here today," Nas stood over him and fumed. He was butt ass naked trying to fight like he wasn't wrong.

"Baby no, please," Stori said as she pulled his arm. She grabbed her robe from the chair in her room to cover herself up. Gavin had seen her naked more times than he could count so that was a waste. It was an insult that she felt more comfortable around another man than she did with her own husband.

"Baby?" Gavin asked incredulously. Stori had never called him baby or any other names other than his own. That shit hurt him more than she knew.

"You good baby?" Nas asked as he walked over to her and caressed her small baby bump.

"Yeah, I'm okay," Stori replied, right before Nas placed a soft kiss on her lips.

"Are you serious right now Stori?" Gavin asked angrily.

"Just leave Gavin. You shouldn't have even come here," Stori replied as she watched him get up from the floor.

"I know I messed up Stori but that's how you do me? Huh? My fucking best friend," Gavin fumed.

"Nigga, I'm not your muthafucking friend! Check your mental rolodex. When have you ever heard me refer to you as such?" Nas questioned as he slipped on his boxers.

Gavin didn't even have to think very hard. Nas had never referred to him as anything more than an associate. Still, no one could have paid him to believe that he would go behind his back and sleep with his wife.

"That's fucked up Stori. I can't believe that you're fucking another nigga while you're pregnant with my baby," Gavin said as he tried his best to remain calm.

"That's my fucking baby nigga. It's mine even if you are the daddy. And stop addressing my girl. Whatever you have to say, direct that shit to me!" Nas bellowed.

Talking to him was what Gavin was trying to avoid. Nas was reminding him so much of Remo and Gavin had never felt that way about him before. Any hope of reconciling with Stori was dead now. Nas looked like he had caught feelings for her already. Gavin knew that Nas and Milan had separated but he was unsure about when he started dealing with Stori.

"Maybe you didn't consider me a friend but I thought we were better than that. You know better than anybody how much I love my wife. I confided in you and you turned around and fucked over me like this," Gavin said angrily.

"That's your whole problem now. You talk too muthafucking much. What kind of grown ass man talks to another nigga about what his wife does in the bedroom? You made me want her even more than I already did. Shit, you gave me a key to the house and the code to the alarm to come get her." Nas shrugged uncaringly.

"Is that my baby Stori?" Gavin asked while ignoring what Nas had just said. The truth hurt and everything that Nas said was real. His mouth was always his downfall and it had been that way since he was a child.

"Don't answer that nigga baby. Give him what he came for so he can get the fuck on," Nas replied.

Stori went to the closet and grabbed Gavin's folder, as Nas put his jeans and shirt back on. She felt bad about how everything went down but she did owe Gavin some answers. She didn't care about how he felt about her being with Nas but he had a right to know about her unborn baby.

"I don't know if this is your baby or not but I will soon," Stori said as she handed Gavin his folder.

"What does that even mean?" Gavin asked.

"We had a test done to determine paternity," Stori said as she opened her nightstand drawer and handed Gavin one of the papers that she got from the lab. It explained the procedure that she had done and everything that he needed to know was on it.

"Why didn't you call me to be tested too?" Gavin inquired.

"Naseem was already tested so you don't have to be. You're the only two that I was with when I conceived. If he's not the father, then we know that you are," Stori said as she looked away in shame.

"Wow. You made me feel like shit for being with Misty but you were no better than I was," Gavin said as he looked at her in disgust.

She wasn't proud of what she'd done and she never intended to hurt Gavin. She was angry about him fathering a child with Misty but she wasn't trying to play catch back with him. She really was attracted to Nas and she had been since the first time she laid eyes on him. She suppressed those feelings when she was with Gavin because she honored her vows. Once it was over between them, she decided to make herself happy for a change. As fucked up as it was, Naseem made her happy. Stori could admit that she moved on way too fast but it was too late for regrets.

"It's time for you to go my nigga. You got what you came here for, so make this your last time popping up over here. Consider this your first and last warning. I can't be responsible for what I'll do the next time around." Nas frowned.

"Is that supposed to be a threat?" Gavin challenged.

"Nah nigga, that's a guarantee," Nas replied.

"You might scare them other niggas but ain't no hoe in my blood. I'm not afraid of you," Gavin said, trying to sound more confident than he felt.

"Yes, you are. You're afraid of me for more reasons than one. Not only will I bust my guns at the drop of a dime but I'll do that shit in broad daylight with a bunch of witnesses around. My don't give a fuck game is strong and I'm the worst kind of nigga for you to go to war with. You're a pussy but niggas like you get false courage when they're pushed to the limit. I took the one thing from you that you had going for yourself. Without Stori on your arm, you're just as lame as everybody always said you were," Nas smirked as he walked closer to him.

"Baby, stop," Stori begged as she walked over to him and grabbed his arm. She was pleading with her eyes for Nas to let it go. The situation was already awkward and she just wanted it to be over with.

"I'm good my love. I'm just about to walk our guest out," Nas replied with a mug on his face.

Gavin walked out of the bedroom with Nas and Stori following behind him. Stori didn't want them fighting and acting a fool in front of Toi. More than likely, she had gone across the street by her friends when Gavin walked into the house. Still, she was probably back out front by now or she would be soon.

Gavin stormed out of the front door and to his truck. He sped away from Stori's house and made his tires burn rubber when he did. His heart was full and he couldn't even think straight. Gavin's hands were shaking so bad that he had to pull his car over to the side of the road. He was bound to have an accident if he kept going.

"Fuck!" he yelled as he pounded the steering wheel and let the tears that he'd been holding in spill from his eyes.

At that moment, Gavin hated everyone. He hated Nas and Stori for betraying him and he hated Misty for starting the downward spiral in his life. He even hated his parents for making him an only child and not giving him siblings that he could lean on in his time of need. He needed money but he hated that he would have to work with and see Nas every day just to get it. Gavin's parents weren't used to having him living with them and he hated it just as much as they did. That was the only reason why they agreed to pay his first three months of rent and deposit. His mother had even agreed to purchase him a living and bedroom set. That was a huge help but he still needed to keep his money flowing. He wasn't about to let Nas run him away from making his money. If he wanted smoke, Gavin would give him some. He wasn't a fighter or a shooter but he wasn't a punk either. With the way he was feeling, Nas could catch a few bullets and Stori could too.

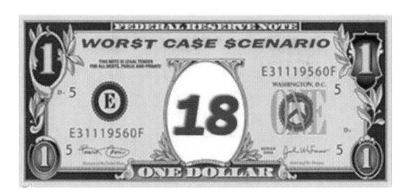

WORST CASE SCENARIO

18

"I'm here bro. Where you at?" Remo said when Nas answered the phone for him.

"I'm on my way nigga. I was sleep." Nas yawned.

"That's all the fuck you do now. Did you even go to work today?" Remo asked him.

"Nope and I probably won't be there tomorrow either," Nas replied.

"I guess you can do that when you're the boss," Remo laughed.

"Stori got me on some cuddling shit like a lil bitch. I ain't never been into no shit like that with nobody else," Nas admitted.

"That's how you know that she's the one. Before Kalani, a bitch was liable to get a bullet if they even tried to kiss me. The right one will make you think twice. What's up with her ole punk ass husband? Nigga dropped out of sight like the hoe he is," Remo said.

He was happy as hell when Nas told him about what happened with Gavin. Remo wanted him to find out and things played out even better than he thought they would. Having Gavin catch Nas and Stori in the act was priceless.

"I don't even know. Nigga ain't been to the shop in a few days. Lil bitch ass is probably scared to face me. I'm good on him though. I got who I want, so he can breathe easy," Nas replied.

"That nigga gon' die when he finds out that you're his new boss," Remo laughed.

"I haven't even been back to the shop since we made shit official. I might go in there Saturday and let them niggas know what's up. I'm not changing the name or nothing, but we do need to update a few things if we plan to rent out the salon part of it," Nas said.

"We need to go up on them niggas booth rent too. That shop is a hot commodity and it's always poppin'," Remo replied.

"Mr. Herbert just hit a nigga with a twenty-five dollar increase a few months ago. We need to wait on that," Nas reasoned.

"Alright bro. You know more about that shit than I do," Remo said.

"I'm pulling up now bro. I'm on my way in," Nas said as he pulled up to Jarvis' house.

The lawyer that Latrice had hired was worth every penny that they paid him. He was making shit happen sooner than they thought he would. He sent some papers home for them to sign and they met by their brother's house to do it. As soon as he walked on the porch, Latrice opened the door for Nas to come in.

"Hey, my love. How's it going?" Latrice asked, as Nas leaned down to hug her.

"I'm good sis. Where your gay ass husband at?" Nas questioned.

"Stop talking about my husband nigga. Trust me, ain't nothing gay about him," Latrice replied.

"Nigga, I know you ain't still in pajamas," Remo laughed as he eyed the Ralph Lauren pajama bottoms and t-shirt that his brother had on. Nas threw on a pair of wheat colored Timbs and left the house in exactly what he had on.

"I told you that I was in the bed. Stori finished doing hair early and we laid up for the rest of the day until it was time to get Toi from school," Nas replied.

"You must really like her," Latrice observed.

"That nigga been wanting Stori for a minute. My bro is in love," Remo beamed.

"Like a muthafucker," Nas acknowledged with a smirk.

"I can't believe what I'm hearing. Naseem and Kareem Donaldson in love at the same damn time. I feel like a proud guardian," Latrice laughed.

"Oh shit bro, I forgot to show you this," Nas said as he handed Remo something that he pulled out of his pocket. Remo looked over what Nas had given him before he jumped up from the sofa.

"Man, I'm happy as fuck right now. Congrats bro," Remo said as he pulled Nas into a tight hug.

"What's going on?" Latrice asked. It always warmed her heart to see the close bond that Nas and Remo shared.

"I'm about to be a muthafucking uncle!" Remo yelled as if he wasn't an uncle already.

"Oh, my God! Congrats Naseem," Latrice smiled as she gave her brother-in-law a hug.

"I hope it's a boy. I want that lil nigga to be bad as fuck," Remo said excitedly.

"Don't say that Remo. We had enough of that with you and Nas. Stori doesn't deserve to go through the same thing," Latrice replied.

"Why didn't you tell me when me and Kalani came over there yesterday?" Remo asked him.

"We didn't check the mail until after y'all left. We talked to Toi about it first though," Nas replied.

"What did Toi say? You know she's been Stori's only baby for a while," Remo noted.

"I know but she's happy as hell." Nas smiled.

"Me too nigga. Shit happened mad fast but I can't wait," Remo said as he grabbed Nas around his neck again.

No one was more excited than Nas was but, in his heart, he already knew. He was experiencing the same pregnancy symptoms as Stori. He didn't have the morning sickness but he slept and ate just as much as she did. Although Stori and Gavin tried to conceive for months, it had never happened. As soon as she started having sex with Nas, she popped up pregnant and he didn't think it was a coincidence. It was meant to be and her getting pregnant so soon confirmed what he already knew. Stori was his soulmate and he felt the connection years ago when he first laid eyes on her.

Toi was so happy that she actually cried. She loved babies and that was proven by how well she cared for Summer. She was excited to know that they would have a baby under the same roof. Stori wanted to wait until it was confirmed before she said anything. She didn't mention it again but Nas had a feeling that she wasn't going to get rid of it no matter what the test said. Her conscience was eating her up and the guilt was starting to consume her. He could see that she was relieved though. Not having to deal with Gavin anymore was the best part of it all.

"The fuck are y'all in here making all that noise for?" Jarvis asked when he walked into the living room.

"You're about to be an uncle baby," Latrice said with a bright smile.

"Aww no! Fuck no man! Which one of you niggas got somebody pregnant?" Jarvis yelled.

"I did nigga," Nas spoke up excitedly.

"Please don't tell me it's Stori," Jarvis said.

"Okay, I won't tell your sensitive ass then." Nas shrugged as Remo laughed.

"This shit is crazy. How do you even know that the baby is yours? The girl is still married," Jarvis pointed out.

"You trying to call my girl a hoe?" Nas frowned.

"Nigga what? I know she ain't no hoe but you have to admit that the entre situation is complicated. That's a legitimate ass question," Jarvis replied.

"It's his nigga. We got the paperwork to prove it," Remo said as he threw the papers at Jarvis.

"Damn man. I feel sorry for Stori already. That damn girl don't deserve that shit. You niggas did not need to have kids no time soon," Jarvis said as he massaged his aching temples.

"Don't say that baby," Latrice replied as she took a seat next to him.

"Are you serious right now Latrice? Them niggas took us through hell. I'm surprised I didn't stroke the fuck out. What can they possibly teach a child? Most of the bad habits that our kids learned came from them two. It ain't even fair that they get to reproduce," Jarvis sighed.

He knew that he and his wife would have to be there for Stori every step of the way. She was never going to get rid of Nas now. God forbid if she had a boy. She would probably lose her mind just like he'd almost done. His prayer from that day forward was going to be for a little niece.

"The fuck is wrong with you, bruh? You need a hug or something?" Nas asked him.

"Fuck a hug. I need a damn vacation," Jarvis replied.

"Book that shit and let us know how much. You need to relax and stop being so uptight," Nas said, as Remo nodded in agreement.

"Let's go to Paris baby!" Latrice yelled excitedly. The twins paid for every vacation that she and Jarvis had ever taken. They spared no expense and they always gave them more than enough spending money to enjoy themselves.

"Book it sis. We got you," Remo said, making Latrice squeal in delight. She jumped up and ran to her bedroom for her laptop.

"What's wrong with you, nigga? You're about to be an uncle for the first time and you don't even seem happy about it," Nas said as he sat down and looked at his older brother.

"I'm very happy about it, but I'm worried too. Having kids is a big responsibility Naseem. You can't be out here on the same dumb shit that you're on now. You need to leave all them hoes alone and do right by Stori if that's who you plan to be with. She's already proving to be better than Milan's trifling ass. You ain't never been with a broad that even thought about helping you build your credit. That alone should make you see that's she different from the rest. It's fucked up how y'all got together but it is what it is. I know y'all think I fuss a lot but I just want y'all to do better. Niggas out here dying for less than the shit y'all be out here doing. I already had to bury mama and daddy. I don't want to have to bury my little brothers too. Don't do that to me, bruh. That shit will kill me if something happens to y'all," Jarvis confessed.

"I understand bruh but we ain't been on no dumb shit. I'm done with all them hoes. It's all about Stori now," Nas swore.

"Yeah man, I've been chillin' too. I can't tell you the last time I had some new pussy but I'm good with that. Dealing with one woman makes my life much easier," Remo replied.

"What's up with that nigga Gavin? I don't want him to be a problem for you either," Jarvis said while looking at Nas.

"Gavin!" Remo yelled as he twisted up his face in anger. "That pussy never was and never will be a problem for us."

"Stop underestimating people Kareem. In his mind, he lost his wife to his best friend. Nas might not have considered him a friend but he obviously felt otherwise. Always be prepared for the worst case scenario. It be the ones that you least expect that become the biggest problems," Jarvis warned.

"Worst case scenario here is he gets a bullet to the head and our problem will be solved." Remo shrugged.

"Just be careful Naseem," Jarvis said while ignoring what Remo had said.

"Always." Nas nodded, right as Latrice walked back into the room with her computer and a file folder.

"These are the papers that y'all need to sign. I read over everything for y'all already," she said as she handed Nas the folder and an ink pen.

"I need a cut too bruh. I was supposed to swing by the shop earlier," Jarvis said as he ran his hand over his hair.

"I wasn't there today but I got you," Nas replied.

"What's going on with that anyway? Are y'all making any changes?" Jarvis asked him.

"Not really but some things need to be updated before we can rent out the hair salon side of it. And speaking of that, I got something else that we can get into," Nas replied while looking at Remo.

"Something legal I hope," Jarvis said as he looked at his two hot headed little brothers.

"It's legal," Nas replied.

"What's good bro?" Remo asked him.

"So, Stori has been trying to find a hair vendor and I think she finally found one that she likes. I was thinking about opening up shop and selling that shit. We can make a fucking killing. She's getting some of that clear shit that she be using to lay their hair down and some fake eyes. That shit is a for sure money maker. All we have to do is give her the money to get started and find a decent spot to open up shop," Nas replied.

"First of all, it's called edge control and lashes. But, that's a great idea. Hair and lashes will definitely generate some good revenue," Latrice spoke up, sounding like the lawyers that she work for.

"It is a good idea and much better than opening a hookah bar. But again, who's going to run it?" Jarvis questioned.

"We'll figure that shit out later. I don't give a fuck if we gotta get grandma to sell some bundles. We gon' get that money," Nas replied.

"Facts." Remo nodded as he gave him dap.

"I better start praying for my niece or nephew right now," Jarvis said while shaking his head.

"How many months is Stori?" Latrice asked.

"Three," Nas replied.

"Damn boy. How long have you been fucking with her?" Jarvis asked.

"Three months nigga. My shit is potent. I wasn't playing no games," Nas replied as he and Remo laughed.

"I'm happy it was her and not Milan." Latrice frowned.

"You and me both," Remo replied.

"I need to go see Stori," Jarvis said.

"For what? Fuck around and Latrice be going to Paris by herself." Nas frowned.

"What you mean for what? She's family now nigga. That's my first niece or nephew that she's carrying," Jarvis pointed out.

"Me and Kalani have to plan the baby shower." Latrice smiled.

"Her mama might do all that shit." Nas shrugged.

Stori told Lady about the baby when she called earlier that morning. She was excited about having a grandchild but she was shocked to find out that Gavin wasn't the father. After having two kids by two brothers, she didn't try to judge her daughter for the decisions that she made. She told Stori that she was coming to visit soon and she wanted to shop for Toi and the baby.

"Go get my clippers baby. I don't want this nigga to leave without cutting my hair," Jarvis said.

"We gotta talk about some shit bro," Remo said as he looked at Nas.

"Come on man. That shit is rude," Jarvis fussed when they started doing sign language.

He regretted not keeping up with the alternate language like his brothers did. He remembered a few things but they did the shit too fast for him to even figure it out. He didn't have a reason to learn it again, so it wasn't that serious to him anymore.

"That's what's up." Nas smiled after he and Remo had silently talked for a while.

"Soon." Remo nodded, right as Latrice walked back into the room with her husband's clippers.

She got on her laptop and looked up some info for their next vacation while her husband got his hair cut. Jarvis was excited about becoming an uncle. He couldn't wait to find out what Stori was having, but he kept referring to the baby as "her" like he already knew what the sex would be. He made Nas call her so that he could congratulate her and everything. He was praying that Stori and the baby would slow Nas down and hopefully Kalani could do the same for

Remo. He knew that all it took was for one of them to do better and the other would follow. Just like always, they were two bodies with one heartbeat.

It had been an entire week since Gavin learned of Nas and Stori's affair. He hadn't been to the shop since then but he wasn't running from anyone. He had moved into his apartment and was getting everything together. His place was fully furnished and he had everything in place. He foolishly thought that he and Stori would get back together, so he signed a month to month lease. Now that he thought about it, that was a stupid move on his part. Stori wasn't that kind of chick. To think that she would take him back after he'd made a baby on her was insane. When she called him a few days ago, Gavin got excited until he found out the reason for her call. Stori had gotten the results of the paternity test and he was not the baby's father. She even took a picture of the paper that the lab mailed to her and sent him a copy. Gavin had no words, so he hung up in her face right after she gave him the bad news. If Stori was trying to hurt him, she exceeded her expectations because he was devastated.

Gavin was heartbroken and angry. Granted, he did cheat on her first but Misty wasn't her friend. People were always saying that he wanted to be like Nas, but it was obviously the other way around. Stori was very beautiful but she should have been off limits to Nas. As angry as he was, Gavin still had something to be thankful for. Although he wanted a child with his wife, he was grateful for the one that he already had. Summer was a beautiful baby and his parents were enjoying getting to know her. Gavin was getting to know her too since he didn't have to hide her anymore.

"The fuck is going on now?" he questioned himself aloud when he pulled up to the barber shop. Mr. Herbert's car was there along with lots of others.

Gavin was dreading going inside but he really had no choice. It was work and he needed to make money. When he got out of his car and walked into the building, he paused when he saw the crowd of people standing in the back. Carlton and another barber were the only ones working because everyone else was in the hair salon part of the shop.

"Damn bruh, I thought you quit on us. You ain't been here in a minute," Carlton said when he saw Gavin.

"Nah man, I had a lot of business to handle," Gavin replied.

"Cool, well welcome back. I'm sure you'll be happy with all the changes that's been made," Carlton said.

"What changes?" Gavin asked as he took a seat at his work station.

"Your boy didn't tell you?" Carlton asked.

"Tell me what?" Gavin countered.

"Shit, I thought you would have known before anybody else," Carlton said, still not getting to the point.

"I'm lost," Gavin replied.

"Mr. Herbert sold the shop to your boy, Nas. Him and his twin are the new owners. Shit ain't gon' be quiet around here no more," Carlton laughed, as Gavin's heart plummeted in his chest.

He was just saying how he didn't want to have to find another job. Now, it seemed as if he didn't have a choice. Nas being his boss was bad enough, but Remo would go out of his way to make his life hell. Gavin just couldn't win for losing. He always did hate Remo, but he never imagined that he would one day feel the same way about Nas. Some niggas just kept winning, even if they didn't deserve to. Gavin made a stupid mistake but he wasn't a bad person. The thoughts that were running rampant in his head wanted him to be though.

"What are they doing back there?" Gavin questioned.

"They got Mr. Herbert a retirement cake and shit. I'm happy his old ass is leaving. We can't even play music up in this bitch when he's here. We needed some young leadership," Carlton replied.

He wasn't a hater and he was happy for Nas and his brother. The shop afforded him many luxuries and he was good as long as he had a job. He'd worked at other shops before but he'd never made as much as he was making now. The area was always busy and that helped out too.

"This shop is about to go down like the Titanic." Gavin frowned. A few months ago he would have been happy with Nas owning the shop. Now, it just seemed like a slap in the face.

"I won't say all that. I just hope they don't try to go up on our booth rent again. Nas said that they're not but his brother might be a problem," Carlton noted.

"Fuck both of them niggas. I'm about to get up out of here," Gavin replied.

He had a milk crate with all of his supplies locked up inside his work station. He didn't have to pack much because the crate contained everything that he needed. He didn't care if he had to cut hair on the go, he was not about to stay there and deal with Nas and Remo calling all the shots.

"Damn bruh, the fuck happened like that? I thought you and Nas were cool," Carlton spoke up.

"Well, you thought wrong," Gavin replied angrily. He was about to gather his things to leave when Nas and Remo came strolling to the front. Nas' face held a blank expression while Remo's wore a smirk.

"What's up lil bitch? Don't you have some work to do? I'm the boss now nigga. Ain't no more slacking on the job," Remo said when he looked at Gavin.

"Fuck you bruh, straight up," Gavin said, feeling fed up with being disrespected.

"That's all I needed to hear. Now I have to fire you for insubordination," Remo smirked.

"Chill out bro," Nas said as he touched Remo's arm.

Shit happened that Nas couldn't take back and he really wasn't trying to. At the same time, he wasn't trying to rub salt in Gavin's freshly opened wounds either. Nas knew that he could be a coldhearted ass nigga but he wasn't all that bad. Not once did he try to get with Stori while she was with Gavin, even though his brother encouraged him to. Remo just didn't give a fuck. Once he got it in his head that he didn't like you, it was over from there. Nas thought it was childish to rub his relationship with Stori in Gavin's face, but Remo was petty.

"I'm good bro, but I can't have the employees talking to me any kind of way. What kind of boss would I be if I allowed that?" Remo asked with a sly smile.

"You can't fire a nigga who already quit," Gavin replied as he grabbed his belongings and made sure that he had everything.

He took the key to his work station off of his ring and threw it on the counter. There was no one that he cared enough to say goodbye to, so he walked out of the shop without bothering to look back. As soon as he opened the door, Gavin almost ran into someone. He almost dropped his crate but the other man caught it before it hit the ground.

"Damn bruh, you quitting?" Corey asked when he saw Gavin leaving with his clippers and all of his supplies.

"Fucking right!" Gavin barked angrily.

"I know it's not because you're not making any money. This shop stay jumping," Corey noted.

"Fuck this shop and the niggas who own it," Gavin said as he walked to his car. He didn't know why the other man was following him because he wasn't in the mood to be friendly.

"You got beef with Mr. Herbert?" Corey asked.

"Nah, that nigga don't own the shop no more. He sold it to Nas and his punk ass brother," Gavin gritted.

"I thought you and ole boy were cool," Corey said.

"Why would I be cool with a nigga that got my wife pregnant? Fuck that dude," Gavin spat furiously.

"Damn man. Now I see why you're so upset. That's fucked up. But, if you're looking for another shop, my boy got one in Gretna. I can put in a good word for you. I can see that you're nice with the clippers and he can use the help," Corey said.

"Yeah? That's what's up. Let me give you my number," Gavin said as he reached into the crate and grabbed one of his cards.

"I got you, fam," Corey replied as he watched him walk away with a sneaky grin on his face.

Gavin had made friends with the enemy and didn't even know it. Corey had been wanting to find out some info on Nas for a minute. Nas and Gavin obviously weren't friends anymore and he was the best person to fill in a few blanks. Corey was shocked to hear that Stori was having his baby though. He never knew his ex to be on no hoe shit but obviously, things had changed.

"I know you see me calling your dog ass Naseem!" Milan yelled into the phone before she hung up on him.

Misty walked into the room and shook her head at how pathetic her sister looked. All Milan did was eat, sleep and smoke. She acted as if she was losing her mind behind Nas and it was pathetic. She refused to work and her money had to be running low. Misty had started dancing at another club and she was stacking her dollars. She had already made the decision to go back home but she didn't want to go back broke. She was trying to get enough money for an apartment and some furniture. Truthfully, she already had enough but she wanted to pay her rent up for a few months and have a nice savings, just in case she needed it. Misty was a licensed real estate agent and she wanted to see about getting her old job back. Following behind Milan had her doing stupid shit and she was tired of it. Their mother was disappointed in them both because she raised them better than that. Misty was happy that nobody back in Texas knew what she had been doing. That would make things a lot easier for her when she returned.

"What the hell is wrong with you?" Misty asked her sister.

"Nas must think it's a fucking game. Look at this shit," Milan fumed as she handed Misty her phone.

Misty gasped when she saw that Nas had posted a date saying that he couldn't wait for the arrival of his first child. He had a pink and blue heart there saying that he was anxious to find out what his girl was having. Misty wasn't even surprised when she saw that Milan had left a bunch of comments cursing him out and acting a fool. She was always going on his page to see what he was doing. Then, she would act a fool when she saw something that she didn't like. Misty checked Stori's page a few times but she only posted pictures of hairstyles that she did or pictures of Toi. Misty smiled when she saw that Toi had turned fifteen and Stori had a spa styled sleepover for her. Misty hated her but she had to admit that Stori was a great big sister.

"Who's having his baby?" Misty questioned.

"How would I know?" Milan snapped angrily.

"Forget him. You need to do what mama said and come back home with me and Summer," Misty replied.

"And do what? I couldn't see myself going back to answering phones for a living. You were always her favorite so she won't miss me. My husband is here and this is where I'm staying," Milan snapped, as Misty shook her head in pity.

Milan was always the wild one or the problem child as their mother put it. She loved fast money and even faster men. She always had to have the most popular man but things never worked out for her. The men that she fell for didn't normally like to have just one woman. Nas made a mistake when he married her because that was something that Milan had always wanted. She was a receptionist at a car dealership back in Texas and she was dating one of the general managers. When he broke things off, Milan almost lost it and began to stalk him and his new woman. They had to get a restraining order on her and she ended up losing her job.

"What are you going to do for money, Milan?" Misty asked her.

"Get it from my husband like I've been doing. That nigga doesn't just work at the barber shop anymore. He owns that bitch now," Milan replied.

She was shocked when she saw the picture of Nas and Remo on Instagram announcing themselves as the new owners of the barber shop. Nas was doing the damn thing and Milan was entitled to whatever he made. She didn't care that he filed for divorce. She was still legally his wife.

"Well, I'm going get ready for work," Misty said as she walked away.

She was so thankful to Gavin's parents for the help that they gave her. His mother was still a bitch but she was trying to get better. She let Misty drop Summer off to her now so that Gavin didn't have to. She even gave Misty her phone number since Gavin didn't live there anymore. Gavin spent time with Summer as well and that was all that Misty ever wanted. He still blamed her for ruining his marriage but he was just as much to blame as she was.

"I'll be back," Milan said as she grabbed her keys and walked out of the house.

Nas had just posted a photo of his last customer, saying that he was done cutting hair for the night. Milan hopped in her car and sped all the way to the barber shop. As soon as she got there, she saw Nas as he was pulling off.

"I got that ass." Milan smiled as she followed right behind him.

For months, she had wondered where Nas was living. Now, she was finally about to find out. She followed him as he got on and off of the bridge. She wasn't surprised when he stopped at the daiquiri shop because Thursday was long island iced tea day. They were too strong for her but Nas and Remo loved them. They always added more liquor in theirs to make it even stronger. When Nas started driving again, she let two cars get in between them before she continued to follow him. She knew the area that he was going to very well and she became even more curious. When he pulled up to Stori's house, he opened the garage and drove his car inside.

"The fuck!" Milan bellowed as her mouth opened in awe.

She thought back to the conversation that she'd had with Misty not too long ago. Pinky told her that Nas and Stori had stayed in the office at the club for a while before they came back out. She didn't want to believe it but the truth was staring her right in the face. Nas was fucking Stori and her blood was boiling at the revelation. Milan sat there deep in thought, trying to come up with a game plan. When the barrel of a gun was pressed to her head, she raised her hands in surrender and fear.

"Stupid ass bitch. I'm a street nigga before anything else. I saw your dumb ass following me ever since I left the barber shop," Nas gritted angrily.

"I'm sorry Nas but I just wanted you to talk to me," Milan said as tears spilled from her eyes. Nas yanked her door open and pulled her out of the car.

"This is my last time saying this, so listen up. Don't call me, follow me or come to any of my businesses. If you do, I'm emptying the clip on your hoe ass and they'll never find your body. Don't come around my girl and stay the fuck away from our house," Nas said through clenched teeth.

"Your girl? Since when Naseem? How could you do this to me, with Stori of all people? That bitch used to do my hair. She's married to your fucking friend!" Milan screamed as the porch light came on. When the door opened and Stori stepped outside, Milan's heart broke even more.

226

Stori had on some leggings with a fitted tank top. Her perfectly round stomach was all the confirmation that Milan needed. That bitch was having her husband's baby.

"Naseem, come inside. Don't cause a scene and get yourself into any trouble," Stori said as she looked around the quiet neighborhood. Nas told her what was up before he even went outside to confront Milan. She heard the other woman yelling and she didn't want her neighbors to call the police. She knew that their relationship couldn't stay a secret forever. She didn't owe Milan an explanation because she was never her friend.

"I'm coming love. Just go back inside and relax," Nas said as he looked over at her and smiled. His entire attitude had switched up and Milan was infuriated.

"You shady ass bitch!" Milan yelled as she charged at Stori. She didn't get very far before Nas grabbed her by her neck. Stori didn't even flinch and she had no reason to. Nas wasn't letting Milan or anyone else get too close to her.

"Go back inside baby. I got it," Nas assured her. He waited until Stori went back into the house before he turned his attention to Milan.

"Let me go Naseem. I can't breathe," Milan choked out as she clawed at his hands.

"Fuck your oxygen bitch. I tried to leave peacefully, but I see that I can't be nice to some of you hoes. Move on and let me be, Milan. Don't awaken the beast in me because you know you won't like it. Don't commit suicide by fucking with me," Nas hissed as he let her go and watched her fall to the ground and inhale some much needed air.

He was tired of playing games with Milan's stupid ass. He let it slide when she tagged him in bullshit on social media. He even let it go when she left all those childish ass comments under all his posts. It didn't even bother him as much when she constantly played on his phone. Following him home was something that he just wasn't going to tolerate though. If she even thought about coming for Stori, pregnant or not, she was gonna get dealt with.

"Why are you doing this to me, Naseem? I've never loved a man as much as I love you," Milan cried as she stood to her feet.

"And I told you that the feelings were never mutual. I never lied to you about shit and I'm not about to start," Nas replied.

"What about all the promises that you made to me? We were supposed to buy a house and start a family Naseem. Our future was planned out and you ruined it," Milan cried.

"I didn't ruin shit. How can you plan for tomorrow when I'm telling you that I don't want your ass today? Get out of your head and your feelings and move the fuck on. Stop testing me, Milan. You already know what I'm capable of," Nas threatened.

"I love you, Naseem," Milan sniffled. Nas cocked his gun in response and she immediately got the hint. Milan hurriedly got into her car and sped away from Stori's house.

"Are you okay boo?" Stori asked when Nas walked back into the house.

"Yeah, I'm good. I'm sorry about that baby. These hoes out here losing their minds," Nas sighed as he laid down on the sofa with her.

"I wonder why," Stori laughed as she grabbed his manhood through his pants and squeezed it.

"That's a wrap on them other hoes. This dick got your name written all over it," Nas laughed.

"It better," Stori replied as he rubbed her belly.

She had just entered her fourth month and they would know the sex of the baby when she went back to the clinic the following month. Stori's stomach had gotten big but her doctor told her that everything was fine. Her appetite was ridiculous and that was probably why. Thanks to the prenatal vitamins that he'd prescribed for her, morning sickness was no longer an issue.

"I'm ready to start shopping for my lil man," Nas said as he stroked her belly lovingly.

"It's a girl. My grandma said that she can tell just by the way I'm carrying. She said that I'm big for four months just like she was with all her girls," Stori replied.

"Man, I don't want to have to kill none of these lil niggas out here for playing with my daughter," Nas sighed.

228

"You'll be fine. Girls are much easier. Look at Toi," Stori noted.

"You and Toi are just naturally sweet. My baby might be on some bullshit like her daddy though," Nas laughed.

"Don't say that Naseem. Me and Latrice have been praying on the phone every night," Stori replied.

"Why are y'all praying over a nigga seed like it's the spawn of satan and shit?" Nas laughed.

"According to Jarvis, it is," Stori giggled.

"That nigga is just soft. Me and Remo weren't all that bad. Jarvis is too damn paranoid. He's scared that he's gonna lose us the same way we lost our mama and daddy," Nas said.

"He said that you and Remo act just like your father used to," Stori replied.

"I don't remember him as good as Jarvis does but I know he didn't play. He was a different person at home than he was in the streets though. He used to sit down and talk to me and Remo for hours every day. I remember how much he loved my mama too. Kind of like the same way that I love you," Nas said as he looked at her and smiled.

Stori didn't know it but he'd loved her from a distance for as long as he could remember. He knew her way better than she knew him but that was cool. He knew her favorite color and what foods she liked to eat. Stori slept wild as hell and he knew that long before they started sleeping in the same bed. He even knew things about Toi and that's what made it easier for him to bond with her. She was the sweetest little girl in the world to him and that was all Stori's doing. He was proud to call her the mother of his child and his brothers were happy too.

"I love you too baby and don't take that lightly. Besides Toi and Kalani, I can't remember the last time I said that to anyone else," Stori replied.

Gavin told her that he loved her all the time, but Stori rarely said it back. He never pressured her and he really didn't care if she said it or not. The only time he ever complained about it was when he was upset or he heard her

Chenell Parker

say it to Toi. For some reason, saying that she loved him always seemed like a lie.

"Damn man. I guess I gotta get ready for sleepovers and all that other girly shit. Toi and her friends almost drove a nigga crazy," Nas laughed.

Toi had a sleepover when she turned fifteen and Stori had a house full of girls. They had Nas at the nail shop and a few other girly places that they wanted to go to. He had fun with them but he was happy when they all went home. He spent over six hundred dollars on them in one day but he didn't mind. Toi was happy and that was all that he and Stori wanted. Stori's birthday was coming up soon and he wanted to do something nice for her too.

"Don't worry about it boo. You'll get used to it," Stori said as she pecked his lips.

They laid on the sofa and watched a movie until Stori fell asleep. Nas carried her upstairs and put her in the bed before lying down next to her and drifting off soon after.

S
tori was a professional and she always
behaved as such. Even though she wanted to
take the woman who was in her chair and lay
her the fuck out, she remained calm as she curled her hair.
The woman was there with her friend and Stori had already
cut and flat ironed the other woman's hair. Both women had
done a consultation two days before to let Stori look at the
nappy shit that was on top of their heads. They were her last
two customers of the day and she was happy for that. She
had to work her wrist something serious to even make their
shit straight.

"I should hook you up with his twin, Remo, and we
can do a double date," Danni said, as Stori continued to curl
her hair.

"If he looks anything like Nas, then you can count
me in," Danni's friend, Gina said.

Gina was a guard at the prison too and she was

always down for some drama. When Danni told her about going to Stori's shop, she was ready to roll with her. They damn near stalked Stori on Instagram and Danni originally wanted to send her a message. When they saw how nice Stori did hair, they decided to pay her a visit instead. Danni wanted to cry when she saw the post that Nas made about becoming a father soon. Stori had posted a picture of herself and Danni didn't have to wonder who the baby's mother was. Stori had a very visible baby bump and she appeared to be at least six months in.

"That nigga got a girl but that don't mean shit. Nas had a wife and I was fucking him almost every night. I don't know why that hoe thought she was special. Everybody knows about that birth mark on his inner thigh," Danni said, making Stori almost drop her flat iron.

"We need to go their club one day soon," Gina replied.

"You're late boo. I'm always over there. I don't really be in the club part though. I always go straight upstairs to the office. And trust me, you don't want to know what goes on up there," Danni laughed.

Stori was furious and she couldn't wait to see Naseem's dog ass. As much as she wanted Nas when she first saw him, she knew that he came with a lot of baggage. Nas and Remo had women falling at their feet but he had Stori fucked up. She didn't care that she was pregnant with his baby. She was nobody's fool and that included Naseem. Whoever the bitch was in her chair had obviously dealt with him before and she wanted Stori to know it. Admittedly, she was cute in the face but she was built like a teenaged boy. Her friend had a bad ass shape but she had the worst adult acne that Stori had ever seen. The fact that they came to her shop with the bullshit really had her heated. Toi usually helped out on Saturdays but she was happy that she wasn't home that day. Stori was sure that her little sister would have had questions about what they were saying. Lady flew in the night before and she took Toi and her friends shopping and out to dinner.

"You're all done boo." Stori smiled as she handed Danni the mirror.

"It's beautiful. I'll definitely be hitting you up again," Danni replied as she handed Stori some money.

"Me too," Gina said as she stood to her feet.

"Thanks ladies. Y'all have a good day," Stori said as she saw them out and locked up. They had her fucked up if they thought they were ever stepping foot in her shop again.

She turned off her open sign and headed upstairs. Nas probably wouldn't be in until later since he and Remo were meeting with a contractor to do a few repairs at the barber shop. That was a good thing because she didn't want to look in his face at the moment. As soon as Stori got upstairs, she heard keys being inserted into the front door. She frowned, thinking that it was Nas. She quickly adjusted her attitude when Toi and Lady walked in instead.

"Hey Stori." Toi smiled. She sat her bags on the floor and gave Stori a hug.

"Hey, my Stanka. Did you have fun?" Stori asked as she took a seat on the sofa. Toi sat down next to her and rubbed her belly.

"Yeah, we got manicures, pedicures and facials. Then, we went shopping and out to eat," Toi replied with a smile.

"I'm ready to shop for my grandbaby too, whenever we found out what you're having." Lady smiled.

"We'll know something soon," Stori replied.

"Mommy wants to know if I can stay the night with her in her hotel suite. Can I go?" Toi asked.

"Yeah, you can go if you want to," Stori replied.

"Hannah and Maddie's mom already said that they can come too," Toi said excitedly.

"Okay baby. Go put your stuff away and pack your bag. Make sure you pack your own soap and towels. Take a separate bag for your dirty clothes too," Stori replied, as Toi grabbed her bags and ran upstairs.

"You're gonna be a great mother Stori," Lady smiled.

"I've had a lot of practice," Stori replied sarcastically.

"I really appreciate the way you take care of Toi. You've done a great job with her and I can't take credit for any of it. I know I wasn't the best mother but I wanna be here for my grandchild. I've been talking to Richard about moving back to New Orleans. He's thinking about retiring and working as a consultant. It's not like he needs the money anyway. If all goes well, we'll be back home in about six more months or less." Lady smiled.

"That's good but Toi is not coming to live with you," Stori noted.

In the beginning, she was scared and didn't think that she could raise Toi on her own. Now that she had done it for eight years, she couldn't imagine not having her around all the time. Lady had her fucked all the way up if that's what she thought. The hardest part was over and Toi could do for herself now.

"I would never take her away from you. Besides, she's already made that clear. She loves you too much to leave you." Lady smiled, right as Toi came back downstairs with her duffel bag.

"I got everything that I need. Bye Stori. I'll call you later and tell Nas that I'll see him tomorrow," Toi said as she leaned down and gave her sister a kiss on the cheek.

"Bye, my Stanka. Love you," Stori replied while giving her a tight hug.

"I love you too," Toi said as she pulled away.

Stori walked her mother and sister outside before locking up and setting her alarm. She took a shower and fixed herself a sandwich before lying down to watch tv. She would usually cook something but Toi wasn't home. Nas could starve and die for all she cared. He was on her shit list and she was happy that he wasn't there. It was almost as if Stori had thought him up because she heard the alarm beeping a few minutes later. When Nas entered the room, he kicked off his shoes and climbed into bed with her.

"I was hoping that you cooked something. I'm hungry as fuck," Nas said as he hugged her from behind.

"Get one of your hoes to cook for you because I'm never doing it again," Stori snapped, surprising him with her reply. Stori had surprised herself too because she was never the jealous type.

"What hoes? The fuck did that even come from?" Nas sat up and asked.

He'd never known Stori to be insecure and he didn't know what was up with her. She wasn't the type to trip for nothing either, so he was wondering what happened to make her snap like she did. Latrice had already warned him about the pregnancy hormones but it seemed to be much more than that.

"I don't think this is going to work out Naseem. We moved way too fast and shit just ain't right. We don't have to be together just because we're expecting a baby. It's a problem when these hoes get comfortable enough to start coming to my shop with the bullshit," Stori said as she got up from the bed.

"Who came to your shop?" Nas asked as he walked closer to her.

"One of the same hoes that you've been fucking in the office at the strip club," Stori spat angrily.

"I'm not about to stand here and act like I'm a saint. I did a lot of shit in the past but somebody got me fucked up if they said I'm doing something now. I haven't touched another bitch since we've been together. Hell, I barely look at these hoes out here," Nas swore.

"The bitch sure seems to know a lot about you though. Talking about your birthmark and everything," Stori noted.

"Are you serious right now Stori? Half the bitches in New Orleans probably saw my birthmark. I've been slanging dick since I was fourteen and you knew I wasn't a virgin when you got with me. But, I swear on my mama's grave, I ain't been on no bullshit since we got together. You know how long I've been waiting for this shit between us to happen? Why would I fuck it up just for a quick nut? Our sex life is good as fuck. I'm not trying to jeopardize what we have for another bitch," Nas swore as he pulled her in for a hug.

Stori wanted to protest but she really had no reason to. Nas had never given her a reason to question or doubt him. She knew his every move because he told her. She wasn't the insecure type, so she never asked. Admittedly, she did feel better after talking to him though. Well, she did until his phone started ringing. When she saw Danni's name pop up on the screen, she pushed Nas away from her.

"But, the bitch is still calling you though," Stori fumed.

"Baby, everybody calls this phone. I have businesses," Nas replied.

"Why didn't you block her then?" Stori asked.

"I'm a street nigga Stori. I don't block people. Shit, I'm not even sure that I even know how," Nas answered honestly. He got several calls from people that he didn't want to talk to. Either he didn't answer or he hung up on them when he heard their voices if he did. He wasn't into all that blocking shit and he had never done it before in his life. He didn't knock niggas who did it but it just seemed like something that a female would do.

"Fuck you, Naseem! Get out of my face and out of my house. You sound dumb as fuck," Stori said as she tried to walk away.

"Nah, fuck that. We're not even about to start this bullshit. I'm not going nowhere and make that your last time saying that shit," Nas fumed as he grabbed her arm.

"Let me go!" Stori yelled as she used her free hand to punch him in the face. When he let her go, she hit him in the face again before rushing out of the room.

"Ahh! The fuck!" Nas yelled as he grabbed his mouth.

Stori was small but she was feisty. Her tiny hands hurt bad as hell and his entire face was burning. Nas rushed into the bathroom and grabbed a small towel. He tasted the blood in his mouth and his lip was throbbing. He knew that it was busted but it was nothing that he couldn't handle. Once he cleaned himself up, he went to see where Stori was. He saw a small sliver of light coming from underneath the door of Toi's bedroom. Had Stori gone anywhere else in the house, he would have taken the door off the hinges to get to her. He didn't want to scare Toi, so she was safe as long as she was in there. Nas was pissed as he headed back to the bedroom and grabbed his phone. He went into the bathroom and locked the door before calling Danni right back.

"Oh, so you did see me calling you, huh?" Danni asked as soon as she answered the phone.

"Yeah, I saw. You got a nigga in trouble and shit. The fuck did you come to my girl's shop for? Nah, fuck all that. How did you even know anything about her or her shop?" Nas asked.

"I got my ways but that's not important. It's sad that I have to do so much just to get your attention," Danni replied.

"Now that you got it, what do you plan to do with it?" Nas flirted.

"What do you have in mind?" Danni asked while flirting back.

"You already know what it is. I gotta get off this phone but you owe me since you fucked it up for me at home. We need to link up tomorrow. Maybe you can get us a room," Nas requested.

"You know I got you boo," Danni said before she hung up.

"Yeah bitch, I got you too," Nas fumed as he stripped out of his clothes and prepared to take a shower.

He didn't understand why everybody was trying so hard to destroy what he was trying to build with Stori. It took him too long to get her and he wasn't letting another bitch cause him to lose her. For the first time ever, Nas was content with being with just one woman. Hoes just wouldn't let him be great. It was all good though. He never did have a problem getting his point across and nothing had changed.

WOR$T CA$E $CENARIO

The next morning, Stori got up and fixed herself some breakfast. When Nas walked into the kitchen, she was sitting at the counter eating while reading a book on her phone. She never did look up at him and he hated to be ignored.

"Where's the rest of the food?" he asked as he looked around the clean kitchen.

"At Waffle House," Stori flippantly replied.

"Stop playing with me, Stori," Nas said as he grabbed her fork and started eating some of her food.

"Move Naseem," Stori whined as he ate most of what was on her plate.

"That shit was good. Fix some more baby. I'll help you," he offered.

"I wish the fuck I would." Stori frowned.

"Stop acting like you're not still hungry," Nas

laughed.

"I am and that's the only reason why I'm about to do it. Don't ever get me confused with these other hoes out here. I'm not your fool," Stori noted.

"I know you're not baby and that's why I love you," Nas said as he pecked her on the lips.

Stori took the steaks out of the freezer while she instructed Nas on how to peel the potatoes and crack a few eggs. Once they ate and cleaned up, they relaxed on the sofa and watched a movie. She didn't want to keep giving him a hard time but she was still in her feelings about Danni coming to her shop. Nas was pissed that he'd slept alone for nothing. Had he known that Toi wasn't there, he would have dragged Stori's stubborn ass right out of her room and in bed with him where she belonged.

"I got a few moves to make," Nas said once they had relaxed for most of the day. He and Stori had just woken up from taking a long nap and he had things to do.

"I bet you do," Stori replied sarcastically.

"Stop acting like that Stori. You know damn well I ain't out here doing you dirty. That bum bitch coming to your shop pissed you off and I can't even blame you for that. But, don't trip. Your man gon' handle it just like always," Nas assured her.

"No Naseem, just let it go. I was upset but I trust you. Your way of handling things is not always the best," Stori said.

"I'm not on no bullshit baby," Nas swore.

"Kalani was right. You and Remo always say that and y'all are always on some bullshit," Stori replied as he laughed.

Nas took a quick shower and got dressed for the day. Once he was gone, Stori relaxed on the sofa until her phone rang. She smiled when she saw that it was Kalani calling her.

"Do you have anything planned for tomorrow?" Kalani asked as soon as Stori answered the phone.

"Bring Toi to school and sleep. Why? What's up?" Stori questioned.

"I just wanted you to come with me somewhere," Kalani answered.

"Oh okay. Where are you going?" Stori asked.

"To the courthouse to get married," Kalani replied nonchalantly.

"Bitch what! You're saying that shit like it ain't nothing serious," Stori replied.

"It's not. We were supposed to go last week until he pissed me off," Kalani said.

"And I thought I was bad by not fixing Nas breakfast. This bitch is calling off whole weddings and shit," Stori laughed.

"What are you mad at Nas for?" Kalani asked.

"Girl, I wanted to call and tell you about it last night but I was too tired," Stori said.

"Come over here. I got ice cream and two spoons waiting on us," Kalani replied.

"Say no more. I'll be there shortly," Stori replied.

Once she freshened up, she called her mother to see what time Toi was coming home. She didn't want to be by Kalani and have her home by herself for too long. When Stori walked into the garage, she was shocked to see that Nas' car was still there. She didn't know what he was up to and she really didn't care. She didn't have the energy to be on his back and it wasn't that serious with her anyway. Almost an hour after they talked, Stori was pulling up to Kalani and Remo's house. She didn't even tell Nas that she had left home and she wasn't going to.

"Girl, my niece is getting big," Kalani said when she opened the door and rubbed Stori's protruding belly.

"Yep and she might not have a daddy if that nigga keeps playing with me," Stori replied.

She and Kalani sat at the island in the kitchen as she ran the entire story down to her. Kalani had seen Danni a few times at the club but it was never that deep with her and Nas. Still, Danni had gone too far when she went to Stori's shop.

"These hoes go too damn far. She better be lucky that Nas is trying to do better." Kalani frowned.

"They both better be lucky that I'm pregnant. My daughter saved them two birds, but she couldn't save her daddy from getting punched in the mouth," Stori replied.

"You hit Nas?" Kalani asked in shock.

"I sure did with his stupid ass," Stori replied, right as Remo walked into the kitchen.

"Why didn't you tell my brother that you were coming over here?" Remo asked while looking at Stori.

"Your brother ain't my damn daddy. He keep trying me with these random ass hoes and he won't be my man either," Stori said.

"You sound just as dumb as your friend. I'm dragging her ass straight to the courthouse tomorrow. As soon as your divorce is final, my bro is gonna drag your ass there too," Remo noted.

"Your brother can't make me do a damn thing," Stori argued.

"Yeah, okay. I see your ass is still pregnant though," Remo snickered.

"What do you have planned for your birthday next week Stori?" Kalani asked.

"Nothing much. It's on a Friday, so I'll probably be working." Stori shrugged.

"Nah, you'll be off all weekend. My bro got some shit planned," Remo said.

"You and your brother have no boundaries. I don't see how Kalani dealt with that shit for so long," Stori fussed.

"Don't worry about it sis. You'll get used to it just like she did." Remo smiled, right as Stori's phone rang.

"I guess you told your brother where I was," Stori said when she saw that Nas was calling her.

"No doubt," Remo replied with a head nod.

"Yes Naseem," Stori said when she answered the phone.

"Come outside baby," Nas replied before he hung up.

Stori slowly slid off the bar stool and made her way outside. When she saw Nas standing next to a black Malibu, her woman's intuition went into overdrive. The car had

Hello Kitty seat covers with the matching sticker decal on the back.

"So, you left your car at home just to go ride around with another bitch?" Stori asked.

"Trust me love, it'll never get that serious. It was one thing for these hoes to play with me. They had the entire game fucked up when they started playing with you too. I apologize though, baby. It was my fault for letting them get too comfortable and I promise that it'll never happen again," Nas said as he grabbed her face and kissed her.

"Okay Naseem, but who does this car belong to?" Stori asked.

"Oh, shit, I'm trippin'. I'm not the only one who owes you an apology," Nas replied as he popped the trunk.

"Ahh! Naseem!" Stori screamed as she jumped into his arms. It was official. Her baby's father was certifiable. She was probably pregnant with the bride of Chucky. Instead of a christening, her baby would probably need an exorcism.

"Calm down baby. She's not dead," Nas laughed as he looked down at Danni.

She was in the trunk of her car with black tape covering her mouth, wrists and ankles. She was shaking in fear as tears rolled down her eyes. Nas had his niece pick him up from Stori's house earlier that day and drop him off to Danni's house. She was shocked when he showed up because he had never been to her house before. Danni had never even told Nas where she lived and he never cared to know. They usually just met up at a hotel, but he obviously had other plans. Danni thought he was about to be on some fucking shit but she quickly found out just how wrong she was. When Nas pulled out his gun and pointed it at her head, she almost lost her bladder. He was livid about her going to Stori's shop and Danni regretted ever doing so. She should have left well enough alone and stopped bothering him when he told her to. She knew what he was capable of but she still tested him anyway. When he hog-tied her, she was crying and begging him not to kill her. He must have been tired of hearing her mouth because he taped it shut before throwing her into the trunk of her own car and speeding away.

"Oh, my God Naseem! What did you do?" Stori asked as she looked down at the frightened woman.

"I had a little talk with Danni. She has something that she wants to tell you. Speak up! You had a lot to say when you showed up to her muthafucking shop!" Nas gritted angrily.

"No, baby, it's okay. I accept her apology," Stori said as he held her bridal style.

"The bitch ain't even say shit yet!" Nas yelled.

"She has tape over her mouth Naseem," Stori pointed out.

"Oh, my fault," Nas chuckled as he ripped the black tape from Danni's mouth, causing her excruciating pain. She didn't let that deter her from what she knew she had to do though.

"I'm so sorry for everything that I did. I'm sorry for coming to your shop and saying everything that I said. Nas and I haven't had sex in months and he cut me off when he got with you. I was upset and I lied. Please, don't let him kill me. I swear that it will never happen again," Danni cried as her tears mixed with the snot that was running out of her nose.

"Let her go Naseem. What if she calls the police? Are you trying to go to jail?" Stori asked him.

"No! Nas, I swear that I won't call the police!" Danni yelled as she cried hysterically.

Stori must have been trying to get her killed. Mentioning the police to a nigga like Nas was a for sure death sentence. Danni had learned her lesson and she was done calling or going anywhere near Naseem Donaldson. He was nice to look at and even better in the bedroom. Still, him or no other man was worth losing her life. Stori could have him because she was done. She was sorry that he knew where she lived and worked. She would be looking over her shoulder forever and that was no way to live. She underestimated how crazy Nas really was but she would never make that mistake again.

"Naseem, please let her go," Stori begged as she wiggled out of his hold.

"You know I love you, right?" Nas asked as he looked down at her.

"Yes, baby, I know," Stori nodded.

"We're a family Stori and nobody is coming in between that. I'll put a bitch and a nigga in the dirt before I let it come to that. Us breaking up for any reason is not happening," Nas said.

"Okay," Stori said as she nodded her head rapidly.

She was sorry for making a big deal out of Danni coming to her shop. She felt partially responsible for what was happening to the other woman but she didn't know that Nas would be so extreme. Stori gasped when Nas pulled a small pocket knife out of his front pocket and moved closer to Danni. She wrapped her arms around his waist, hoping that he didn't do anything crazier than he'd already done.

"Are me and my wife gonna have any more problems out of you Danni?" Nas asked as he frowned down at her.

"No, I swear to God, you will never ever see me again," Danni sobbed.

"What's my number Danni?" Nas asked her.

"I… I don't know it," Danni replied, saying what she hoped he wanted to hear.

Her entire body trembled when Nas came at her with the knife. She relaxed a little when she saw that he was only trying to cut the tape. Once she was free, Danni just laid there, afraid to speak or move. She didn't want him to change his mind and end up putting a bullet in his head.

"Bitches have died for less. Enjoy your second chance at life and make the best of it," Nas said, giving her the okay to get out of the trunk. Danni's body was sore from the position that it had been in but she ignored the pain and hurriedly got up.

"I'm so sorry Stori," Danni said as she looked at her regretfully.

"Did I say that you could talk to my wife? Fly away like the bird you are," Nas said with a menacing glare. He didn't have to tell Danni twice. She hopped in her car and sped away from her troubles. As far as she was concerned, Naseem Donaldson didn't even exist anymore.

"Naseem, that was not okay. God! What the hell is wrong with you?" Stori asked once they were alone.

"I'm in love," Nas replied as he grabbed her hand and kissed it.

"She looked scared out of her mind," Stori noted.

"Fuck that bitch. You did a good job on her hair though. That was the best her shit ever looked," Nas said while leading her inside the house.

"What's up bro? You good?" Remo asked as soon as he walked in.

"I'm straight now," Nas replied with a head nod.

"The fuck happened to your face?" Remo frowned as he took in his brother's busted lip and the bruise that was on the side of his face. They both had light colored skin, so that made everything easier to see. He was out handling business with Kalani earlier and that was the only reason why he wasn't with Nas on his mission. He was pissed to think that Danni had put her hands on him though.

"She happened," he replied while nodding his head towards Stori.

"What! You beating on my brother girl?" Remo asked while looking at her.

"Maybe Kalani needs to start beating on your ass," Stori replied with a roll of her eyes.

"What's going on with this wedding? I hope you ain't change your mind again," Nas said while looking over at Kalani. Remo told him about his plans to marry Kalani when they were at Jarvis' house that last time. He told him in sign language because he wasn't in the mood for another lecture from their big brother.

"Man, fuck that. Ain't no more mind changing around this bitch. We got some more black tape and my trunk is big enough," Remo smirked.

"I should have known that you were in on it too." Stori frowned.

"In on what?" Kalani asked.

"You don't even want to know," Stori replied while shaking her head.

"So, check it, we're going to the courthouse tomorrow around ten. Then, we're going get things straight for Stori's birthday. We got a spot to look at for the hair stuff and we can grab some food once we're done. Me and Kalani can do the honeymoon thing after all that," Remo spoke up.

"That's cool with me," Nas said while nodding in agreement.

"What are we doing for my birthday? Why do you always make plans without telling me? I have to let my clients know when I won't be working and make arrangements for Toi," Stori replied.

"I already took care of it," Nas said.

"How Naseem?" Stori asked.

"Your grandma said that Toi can stay with her and she'll make sure that she gets to and from school," Nas answered.

"When did you talk to my grandma?" Stori asked.

"Don't worry about all that. Just know that it's handled," Nas replied.

"What about the shop?" Stori questioned.

"Stop asking so many questions and check your Instagram. Come on, let's go. I'm hungry," he said while grabbing her hand.

"See y'all tomorrow and don't be late," Kalani yelled as they walked out of the house.

Nas grabbed Stori's keys and opened the door for her to get in the car. She was too busy looking at her phone to even care about anything else. When Stori got on her page, she was shocked to see a flyer posted with the dates that she wouldn't be working. She hadn't been on social media since two days before and she knew that she didn't post anything.

"The fuck? How did you get my login info?" Stori asked while looking over at Nas.

"I'm your man Stori. It's my job to know that kind of shit," Nas replied.

He always made it a point to find out whatever he needed to know. Remo was always quick to act but Nas liked to think things through and be prepared. His contact person at the DMV helped him out with a lot of stuff and that was how he got Danni's address.

"You have to stop this Naseem. Didn't we just have a talk about boundaries?" Stori inquired.

"No, you talked and I pretended to listen. Don't trip though, baby. You'll get used to it just like Kalani did," Nas said like it was no big deal.

"And that's exactly what I'm afraid of," Stori sighed.

"You don't ever have to be afraid of anything with me. In any situation, just know that I always got you," Nas assured her.

"I know you do." Stori smiled.

"Okay, now what do you feel like eating?" Nas asked.

Stori called Toi to see if she had eaten before she and Nas decided on what they wanted. Since Toi was okay, they decided to go sit down in a restaurant to enjoy their meals instead of taking it to go. Getting used to a man like Naseem was going to take some time. He was all about a man being the head and Stori had no problem with that. The way he did things wasn't normal and that's what she needed him to be mindful of. She would never try to change him but she would definitely encourage him to do better.

FEDERAL RESERVE NOTE

WOR$T CA$E $CENARIO

E31119560F

WASHINGTON, D.C.

22

E31119560F

ONE DOLLAR

"**D**amn bruh. This nigga out here living his best life with your wife by his side. That's some fucked up shit right there," Corey instigated as he sat in his friend, Irvin's, barber shop and talked to Gavin.

Corey and Irvin were locked up together at one time, but Irvin got his shit together after a while. He used some of his dope money and opened up a barber shop and rented out booths to other barbers. Gavin had recently started working there since Corey put in a good word for him. Irvin's shop wasn't that big but working there was okay. The money wasn't as nice as he was used to and the crowd was never as thick. Irvin and the other barbers were cool but Corey was starting to be a pain. He was a low level hustler who was always looking to get something free. Irvin didn't play that shit with him and he couldn't even get a free haircut out of him. That's why he was always at the other shop because his cousin didn't charge him.

"Man, fuck that dude and fuck Stori too. Nobody comes before Toi and he'll see that for himself," Gavin replied.

"That lil bitch used to be spoiled rotten," Corey pointed out.

"And nothing has changed," Gavin replied, wondering how he knew that.

"Damn, they opening up a hair spot and everything. That nigga money must be long as fuck," Corey said as he fished for information.

"Who?" Gavin questioned.

"Your boy and his wife. I mean, your wife," Corey laughed.

"That bitch ain't my wife. We're divorced," Gavin said, telling half the truth.

He and Stori didn't have very long before their divorce would be final though. After what she'd done to him, he didn't even care anymore. He hated Stori and everything about her now. At least that's what he always tried to make himself believe. Gavin tried, but it was hard for him to forget seeing Stori and Nas in the act. It messed with him mentally and he even had a dream about it once before. It replayed over and over in his head like a pornographic film.

"That nigga is doing it big for her though. They look like some Instagram celebrities. People are calling them a power couple and shit," Corey said, hoping that Gavin would take the bait.

When Gavin grabbed his phone from his front pocket, Corey smiled. He saw the anger flash across his face and he knew that his plan was working. Nas had posted pictures of him and Stori on a yacht for her birthday. He'd rented it out for an entire weekend and they looked like hood royalty standing on the deck. He had a video of her opening all the gifts he got her and they looked genuinely happy with each other. Nas also posted pictures of his brother getting married and he was on the boat with them too. Corey wasn't surprised to see that Kalani was there but he didn't know that she was messing with Nas' twin. It was more than that now because she was his wife. The last photo was of a suite that Nas had rented out, saying that it was the future home of their new hair store. He was making money moves and Corey wanted in. Not in a legal way though. He wanted to mask up and take it.

"Fuck them. Bitch stacked her chips while I was paying all the bills. She got with that nigga and want to open up businesses and shit," Gavin argued bitterly.

"You're better than me, fam. A nigga like me would take their shit and live just as good as they're living. You lost too much because of him. Nigga took your wife and your job. Ain't no way in hell are you supposed to let that slide," Corey rambled.

He was happy that nobody else was in the shop at the time because he didn't want to be interrupted. Gavin was easily swayed and that wasn't hard to see. He wore his heart on his sleeve, even though he tried to act unaffected. Gavin still loved Stori and Corey could easily identify with how he felt. She was his first love and his first heartbreak too. Stori felt like she was too good to even hold a conversation with him now and he didn't like her new attitude. Truthfully, he wanted her to suffer just as much as he did all those years ago. Hurting her man would hurt her too and that was like a two for one special.

"That nigga didn't take shit from me. I already got another job and finding a bitch is just as easy. I just married an undercover hood rat and didn't know it. I should send somebody in that shop to rob her hoe ass. Bitch never locks up so it won't be hard," Gavin fumed.

"I'm sure that lil shop ain't even making enough for a nigga to rob," Corey said as he sat up and gave Gavin his undivided attention. He'd pissed him off just enough to get some information out of him. That was his goal and it had been accomplished.

"Believe that if you want to. She never walks away with less than five hundred and that's on a slow day. Besides that, she be selling edibles and shit and that makes a killing all on its own," Gavin replied.

He knew that she went into some kind of business arrangement with Nas and Remo but he didn't know too

251

much more. Now that he thought about it, he really didn't know much about Nas at all. Besides him being a barber and owning the strip club, Nas was a mystery. Gavin was mad with himself for not putting a stop to Stori's business dealings with Nas and Remo when it first started. Now, his soon to be ex-wife was making power couple moves with a nigga that he once considered his best friend. She was probably fucking Nas back then too and he was too dumb to see it. Every time Gavin thought about it, he got sick to his stomach. He'd basically given Nas an open invitation to his life and his wife too. The shit was embarrassing and made him look weak. With each comment that he read, Gavin got even angrier. People were talking like they were Jay and Beyoncé or some shit. They were both still married to other people but nobody mentioned or cared about that.

"Is her shop still in her house?" Corey asked.

"How do you know all that?" Gavin countered.

"I'm from the hood nigga. I know a lot of shit," Corey replied.

"Yeah, it is. What you got in mind?" Gavin asked him.

"What makes you think I got something in mind?" Corey smirked.

"Stop trying to play me for a fool. I can see the wheels in your head turning. Whatever it is, I want a piece of the action. They owe me." Gavin frowned.

"You scratch my back and I'll scratch yours," Corey replied with a sneaky grin.

Once Irvin came back to the shop, Corey and Gavin left to go have drinks. Gavin was all smiles thinking that he and Corey were putting a plan in motion, but he was too dumb to see shit for what it really was. Corey was a greedy nigga and he didn't like to share. All he needed Gavin to do was give up the info and he would take it from there. Gavin was making a deal with the devil and Corey wore the horns.

"Hey ma, just calling to let you know that we made it home safely. I know it's kind of late, so I'll call you tomorrow. Love you," Misty said as she spoke to her mother's answering machine.

She and Summer had just made it back home from Beaumont and she was drained. The drive was only a little over four hours but Misty left later than she wanted to. Her mother didn't want Summer to leave and she prolonged their stay. Misty had been there for three days and she got a lot accomplished in that short time. She'd spoken to her old supervisor and she was thrilled that Misty wanted to come back to work. They always got along great and Misty did her job well. She didn't have to worry about a babysitter because her mother was all too happy to do it. She'd put in for a two bedroom condo and she was waiting to hear back from the leasing office. She looked at furniture and had a good idea of how she wanted to decorate if she got the house. It was two streets over from her mother and things couldn't have been better. Misty had more than enough money saved and she was hoping to be back in Texas in no more than two weeks.

"Let's go pretty girl. We need a bath and a bed," Misty said as she got Summer out of the car.

She grabbed Summer's bag and decided to leave hers in the trunk. Misty groaned when she walked up on the porch and heard the loud music and laughter coming from inside. For the past few weeks, it had been the same thing with Milan. She always had a bunch of niggas in the house and all they did was drink and smoke. Her attitude had been fucked up lately and Misty tried hard to stay out of her way. She was shocked to learn about Stori being pregnant with Naseem's baby but Milan was taking it hard. She tried for months to give Nas a baby and she was never successful. Gavin pretended like he didn't care but Misty knew that he had to be crushed. Stori was his world and he loved Nas like a brother. He used to get mad with Misty when she told him the truth. Nas didn't fuck with him the same way but Gavin didn't want to believe it. Besides Remo, he didn't really fuck with nobody.

"What's up beautiful? You got a man?" one of lil boys who was sitting in the front room asked as soon as Misty walked in.

He looked like he was no more than eighteen and missing a few meals. Corey was sitting next to Milan looking like he was up to no good. He was a snake and that wasn't hard to see. Milan always got weed from him but letting him hang around her house so much was something new. Corey never came over by himself. He always had at least three other lil boys with him. They were childish and always loud as hell.

"Lil boy get out of my way. I already got a baby to breastfeed," Misty snapped as the other men laughed. She fanned the weed smoke away from Summer as she made her way to her bedroom.

"She's acting all stuck up like she ain't a stripper. I bet you pull out some singles and she'll get her mind right real quick," Corey said as he puffed on his blunt.

"This is my house. Fuck her." Milan frowned.

"What's up Milan? You trying to fuck me too?" Corey asked flirtatiously as he rubbed her thigh.

"Nigga please. You can't even afford to sniff this pussy. My husband got bank and he took care of me. I can't downgrade," Milan replied as she moved his hand away.

"Your husband? Maybe you missed the memo but that nigga is in love with the next bitch. Besides, with this lick that I'm about to hit, you'll be begging me for the dick," Corey replied.

"You've been hitting licks since we first met and ain't come up yet," Milan pointed out.

"That's because I haven't been hitting the right ones. Your husband is about to be the nigga to get me right though," Corey noted.

"How so?" Milan asked.

"Him and his bitch are my next two licks. I already got the inside scoop and everything," Corey answered.

"From who? Nas don't even talk to nobody like that. Somebody is sending you on a straight up dummy mission," Milan said.

"Maybe he doesn't but his bitch does. I got a few things in the works," Corey replied.

"Good and make sure that bitch is no longer breathing while you're at it." Milan frowned.

"And what do I get?" Corey asked with a devious smile.

"You make Stori a distant memory and you can get whatever the fuck you want," Milan swore, right as Misty walked back into the room.

"Can y'all turn the music down please? My baby is trying to sleep," Misty said as politely as she could.

"I guess that's our cue to get going," Corey said as he and his cousins stood up.

"Y'all don't have to go nowhere. This is my damn house," Milan argued.

"We got some moves to make but I'll be in touch," Corey said as he and his crew walked out of the house.

"Don't be coming up in my muthafucking house trying to run shit!" Milan jumped up and yelled at her sister.

"How am I trying to run shit? I only asked y'all to lower the music so my baby can sleep. I don't know what the fuck has been up with you lately, but I can't wait to get out of your house," Misty replied.

Milan had been snapping on her more and more and she didn't have time for it. She seemed to be trying to provoke her but Misty never took the bait. They barely even talked anymore and Misty hadn't done anything to make her sister act differently.

"Why wait? Get you and your baby's shit and get the fuck out right now," Milan snapped angrily.

"No worries, I'll be gone for good in another week or two," Misty assured her.

"I want you gone tonight. It's because of you that my husband is no longer here," Milan argued.

"You can't be serious. What do I have to do with Nas leaving you?" Misty inquired.

"If you wouldn't have fucked with Gavin, Stori wouldn't have fucked with my husband. She was trying to get back at you and Gavin and she used my husband to do it. All of this shit is your fault. I'm happy that you're going back to Texas. I don't know why I even begged you to come here," Milan cried.

"I know you're hurt and upset but none of this is my fault. I don't know how Stori and Naseem ended up together, but it has nothing to do with me. He left you before Stori even found out about Summer anyway. That's not on me," Misty noted.

"I don't give a fuck, just get out. I don't even want to look at you anymore," Milan sobbed. She was having a complete meltdown and Misty didn't know what to do.

"Where am I supposed to go with Summer? You know that we don't have any family here," Misty said as her eyes filled with tears.

"I don't know and I don't give a fuck!" Milan snapped.

The more she sat down and thought about it, the angrier she became. She had never had any problems with Stori and she was a faithful customer at her salon. It wasn't until Misty had Summer that everything started to go left. Milan felt like she was being punished for the sins of her sister and she hated her for it. She was so hung up over Remo that she ruined everybody's life. All she had to do was get the abortion like he told her to and things would have ended differently.

"I have nowhere else to go Milan. I can't believe you're doing this to me. Summer is your only niece. How can you throw an innocent baby out on the streets?" Misty questioned as she cried. Milan was a piece of work. She wasn't saying all that when Misty was getting pissy sticks from her co-worker to help her fake a pregnancy. She loved her to death as long as she was doing something for her.

"I don't care! Just get out!" Milan yelled like a crazy person.

Misty wasn't about to keep begging her sister to let her stay. She walked down the hall to her bedroom and started packing a bag. She still had the bag that she took to Texas in her car but she needed a few more items. There was no way that she could take it all but she could always come back for the rest. Misty played a huge part in the demise of Gavin's marriage but that was all that she was taking responsibility for. She had lots of regrets but Summer wasn't one of them. Her daughter made her want to do better and she was trying. Milan was trying to blame everybody else for Nas leaving her when it was her own fault.

Once Misty was done packing, she picked Summer up and headed down the hall. Although she wanted to break down and cry, she held her head high as she walked out of the front door. Misty wanted to call her mother back as she drove away, but it was too late. Instead, she called the one person who she dreaded calling the most.

"Yeah Misty," Gavin answered with an attitude.

"I need a huge favor Gavin. Milan put me and Summer out of her house and we have nowhere else to go. I only need somewhere to stay for a week or two before we leave for Texas," Misty sniffled.

Gavin's first mind told him to curse her out and hang up the phone. Since he had Summer to think about, he had to behave like a mature adult. He still couldn't stand Misty but she was the mother of his child. He hated that she was moving Summer four hours away but he couldn't let her be homeless until then.

"Make no mistake about it, I'm only allowing you to come here because of my daughter. I'll send you the address," Gavin replied before he hung up.

"Stupid ass," Misty mumbled as she continued to drive. She was mentally and physically drained and her move to Texas would probably happen sooner than she anticipated. She loved the food and culture in New Orleans but it was no longer the place for her.

"What happened?" Remo asked as he looked over at Kalani.

"The voicemail picked up again," Kalani replied.

"Man, Fuck! Something is wrong. It's not like Nas not to answer my calls," Remo replied nervously.

"Calm down baby. Stori would have told me if something was wrong when she sent the text. Maybe their clinic appointment ran over. That's probably why she wants us to get Toi from school," Kalani reasoned.

"Damn man. I hope nothing is wrong with my niece. Roll me up something baby. My nerves are bad as fuck," Remo said as he drove towards Toi's school.

"Pull over in the Walgreens parking lot so I can drive. You're not even focused," Kalani noted.

Remo couldn't even argue with that. He pulled over

into the half-empty parking lot and got out of the car. He knew that Kalani wasn't going to stop in front of a store and not go inside. Knowing her, that was her motive all along.

"Don't be all day Kalani and bring me back something to drink," Remo requested.

"Okay," Kalani replied as she got out of the car.

She wanted some candy and she wanted to grab Toi a few snacks while she was in there. She got a small hand basket and made her way to the candy aisle. Once she was done there, she went to the coolers and got Remo something to drink.

"Kalani Simmons. It must be my lucky day," a deep voice boomed from behind her.

Kalani spun around and smiled when she saw her ex-boyfriend Jamar standing there staring at her. She hadn't seen Jamar in a while and she was shocked to see him standing there in a police uniform. He was a lot more muscular than she remembered him but he looked great.

"It's actually Kalani Donaldson now." She smiled as she flashed the huge rock that was on her finger.

"Wow. I know I'm supposed to congratulate you but it wouldn't be sincere. Who's the lucky man?" Jamar asked.

"Who do you think it is?" Kalani countered.

"Please don't tell me that you married that crazy ass twin," Jamar said as he looked at her with wide eyes.

"My husband is not crazy," Kalani laughed.

"That nigga came to my job and was already sitting in my car when I got in there. You're absolutely right. Crazy is too good of a word to describe him," Jamar replied.

"He can be a little extreme sometimes," Kalani shrugged.

"How is your mom?" Jamar asked.

"She's good, thanks for asking," she smiled.

"What about Stori and Toi?" Jamar asked.

"They're good too. Stori is five months pregnant," Kalani replied.

"Wow. Tell her that I said congrats. Besides being married to a lunatic, how have you been?" Jamar asked as his eyes roamed her curvaceous frame.

"Not too much on my husband. But, I've been fine," Kalani replied.

"You look great," Jamar complimented. Kalani was about to reply but she heard Remo's voice before she even saw him.

"So, you want me to kill a policeman? Huh Kalani? Is that what you want?" Remo questioned as he stood in front of her with a menacing glare.

"Calm down Kareem. Jamar was just saying hello," Kalani replied as she grabbed his hand to make sure he didn't swing.

"Let that fuck boy go say hello to somebody else's wife. Let's go," Remo fumed.

"Still insecure I see," Jamar spoke up as he smirked at Remo.

"Don't start feeling yourself because you got on that clown suit nigga. You'll be getting buried in that same outfit. Fuck with me," Remo gritted.

"Are you threatening me?" Jamar asked incredulously.

"Nah nigga, I'm promising you," Remo answered.

"We'll see each other again, trust me," Jamar noted.

"Most definitely," Remo smirked menacingly as he grabbed Kalani's hand and walked away.

"Did you have to do all that?" Kalani asked him as they went to the counter to pay for their items.

"You should be happy that I didn't do more. I'm stressed the fuck out worried about my brother and sister-in-law while you're in here reminiscing with your ex. If you thought I cut up when you were my girl, I'm fucking shit up now that you're my wife," Remo noted.

"You need to relax. You always get crazy whenever you don't hear from your brother. Nas and Stori are fine," Kalani assured him.

Remo dialed his brother's number again and got even more worried when the voicemail picked up. Once they left the store, Kalani drove as he sat in the passenger side smoking and worrying. Once they got Toi, Kalani broke the speed limit getting to Stori's house. When they saw Jarvis' car parked out front, Remo almost lost it.

"I told you that something was wrong!" he yelled as they all jumped out of the car together.

Toi used her key to get inside and they all paused as soon as they walked in. Stori was sitting on Nas' lap crying while Jarvis and Latrice sat next to them. Jarvis was holding her hand while Latrice lovingly rubbed her back.

"What's wrong Stori? What did the doctor say?" Toi asked when she walked over to her.

"Why didn't you answer your phone bro? You had a nigga going crazy," Remo said as he looked at Nas.

"My bad bro. I left it in the car," Nas replied, as Stori got up to grab a paper towel.

"Come sit down baby. I could have gotten that for you," Nas said as he got up and wiped Stori's eyes.

"What's good bro? Is my niece okay?" Remo asked.

"You're not having a niece," Stori sniffled.

"Oh shit! It's a boy?" Remo asked excitedly.

"Yeah, two of them," Nas replied as the entire room got quiet.

Toi and Kalani stood there in shock as they digested the news. Jarvis looked worried and Stori was a mess.

"We're having twins?" Remo asked, just to be sure.

"Two boys." Nas nodded.

"Two babies," Toi repeated as she took a seat on the love seat.

"That's what the fuck I'm talking about! Nas and Remo reincarnated around this bitch!" Remo yelled happily as he wrapped his arms around his brother and hugged him tight.

"Oh God," Stori groaned as she started crying again.

"Chill out with that shit Kareem. The damn girl is already traumatized and I can't even blame her," Jarvis said as he got up to hug Stori.

"Traumatized for what? That's about to be me and Nas all over again baby." Remo smiled.

"God no. I don't want my kids to be like you and Naseem," Stori sobbed.

"Kareem stop. That is not a compliment," Kalani said as she fussed at him.

262

She pulled Stori over to the sofa and sat her down. Nas and Remo were secretly celebrating while Jarvis paced the floor. Nas was in shock when the doctor first told them that they were having twins. Stori asked them to do the ultrasound again and, again, the results remained the same. Nas ended up calling Latrice and she told them to get a second opinion in the form of a three-dimensional ultrasound. She called around and found a place that took walk-ins and she and Jarvis met them there. Stori asked Kalani to get Toi from school because she didn't know how long it would take. The first doctor couldn't confirm the sex of the babies but the second doctor did. When they told Stori that she was having two boys, she almost lost it. Jarvis didn't make it any better by telling her stories about Nas and Remo. She hadn't stopped crying since they left the appointment. Nas was happy as hell and he knew that Remo would be too.

"My bro wasn't playing. That nigga dropping babies two at a time around this bitch," Remo said as he gave Nas dap.

"Don't worry about nothing Stori. You know we got your back," Latrice assured her.

"Yeah and I'll help out too," Toi said as she squeezed into a spot on the sofa right next to her sister.

"Aww, thank you my Stanka," Stori said as she smiled through her tears. When Toi hugged her, she felt as if everything would be okay. It was crazy how her baby sister could always make her feel better.

"They gotta be close too bro. We have to make sure of it," Remo said seriously as he looked over at Nas. He took his bond with his brother seriously and he wanted his nephews to do the same.

"Most definitely." Nas nodded in agreement.

"They gon' be bad as fuck too. I can feel it," Remo said like that was something to be proud of.

"Kareem!" Kalani yelled angrily. Every time Stori seemed to start feeling better, he said something else to make her cry again.

"Let's go outside," Nas said as he headed for the front door with his twin following right behind him.

"What's good?" Remo asked him.

"We got a lot of shit to figure out," Nas said.

"Like what?" Remo questioned.

"Like who we're gonna get besides Bee to help run all these damn businesses. You're married now and I'm about to be the father of two soon. We can't do all the long days and nights no more. I'm not too worried about the barber shop because I can close that up early. I can probably do the club two nights a week and that's only if Stori don't trip. We got the location and all the inventory for the hair spot with nobody to run it," Nas pointed out.

"Yeah, that's true. Don't even worry about the hair spot though. I'll take care of that. Bee can run the club with his eyes closed but we need to get somebody else that we trust to help him," Remo said.

"Nigga, besides each other, who else is there that we trust?" Nas asked.

"Shit, that's the damn problem," Remo sighed.

"We need to keep our eyes open and make something shake soon," Nas said.

"I'm on it bro. But, check it. We ran into Kalani's ex nigga at the store a few minutes ago. The nigga is a cop now and I feel like he might be a problem in the long run," Remo stated.

"What ex? Dude that she was with before you?" Nas asked.

"Yeah, that fuck boy was talking sporty because he wears a badge now." Remo frowned.

"What's his name?" Nas asked.

"How the fuck should I know? I wanted his girl and I got her. I never asked the nigga his name because I didn't give a fuck," Remo replied.

"What parish does he work in?" Nas inquired.

"Jefferson," Remo answered as he remembered the kind of uniform that the other man had on.

"I need a name. Even if it's just a first or a last. I need something," Nas said.

"I'll ask Kalani when we get home tonight," Remo noted.

"Nah, don't ask her nothing. I'll figure it out," Nas assured him.

"I was worried when you didn't answer the phone. That's the only reason why her and that nigga got a pass. She was standing there smiling in the nigga face like I won't put her ass in a wheelchair," Remo fussed.

"Fuck that nigga. You know Kalani ain't going nowhere," Nas said, waving him off.

"Man listen, you just don't know how happy I am. We're having muthafucking twins!" Remo yelled out.

"Yeah man, but I think my baby is in shock. She wasn't expecting to hear that shit and neither was I," Nas laughed.

"I think we may have traumatized Jarvis. That nigga is shook," Remo said.

"His stupid ass is the one who got her to crying and shit. He was telling her all that shit that we did when we were younger and now she's scared to death. I can't let Stori be on no soft shit with my sons though, bro. They gotta be tough just like daddy had us," Nas replied.

"Damn right," Remo nodded, right as Jarvis opened the front door. He and Latrice were preparing to leave and bring their girls to the movies.

"Stori is calm now Kareem. Make sure she stays that way," Latrice warned.

"I got you sis," Remo replied.

"Two more of these muthafuckers on the way. I need a damn drink," Jarvis mumbled, as Remo and Nas laughed.

"You need a hug bro? Come here and let's hug this shit out," Nas said as he opened his arms wide.

"Fuck you!" Jarvis yelled right before he got into his car and pulled off.

"What you and Kalani got going on for the rest of the day?" Nas asked his brother.

"We ain't doing shit. Why? What's up?" Remo inquired.

"Let's go somewhere and eat," Nas suggested.

"I'm good with that." Remo shrugged as he followed his brother back into the house.

Stori was smiling as Toi animatedly dominated the conversation. She was looking at something on her phone that she kept showing to Stori.

"Nas, I found some names for the babies. Well, one of the babies since the first one out will be named after you," Toi said.

She was so smart to be fifteen years old and that always amazed Nas. He couldn't believe that Gavin was so jealous of a child. Nas loved her and Stori's relationship and that shit was just ridiculous. He had a niece Toi's age and he was hoping that they could link up sometimes.

"I don't know about that second name Stanka." Stori frowned.

"I think it's cute," Kalani spoke up.

"So do I. What do you think about Naseem and Nakeem?" Toi asked.

"They sound too identical," Stori noted.

"Duh Stori. You're having twins," Kalani noted.

"Don't even remind me," Stori said as she rubbed her big belly.

"I like it." Nas smiled.

"Yeah, that's straight." Remo nodded in agreement.

"Well, it's settled. We're going with the names that Toi picked." Nas smiled as he winked at her.

"Yes! I can't wait to tell everybody that I named the babies," Toi cheered.

"Do you have homework baby?" Stori asked her.

"No," Toi replied while shaking her head.

"Good, let's go somewhere and eat," Nas said.

"Can I go in my uniform Stori? I don't feel like changing," Toi said.

"You don't have to change," Nas replied, right before Toi ran upstairs to put her backpack away.

"Let me run to the bathroom before we go," Stori said as Nas helped her up from the sofa.

"My poor friend," Kalani said once Stori wobbled away.

"If you don't know nothing else, just know that I got her, my kids and Toi too," Nas replied.

"I know you do and that's the only thing that makes me feel better," Kalani noted.

Once they ate, Nas, Stori and Toi went to his grandmother's house to tell her and Mr. Herbert about the twins. Everybody offered their assistance and that seemed to make Stori feel better. Her grandmother and aunties were excited too but nobody was happier than Lady. She'd always wanted a son but she was getting two grandsons instead. Her mother was a twin, but it skipped a generation and fell on Stori. She was trying to hurry her husband along with their move to New Orleans. She already knew the area that she wanted to live in and she wanted to make it happen before her grandsons came. She had already contacted an event planner to do the baby shower and she was about to go crazy with her husband's money.

"My mama is too excited. She fucked up with me and Toi, so maybe she's trying to be a better grandmother," Stori said as she and Nas laid in the bed that night.

"Yeah, I saw how happy she was. I know you're nervous baby but you don't have a reason to be. We got this," Nas assured her.

"I know we do. I just know that a lot of things are going to change," Stori said.

"Change is a good thing. Look at how much I've changed since I got with you," Nas replied.

"Boy bye. You might do things a little differently but you haven't changed," Stori said.

"Girl, I'm faithful as fuck. I can't remember a time when I didn't deal with more than one woman. Shit, I don't think I ever have. So yeah, a nigga made some serious changes," Nas replied.

"Nigga, you better be faithful. Pregnant or not, you can still get it," Stori threatened, making him laugh.

Stori didn't mind poppin' off, so he believed her. She didn't have to ever worry about him going astray though. She was everything that he ever wanted in a woman and she was about to give him, not one, but two kids. Nas was ready to settle down long before they got together. Having the woman that he'd always wanted only made things better. Stori was his soulmate and her having his kids only confirmed what he already knew.

"Did you eat baby?" Nas asked as he talked on the phone with Stori.

"One of my clients got me something when I finished her hair. I only had five people today but they all wanted a sew-in," Stori replied.

She wasn't complaining because she had made over a thousand dollars in just a few hours. Nas got her some comfortable clothes and shoes and she was good to go. She limited her clients to five a day because he didn't want her to overdo it.

"I told you that you don't even have to work no more if you don't want to. You can just chill at home," Nas said.

"And do what Naseem? Sit around the house all day and get fat. I need to stay as active as I can. I cut down on the number of people I take like you asked me to but I'm not ready to stop working yet," Stori replied.

"See, that's why I love you, baby. You out here grinding with your man trying to get this money. I'm trying to buy us a house in the next few months," Nas said.

"I already have a house," Stori pointed out.

"Fuck that house. I want us to make some new memories in a new spot. Besides, I'm not feeling the idea of laying my head in the same place where you run your business. That's not a good look," Nas said.

"I guess. Did you eat anything?" Stori asked him while changing the subject.

"No and I'm hungry as fuck. I'm in the office now but we still got a few niggas waiting to get cut," Nas replied.

"Okay boo. Well, I'll have something cooked for you by the time you're done. My auntie is picking Toi up from school. It's her daughter's birthday and she's taking them all out to eat," Stori said.

"Alright baby. Let me go help them knock this crowd down and I'll be there when I'm done," Nas replied before they disconnected.

When he walked back to the front of the shop, all of the barbers were hard at work. He didn't know what was up but it was kind of crowded to say it was a Thursday. They had six men waiting, so Nas called whoever was next over to his chair. Eric was busy sweeping the floor and making sure the bathrooms stayed clean. The dude who Nas and Remo had hired was almost done putting the finishing touches on the hair salon side of the shop. He'd replaced the four shampoo bowls and put down a new floor. Nas got some new chairs for the customers and Latrice hung some pictures on the walls. Everything else looked almost new and Nas was ready to start advertising for stylists.

"Can I get a lining Nas? I don't want a cut because I'm trying to let my hair grow out. I think I want a mohawk," Eric said once he finally took a seat in one of the chairs against the wall. Nas was busy with a customer but he was almost done. Only two men were waiting to be cut now and Nas was thankful that no one else had walked in.

"I got you," Nas replied, right as he heard the front door chime.

He was tired as hell but he had a business to run. Even if all the other barbers left, he would still have to stay and take the last person. That alone let Nas know that he was maturing or at least trying to. A few months ago, he wouldn't have cared about nothing like that. He had Stori and his sons to think about now and that had him moving smarter.

"Damn, she fine as hell," one of the barbers said, making Nas look up to see who he was referring to. He had to do a double take when he saw his ex-girlfriend, Alissa, walking his way. Nas couldn't even front, Alissa was still fine and her face was just as pretty as he remembered.

"Hey stranger." Alissa smiled while walking over to Nas.

"Shit, I'm not the one who up and disappeared. You're the stranger," Nas replied.

"You know I travel a lot Naseem but you didn't give me a reason to stay," Alissa said.

"What's been up with you?" Nas asked as he continued to cut his customer's hair.

"Nothing much. Just working and enjoying life. Being a traveling nurse lets me see the world on somebody else's dime. I see you've been very busy though. Twins huh?" Alissa asked.

"I see you've been keeping up with a nigga," Nas smirked.

"I always keep up with the ones I love." Alissa smiled seductively.

Nas looked even better than she remembered. It had been over a year since she'd seen him and time had definitely been good to him. She kept up with everything via Instagram and Nas always did post a lot. He had a business so that wasn't surprising. What did surprise her was when he announced that he was going to be a father. Alissa was sick to her stomach to think that Milan was going to be the mother of his child. After all, he'd cheated on her with the other woman and married her too. The big shocker came when he posted his new woman and she saw who it was. Alissa had been to Gavin and Stori's house with Nas before and she was shocked to know that they were together now. She hadn't been gone that long but it was obviously long enough. Nas had Stori on yachts and was showing her off like she was a prize. Although she had a man now, Alissa wouldn't turn Nas down if he wanted another chance with her.

"How long are you in town for?" Nas asked as he finished with his customer and collected his payment.

He took a seat in the chair when his customer got up. He was happy that the other barbers took the remaining men who were waiting because he wasn't in the mood.

"Why? Are you trying to take me somewhere?" Alissa asked as she walked over to him.

She was trying to stand in between his legs, but Nas turned the chair around and put his feet up on his work station. He wasn't trying to be rude but he didn't want to send her mixed messages either. He was good on other women and that included Alissa. Before he got with Stori, he would have had her bent over the desk in his office. Now, he had too much to lose to even risk it.

"Nah sweetheart. I'm already taken," Nas said.

"That never stopped you before," Alissa noted.

"I've never been in love before." Nas shrugged.

"Are you trying to hurt my feelings Naseem?" Alissa asked.

"Not at all, I'm just being honest," Nas replied.

"So, you were never in love with me?" Alissa asked.

"No but I came close. I guess I wasn't ready to settle down back then," he answered truthfully.

"I asked you once before if you were attracted to Stori and you said no. Gavin might have been oblivious but I paid attention to the way you looked at her. You lied to me," Alissa accused.

"No, I spared your feelings. That alone should let you know that I cared," Nas said.

"Do you still care?" Alissa asked.

"Yeah, about Stori," Nas replied honestly.

"How did that even happen with you two?" Alissa asked.

"It just did." Nas shrugged, not caring to elaborate.

"What did she do to make you want to be faithful? Why her?" Alissa wanted to know.

"She's the one Alissa. I can't explain it and I won't even try," Nas replied.

"You've changed Naseem. Even your appearance. I love what you've done with your hair," Alissa flirted as she ran her hand through his mohawk.

"Aye, Nas," Eric called out to him.

"Chill out Alissa. I promise, I ain't got nothing for you," Nas said.

"Yo, Nas," Eric said, once again trying to get his attention.

"Stop acting like you don't miss me," Alissa purred.

"Naseem!" Eric yelled nervously.

"What!" Nas yelled back but it was too late. Stori was already right there in his face. Nas was about to explain but a left, then a right hook to his face, made him lose his voice.

"Oh shit!" one of the barbers yelled out.

"Baby, chill out," Nas said as he jumped up and grabbed Stori's hands. His eye was burning and watering up from her licks. Alissa jumped back and got ready, just in case she was next.

"Fuck you, Naseem! Nigga, let me go! I'm going get my gun out of my car and shoot you and that hoe," Stori yelled angrily.

She was acting like she wasn't pregnant with two babies and Nas was having a hard time controlling her. Stori felt bad that he hadn't eaten and she wasn't in the mood to cook. She took a shower and decided to bring him something to eat instead. What she didn't expect was to see his ex-girlfriend standing there running her fingers through his curly hair. Eric tried to warn him, but he was too busy smiling up in her face to care.

"Miss, you better leave. She really will shoot you," Eric said as he looked at Alissa.

Eric had only met Stori a few times, but Nas was always saying that she had a lot of guns. She was always nice to him but that didn't mean a thing. Stori looked like she would do exactly what she said. He didn't have to tell

Alissa twice. She rushed out of the shop right as Nas carried Stori to the office in the back. She had a career to think about and he wasn't even worth it.

"The fuck you always acting crazy for Stori? I didn't even do shit," Nas said once they were alone.

"I saw that bitch running her fingers through your hair and shit. And your stupid ass sat there and let her," Stori fussed as she mushed his head.

"Man, fuck that bitch. Do I need to grab the black tape and throw her ass in the trunk too? I haven't seen that damn girl in over a year," Nas swore.

"I don't give a fuck. You shouldn't have let that hoe touch you. Bitch playing in your hair and shit," Stori fumed.

"The fuck Stori! You want me to cut the shit off? Will that make you happy? You be going crazy for nothing," Nas replied.

"Fuck you nigga and I hope you choke on your food," Stori fumed as she tried to walk away.

"I love you, baby. I swear on my mama's grave that I didn't do shit. I got your pictures all over my Instagram. I didn't even have to tell her nothing about us because she already know what's up," Nas said as he tried to calm her down.

He hugged Stori from behind and rubbed her stomach. The babies were moving like crazy, just like always. Stori relaxed in his embrace and allowed him to comfort her.

"I'm fine Naseem. You don't have to hold me. I'm not trying to swing on your stupid ass no more. Go eat your food before it gets cold," Stori said.

"My damn eye is throbbing. You better stop putting your hands on me girl," Nas fussed.

"Or what nigga?" Stori challenged as she turned around to face him.

"Why you gotta be so damn sexy?" Nas asked as he pulled her close and kissed her.

He picked Stori up and sat her on top of his desk. Their kisses became more aggressive as she rushed to remove his shirt. Stori lifted up her dress and Nas pulled her underwear off. They both moaned when he held her legs in the crook of his arms and entered her. They didn't care about the few people who were left in the shop. They stayed in his office for over an hour and Eric was the only one in the shop by the time they came out. He was almost done cleaning up and Nas gave him a lining soon after. Once he locked up for the night, he dropped Eric off home and rushed back to Stori to finish what they had started.

"You look so handsome boo." Stori smiled as she looked over at Nas.

"Yeah, okay," he blushed as she ran her hand across his freshly cut hair.

He was only joking when he asked Stori if she wanted him to cut his hair. She was still pissed about seeing Alissa touching him and she told him that she did. Nas got up early that Sunday morning and made it happen. Toi held the mirror for him while he gave himself the best fade ever. He had a full beard and he was liking the lower, wavy cut.

"Where are we going? You know I don't like to leave Toi home by herself too long," Stori noted.

"I know baby but we won't be too long," Nas said as he pulled up to their destination.

"Seriously Naseem? I'm almost six months pregnant with two babies. You know damn well I can't get no tattoo," Stori fussed.

"Get your whining ass out of the car," Nas laughed.

When Stori reached for the handle, he slapped her hand and jumped out of the car to open her door. He grabbed her hand and walked her up the steps to the tattoo shop. The place was fairly empty but it was still early. Usually, they would have to start a sign-in sheet and he wasn't in the mood to deal with a crowd. Nas smiled when he saw the owner and the other man's smile was just as bright.

"Man, I must be seeing things. Where your crazy ass been hiding at? It's been a minute." Bryce smiled as he walked over and embraced Nas.

"I pass through to holla at that nigga Jaden all the time. You don't be open most of the time though," Nas replied.

Bryce and Jarvis were cool and had been for years. His wife, Taylor, used to do Latrice's hair until she stopped working. Bryce's younger brother, Jaden, was a barber and he was who taught Nas most of what he knew. Nas worked under him for a while until he became a licensed barber. Jaden had chilled out over the years but Nas and Remo made sure to stay in touch with him. He always said that the twins reminded him of himself when he was younger. They were wild and crazy just like he used to be. Bryce and Jarvis still hung out too and it was always love between all of them.

"How you doing sweetheart?" Bryce said as he reached his hand out to Stori.

"I'm fine, thank you." Stori smiled.

"Baby, this is Jaden's brother, Bryce. This is my girl, Stori, and our sons," Nas said as he rubbed her stomach.

"Sons? Y'all are having twins?" Bryce asked.

"Yep." Nas smiled brightly.

"Nas and Remo all over again. You're in my prayers baby girl," Bryce said as he shook his head. He remembered all too well how much shit the twins used to get into. They damn near drove Jarvis crazy and it was a miracle that he didn't have a nervous breakdown. He knew that Nas had a baby on the way but Jarvis never told him that it was twins.

"Don't tell her that shit bruh. I don't need her to start up with all that crying again," Nas replied.

"What you getting today bruh?" Bryce asked as he pulled up a chair for Stori to sit down.

276

"You got some lipstick baby?" Nas asked as he looked at Stori.

"Yeah, why?" she asked while looking at him sideways.

"Put some on," Nas requested.

"For what Naseem?" Stori asked.

"Because that's my tattoo," he replied, confusing her even more.

"Oh, okay. You have to put on some lipstick and kiss the paper for the tattoo that he wants," Bryce explained.

Stori did what they asked her to do but she was still confused. She and Nas made small talk with Bryce until he was ready to do the tattoo. Once it was done, Stori smiled when she saw the finished product. Nas had gotten a tattoo of her lips on his neck with her name underneath it. The colors showed up great on his light colored skin and she loved it.

"You like it baby?" Nas asked when he saw her admiring his ink.

"I love it." Stori smiled, right as someone else walked into the shop.

"Nigga, I thought you faked me out," Nas said as Jaden walked over to them. Stori had already met him and his wife before, so she smiled and waved at him.

"I had to duck my granddaughter man. Nigga can't even leave the house without her ass no more," Jaden laughed.

"Don't listen to that nigga. He got that baby spoiled rotten," Bryce laughed.

"You ready to drop them boys?" Jaden asked as he looked over at Stori.

"Hell no," she replied as they all laughed.

Nas paid Bryce what he owed him before he and Stori walked outside with Jaden.

"Did you handle that for me?" Nas asked him.

"Yeah man. That nigga is on board. He just got laid off so this shit is right on time. I gave him your number and he said he's gonna call you tonight," Jaden replied.

"Good looking fam." Nas nodded.

"Nah bruh, I appreciate you and Remo for showing love. That's my favorite uncle, so I got him regardless. I know he would feel better if he was making his own money though," Jaden said.

Nas and Remo had been going crazy trying to find somebody else to help manage their club. When Nas called Jaden a few nights ago, he told him about his uncle Shaq being laid off from his job. Nas knew Shaq very well and he was just what they needed to help Bee out at the strip club. Jaden thought it was a good idea and he was happy that Shaq was on board.

"You know we don't fuck with too many people," Nas pointed out.

He stood out there and talked with Jaden for a while until Remo called. He and Kalani were getting food and coming over to the house to chill. When Nas and Stori pulled up, Remo and Kalani were just getting out of the car. They all walked into the house together and sat in the front room.

"Look at this bullshit," Kalani fussed as she handed Stori an envelope.

"What is this?" Stori questioned.

"I gave this nigga my hand in marriage and he gave me a pink slip," Kalani fumed.

"You fired my friend?" Stori asked while looking over at Remo.

"I don't want my wife being a bartender at a strip club," Remo replied nonchalantly.

"I was a bartender when I was your girl," Kalani noted. "You fucking up my money."

"So the fuck what Kalani! It ain't like you pay no damn bills. The fuck you getting mad for? Besides, I told you that I need you to help out with something else," Remo said.

"Whatever Kareem. You can be prepared to be the only income in the household too nigga," Kalani argued.

"I'm already the only income in the household. I don't see a dime of your money," Remo replied.

"Ooh Nas, I love your haircut," Kalani cooed as she ignored her husband.

"The fuck you mean you love his haircut? So what, you don't like the dreads no more?" Remo frowned.

"Yes baby, I love the dreads too," Kalani said as she rolled her eyes.

"Yeah okay. The fuck happened to your eye bro?" Remo asked as he looked at the fading purple colored bruise under his brother's eye.

"The fuck you think happened?" Nas countered as he looked at Stori.

"Aye girl, you better calm your wild ass down. I'm not gon' keep sending my brother back into this abusive situation," Remo said seriously as he looked at Stori.

"Tell him to keep his hoes and ex hoes in line and he wouldn't be getting beat," Stori said as Kalani laughed.

"You good bro? Domestic violence is not okay. You need to speak up," Remo said, as Nas laughed.

"You got another tattoo Nas? I love it." Kalani smiled as she looked at his new artwork.

"You loving all kind of shit today, huh?" Remo asked as he looked at her and frowned. He had her name in big bold letters going down his arm, so he wasn't surprised to see that Nas had gotten Stori's name too.

"Aye bro, I just talked to Jaden and Shaq is with it. All we have to do now is find somebody to manage the hair spot and we're all good," Nas said.

"We already got somebody for that," Remo said as he looked at Kalani.

"Wow. When were you going to tell me?" Kalani asked.

"I'm telling you right now. I don't want you working at night no more. You need to be at home in bed with your husband," Remo replied.

"Facts," Nas said while nodding his head.

"Fine and, since we're making demands, I want your hair cut. I'm sick of the dreads," Kalani snapped as she rolled her eyes.

"What?" Remo mumbled like he was in shock.

"I got you, bro," Nas said as he laughed at the expression on Remo's face. His brother loved his dreads but, for Kalani, he knew that they were about to go.

"Okay, now that all of that is settled, what did y'all get to eat?" Stori asked.

Toi came downstairs and they all sat in the front room eating and watching movies. Once they were done, Kalani cleaned up their mess while Nas gave Remo a cut that was exactly like his. He loved it but, even more than that, he loved that he and Nas were identical once again.

S tori took pride in her work and she was never one to rush on a customer. There was a first time for everything and she found herself moving a little faster than usual. It was still early but it was dark outside. She wasn't expecting Nas home so soon on a Saturday, but he was in their bed butt ass naked waiting for her. Stori was on her last customer and she had already turned off her sign. Toi was staying the weekend with their grandmother and she was ready to lay up with her man for the rest of the night.

"Thanks Stori, I love it. I'll see you in two weeks," her client said as she looked at her hair in the mirror.

"You're welcome boo. See you in two weeks," Stori replied, right as her phone rang.

She collected her payment and waved to her customer as she answered the phone for Toi.

"Hey Stori," Toi said as soon her big sister answered

for her.

"Hey, my Stanka. What are you doing?" Stori asked as she made her way up the stairs.

"Nothing, but grandma and mommy just had a fuss," Toi giggled.

"For what?" Stori asked as she opened the fridge and grabbed some strawberries. She knew that Nas was upstairs waiting for her but she wanted to hear what Toi had to say first.

"Mommy called me and we were talking. She heard grandma talking in the background and she told me to tell her hello. Grandma called her an unfit mother and a gold digging tramp and they started arguing. Grandma snatched the phone from me and everything," Toi laughed.

"That old lady needs to stop," Stori snickered, right before her grandmother snatched Toi's phone again.

Stori sat there and listened as her grandmother told the same story that she'd been telling for years. According to her, Stori and Toi were the best things to ever come from Lady. Lorraine always said that Stori's father went to his grave not knowing that he was dealing with a hoe. Toi's father knew it because he had her after his brother. Lady was selfish but Stori wouldn't exactly say that she was unfit. She took care of them financially. She just wasn't there physically.

"The hell?" Nas questioned when he walked downstairs and saw Stori siting there on the phone. He had been waiting for what felt like forever and she still hadn't come to the room. He didn't know if she was still in the shop, so he put his clothes back on so that he could go see.

"I'm sorry boo. Thirty-seven minutes of listening to my grandma call my mama an unfit hoe and I'm over it," Stori said as she muted the phone.

"Man, I dozed off and everything," Nas said as he ate some of her fruit.

"I'm about to get rid of her," Stori promised.

"I hope so," Nas replied. He laughed when Stori put the call on speaker and he heard some of what her grandmother was saying. Stori kept trying to interrupt but she wouldn't let her get a word in.

"Okay grandma, Naseem just came home and he wants to talk. Love you and tell my Stanka that I love her too," Stori said before she was finally able to hang up.

"It's about damn time. I thought I was gon' have to beat my shit," Nas fussed as he picked her up from the bar stool.

Stori grabbed her phone from the counter and wrapped her legs around his body as they kissed and made their way upstairs. When Nas laid her in the bed, he pulled her leggings off right before he removed his shirt. Stori lifted her body up and made it easier for him to remove her underwear. He kissed her belly first and made his way down her body.

"Basement door," the alarm chimed, halting their movements.

"I thought you were done for the day," Nas said as he looked at her.

"I am done. My last customer left almost an hour ago," Stori replied as she grabbed her phone to look at the camera.

"Did you lock the door?" Nas asked as he put his shirt back on.

"Nas! Oh, my God!" Stori screeched.

"What's wrong?" he asked when he took in the panicked look on her face.

"Look," Stori said as she showed him her phone.

"Fuck!" Nas bellowed as he saw three masked gunmen downstairs in Stori's shop.

They were opening drawers and looking to see what was inside. It was an amateur's move but that bought him some time. Stori jumped up and put her clothes back on right before running to her closet. Nas went under the bed for his gun as he continued to watch the camera.

"Who the fuck is that?" Stori whispered.

"I don't know baby, but I need you to hide. I don't give a fuck about what they do to me, but I can't let nothing happen to you and my boys," Nas said in a hushed tone.

"Fuck that Naseem! My sons are going to know who their father is. We're not visiting your grave on Father's Day and birthdays. Them niggas came into the wrong house today," Stori fussed as she threw two big ass guns on the bed.

"I love the fuck out of you," Nas said as he walked over and kissed her.

"I love you too boo," Stori said as she grabbed two handguns and stood behind the closet door.

"Stay there baby. Whatever you do, don't come out of the closet. One of them niggas is coming up the steps," Nas said as he continued to look at the phone.

He wasn't about to give them a chance to come up to the bedrooms. He was about to meet them niggas halfway. He handed Stori the phone and made sure the guns that she gave him were fully loaded. Stori looked at the phone and held up two fingers, letting him know that two men were coming up the stairs. Nas nodded his head as he crept out of the room. Stori kept looking at the phone and less than a minute later, she heard gunshots rang out. The two men who were coming up the stairs ran for their lives as Nas let his guns rip. The third man who was still in the basement ran out of the house before they even got back down there. One of the other two must have felt brave because he turned around and starting shooting back. Stori gasped when Nas held his side and dropped one of the guns that he was holding.

"Fuck!" she yelled as she bolted from the closet like she wasn't carrying a double load.

Stori had two guns in her hands as she ran down the stairs and started shooting alongside her man. She hit one of them in the arm and he dropped his gun. Nas hit the other one in the back and he went down briefly. The men were done shooting but Nas and Stori weren't. They emptied their guns on the two men, hitting them both at least one more time. They left a trail of blood behind as they ran out of the house and away from the hail of bullets.

"Shit," Nas hissed as he held his bleeding side. He had never been shot before and it felt like fire was traveling through his body.

"Here baby. Apply pressure to it," Stori said as she grabbed a bunch of towels and pressed them to his side.

"Ahh! Fuck!" Nas groaned in pain.

"I'm sorry baby but I have to make sure you don't bleed out. I need to get you to a hospital. We can't call the police," Stori said as she helped Nas up the basement stairs.

He leaned up against the wall as Stori rushed to her bedroom to get her purse and keys. Remo was calling Nas' phone, but she didn't have time to stop and answer it. He seemed to always know when something was wrong and he was right on point that time. When Stori got back to Nas, he was lying on the kitchen floor motionless.

"Nas!" she yelled as she rushed over to him.

"I'm good baby. This shit hurts bad as fuck but I'm still breathing," he said as he slowly stood to his feet.

Stori helped him to her car in the garage and sped all the way to the hospital. She kept apologizing to Nas for what happened because she felt like it was all her fault. She was too careless and everybody always fussed at her about locking up. She had learned the hard way that she should have taken heed to their warnings.

"What do we tell them Nas?" Stori asked as she got closer to the hospital.

"Attempted robbery," he replied, knowing exactly what she meant.

They didn't do anything wrong, but Nas didn't want the police to know what really happened. Whoever was bold enough to come into Stori's house were as good as dead. Jail was too good of a punishment. Stori was mad with herself but he didn't blame her. If niggas really wanted to come in there, a locked door nor an alarm was going to stop them. Nothing like that had ever happened to her before, so he knew that he was who they were after. Putting his girl and sons in harm's way was a mistake that they were going to regret making.

"We're here baby. I'm going get somebody to come out and help you," Stori said as she jumped out of the car and ran into the hospital.

A few minutes later, three men came running outside with a stretcher. Stori was told to sit outside in the waiting room while they rushed Nas to the back. She used that time to call Remo and Jarvis to let them know what was up. She also closed her eyes and said a prayer for Nas and whoever was dumb enough to come after him.

Kalani was happy that she was wearing tennis shoes because Remo was dragging her down the hall of the hospital. His intuition was at an all-time high and he had been calling Nas for almost two hours. He and Kalani had just got dressed to go to Stori's house when she called and told him that Nas was in the hospital. Remo couldn't even drive and Kalani had to get them there in one piece. He sat on the passenger's side of the car smoking a blunt and staring out of the window.

"Excuse me but you can't smoke in here," one of the nurses said when Remo walked by the nurse's station.

"Fuck you. Try to stop me," he snapped as he continued to rush down the hall to where Stori said she was.

"I'm calling security," the nurse warned.

"Fuck them too! I'm ready for whatever!" Remo yelled as he continued to his destination.

"Baby, you can't smoke weed in the hospital," Kalani tried to reason.

"Man, fuck these people Kalani. My nerves are bad as hell right now. Weed and pussy are the only two things that can calm me down. Unless you're trying to fuck me in the hospital hallway, let me smoke," he replied.

"Just calm down Kareem," Kalani said as she squeezed his hand.

Her husband was in a foul mood and she didn't want anybody to set him off. Still, he couldn't be in the hospital around sick people putting loud in the air. When they got to the waiting room, Stori and Latrice were sitting there quietly. Stori's clothes were full of blood but she looked fine other than that. Kalani was surprised that Jarvis wasn't there but she knew that he wasn't too far away.

"Where's my brother?" Remo asked impatiently.

"He'll be fine Kareem. Jarvis spoke with the doctor a little while ago. They were able to remove the bullet and he didn't lose a lot of blood. They're getting him set up in a room and then we can all go back there. Now, I know that you're worried but you can't be in here smoking weed. Put it out and give it to me," Latrice demanded in a stern, yet calm voice.

Remo and Nas had mad respect for Latrice. Not many women would have done all that she had done for them. They were a handful but she stuck by her husband's side and helped him raise them. She treated them like her own and had always been there when they needed her. For that, they would always be grateful and do whatever she asked them to. Remo put the blunt out on the floor and handed it to his sister-in-law. Kalani visibly relaxed as she took a seat next to Stori.

"Are you okay boo?" Kalani asked as she grabbed her best friend's hand.

"I am now since I know that Naseem is good," Stori replied.

"What happened sis?" Remo asked her in a low tone as he squatted in front of her to make eye contact.

Stori looked around to make sure no one else was in the room before she ran the entire story down to him. Remo's face was a mask of anger and confusion. He was angry that someone was bold enough to run up on his brother and he was confused about who would do it. Nas didn't have any enemies that he knew of. Gavin wasn't a threat but that was an easy fix if he was.

"I just feel like this is all my fault. I got distracted on the phone and forgot to lock up after my last customer left," Stori said.

"This is not your fault Stori. You've been doing that for years and nobody ever did no shit like that before," Kalani noted.

"Exactly. But, man, I appreciate the fuck out of you, Stori. This shit could have went left real quick if you weren't using your head," Remo commented.

"Family of Naseem Donaldson!" the doctor yelled when he walked into the room.

"Yeah, I'm his brother," Remo said as he rushed over to him.

"Indeed you are. Wow. Identical twins. Well, you guys can come on back to visit. Mr. Donaldson will be sore for a while but, if all goes well, he'll be able to go home sometime tomorrow. We just want to monitor him overnight for bleeding and infection." The doctor smiled as he led them down the hall.

"Thank you so much." Latrice smiled as they opened the door and went into Nas' room.

Nas was sitting up in the bed with some pillows propping him up. His eyes looked low and droopy and they knew that he was full of pain meds.

"They got you on the good shit huh, bro?" Remo smiled as he walked over to his bed. Kalani shook her head when he moved the covers back and climbed in with him.

"Hell yeah," Nas said as he reached his hand out for Stori. She sat on the bed next to him and kissed his lips softly.

"How do you feel baby?" Stori asked as she rubbed his head.

"High as a kite," Nas smirked.

"Boy, Stori is the muthafucking truth. I need to let her train my baby to bust them guns. I already know I'm a dead man if niggas ever come in the house on us," Remo said while looking at Kalani.

"I'm glad you know it my nigga. My mama is a boring ass school teacher who lived a boring ass life. She never dated dope boys and we didn't own a gun. I didn't know nothing about the street life until I started hanging with Stori. The only thing I can bust is your car windows," Kalani said, making everybody laugh.

When the door opened a few minutes later, Jarvis walked in carrying some bags from Target. The store was right next to the hospital and he went there as soon as he

288

learned that Nas was okay. Hearing that his brother had been shot was one of his worst fears. He was thankful that it wasn't fatal though.

"Aww, fuck no! When did you niggas cut your hair?" Jarvis asked as he looked back and forth between his brothers. He knew which one was Nas because Stori was holding his hand. Other than that, he would have been lost.

"Calm down bro. Just check the tattoo," Nas said as he showed him his latest artwork.

"Here Stori, I got y'all some changing clothes and stuff. Y'all can come stay with us until y'all figure everything out," Jarvis said as he handed her the bags.

"You sound dumb as fuck. They're coming to stay with us. We got more than enough room for everybody," Remo replied.

"I really don't want to stay with anybody. I hate that I have to up and move Toi around like that," Stori replied.

"I know baby but it's only temporary. I told you that I was going to buy us a house. It'll just have to happen sooner than I thought," Nas said.

"I know Nas but, soon, it'll be five of us instead of three. I can't have two babies and not have a stable place to stay," Stori sighed worriedly.

"You know we got you, sis. Don't stress yourself and my nephews out worrying about that," Remo said, right as the door flew open.

Two policemen walked into the room and he smirked when he saw who one of them was. The nurse who he cursed out was right there with them with her snitching ass. She didn't call the hospital's security, she called the police instead. She could see that Remo was going to be trouble and their guards weren't equipped to handle that. Remo locked eyes with Kalani's ex, Jamar, and he seemed happy that he had the upper hand.

"There he is. He walked into the hospital smoking weed and he disobeyed my orders when I told him to get rid of it," the nurse said as she pointed at Remo. She was confused for a moment seeing another man who looked exactly like him. She remembered what Remo had on and was quickly able to identify him.

"Bitch!" Kalani yelled as she lunged at her. Thankfully, Latrice was right there to hold her back.

"Relax baby. No need in both of us going to jail," Remo replied as he blew her a kiss.

"I can't believe you, Jamar. You're really acting like a bitter bitch right now," Kalani argued.

"I'm just doing my job. Your husband needs to learn how to follow rules and so do you," he replied.

"Stand up and place your hands behind your back," one of the officers said as he walked over to Remo. Kalani started crying and Latrice rubbed her back in comfort.

"Are you fucking serious right now? Our brother is laid up in the hospital and y'all are trying to arrest him for a small misunderstanding?" Jarvis barked angrily.

"This hospital has a strict no smoking policy. We have sick people in here. Besides, he wasn't just smoking a regular cigarette, he was smoking weed," the nurse acknowledged.

"So what? He's not smoking it now. You can't be that concerned about the sick patients if you're coming in here harassing my brother. Miserable ass muthafucker. Don't worry about nothing bro. You know I'll be down there to get you. Niggas getting killed left and right and these stupid bitches up in here on this dumb shit," Jarvis fumed.

"You need to watch your mouth," Jamar warned.

"Or what? Freedom of speech muthafucker!" Jarvis snapped angrily.

"Damn bro. I knew you had it in you. I feel like a proud little brother right now." Remo smiled.

"Aye!" Nas called out to Remo as he said something to him in sign language.

"I got you, bro," Remo said with a smirk.

"This is some straight bullshit!" Kalani yelled angrily.

"Calm down baby. Trust me, I'll be sleeping in bed right next to you tonight," Remo assured her as he was led out of the room in cuffs.

"I told you that we would be seeing each other again," Jamar said as they stopped in the hallway. His partner was talking to the nurse and he used that time to taunt the man that he hated so much.

"Yep, you sure did." Remo nodded.

"You fucked with the wrong nigga," Jamar gritted as he gripped his wrist tighter.

"Nah fam, I think you did. Tell me, does your mother still work at city hall? I'm sure she does. That's probably how you got this job. What about your sister? Does she still work for the post office? I know your brother is a coach at the high school. Your mama got a nice ass house too. I'm sure your late father would be proud," Remo smirked as he watched all the color drain from Jamar's face.

"How… you… look, leave my family out of this. They didn't do anything to you," Jamar stammered as he looked at Remo in fear.

"And I won't do anything to them either. At least I hope I won't have to. I'm a fair man though, Jason. You leave me and mine alone and I'll be happy to return the favor. I can be nice when I want to be but that all depends on you." Remo smiled.

"The name is Jamar," he corrected.

"Yeah, I'm pretty sure you know that I don't give a fuck." Remo shrugged as the other officer walked back over to them.

"Uncuff him," Jamar said to his partner.

"What?" the officer yelled.

"You heard me. Uncuff him," Jamar repeated.

"You know I can't do that. We have a formal complaint that we have to address. I can't let him go just like that," the other officer objected.

"You can let him go the same way I let your sister's husband go two weeks ago. Uncuff him!" Jamar bellowed as his partner frowned. It pained him to do it but Jamar needed to be smart about everything. Remo was serial killer material and going to war with him wasn't worth it. His family meant everything to him and he would never put their lives in danger because of a childish vendetta. He had too much to lose and it wasn't that serious.

The other officer grabbed Remo roughly and took the cuffs off before storming away. He didn't like Remo's attitude and he hated that he had to let him go.

"You're a smart man Johnathan. Much smarter than you look." Remo smiled as he slapped him on the back and went back to his brother's room.

"Kareem! What did you do? Oh God. Please don't tell me that you escaped," Kalani worried as she rushed over to hug him.

"Hell no, girl. I told you to relax. I'm good. The nigga let me go," Remo replied as he gave his twin a knowing look.

Nas was that nigga. Remo didn't know how his brother found out some of the shit that he knew and it wasn't important. Nas had all kinds of connections and they always paid off. Nas was the friendlier one of the two and Remo needed to work harder at being nice. He wasn't much of a talker but Nas could use his words to finesse his way out of any situation. They both had different approaches to situations but it always benefitted them both in the end. Now, they had to put their heads together once again to figure out who had shot Nas. Once they did, it was lights out for them and anybody around them.

"Come on baby, I hate when you be looking like that," Nas said as he grabbed Stori's hand and kissed it. A little over a week had passed since he'd been shot and he felt like his old self again. He and Stori had just come back from her six month checkup and his sons were doing fine. Stori hadn't done hair since the incident at the house and he was returning to the barber shop for the first time once he dropped her off home. Mr. Herbert was the only one who knew what happened to him and he agreed to run things at the shop until he returned. They had been staying with Remo and Kalani, but they hadn't made a move to secure a permanent place of their own yet. Stori hated the way things were and he didn't know what to do to cheer her up. Lady was worried sick about her and Toi and she had been in town for the past week, making sure they were okay. Remo got Bee and Eno to help him clean up the house and it looked as good as new.

"I'm okay," Stori replied with a forced smile.

"I know that this is stressful baby but I got us. You be so worried about Toi and she seems happier than you are," Nas pointed out.

"Toi just loves you and Remo. All of us being under the same roof is like a dream come true for her. I just hate that I'm not able to do hair like I want to. I don't like turning my clients down," Stori sighed.

"Why can't you do hair? I got a whole beauty salon in the barber shop. You can even hire more stylists to work in there with you. We can be on some power couple shit and secure the bag together," Nas pointed out.

"Hell no Naseem. We cannot work together," Stori replied.

"Why not? You got something to hide?" Nas asked with a frown.

"Because Nas. We talk about shit in the hair salon. I don't need you all up in my mix like that," Stori replied.

"I'm happy to know that. You don't get to choose now. Working with me is your only option," he scowled.

"Boy, you got me fucked up. My clientele is huge and I can go work anywhere. I can have another shop by tomorrow if I wanted to," Stori noted.

"I hope you put some good insurance on that bitch too," Nas said.

"What does that have to do with anything?" Stori asked.

"Did I ever tell you that I used to play with fire as a kid? I'll have that shit looking like an abandoned building in less than an hour. Fuck with me if you think it's a game," Nas warned.

"You need help," Stori said while shaking her head.

"And you need to stop fighting me on everything. I got too much dick in my boxers to let you wear the pants. Ain't no need for you to trip anyway. The salon is all the way in the back with a separate entrance. We won't see your customers and we won't be able to hear what y'all are saying. I'll get the office redone and we can share it. I'll do whatever I need to do to make you feel comfortable. You can even change the name if you want to," Nas offered.

"No, the name is fine. I guess I have to start advertising the new location on Instagram. I still need at least another week to set everything up how I want it," Stori replied.

"I got you, baby. Whatever you want, I got you," Nas swore.

He took Stori to get something to eat before dropping her off at Remo and Kalani's house. No one really knew about Nas getting shot and that made it harder for him and Remo to get info. When Nas pulled up to the shop, Mr. Herbert was standing outside talking but he walked over as soon as he saw him.

"How you feeling Naseem?" the older man asked.

"Back like I never left. I get a lil ache every now and then but it's nothing that I can't handle," Nas replied.

"I'm happy that your ass is back. I'm over all this mess. I was about to go inside but I'm bringing my old black ass right back home," Mr. Herbert laughed.

"I appreciate you for looking out," Nas replied.

"Always. How is your girlfriend and those babies?" Mr. Herbert questioned.

"Everything is all good. We just went to the doctor before I came to work. I just convinced her stubborn ass to come work with me and run the salon part of the shop," Nas said.

"That's a good look. Keep all the money under one roof." Mr. Herbert nodded in approval.

"Facts," Nas said as he saw him off. Once Mr. Herbert was gone, Nas walked into the shop and greeted everybody.

"Man, I'm so damn happy to see you. I almost fainted when I saw that Mr. Herbert old ass was back," one of the barbers said as everyone else laughed.

"Nah, I just needed a lil vacation but I'm back," Nas replied as he walked to his work station.

He was very observant and he immediately noticed that something was different. The work station that once belonged to Carlton had been cleared and the key to the locker was dangling from the lock. One of the barbers noticed Nas staring and decided to speak up.

"That nigga Carlton just up and quit while you were off. Dude didn't even say nothing. He just packed up his shit and bounced." The man shrugged.

"I heard niggas talking at the pool hall and they said that his two lil brothers got shot. Them lil bad ass niggas be into all kinds of shit. Nobody is saying how it happened but that's what the word on the street is," another barber said.

"Yeah, I heard that too," one of the customers chimed in. Nas didn't even bother with a reply. He went straight to his office and called his brother.

"What's good bro?" Remo asked when he answered.

"I'm at the barber shop. Come fuck with me," Nas requested.

"I'm on my way," Remo assured him before he hung up.

He knew that Nas didn't like to discuss certain things over the phone. Whatever he had to say must have been important and he wanted to know what was up. Nas sat there deep in thought until his phone started ringing. He didn't recognize the number so he ignored it. When it rang two more times with the same number, Nas decided to see who wanted to talk to him so badly.

"Yeah!" Nas yelled into the receiver.

"Hello Naseem. How are you?" a deep voice echoed on the other end.

"The fuck is this?" Nas barked angrily, making the man on the other end chuckle.

"This is Latoya's husband, Richard," he replied in an unbothered tone. Nas had been around Lady's husband a few times when they invited them out to dinner. He was still baffled as to why the other man was calling him though.

"What's good Richard?" Nas asked.

"I'm in town until morning and I was wondering if we could meet up to discuss a few things," Richard replied.

"Yeah, I can meet you but I'll need about an hour," Nas said.

"That's perfect. I'll send you the address and I'll see you in an hour," Richard replied before hanging up.

296

Nas didn't know what that was all about but he was curious. He waited around for his brother and they sat in the office and talked once he got there. Nas told Remo everything that the other men had said and he too found the situation very strange. It was no coincidence that Carlton's two brothers got shot and he just up and disappeared. Nas instructed Remo to keep his eyes and ears open and he was going to do the same.

About an hour later, Nas was pulling up to the address that Richard had given him. Nas had never been in the ducked off area before and he had to check the address to make sure he went the right way.

"Lake Villa Estates," Nas said out loud as he read the sign. He came up on a security gate with a booth that looked like a small apartment. Nas was about to call Richard until one of the guards walked up to his car. Nas rolled down his window to see what the other man wanted.

"Good afternoon Mr. Donaldson. Mr. Hampton is waiting on you. Please follow me," the man said as he got in a security cart and opened the gate.

Nas followed behind him until they got all the way to the back of the estates. He stopped in front of a huge three-story white house that looked like a mini castle. Nas was even more confused than he was before. They had three cars parked in the driveway but he didn't recognize any of them.

"The fuck?" Nas mumbled as he looked around the beautiful home with the elaborate landscaping. He got out of the car at the guard's insistence and followed him to the huge double doors. He rang the bell once before Lady opened the door and smiled.

"Thank you, Douglas. Hello Naseem. Come on in," Lady said as she gave Nas a hug.

"Whose house is this?" Nas asked as he looked around in awe.

The outside didn't do the place justice and the inside was simply amazing. The floors were marble and they looked too perfect to even walk on. The ceilings were high and looked like they belonged in a cathedral. They had a staircase on both sides of the room that were the same marble print as the floors.

"As of thirty minutes ago, it's mine." Lady smiled. It wasn't hard to see why so many men were crazy about her. Lady was beautiful and so were her daughters.

"Damn," Nas mumbled as he continued to look around.

"Do you think Toi and Stori will like it?" Lady asked him.

"Hell yeah. This bitch is nice," Nas said, not bothering to hide his true colors in front of Lady. He didn't know it but his realness was what won her over.

"You're raw and honest Naseem. That's one of the things that I like about you. I told Stori from day one that Gavin was a pretender. He put on airs for other people and he wasn't husband material. A husband is supposed to be the head and I didn't see that leadership quality in him. I asked her not to marry him but I stood by her decision. I really didn't expect her to listen to me anyway. As you might have heard, I wasn't the best mother to her and Toi. Truthfully, I really didn't know how to be. I was an only child and I was spoiled and selfish. Taking care of somebody else besides myself was something that I never got used to. I love my babies but the only way I knew how to show it was through gifts and money. I want to be a good grandmother though, Naseem. I want to put somebody else first for a change and I'm gonna start with my grandsons," Lady replied.

"I understand," Nas said for lack of anything better to say. He followed Lady into a huge room where two women sat along with her husband.

"Naseem, I'm glad you could make it," Richard said as he stood up and shook Nas' hand.

Richard was a tall, slender man with specks of gray hair and greenish blue eyes. He looked intimidating to most, but he was always cool every time Nas was in his presence. Richard kept a smile on his face and an expensive cigar in his hand. He looked like the kind of man who would be married to an older white woman and he and Lady didn't really look compatible. Looks were deceiving though because Richard loved Lady endlessly. You could see it in his eyes whenever he looked at her. Nothing was too good for Lady or her girls.

"I'll leave you two to talk. Come on ladies. We can continue our discussion out on the patio," Lady said as she escorted the two women out of the room.

"Do you smoke cigars Nas?" Richard asked as he offered him one from a gold case with his initials on the front.

"Yeah, but not the same kind that you smoke," Nas smirked. The cigars that he smoked weren't as expensive and they were always filled with something loud.

"I know that you're a busy man Naseem, so I'll just get right to the point. I was made aware of the incident that happened at the house and I wasn't too happy about it. I don't have any biological kids but Toi and Stori are like my babies," Richard said.

"Okay," Nas said, encouraging him to go on.

"My wife is unhappy and that's a huge problem for me. Everything I do is to put a smile on her face and that's been missing lately. She's worried about the girls and she hasn't been sleeping too well at night. I need to rectify this issue and I want to help," Richard replied.

"Help how?" Nas questioned.

"I'm a man Naseem and I know how prideful we can be. That's why I'm willing to leave whatever we discuss just between the two of us. Stori doesn't have to know about this conversation," Richard said.

"What conversation? What are we even discussing? I'm confused." Nas frowned.

"I want to buy and decorate you and Stori a house. One of the ladies out back is our interior decorator and she and her team are ready to work. The other is our realtor and she's ready to show you a few of the available properties on the estates," Richard said like it was nothing. He spoke like a man who had more money than he'd ever spend. He was speaking of buying them a house as if he were buying them lunch or dinner. It wasn't a big deal to him but it was huge to Nas.

"Wait," Nas said as he held up his hand. "What estates?"

"These estates. I'm not trying to step on your toes Naseem. Stori told her mother that you were going to buy another house and I just wanted to offer my assistance. I make millions every year from other people's fuck ups. And believe me, they fuck up a lot. I just want my wife to be happy again. In no way am I trying to offend you," Richard noted. As crazy as it sounded, that was his first time being a homeowner too. He moved around too much to ever buy a home of his own.

"Shit, I'm not offended at all. I'm definitely taking you up on your offer but I have to let Stori know what's up. I can't make a decision on a house without her," Nas replied.

He would be a damn fool to turn down such a gracious offer. Pride was the sign of a foolish man and there was nothing stupid about him. People opened doors but it didn't make him less than a man to walk through them. He had to put his family first and he was thankful to Richard and Lady for their help.

"I understand and we can do this however you and Stori want to do it. Lady and I are just here to write the checks. All you and Stori have to do is tell them what you want and they'll make it happen. Hopefully, we can get everything done before the boys get here," Richard said.

"Definitely. I know Stori will be ready. We've been staying with my brother and she's not feeling that too much.

What do you and Lady plan to do with the other house?" Nas asked.

"It's Stori's house, so that's up to her. I can get my realtor on that too if she wants to sell it. With her having a fully functioning salon in the basement, I'm sure it'll sell in no time," Richard said.

"Yeah, she can get on that too because she's definitely selling it. I was never too fond of her having her business in the same place where she sleeps," Nas said as he stood to his feet.

"Is everything okay?" Lady asked when she walked back into the house with the two ladies following behind her. Richard stood up and hugged her as he smiled at her lovingly.

"Everything is perfect sweetheart. We're ready to proceed," he replied, making her visibly relax. Lady wasn't blaming Nas for what happened but she needed her daughters to be safe. She knew all about the lifestyle of a dope boy because she'd dealt with more than a few of them. Although Nas had a job, she knew that he still did his thing on the side.

"Thank you, baby." Lady smiled happily.

"Anything for you my love," Richard replied as he kissed her cheek.

"Hi Naseem. I'm Meredith and I'm the realtor who you'll be working with. Here is my card and I'll make myself available whenever you're ready." The woman smiled as she handed Nas her business card. The interior decorator introduced herself and handed Nas her business card too.

"I'm so excited. Both of my babies and my grandsons will be living close to me. I hope Stori likes the house next door. That would really make my day," Lady said as Richard smiled at her. Seeing his wife happy was all that mattered to him. Richard walked Nas outside, as Lady stayed behind and continued to talk.

"Stay in touch Naseem and let us know if you or the girls need anything," Richard said as he shook his hand.

"Will do and thanks for everything. I appreciate it and I know that Stori will too," Nas replied.

"It's my pleasure. And if you can, try to convince her to get the house next door," Richard replied with a hearty laugh.

Nas laughed too, even though he knew that the other man was serious. If Lady wanted it, Richard tried to make it happen. Nas got into his car and pulled off. He stopped at the house next door to theirs and it was just as nice. It wasn't as big but it was big enough. He wasn't sure how Stori would feel about it and he wasn't making a decision without her. Nas pulled out his phone to tell her the good news as he drove back to the barber shop.

Carlton pulled up in front of his house and parked in his driveway. The last two weeks had been hectic and he was happy that it was over. He had just gone with his mother to put his two little brothers on a plane to Kentucky. Their father lived there and he insisted that they come to live with him for a while. They were getting into too much trouble in New Orleans and they needed a change of scenery. The last straw for him and everyone else was learning that they had both been shot. One of them was worse off than the other and he had to undergo two surgeries to remove the bullet from his back. Carlton just assumed that they had gotten into their usual bullshit again until his little cousin told him what happened. Apparently, his two dumb ass brothers and cousin listened to Gavin and Corey and tried to rob Nas and his girl. Corey put together the entire plan and they were too stupid to see it for what it really was. They never even stopped to ask themselves why he didn't go with them if the plan was so solid. He sent them on a dummy mission and they failed miserably. Corey was known to hang with younger men because they were so much easier to manipulate.

As a result of their carelessness, Carlton had to quit his job at the barber shop and resort to making house calls to his customers. He was trying to find another shop to work in but he had been too busy dealing with his brothers to really focus. Thankfully, the streets weren't talking, so that was a good sign. All three of them wore masks and, hopefully, no one knew that they were behind it. Carlton had heard stories about Nas and his twin brother and he didn't need that kind of trouble. He didn't even give notice before he left the shop but he was sure that Nas didn't care. His booth rental was paid up, so he didn't owe him anything.

After finishing off the last of his blunt, Carlton got out of his car and headed inside. He saw the lamp on in the front room and his wife was sitting on the sofa when he opened the door. Their kids were with her mother and she was usually in the bed at that hour. When Carlton looked at the tears falling from her eyes, he knew right then that something wasn't right.

"What's wrong Drina?" he asked while looking at his wife. She didn't reply but he got his answer when the barrel of a gun was placed to the back of his head.

"Have a seat my man," Nas said as he pushed Carlton towards the sofa. Remo emerged from the darkness of the kitchen and stood right next to his brother. Drina was shaking and Carlton grabbed her hand to calm her down.

They caught Drina taking trash out of the house and they forced her back inside at gunpoint. She was scared and she told them exactly where Carlton was and what he was doing. Nas wasn't surprised to know that the lil niggas who shot him went out of town. Running was what most cowards did.

"Let's talk fam. And please, don't lie to me because I'm really not in the mood to play games," Nas said as he looked at him sternly.

304

"Man Nas, I swear, I didn't have shit to do with what happened to you," Carlton nervously denied.

"Maybe not but you know who did it. You showed your guilt when you up and left the shop with no word or explanation. That was a coward's move if I've ever saw one," Nas replied.

"I just didn't want to be implicated in some shit that I didn't have nothing to do with. I've never had any problems with you, Nas, and you know that," Carlton said.

"And you won't have any problems with me now if you tell me what I want to know. I already know that it was your little cousin and brothers who came in on me and my girl but them lil niggas are irrelevant to me right now. They don't know me but somebody else obviously does," Nas argued.

He had been asking around about Carlton and his family and he learned a few things. Carlton's brothers were lames who tried to sell weed just to get shoe money. They were dumb criminals and that was proven by the way they came into the house. Their moves were uncoordinated and they had no strategy. They were kids playing grown man games and they were going to lose their lives behind it. Nas really didn't want them though. He wanted whoever it was who put them up to it. The puppet was nothing without the puppet master.

"They're gone bruh. You won't have to worry about them ever again. They didn't have no beef with you, Nas. You just said yourself that they don't even know you," Carlton said. His little cousin was in Dallas by his aunt, so he was out of the picture too.

Remo was done listening to the bullshit that he was spitting. He cocked his gun and put it to Carlton's wife's head. They needed to know just how serious he was about his brother. He wouldn't hesitate to paint the walls with her thoughts if her husband didn't come clean soon.

"No! Please!" Drina cried.

"Come on man. She don't have nothing to do with this shit," Carlton pleaded.

"Last chance nigga. I would hate to take a mother away from her kids but shit happens. My brother is not as nice as I am, so you might want to start talking," Nas sighed.

"It was Gavin man. He was mad at you and Stori and he set that shit up," Carlton snitched.

He would never give up his cousin but Gavin was on his own. Although Corey put him in a fucked up position, he was still family.

"What else do you know?" Nas questioned.

"That's it man, I swear," Carlton answered.

"That's bullshit. I used to see you and that nigga Gavin talking all the time. For all I know, you could be in on it too," Nas snapped.

"I haven't seen or talked to Gavin since he left the shop. I didn't even know that my little brothers knew him," Carlton swore.

"Just kill the nigga and his bitch so we can go. He's obviously trying to protect somebody," Remo barked angrily as Drina cried hysterically.

"All I know is that Gavin works in Irvin's barber shop now. My lil brothers hang around that way selling weed. That's probably how they met Gavin," Carlton lied, trying hard to spare his cousin's life.

"Make no mistake about it, if I find out that you're lying to me, you'll be seeing me again. And don't think your brothers will be safe out there in Kentucky either. Even your kids who are spending the night in Harvey by your mother-in-law can get it," Nas warned, as Carlton's eyes grew wide with fear. He started shaking just as much as his wife was when Nas mentioned that.

"And the nigga is cheating on you, baby girl. He was at the hotel with some strong face, drag queen looking bitch a few days ago," Remo said, as Carlton looked at him in shock.

Those niggas were like the modern day Sherlock Holmes. They knew shit that other people wouldn't normally care about. Carlton hadn't cheated on his wife in years but the temptation was too great. His wife swore that she would divorce him if he cheated again and that scared him straight for a while. The fact that he'd started dealing with the mother of one of his young customers a month ago wasn't public knowledge. They were very discreet and careful. How the twins knew was a serious mystery to him.

"You're confused, huh? You're torn between calling the police on us and beating the dog shit out of your husband for cheating on you. I can see it all in your eyes. Trust me, fucking him up is a wiser decision than calling the police on us. You won't lose your life that way," Nas smirked as he looked at Drina before he and Remo made their way out of the house. They heard the roaring of motorbikes a minute or so later and Carlton jumped up to lock the door.

"I'm sorry about what just happened baby but you know we can't get the police involved. We'll be dead before they even get behind bars," Carlton said.

"I'm staying the night at my sister's house," Drina said as she rushed down the hall to their bedroom.

"You don't have to do that baby. I'll get us a room for the night," Carlton offered.

"I don't want to be anywhere around you right now," Drina snapped angrily.

"What! I know you don't believe that shit that them niggas just said," Carlton fussed.

"It's crazy, right? Them niggas had a gun to my head and threatened my life. But yeah, I believed every word they said. They have nothing to lose Carlton. What would they gain by telling me that you're cheating? You're a fucking liar and you lied to them too. I know you're trying to protect Corey, but it's fucked up that you would risk our lives to do it. I can bet my last dollar that his shady ass wouldn't have done it for you," Drina fumed as she packed her a bag.

Carlton and his entire family better pray that she never ran into the psycho twins again. If she did, she was giving Corey up and anybody else who she thought had anything to do with what happened. Unlike her husband, she didn't give a fuck about Corey because he didn't give a fuck about anybody else.

Irvin turned off his sign, alerting would be customers that he was closed for the night. He had a crowd earlier that day and two of his barbers weren't even at work. Gavin had been off for the past week and the other man was always unreliable. It was cool with him either way because he'd made enough money to get him through the rest of the month.

"I'm closed!" Irvin yelled when he heard the front door to his shop chime.

He was sweeping up the floor when two men walked in, making him do a double take. He had seen twins before but they looked too much alike. The shit was eerie if he had to say so himself.

"Do it look like we need our hair cut nigga?" Remo asked as he took a seat in one of the barber chairs.

"How can I help you?" Irvin asked.

"We're looking for Gavin. And before you lie, please keep in mind that I'm tired, hungry and in need of some pussy. Make this easy on yourself and answer the question. I'm trying to get home to my girl," Nas said as he sat in the chair next to his brother and put his gun on his lap.

The past week had been hectic but in a good way. Stori and Toi were excited about getting another house and they picked one that they fell in love with. It wasn't the house that was next door to Lady's but it was on the same street. Lady and Richard's house was the second one on the block and theirs was about five house down. It was walking distance and she was satisfied with that. The place was huge, but Richard wrote the check without even blinking an eye. Toi was sold on the endless pool in the yard and Stori fell in love with the enormous kitchen. The interior decorator had been meeting with them every day and they were looking over some things that Stori wanted done to the house. Nas really didn't care about any of that. The only time he voiced his opinion was when it came to his boys. Stori was trying to do some Disney bullshit in their room and he wasn't feeling it. Other than that, she was happy and that was all that he cared about.

"Gavin is not here," Irvin said, stating the obvious.

"Duh muthafucker," Remo spat angrily.

"When do you expect him to return?" Nas asked calmly.

"I really don't know man. He just told me that he was taking a week off. He didn't say why and I didn't ask," Irvin swore.

He was pissed that Corey had recommended Gavin to him. The nigga looked goofy as fuck but he was obviously in some bullshit. The niggas who were sitting in his shop did not come there to play. Irvin was done with the street life and he didn't want to get pulled back in.

"That's your story?" Nas asked him.

"That's all I know. I don't really know dude like that. The nigga told me that he was looking for a job and I hired him. He's my employee, not my friend," Irvin replied.

Nas stared at him for a while, trying to see if he detected any nervousness. The man seemed to be telling the truth but he still needed answers. Going to Irvin's shop wasn't on his list of things to do, so he didn't have time to ask around about him. He was definitely going to get some info from his sources for future references though.

"Call him," Nas demanded as he looked at Irvin.

"And say what?" Irvin asked.

He had been in the streets for a while before he went legit and he knew how it went. He wasn't afraid of the two men in his shop. He knew that if they wanted to kill him, it would have already been done by now. They wanted answers and a dead man couldn't talk.

"Fire his bitch ass. After this, I'm sure you don't want him working in your shop no more anyway," Nas replied.

"Fuck no. I got kids to think about," Irvin replied angrily. He dialed Gavin's number and waited for him to pick up.

"What's good Irvin?" Gavin asked when he picked up the phone.

"Where you at nigga?" Irvin asked.

"I'm on my way back from Texas. I had to help my daughter's mother move. That's why I needed the week off," Gavin replied, as Nas and Remo looked at each other.

They knew that Misty and Milan were originally from Texas, but they had no idea that they had moved back. Nas was hoping that Milan's disgusting ass left too. Maybe that's why she hadn't been bothering him. That and the fact that he threatened to end her miserable ass life if she did.

"Tell that nigga that Nas and Remo came here looking for him," Nas whispered, as Irvin nodded his head in understanding.

"Aye, some niggas named Nas and Remo came here looking for you. I don't know what the fuck you did but I can't have that around my shop," Irvin said.

"What did you tell them?" Gavin asked nervously.

"The fuck you mean nigga? I don't know shit about you other than your name and phone number. But, I need you to come get your shit. This ain't gon' work. I don't need my shop to be hot like that," Irvin replied.

"Man, fuck them niggas. They ain't gon' do shit but talk. It's cool though, fam. I'll send somebody to get my shit soon," Gavin said before he hung up in his face.

He was talking all that shit but he was scared to death. He knew that Nas and Remo were more than just talk. He had never witnessed them do anything but a lot of niggas feared them. He would never admit it but Gavin was one of them. He was no fool and he wasn't going anywhere near Irvin's shop again. He needed his supplies but he would have to ask one of his parents to get it for him.

"We're all talk but his bitch ass is scared to come get his shit. I bet you a stack that his hoe ass gon' send his mama or daddy to get it for him," Nas said, as Remo laughed.

"Good looking fam. This is for your trouble," Remo said as he sat three crisp hundred dollar bills on the counter for Irvin.

"Enjoy this and, if you want more, come to Twin Tails Strip Club and fuck with us," Nas said as he handed Irvin some weed that smelled good as hell.

He nodded at both men in admiration as they left his shop. He'd heard about the twins before but he'd never seen them. He'd been to their club a few times and it was always lit. Irvin locked up his shop once they left and finished sweeping. Once he was done, he grabbed the weed that Nas had left him and rolled himself a blunt.

"Damn! This shit is official. Them niggas just got a new customer," Irvin said as soon as he took his first hit. He grabbed his keys and prepared to leave. He wasn't about to go home though. He was about to hit up Twin Tails and spend some money with his new weed suppliers.

"Good looking fam," Gavin's customer said when he paid him and got out of his chair.

Two weeks had passed since he stopped working at Irvin's shop and Gavin had another job already. It was at an old, outdated barber shop but he quickly became the man to see. The shop was owned by two brothers and they couldn't cut for shit. Gavin had taken all of their customers and gained a few of his own. He was making some nice money and the older crowd were good for tipping. His father had gone to Irvin's shop to get his supplies and he put a word in for Gavin with one of his old friends. Before Gavin became a barber, his father had been a faithful customer at that same shop for years.

Gavin had been laying low and staying out of the way. He felt like a damn fool for trusting Corey and now he had Nas and Remo gunning for him. Corey never once mentioned his previous history with Stori. He just had Gavin believing that he was trying to hit a lick. Gavin never knew that he had a personal vendetta against her, even though he swore he didn't. Not to mention he had Milan in his ear calling all the shots. She hated Nas and Stori more than anybody and she wanted them both dead. Corey's stupid ass sent kids to do the job of a man and they fucked everything up and almost lost their lives instead. Gavin ran into Carlton at the gas station and he gave him the rundown of everything that happened. Gavin never knew that Carlton was the one who had the twins gunning for him. He was too trusting and that was proving to be his downfall.

"It's closing time young man. These old bones can't take standing up all day no more," one of the brothers said as he looked over at Gavin.

They usually closed the shop before dark. Since Gavin started working there, they started staying open later and making more money. It didn't matter that they lost a few of their customers. They were happy to have someone young in the shop with fresh new ideas.

"That's cool with me. I'm tired as hell my damn self," Gavin replied.

He felt like he'd been on the go more than usual lately and he needed a break. After spending two weeks at his house, Misty and Summer finally made the move back to Texas. Gavin and his mother went there for a week to keep Summer while she got settled. They stayed in a hotel and let Misty do what she needed to do. Gavin had never been to Beaumont but it wasn't that bad. He went to a club and enjoyed being in a place where no one knew him. He'd even met a chick while he was there and took her on a date. The only reason why he even approached her was because she reminded him of Stori. Gavin thought about Stori often and it always left a bad taste in his mouth. He'd never loved another woman the way he loved her and she broke his heart in the worst way imaginable. He and Stori would be officially divorced soon and that was something that he never fathomed.

"Maybe we can see about giving you a key to the shop soon. We'll give it a little more time to see how everything goes," one of the old men said as they all walked out together.

As soon as Gavin got into his car, he called his friend who he met in Texas. He and his parents agreed to visit Summer at least twice a month. If all went well, he would be visiting his female companion too. She had never been to New Orleans, so she and Gavin made plans for her to visit whenever time permitted. They always had lots of festivals in the city and he wanted to show her around. He couldn't do that if someone was after him though. He hadn't seen or heard anything from Nas and Remo since Irvin called him and he was hoping that everything blew over soon.

Gavin had just hung up the phone when he pulled up to the gates of his apartments. He entered the code to get in right as a black car pulled up on the side of him. When two masked figures jumped out of the car with guns, Gavin tried to duck. His car was sprayed with bullets and a few of them hit his body. Gavin had never felt anything so painful before and he prayed that he never had to again. He seemed to think about everything that he'd ever done wrong and he found himself repenting for his sins. It was crazy how he felt like enjoying life at a time that he could possibly be dying. The pain had him going into shock and everything faded to darkness soon after.

"The fuck we got on masks for? I wanted his bitch ass to see me," Remo fussed, as Nas sped away from the scene in Bee's car.

"No face, no case," Nas replied as he took the mask off and threw it in the back seat.

"I hope the nigga ain't dead. That way we can come back and do the shit all over again." Remo frowned.

"Stupid ass probably thought he was home free since niggas ain't been saying shit about him," Nas fumed.

Just like he'd assumed, Gavin sent his pops to Irvin's shop to get his shit. Nas and Remo had been lurking around the shop for days waiting for it to happen. They followed Gavin's father to his house and Gavin showed up a short time later. Nas had been knowing where he lived and worked for over a week but he wasn't in a hurry. He wanted to catch Gavin off guard and that's exactly what he did.

"I don't know bro, I still feel like some shit ain't right. That nigga Gavin is a duck. I just can't see him sending some lil niggas at you like that on his own," Remo spoke up.

"I said the same thing. Somebody is in his ear. I just have to find out who. Shit, I don't have time to focus on that right now. We're in the process of moving and Stori's baby shower is coming up. Fuck them niggas for right now," Nas replied.

"You think Stori's stepdaddy might wanna adopt me? Ole boy out here buying houses and shit. That's my type of dude," Remo said, as Nas laughed.

"You're focused on the wrong thing right now. You need to do what I told you to do," Nas replied.

"Yeah bro, I am. I hate school man. You know a nigga got ADD. I can't sit still for too long. And you know I get anxiety when it's time to take test. I be knowing the shit but my mind go blank the minute it's placed in front of me," Remo pointed out.

"That's why you need to work on being nicer. All you have to do is find a nigga like Gavin to do the shit for you," Nas laughed.

"Hell no, bro. You know I don't really like people." Remo frowned.

"Don't even trip bro. I'll come through that bitch and take the test for you. It ain't like I don't already know the shit. We got this," Nas assured him.

"You know I'll follow wherever you lead." Remo nodded.

"I'm trying to think of the bigger picture. All we need is for you to become a licensed barber and shit will be sweet from there. Truthfully, I can teach you how to cut but you need that certification under your belt," Nas noted.

"I'll sign up for classes tomorrow," Remo promised him.

Nas was trying to make some things happen. The building that was right next to the barber shop was going up for sale. He was cool with the owner and Nas told him that he was interested in buying it. If all went well, Nas planned to knock down some walls and expand the shop. That way,

316

he could sell the hair and other hair products right in the shop and he wouldn't have to worry about renting out another space. Kalani could still run it but she would be in the same shop with them. Once Remo got certified to cut, he could work in the shop and they would all be getting money together. Although Remo loved the idea, the thought of going to school annoyed him. Still, to make sure that he and his family ate well, he would do what he had to do just like always.

Gavin's eyes fluttered a little before he finally opened them fully. His vision was blurry and it took a while for him to really see clearly. When he did, he tried to sit up. The pain that coursed through his entire body made that almost impossible.

"No baby, don't try to sit up," his mother, Karen, said as she gently pushed him back down.

"How do you feel son?" his father asked him.

"Like shit," Gavin managed to say through his aching, dry throat.

"Well, after being shot five times and in a hospital bed for three days, that's to be expected," his mother noted.

"Three days?" Gavin questioned in shock.

"Yes, you've been doped up and sleeping so much," his mother replied.

Besides being shot up, Gavin couldn't remember much else after that. He remembered the pain being so bad that he passed out but that was about it. He didn't remember how he got out of the car and he didn't remember being taken to the hospital.

"What happened son? Do you know who did this to you?" his father asked.

"I just want to know why," Karen said.

Gavin knew who had done it to him and he definitely knew why. Unfortunately, he would never tell that to his parents. Although the shooters wore masks, Gavin could recognize Nas and Remo's build from a mile away. He should have known that they weren't going to let him off the hook so easily. Gavin was just pissed that he was the only one that was being punished. He needed to get at Corey to let him know what was up.

"No, I don't know what happened or why. I had just pulled up to my gate when a car pulled up and started shooting. It might have been a case of mistaken identity," Gavin grunted as pain shot through his body.

"That's bullshit Gavin. Now, I don't doubt that people are victims of mistaken identity, but I seriously doubt that you were one of them. You did something to piss somebody off. I just hope they don't come after me and my husband behind whatever mess you made," Karen fussed.

"Maybe he needs to go visit my mother in Charlotte for a while," his father suggested.

"What good would that do Gordon? If they wanted him to come out of hiding, they would use us to do it," Karen pointed out.

"Can y'all stop talking about me like I'm not right here? Nobody is after me and nobody will come after y'all." Gavin frowned in annoyance.

One thing his father said resonated within him though. Leaving New Orleans wasn't such a bad idea. Besides his parents, there was nothing left for him there. He had no friends and, soon, he would no longer have a wife. He couldn't see himself moving to Charlotte though. He liked the area when he visited but staying with his grandmother wasn't happening. If anything, he would relocate to Beaumont to be closer to his daughter. As if on cue, his hospital room door opened and Misty walked in carrying Summer.

"Hi," Misty spoke as she smiled awkwardly.

Gavin's parents tolerated her because of Summer but they weren't too fond of her. She was a whore in their eyes and their son was too. They loved their granddaughter and that was the only reason they were cordial with her. Summer was a year old and they had already missed out on so much of her life. Karen put her disdain for Misty aside and called to tell her what happened. She deserved to know since Gavin was her daughter's father. Karen didn't expect her to come but she was happy to see Summer.

"Hey grandma's baby. You look so pretty," Karen said as she smiled at Summer.

Her heart was filled with joy when Summer reached her hands out for her grandmother to hold her. She had been around them enough to know them and that was all that Karen wanted.

"Did she eat anything? I'm about to head to the cafeteria," Karen said.

"She ate while we were on the way but she's probably hungry again," Misty replied.

"Come on, I'll walk with y'all," Gordon said as he opened the door for his wife and granddaughter to walk out of.

"How do you feel Gavin?" Misty asked.

"How do you think I feel? I got shot the fuck up," Gavin snapped.

"You can kill the attitude after I drove for four hours to come check on your ungrateful ass," Misty replied.

"My bad Misty. Shit is just all fucked up right now," Gavin said as he ran his hand across his face.

Even that hurt to do and he grimaced in pain. He was happy to be alive but he was sure he wouldn't stay that way if he stayed in New Orleans. Nas might have a little heart, but Remo would kill him and feed his remains to the sharks. After being shot, Nas would probably want to do the same.

"Do you know who shot you?" Misty asked.

"Those identical psychos," Gavin replied.

"Nas and Remo!" Misty shouted.

"Stop talking so damn loud girl. And don't tell nobody else that shit either," Gavin ordered.

"What did you do?" Misty asked.

"I got caught up in some bullshit with Corey and your shady ass sister." Gavin frowned.

"Damn Gavin. If they find out that you're alive, you won't be for very much longer," Misty pointed out.

"I already know and that's why I need your help," Gavin said.

"With what?" Misty inquired.

"I need to get the fuck out of New Orleans. I might need to crash by you for a little while until I can get my shit together. I got some money saved up so I can pay you," Gavin stated.

"I'll tell you like you told me when I needed a place to stay. I'm only allowing you to stay with me because of our daughter. And I would never charge you anything. You made me feel very welcome at your house and didn't charge me a dime. A favor for a favor," Misty replied.

"Corey and your sister better sleep with one eye open," Gavin said.

"Fuck Milan. I don't give a damn what happens to her. That bitch was willing to let me and my baby be homeless." Misty frowned.

"I can't lie and say that I didn't do nothing, but I shouldn't be the only one in the hospital. All I did was provide a little info. They were the ones who planned it out. Shit still went left and I almost lost my life behind it," Gavin replied.

"Well, I'm happy that you're okay. I got a room for the night but me and Summer are leaving in the morning. Just let me know whenever you plan to come," Misty replied.

"Shit, I'll be there as soon as they let me out of this damn hospital. I'm getting the fuck out of New Orleans," Gavin swore.

He was happy that he still had a cordial relationship with Misty because he needed her right now. He would never deal with her romantically again but they had to see each other because of Summer. Gavin had some money saved up but it wasn't much. He knew that his parents would help him out and he needed that now more than ever. If all went well, Beaumont was going to be his new home for a while. He was happy that he'd met someone on his visit there, so he wouldn't lack companionship. His daughter was in Texas and, hopefully, his new woman too.

"Fuck baby. This shit feels so good," Nas moaned as he bit and sucked on Stori's neck. She had her legs wrapped around his waist as he bounced her up and down his length.

"They're calling us Naseem. We have to go open up the gifts," Stori replied as she threw her head back in pleasure.

Stori was a little over seven months pregnant now and they were at their baby shower. She wasn't expected to go full term with the babies and Lady didn't want to take any chances. The hall was packed with all their family and friends, but Nas didn't care. He wanted some and nothing was going to stop him from getting it. The bathrooms seemed to always be crowded, so Nas pulled her into a small storage closet in the kitchen. Lady had all the food catered, so they weren't worried about anyone coming in there. They really didn't have a reason to unless they needed more cups or napkins.

"I'm almost done baby," Nas said as he quickened his pace. They were on the microphone calling for them but they were too busy to answer.

"Where the fuck is my brother? I know I didn't see him leave!" Remo yelled when he walked into the kitchen. Nas knew that if anybody was gonna come looking for him, it would be his overly protective brother.

"I checked the women's bathroom and Stori wasn't in there," Kalani replied.

"I checked the men's bathroom too. Is there a back door around here somewhere? Maybe he went outside to smoke," Remo assumed.

"I don't know but he wouldn't have taken Stori outside with him for that," Kalani pointed out.

"Man fuck! Roll me up something baby. You know my nerves are bad as fuck right now," Remo said as he paced the floor.

"Relax Kareem. They didn't leave because the car is still outside," Kalani noted, right as something fell in the kitchen.

"The fuck was that?" Remo questioned.

He and Kalani looked around, trying to figure out where the noise had come from. Kalani walked over to the storage closet and tried to open the door.

"Who's in there?" she yelled as he continued to twist the knob. When the door opened slightly, Nas stuck his head out with a frown covering his face.

"Stall them for me, Kalani. I need like five more minutes," Nas begged.

"The fuck!" Remo yelled as he walked over to where his brother was. He didn't see Stori's face but he saw her legs wrapped around his brother's waist. Remo fell out laughing while Kalani only shook her head.

"These dummies went missing at their own baby shower just to sneak off and fuck," Kalani said.

"Did y'all find Nas and Stori yet?" Toi asked when she walked into the kitchen. Remo hurriedly closed the door to the storage closet, so she wouldn't see anything.

"Come on baby girl. They said that you can start opening the gifts until they come back," Remo said, making Toi smile.

He led Toi back into the room and told everybody what was up. About twenty minutes later, Nas and Stori reappeared and started helping Toi open everything. Lady was always so extreme with everything that she did. She hired a moving company to pick up all of Stori's gifts and deliver them to the house. Although it wasn't completely done, most of the house was livable. The only thing that had to be decorated now was the living room and two of the spare bedrooms. They had moved in about a week ago and Stori was happy that they were stable once again.

"Who the fuck bought these non-matching ass outfits? Why would they buy them something different when they know they're twins?" Remo fussed as they put the babies stuff away.

He and Kalani were helping Nas and Stori fold and hang up the babies clothes. Every time Remo saw something that didn't match, he tossed it to the side angrily.

"Put that stuff in the closet Kareem. Just because they're twins doesn't mean that they have to match all the time," Kalani noted.

"Don't be trying to cause a division between my nephews Kalani." Remo frowned.

"You can't be serious. They're not even here yet," Kalani laughed.

"It doesn't matter. Don't be trying to break their bond," Remo said.

"What bond Kareem?" Kalani inquired.

"The one that they're forming right now. Bonding starts in the womb. See, you came into the world by yourself, so you wouldn't understand that," Remo said.

"What do you plan to do with all the stuff that you put to the side?" Kalani questioned.

"Donate that shit," Remo answered.

"What! Hell no, Remo. Nothing is even wrong with it," Stori argued.

"Maybe not but it doesn't match," he shrugged.

"Don't worry about it baby. It'll be replaced," Nas said, not wanting to argue with his twin.

He understood Remo in a way that Stori and Kalani never would. Remo wanted to make sure that his nephews shared a bond like the one he had with Nas. That was as important to him as breathing. They wore matching clothes up until the day their parents were killed. Jarvis stopped doing it after that because their clothes helped him to tell them apart.

"You need us to do anything else while we're here friend?" Kalani asked Stori.

"No, that's it for now. All those diapers and wipes will have to stay in the garage for now. I don't want their room to be too cluttered," Stori replied.

She and Nas walked Kalani and Remo outside and saw them off. Once they got back inside, Stori took her shower and went straight to the bed.

"Are you awake Stori?" Toi asked when she knocked on the door.

"Yeah Stanka, come in!" Stori called out.

Nas was out back smoking, so she pulled back the covers for Toi to lay in the bed with her. A lot had changed over the past few months and Stori made it a point to always see how Toi was feeling. Not only had she and Gavin separated, but she had started dating Nas soon after. They moved out of their house suddenly and they were working in a different shop now too. Not to mention the two baby boys that she had growing in her belly. They'd had a busy year and she didn't want her baby sister to be affected by any of it. Toi seemed happy about all the changes, but Stori always had to be sure.

"Seemi and Keemi got so much stuff from the baby shower," Toi said, referring to the babies.

"They did but we have to work on some better nicknames Stanka," Stori laughed.

"I can't give them a nickname until we meet. Remember what you said? You had to see me first before you decided what you wanted to call me," Toi said.

"Yep and you've been my Stanka ever since then," Stori said as she kissed her cheek.

326

"Can I ask you something Stori?" Toi inquired.

"Always," Stori replied.

"Am I old enough to talk on the phone with boys?" Toi asked, making Stori's heart skip a beat.

"Why? Did a boy ask for your number?" Stori questioned.

"Yeah," Toi blushed.

"Did you give it to him?" Stori inquired.

"No, but he gave me his. I wanted to ask you first before I gave him mine," Toi replied, right as Nas walked into the room.

"What's up pretty girl?" Nas asked as he smiled at Toi.

"Nothing. I was just talking to Stori about something," Toi replied.

"You good?" Nas questioned as he looked at her.

"Yeah, I'm good. Do you think I'm old enough to talk on the phone with boys Nas?" Toi asked him. Stori was shaking her head saying no, but Nas ignored her.

"Yeah, I don't see nothing wrong with it. Just make sure you let that nigga know about me and Remo. He don't want no smoke," Nas replied.

"He's nice. He won't cause any problems." Toi smiled as she got out of the bed and rushed out of their bedroom.

"Why did you tell her that Naseem? I don't want my baby dealing with none of these dirty ass lil boys," Stori fussed.

"Don't do that Stori. I know girls Toi's age that already have babies. She didn't even have to tell you anything. Don't have her scared to come talk to you. Y'all have a good relationship and you want it to stay that way," Nas said as he laid down next to her.

"I'm so not ready for this. Next thing you know, she'll be wanting to go out on dates." Stori frowned.

"And you should let her," Nas replied.

"You must be crazy!" Stori yelled.

"Would you rather her date with your blessing or start fucking without it? I'm telling you baby, don't fight her on something so simple because she won't come to you the next time around. Shit, I already had three sex partners by the time I was her age. Talking on the phone ain't nothing," Nas said.

"Oh God. I hope I don't have to go through that with my babies," Stori sighed.

"Man, I'm not stressing myself out with that shit. I'm giving them niggas some condoms and sending them on their way," Nas said.

"Really Naseem?" Stori replied.

"Really what? Me and Remo gave Jarvis hell. I already know the shit gon' come back on me and I'm ready for it." Nas shrugged.

"But, how is that fair to me? I wasn't a problem child. I didn't give my mama no trouble at all. Why do I have to suffer because of the shit you did when you were younger?" Stori questioned.

"You should have checked my resume first," Nas laughed.

"I'm getting my tubes tied after this," Stori huffed.

"Nah, we need a girl first and then you can close up shop. And when are we getting married? I'm tired of asking the same damn question," Nas argued.

"Calm down Naseem. Both of our divorces were just finalized," Stori laughed.

"That don't mean shit to me. I'm not waiting forever Stori. Don't make me force your hand," Nas warned.

"You can't make me marry you," Stori said as she laughed harder.

"The only nigga you gon' be playing Bonnie and Clyde with is me. I should have took you from that nigga when Remo told me to. We would have already been married by now. That's what I get for being nice and shit," he frowned as he spoke of her ex-husband.

Nas got word that Gavin wasn't dead but he really didn't care. Remo wanted to finish him off but it wasn't even worth it. He got the message and that much Nas was sure of. Being as hardheaded as he was known to be, Remo still crept over to his house to finish the job. Gavin was a lucky ass nigga because he had already moved and cleared the house out by then. A few people said that he moved out of town but Nas wasn't so sure. What he did know was that they hadn't seen or heard from him since they riddled his car and body with bullets. They were still curious as to who Gavin was working with because he wasn't smart enough to plan anything on his own. That was a mystery that Nas wasn't sure would ever get solved.

"I should have my body back right by the time the twins make six months. We can start planning something then," Stori conceded.

"Six months! I'm not waiting that long Stori," Nas argued.

"You really don't have a choice. Too much is happening too fast and I need time to process it all. I don't even have a ring and you're talking about getting married," Stori noted.

"That's an easy fix. No worries love, you'll have one tomorrow," Nas assured her.

"We're still waiting Naseem. I let you have your way with everything else but I'm not compromising on this one," Stori replied.

"Alright baby, I'll wait." Nas smiled as they cuddled in the bed and watched some tv.

He gave in too easily for Stori but only time would tell what his motive was. She knew Nas well enough to know that he always had one. There was always a reason why he did everything. Unfortunately, Stori didn't always understand or like it.

WOR$T CA$E $CENARIO

E31119560F

E31119560F

30

ONE DOLLAR

"S hiiiiit!" Milan screamed as she came and her entire body shook.

Corey was like a famished kitten lapping up milk as he slurped up her juices. If he wasn't good for nothing else, he could eat pussy like a pro. That and the bomb ass weed that she now got for free had Milan keeping him around longer than she should have.

"Come on man, let me hit it one time," Corey begged as he climbed on top of her.

"Nigga please. Your head game is official and your weed is bomb, but I'm worth way more than that. You need to step your game all the way up before you can get this pussy," Milan replied as she pushed him away from her.

"Your ass wasn't saying all that when I gave you the deposit to move though," Corey snapped angrily.

"That lil five hundred dollars wasn't shit. I used to make more than that in a few hours when I was dancing,"

Milan replied.

Corey had her all the way fucked up. She didn't have as much as she used to but she wasn't broke. Without Nas and Misty's help, she couldn't afford to keep her three bedroom apartment, so she moved into a smaller one. She now lived in a one bedroom fourplex in a quiet neighborhood. Milan finessed the deposit money out of him only because she didn't want to use her own money. She had another nigga pay her rent up for three months and she was straight. She sold the extra furniture that she didn't need and added that money to her stash too. She was a hustler, so she would never go without. Corey was too dumb to see that he was being used.

"Whatever man. I'm not begging for no pussy when I get the shit thrown at me damn near every day," Corey fumed as he got up and started to get dressed.

"If it's being thrown at you so much, maybe you need to catch that shit. Then, you can stop asking me all the time," Milan said as she scrolled through her Instagram.

She had stop commenting under Nas' posts for a while but she was back at it. That nigga had Stori living in a mansion, but he refused to even buy a house with her. Stori was having twins and Milan was furious. They were on some power couple shit and she now worked in the shop with him. Stori's stomach was huge but she still looked cute. That was something else that pissed Milan off. Corey was supposed to handle them but his stupid ass couldn't even get that right. He talked all that shit but he wasn't about that life. He sent his cousins to handle business and they fucked everything up. Nas took a bullet to the side and their scary asses moved out of town.

"Fuck you!" Corey spat angrily.

"Nah nigga, I already told you no," Milan laughed, as he walked into the bathroom and slammed the door behind him.

"Stupid ass bitch," Corey fumed as he grabbed a towel to wash his face.

He felt played but it was all good. He had gone down on Milan a few times, but she never let him hit. He was giving her money and free weed and she was treating him like a fuck boy. Corey had baby mamas that he didn't do as much for but it was cool. Milan was a bad bitch, but he was good on her. He started to take the pussy when she laughed at him but he wasn't about to stoop that low. He had too many other hoes that he could get it from.

"This cheap ass pre-pay phone is ringing!" Milan yelled as she laughed at her own joke.

She was always calling him broke but she was always smiling up in his face. Corey got pissed all over again when he walked out of the bathroom and saw Milan smoking a blunt filled with his shit. Bitch was holding the pussy hostage but wanted to smoke for free. He was losing out on money but that was her last freebie from him.

"The fuck this nigga keep calling me for?" Corey snapped when he saw that Gavin was calling him yet again.

Shit didn't go the way they planned with Nas and Corey was over it. His cousins almost died behind that shit and he didn't want no parts of it. Carlton told him about Nas and Remo coming to his house, but Corey was in the clear. His cousin threw Gavin under the bus and Corey assumed that's why he was calling.

"Who is that?" Milan asked.

"That's Gavin with his stupid ass." Corey frowned.

"I heard that he moved to Beaumont with Misty's desperate ass," Milan said as she blew smoke from her nose and mouth.

"Who told you that?" Corey asked.

"One of my cousins told me. She said that Misty's baby daddy lives with her now. Gavin is her baby daddy, so it must be him." Milan shrugged.

She didn't talk to Misty or her mother anymore. Once she put Misty out, their mother called her going off and Milan ended up cursing her out. Their mother had always favored Misty and Milan was sick of it. Granted, she was always good to them both but Misty was her golden child. Milan had gotten into some trouble and their mother never let her forget it. When Corey's phone rang again, Milan was shaken from her thoughts of the past.

"Yeah bruh," Corey said, deciding to answer for Gavin.

"Damn nigga. The fuck you been at? I been trying to call you for weeks," Gavin replied.

"I been out here trying to get this money. What's good?" Corey asked.

"Man, shit is all fucked up bruh. I left New Orleans and I seriously doubt if I'm ever coming back," Gavin answered.

"I told you," Milan whispered.

"Why? What happened?" Corey asked.

"Man, I got shot the fuck up is what happened. Niggas hit me up five times and almost killed me," Gavin said.

"Shot by who?" Corey asked.

"Who the fuck you think? You better be careful fam. Them niggas rode down on me when I pulled up to the gates of my apartment complex and lit my car up," Gavin said.

"The fuck you mean I better be careful? You told them niggas something about me?" Corey asked as he stood up and paced nervously.

"I wasn't able to say shit. Them niggas hopped out the whip and just started shooting. Niggas was masked up, but I know it was them because Irvin said they came to the shop looking for me," Gavin replied.

"Oh, well that's all on you fam. You must have pissed them niggas off," Corey said as he laughed.

"The fuck you mean that's all on me? All this shit was your idea. You didn't tell me that Stori used to be your bitch back in the day. That's real fucked up how you played me. Trust me, them niggas can find you the same way they found me!" Gavin barked.

"It don't sound like they're looking for me though, fam. I didn't play you. You played yourself," Corey said as he and Milan both laughed.

Gavin was heated and he knew right then that something wasn't right. He thought back to his conversation with Carlton and began to put it all together. When Nas and Remo confronted Carlton, he must have sold Gavin out. Corey was his blood and he was almost sure that he wouldn't give him up. Gavin was thankful that he was alive but it pissed him off that Corey got away with no consequences for his actions. He and Milan were just as guilty and they needed to pay.

"Yeah, you're right. I did play myself but it's all good. You live and you learn. You be safe out there fam," Gavin replied before he hung up the phone.

"I got a plan," Milan said as soon as Corey was off the phone.

"Fuck you and your plan," Corey snapped angrily.

"Don't be like that Corey. If all goes well, you can have all the pussy you want," Milan promised with a seductive grin.

"I'm listening," Corey said he looked over at her.

Milan got up and climbed onto his lap, making him rock up instantly. When she started whispering in his ear, Corey had to stop himself from taking the pussy. Milan was tempting him, but he remained cool. He listened to what she had to say and her plan wasn't half bad. He wasn't sure if they could get away with it but it was worth a try.

"Thank you, my Stanka." Stori smiled when Toi came back and handed her the drink that she went to the store and got for her.

"You're welcome. Are you okay Stori? Your stomach is huge," Toi noted as she watched her sister moving around the salon.

"I'm fine baby. I only have one more week and I'm officially on maternity leave." Stori smiled.

"I'm so excited that the babies are almost here." Toi smiled.

"Me too but I'm happier that I won't be pregnant anymore," Stori replied.

"I wonder if Riya or Cami want me to still come help them out when I get out of school," Toi said, referring to the other two stylists that Stori had hired. She had space for two more and she was hoping to have them filled before she left. Toi was making good money by helping them out, but Stori knew that wasn't why Toi wanted to hang around. She didn't know that the little boy who asked Toi for her number was Eric. He was at the shop every day just like she was and they developed a crush on each other. Toi walked around with her phone glued to her ear all day when they were at home. She didn't lack in her responsibilities, so Stori let her be.

"I don't know but I'll ask. I thought you would have wanted to be at home with me," Stori pouted.

"I do wanna be at home with you but I like helping out at the shop too," Toi replied.

"It's cool, as long as Nas is here," Stori said.

"I have to tell you something," Toi smirked.

"Tell me what?" Stori asked as she looked over at her.

"Eric kissed me." Toi smiled.

"When?" Stori asked.

"It happened twice. He kissed me and…" Toi said as her words trailed off.

"And what!" Stori yelled as her heart started thumping in her chest.

"I don't know Stori. I liked it but I felt weird afterwards," Toi admitted.

"What do you mean Stanka? Did he do something that you didn't want him to do?" Stori asked as she sat down to calm her nerves.

"No, it was nothing like that. You remember when we had the talk about my body parts?" Toi asked.

"Yeah, I remember." Stori nodded.

"Well, I felt weird down there but in a good way," Toi said as she looked down at her vaginal area.

Nas told her that the day would come, but Stori wasn't ready. Toi was at the age where her hormones were raging and she was experiencing it sooner than Stori wanted her to. She knew that she couldn't shield her from it and that's why she always made sure to keep the lines of communication open between them. She wanted Toi to feel comfortable talking to her about anything, no matter how uncomfortable it made her.

"I understand what you're saying Stanka and we've talked about this several times before. What you're feeling is very normal but you're way too young to act on those feelings," Stori replied as calmly as she could.

"I'm not ready to have sex or nothing like that," Toi said, making her visibly relax.

Stori knew how that could go though. Although Toi said that she wasn't ready, things took a different turn all the time. If ever the opportunity presented itself, she knew that anything was possible.

"Well, I'm happy to hear that but I need you to let me know whenever you are. Remember what I told you about being careful. It's not just about pregnancy. You have diseases to worry about too. Nas and I were careless and that's exactly why we're about to have two babies. I don't want that for you though," Stori told her.

"I don't want that either. I want to graduate college and be married before I have kids. You and Nas are getting married, so it's not so bad," Toi replied, right as Eric walked into the shop.

"You wanna walk with me to the store Toi?" he asked as he smiled at her.

"Didn't y'all just go to the store?" Stori countered with a slight attitude.

"Yeah but Nas wants me to go back to get something for him," Eric replied.

"Can I go Stori?" Toi asked her.

"Yeah, you can go," Stori replied as she discreetly rolled her eyes at Eric. He was a sweetheart but he could be sweet for somebody else's little sister and leave hers alone.

"I got one more head to cut baby and then we can dip," Nas said when he walked into the salon. He leaned in to give Stori a kiss, but she grabbed him by his barber's smock and pulled him closer to her before he could.

"You tell that slow talking bastard to keep his lips off of my Stanka before I shoot his lil dick off," Stori gritted through clenched teeth.

"Who?" Nas questioned.

"Eric, that's who. Bastard got my baby getting all hot and bothered because he can't keep his lips to himself," Stori fussed as she pushed Nas away.

"Why am I getting fussed at though?" Nas laughed.

"That's not funny Naseem. You better tell his ass something," Stori fumed.

"I'm not telling him shit and neither are you. We already talked about this Stori. Leave them damn kids alone. Eric is an honor roll student who don't do nothing but go to school and hang around the shop all day. He's not out here selling dope and robbing people like some of the boys his age. Be happy that it's him who got Toi's attention and not one of these other lil niggas out here," Nas said as he grabbed her face and kissed her.

"Toi is too young for a boyfriend and I'm not ready for her to have one," Stori replied.

"Too late. That's what he's walking her to the store to ask her," Nas laughed.

"What!" Stori yelled as she jumped up from the chair.

"Sit your ass down before you fall with that big ass belly," Nas laughed as he grabbed her arm. He sat down in the chair and pulled Stori down on his lap.

"I can't believe you right now Naseem." Stori frowned.

"Let my boy do him. He said that he's really feeling Toi and I told him to go for it. Eric is a good dude. He wouldn't be hanging around me so much if he wasn't. He had it rough at home but he didn't let that stop him from making the grades in school. I think he's a good fit for Toi," Nas said.

"Okay, I'll let it go but you better be right," Stori said, right as his phone rang.

Nas smirked when he saw a familiar number flashing across his screen. Stori looked confused but she was curious as to what the call was about.

"I guess my aim ain't as good as it used to be," Nas said when he answered the phone for Gavin.

Stori already knew what happened because Nas told her about it when he came home that night. Gavin was bitter like a bitch, so she wasn't even surprised to hear that he had something to do with the break-in at her house. Gavin was an only child, so she was happy that he didn't die. His parents were always good to her and Toi and she would have hated for them to go through that.

"Man, that was fucked up what you and your brother did but real niggas don't die that easily," Gavin bragged.

"You moved out there to Texas and decided to get some heart, huh nigga. You were a bitch in New Orleans and you're still a bitch in Beaumont. Four hours ain't too far for me to drive to finish the job. Act like you got some sense nigga," Nas threatened, making Gavin slightly nervous. He didn't know how Nas found out so much shit about everybody but it was unnerving.

"I'm not calling to beef with you, bruh. You and Stori did me dirty and I can admit that I was in my feelings. I made a stupid decision and I paid for it with five bullets. I just want you to know that I wasn't the only threat to your life," Gavin noted.

"Speak facts nigga. Your hoe ass was never a threat to me at all," Nas clarified.

"Maybe not but you and Stori's exes are. Milan and Corey are who you should be worried about. They tried to pin the shit on me but they're the masterminds behind everything. I know that Carlton was the one who sold me out, but Corey is his first cousin. You tried to kill the wrong man," Gavin said.

"Nah, I wanted you dead too. But, you get a pass since you snitched on the nigga that I really want. Enjoy your new life in Texas. You came too close to death for you not to," Nas replied before he hung up.

"Wow," Stori mumbled as she thought about everything that Gavin had just said.

"Tell me everything that you know about this Corey nigga," Nas said as he looked at Stori. He knew of Corey just from seeing him in the shop a few times. He just assumed that he was one of Carlton's regulars. He never knew that they were related.

"Naseem, no. I'm less than a month away from giving birth to two babies. I need you to be here in one piece when I do," Stori replied.

"I got you, baby. I'm not on no bullshit," Nas swore.

"Oh, my God! I hate when you say that!" Stori yelled as she stood up.

"What?" Nas asked as he held his hands out innocently.

"Every time you say you're not on no bullshit, bullshit is exactly what you're on," Stori pointed out.

"Alright baby. You got my word. I'll let the nigga make it just a little while longer. I'm really in my feelings right now though. Me and Remo said that somebody else was involved but I didn't suspect him or Milan. I don't really know him but that bitch got a serious death wish. Maybe I wasn't clear enough for her the last time," Nas said, as Toi and Eric walked back into the shop.

Stori didn't miss that they were holding hands but they let go as soon as they walked in.

"Come on and let me cut you up so we can go," Nas said while looking at Eric. He was the last head that he had to cut before he called it a night.

As soon as they walked away, Toi walked over to Stori and rubbed her stomach. She missed Summer a lot but she was happy to have her two nephews coming soon.

"I have something to tell you, Stori," Toi blushed and smiled.

"Okay Stanka. What's up?" Stori asked, even though she already knew.

She took a seat and braced herself for the news that she wasn't prepared to hear. Her baby sister was about to tell her that she had her very first boyfriend and Stori just wasn't ready. She knew that she had raised Toi right and she trusted her to make the right decisions. Maybe Nas was right and Eric was a good boy. If not, Stori had no problem making good on her earlier threat.

"**N**igga, fuck you, your bitch and them ugly ass babies that she's about to push out!" Milan yelled at Nas over the phone.

It was crazy of her to get excited when he called because she knew that it couldn't have been anything good. She and Nas were divorced now and he never gave her any indication that he wanted her back. Milan had just saw her male friend out when she got the call. She was about to hop in the shower to wash the smell of sex from her body. She paced around her bedroom butt ass naked arguing with her ex-husband instead.

"See, you just be playing dumb but I'm real life stupid with this shit. Putting a gun to your head wasn't good enough. You must want a nigga to pull the trigger," Nas replied.

"Why are you calling me, Naseem? You wanted a

divorce and you got one," Milan noted.

"It's not too often that I give passes Milan but I'm trying to be the bigger person here. Even though you and that hoe ass nigga Corey came at me and my wife on some bullshit, I'm willing to let you walk away with your life. I got a wife and two sons to think about and I'm trying to do better," Nas said.

Although they'd done a lot of unforgivable things, Stori begged Nas to squash the beef that he had with Milan and Corey. Remo was heated, but Kalani begged him to let it go too. Remo was begging his wife for a baby but she swore that it wasn't happening until he calmed down. Milan had started up with the keyboard thugging on Instagram again, but Nas ignored that too. Stori kept reminding him of the bigger picture and he was trying to do better. She kept telling Nas how blessed he was and he had to agree. His credit score was improving and his criminal record had been wiped clean. They had a beautiful home, thriving businesses and two sons that were due to arrive any day now. He had too much to lose to keep playing the same childish ass games. He and Remo even went to Milan's house but God was once again looking out for her. Milan had moved and that was the only thing that saved her pathetic ass life.

"That bitch ain't your wife. You better test them lil ugly muthafuckers when they get here. Ain't no telling who their real daddy is. And as I stated earlier, fuck you, your kids and your bitch. Y'all did me dirty, not the other way around," Milan snapped, pulling Nas out of his thoughts.

"Hang up on that childish hoe. I'm sorry for even trying to get you to be the bigger person," Milan heard Stori say in the background.

"Fuck you, bitch. I'm not the one who was fucking friends, hoe. You need to be trying to find your babies a daddy. Their real daddy hoe because it's not Naseem!" Milan yelled.

"Don't be mad because I'm really pregnant boo. Ain't no faking over this way bitch," Stori laughed.

"Laugh now bitch but I got something for both of you hoes," Milan warned.

"Hang up Naseem. I tried but it's whatever now," Stori said.

"You got that sweetheart," Nas replied before the phone line went dead.

"Stupid ass bitch got the right one," Milan fumed as she dialed Corey's number on her phone.

"What's good Milan?" Corey asked when he answered for her.

"That's what I'm trying to find out. What's up with what you were supposed to be doing?" Milan questioned.

"I got this shit under control. You just make sure you got that fat ass in the air once it's done," Corey replied.

"I'm a woman of my word. You got me and I definitely got you," Milan cooed seductively.

"Come open the door. I just pulled up," Corey said, right before he hung up the phone.

Milan frowned because she was not in the mood to be bothered with his disgusting ass. Corey was starting to annoy her with the pop up visits and she was tired of telling him about doing it. Milan was still naked but she grabbed some feminine wipes from her bathroom and quickly wiped the scent of her previous lover from between her thighs. She sprayed some air freshener to mask the smell of fresh sex in her bedroom. When Corey knocked on the door, she didn't even bother getting dressed before she went to open it. He needed a little persuading and she was a master of persuasion.

"I don't do unannounced visits my love. I've made this clear to you before," Milan stated when she let him in.

"I did announce my visit," Corey said as he stared at her body lustfully.

"No, not when you're almost here," Milan admonished while walking to her bedroom with him following behind her.

"Damn," Corey said as he walked up on her. He grabbed a handful of her ass, but Milan slapped his hand away.

"No touching. You claim to want me so bad but you can't even follow simple instructions," Milan said as she sat on her bed and crossed her legs.

"I told you that I got shit under control. My lil niggas gon' handle that," Corey assured her.

"I hope they don't handle it the same way your cousins handled it. It was three against one and Nas should have been dead. How the fuck did he walk away with a single gunshot wound?" Milan questioned angrily.

"Nah, these lil niggas are some straight savages. They gon' handle it," Corey assured her.

"Remember the reward you'll receive for a job well done," Milan said as she opened her legs to give him a better view.

Corey was a dummy and that wasn't hard to see. He was older than Milan, but she got him to do whatever she wanted him to. Besides Stori, Corey was used to fucking with hood rats. Milan was a bad bitch and in a higher class than all the others. Getting a piece of her was equivalent to getting a little piece of heaven on earth.

"That shit better be bomb as fuck too," Corey said as he licked his lips.

"Trust me, it is," Milan replied as she grabbed his hand. She inserted one of his fingers inside of her and squeezed her vaginal muscles around it.

"Fuck," Corey hissed as he removed his finger and stuck it in his mouth.

"It's all yours, any and every way you want it," Milan replied seductively.

"You better stop teasing me," Corey warned as he salivated at her freshy waxed middle.

Corey had never done so much to get pussy before, but Milan had him intrigued. She was like the one who got away and he had been trying to get with her for a while. Even though she received pleasure from it, he was shocked when she let him go down on her. Milan only fucked with a certain type of nigga and Corey felt like it was a privilege. Truthfully, he was skeptical to do what she was asking of him but she was making it hard to say no. Corey was about to take a huge risk and he was hoping that Milan was worth it.

"Calm down baby. What's the difference if he kept you this week or the next?" Nas asked as he helped Stori change into a hospital gown.

A simple visit to her doctor turned into her being admitted to have the babies. Stori was right at thirty-five weeks and her doctor didn't want her to go any further. He was telling them about all of the complications that could arise if a twin pregnancy went too long. Stori was in great health and the babies were in a good position to be delivered vaginally. Both babies were over five pounds and the doctor wanted to induce.

"I know Naseem but we're not prepared," Stori cried.

"What else do we need to do Stori? Their room is done and so is the rest of the house. They have everything that they need and more," Nas said as he wiped her eyes.

"That's not what I meant. We were just supposed to be coming for a visit. I don't even have our bags and Toi is at school," Stori sobbed.

Stori was an emotional mess since she'd been pregnant. It didn't bother Nas though because he knew how to deal with her. She was always worried about other people and not enough about herself. Nas had everything under control and he needed her to relax.

"Relax baby. Remo and Kalani are getting Toi out of school early and she's coming up here with them. Your mama is getting our bags and the car seats from the house.

I already handled everything, so you don't have nothing to worry about," Nas said.

"Tell them to make sure that Toi eats something too. I don't know how long we'll be here," Stori replied.

"Kalani knows what to do baby. Just relax," Nas said.

"I'm trying to relax Naseem but I'm nervous. I just thought I had a little more time. I wasn't mentally prepared for this today," Stori noted.

"I'm happy that you're having them today. You're miserable and you can barely sleep at night. Your back is always hurting and your stomach is huge. It's time for them lil niggas to come up out of there," Nas said, right as he received a text message.

"Getting rid of this big ass belly is the best part of it all," Stori sighed.

"Jarvis and Latrice are on their way up here. That nigga is happy as fuck." Nas smiled as he typed his reply.

"Why?" Stori asked as she looked at him.

"Today is his birthday," Nas answered.

"I thought his birthday was last week," Stori said.

"No, we gave him his gift and celebrated last week. Him and Latrice were supposed to be driving to Florida today. That's why we did it early," Nas replied.

She forgot all about it being Jarvis' birthday because Nas and Remo gave him his gift a week early. They had a seafood boil at Remo and Kalani's house and there was a cake there too. Since they celebrated early, Stori forgot about the actual day.

"I really feel bad now. Jarvis can't even celebrate his birthday because Dr. Jekyll wants to deliver the babies today," Stori said as she rolled her eyes.

"That nigga is happy. He don't care about none of that. All he wanted was another car and me and Remo made that happen last week," Nas replied.

Nas and Remo got him a sports car and he was like a kid in a candy store when they took him outside to see it. Jarvis had a sports car before their parents died but he had to give it up to get something bigger. He was always talking about getting another one and his brothers made his dream a reality.

"Y'all talk all that shit but you and Remo are crazy about Jarvis," Stori laughed.

"That nigga is disgusting as fuck but we love his ass. He was young but he handled business with us. We always had the best of everything and he made sure of it. Me and Remo didn't even have to know nothing about the money that our parents left, but he looked out and made sure that we got our share. I appreciate him more than anything," Nas said, as Stori smiled at his sentimental moment.

"I need to call my grandma," Stori said.

"I already called her. I told you that I handled everything. Your man got you, baby," Nas assured her with a kiss on the lips.

About an hour later, everybody had arrived and the doctor induced Stori's labor. It was only eleven that morning and they didn't know what time the babies would make their grand entrance. Their family and friends took turns coming in and out of the room, but Toi refused to leave Stori's side. When Stori's labor pains started, Toi cried right along with her. The pain was like nothing that Stori had ever felt but it was worth it when her identical twin babies entered the world about five hours later. Stori had heard horror stories about cesareans and she was happy that she didn't have to get cut. Jarvis was ecstatic that his first and only two nephews were born on his birthday. In his eyes, that was the best gift ever. Remo was almost in tears as if Kalani was the one who had given birth.

"These lil niggas look just like us." Remo smiled as he sat in the chair in Stori's hospital room and held one of the babies.

"They damn sure do. Make it easy on yourself Stori. Find something to differentiate them from one another," Jarvis said as he held the other twin.

"She's their mother. She'll be able to tell them apart if nobody else can. Everybody had a problem telling Nas and Remo apart but Summer always knew," their grandmother pointed out.

"She sure did. I don't know how she did it but she could always tell them apart," Jarvis replied.

"A mother knows," their grandmother shrugged.

"At least she didn't have to pull our pants down to do it," Nas smirked as he looked at Jarvis.

"Say what you want nigga. I had to do what I had to do," Jarvis laughed, right as the nurse walked into the room with another woman.

"Sorry to interrupt. We just need your signature for their birth certificate Mr. Donaldson." The nurse smiled as she walked over to Remo.

"Nah, that's me," Nas replied.

"Oh, I'm sorry," she replied as she walked over to him instead.

"I could have signed for you, bro. They got my DNA floating around in them too," Remo laughed.

"Boy please," Stori hissed.

"Think it's a game if you want to. I bet if they give me a paternity test on your kids, it'll come back that I'm the father too. Me and Nas have identical DNA," Remo pointed out.

"Is that true?" Stori asked the nurse.

"Yes ma'am, it is. You would have to do a more extensive test to determine paternity because a normal DNA test wouldn't work," the nurse replied with a smile.

"Stop trying to play me, Stori. I paid attention to some things in school," Remo laughed.

"Damn, so that would be true for my kids too," Kalani spoke up.

"What kids? I think your sneaky ass be popping pills behind my back. You should have been pregnant by now. You better not let me find out," Remo said with a frown.

"I dare you to start acting stupid in here," Kalani said as she threatened him with her eyes.

"Get him Kalani," their grandmother laughed.

Nas signed the papers for his sons and sat around talking to their family for a while. Toi ended up going home with their grandmother, although Lady wanted her to come to her house. It was sad that Toi didn't really know her and didn't really feel comfortable being around her. She was fine as long as her friends or Stori were there, but she didn't like to go alone. Lady tried to get Stori to intervene but she refused.

"Your mama looked like her lil feelings were hurt when Toi left with your grandmother," Nas said once he and Stori were in the room alone.

"That's all on her. That's what being selfish gets you. I'm not making my baby go with her if she doesn't want to. I don't know what she expected to happened when she left her eight years ago. Toi doesn't know her like that," Stori replied.

"I can't see it baby. The only way I'm leaving mine is if I'm dead and gone," Nas swore.

"Don't say that Naseem." Stori frowned.

"I'm just saying baby. I couldn't see me leaving my boys behind for nothing less than death." Nas shrugged.

"I feel the same way but Lady only cares about herself. I appreciate her for taking care of us but being a mother is more than just financial support. I've been having Toi since she came home from the hospital. I was a damn baby myself. My mama didn't give a fuck though. She packed her shit and left like it was the easiest decision in the world. It's sad when bad habits are the only thing you can say your mother ever taught you," Stori said while shaking her head.

"She taught you how to shoot and make money. That's some gangsta shit right there," Nas laughed.

"That's some bullshit is what it is. I'm happy that Toi wasn't exposed to all that mess. I was sixteen years old making edibles like that shit was normal," Stori argued.

The only reason why she'd stopped was because she got pregnant. Nas wanted her to teach him and Remo how to do it but she never got around to it. They still had Eno pushing product in the club and they were seeing a nice bit of profit from that too. They were even looking into buying more rental property but they weren't sure where yet.

"It's all good baby. We both got skills to ensure that we'll never be broke," Nas said.

"Yep, we're a team." Stori smiled.

"And that's exactly why we need to make this shit official," Nas said as he pulled a blue velvet box from his pocket. He opened the box and Stori gasped when she saw the ring.

"Aww, baby, I love it," Stori said as he slipped the ring on her finger.

"Just tell me when." Nas smiled as he kissed her.

"Give me about six months. Since I didn't get cut, I should be able to exercise after two weeks. I got to get my body back right," Stori replied.

"Nah, I'm not waiting that long Stori. You didn't even really gain that much weight," Nas noted.

"Stop lying Naseem. My ass is huge." Stori frowned.

"The fuck! I know you ain't trying to get rid of that!" he yelled.

"No baby but I need to tone up," Stori said as she laughed at his facial expression.

"I hear you but I'm still not waiting that long," Nas replied.

"You can't make me walk down the aisle Naseem," Stori chuckled.

"I'm not trying to but don't force my hand," Nas replied.

He and Stori talked for a while longer before she drifted off to sleep. The babies were sleeping too but Nas had a million things on his mind. He wanted to do what Stori said and let the situation with Milan and Corey go, but that was easier said than done. He hated when anything kept him awake at night. He knew that those kinds of problems didn't go away on their own and he had his family to think about now. As he looked at Stori and his boys sleeping, he felt an overwhelming need to protect them and keep them safe at all cost. Toi wasn't his but she was just as much of his responsibility as his boys were. He didn't like loose ends and that's exactly what Milan and Corey were to him. It didn't matter if they stayed quiet for a while, he wanted them silenced forever. Nas had to get with his people to see where Milan was staying now. He had a feeling that he would be paying her a visit sooner or later.

"My legs hurt," Toi complained when she and Stori got into the car.

"Mine too Stanka," Stori replied.

It had been seven weeks since Stori had the babies and she had been going to the gym every day. Her doctor cleared her at her six-week checkup and she started her diet and workout plan soon after. Stori had dropped a lot of the baby weight from breastfeeding but she had about twenty pounds to go before she was back to her pre-baby weight. She liked her thicker frame, so she only planned to drop ten. She usually worked out with Kalani but she and Remo were having a date night. Jarvis and Latrice were at the house with the boys and Nas was at work. Lady and Richard were having an all-white party in another month and Stori had to make sure that she was on point before then. It had been a while since she was able to unwind with a few drinks and she was looking forward to it. She was happy that her boys drank formula too because she would have too much liquor in her system to pump.

"Let's go to Burger King. I'm hungry," Toi said.

"We just finished working out and you want a hamburger," Stori smirked.

"And a milkshake," Toi laughed.

"I guess I can get me a salad. I wonder if Nas ate anything," Stori said.

"Can we go to the shop Stori, please?" Toi begged excitedly. She missed Eric and she wanted to see him.

"I don't know Stanka. Look at how I'm dressed. You must want Naseem to kill me," Stori laughed. She had on Nike leggings with the matching muscle shirt and Nas wouldn't like that at all. It was dark outside but it was still early. Stori was sure that the barber shop was still packed because it always was on Saturdays.

"He won't kill you. And we don't even have to stop for food. I can get a shrimp plate from the corner store," Stori said.

"Okay but we can't stay long. We both smell like gym sweat," Stori said as she turned around and headed for the shop.

She had hired two new stylists before she left to have the twins and she wanted to see how they were making out. Nas said that everything was cool but he wouldn't know if there was a problem anyway. He stayed home with her and the babies for a few weeks and he was just now retuning. Mr. Herbert ran things in his absence and everybody hated that. Remo was back in school and Nas was excited about them eventually working together. That had always been his dream and it was finally becoming a reality. He was in the process of purchasing the space next to the shop and expanding the building. Kalani was running the hair store and business was booming. They were making money all kinds of ways and that was what Nas wanted.

"Can I have some money? I left my purse at home," Toi said when they pulled up to the shop.

"I'll walk over there with you," Stori offered.

"You don't have to. I'll get Eric to come with me," Toi replied.

Stori reached into her purse to get her some money before they got out of the car. When they walked into the shop, it was jumping as usual. The music was blasting and they had a crowd of men waiting to get their hair cut. Toi spoke and went straight to the salon while Stori walked over to greet her man. Nas was finishing up with a customer when he looked up and saw Stori. The frown on his face let her know that he was not too pleased to see her.

"Come here," Nas demanded as he walked off towards the office.

"What's good Stori?" one of the customers asked.

"You must not be trying to get your hair cut today, huh nigga?" Nas barked as he abruptly stopped walking and turned to face him.

"My fault Nas. I was just speaking. I didn't want to be rude," the man replied.

"Be rude next time nigga. Keep your muthafucking eyes on the floor when you see this one," Nas snapped in anger.

"Really Naseem?" Stori asked when she walked into the office behind him.

"The fuck you mean really? Why did you come in here dressed like that?" Nas asked angrily.

"We just came from the gym and Toi wanted to come over," Stori replied.

"You should have went home and changed first. You must be trying to get one of these niggas fucked up in here," he fumed angrily.

"Bye Naseem," Stori said as she turned and tried to walk away.

"Stop playing with me," Nas said as he pulled her close and kissed her.

"Move Naseem, I'm sweaty," Stori giggled as he picked her up and sat her on top of the desk.

"Girl, I saw you push two babies out, two minutes apart. You think I give a fuck about a lil sweat. I don't know how the doctor did it but he snitched that shit up extra tight," Nas said as he ran his hand in between her legs.

"Shut up boy," Stori laughed as she slapped him.

Nas was happy as hell when Stori got cleared by her doctor. He was like a crack head waiting for those six weeks to be over with. He swore that sex with Stori was even better than it was before the twins came. He told her that the doctor stitched her up and made her even tighter. Stori laughed every time he said it but he was dead ass serious.

"Who's at home with my boys?" Nas asked.

"Jarvis and Latrice. I was gonna skip the gym today but I'm happy that I didn't have to," Stori replied.

"I'm about to start charging that nigga rent. He comes over there every day," Nas said, speaking of his older brother.

"Leave him alone. He's excited about his nephews," Stori replied.

Jarvis came to their house every single day without fail. Most times, he came straight from work and stayed for hours at a time. It had been a while since they had a baby in the family and he was enjoying being a first time uncle.

"I'm going to the store Stori!" Toi yelled as she knocked on the door.

"Okay Stanka," Stori replied.

Eric wasn't in the shop, but Toi sent him a text letting him know that she was there. He was playing basketball but he swore that he was on his way. The court where he played was right around the corner and he was taking too long for her. Toi was hungry and she ended up going to the store alone to get her something to eat. She knew that Stori would kill her for going by herself at night but she didn't want to disturb her or Nas.

"What's up beautiful?" a young dude asked Toi when she walked up to the store.

"Hey," Toi replied politely as she walked inside.

The dude walked in behind her and followed her to the back. Toi saw him staring from the corner of her eye and got paranoid. He was talking on the phone with somebody but he was whispering. The entire situation was weird and she was ready to go. Instead of ordering her food, she called Eric's phone as she prepared to go back to the shop. When he didn't answer, Toi got even more frightened. The dude was trying to play it off but he was clearly following her.

Toi slipped her phone in her front pocket and was prepared to run back to the shop. As soon as she walked outside, she was about to take off until she was grabbed from behind.

"You ain't going nowhere lil bitch," a man gritted as he pulled her to an all-black car.

"No! Let me go!" Toi kicked and screamed as she was forcefully shoved inside.

The man who had followed her around the store came running outside and hoped in the driver's seat before quickly pulling off.

"I told you, nigga. All we had to do was be patient and wait. I knew we would catch them bitches slipping one day. Nobody is on point that much," the man from the store said excitedly as he drove.

"Let me out of here!" Toi yelled as she swung and kicked her legs wildly.

"Ahh! Fuck! This bitch kicked me in the mouth!" the man who sat in the back seat with her howled. He raised his hand high in the air and slapped Toi across her face.

"You better calm the fuck down back there girl," the driver ordered.

"Don't tell this bitch nothing. I got something for her ass if she try that shit again," his accomplice said as he pulled out a silver gun and sat it on his lap. Toi was paralyzed with fear as she held her stinging cheek. She had never seen the two men before but they looked kind of young. She regretted walking to the store alone and now she knew why Stori had her on such a short leash. Her big sister was overprotective for a reason and she now understood why.

"Let's go get something to smoke before we head over to the spot. This bitch ain't gon' be a virgin for long," the driver said excitedly, as Toi's heart thumped loudly in her chest.

Her phone was in her front pocket but she was too scared to move. The man was staring at her menacingly as he held on to the gun that was on his lap. Toi was praying for a miracle but she didn't know how she was going to get out of the mess that she was in.

Eric dribbled the ball that he was holding all the way to the barber shop. He hadn't seen Toi in a few days because Stori was out on maternity leave. They talked on the phone and Facetimed all day but it wasn't the same. Eric never had a girlfriend before and he really liked Toi. He could tell that Stori wasn't too happy about the idea at first but she was starting to come around. She even let Eric come over there a few times to see Toi since they hadn't been at the shop. Nas would pick him up early Sunday and let him spend the entire day at their house. He and Toi only watched movies or swam but he loved spending time with her.

"Good evening," Eric spoke when he walked into the shop.

He didn't see Nas but he walked straight to the hair salon to find Toi. The entire shop was busy but he didn't see Toi anywhere. He knew that they were still there because Stori's car was parked out front. When he walked back up front, Nas and Stori were walking out of the office hugging and smiling.

"Hey Stori. Where's Toi?" Eric asked, wiping the smile from her face.

"I thought you walked with her to the store," Stori replied.

"No, I was playing ball when she called and I just came back," Eric said.

"I know damn well Toi didn't walk to that store by herself this late," Stori fussed.

"Calm down baby. It's not that late," Nas said.

"Maybe not but it's dark outside," Stori pointed out.

"I'm going run over there," Eric said as he put his ball down and hurried out of the shop.

356

"She knows better than to do something like that," Stori said as she walked into the salon.

The stylists were busy with their clients but they were happy to see her. Stori smiled when they complimented her on how well she looked after just having two babies. They didn't know her before pregnancy, so they didn't know that she used to be smaller.

"The fuck you mean!" Nas yelled from the front of the shop a few minutes later. Stori got up from where she was seated and rushed to see what had him so upset.

"What's wrong baby?" Stori asked when she walked up to him.

"She wasn't in the store and nobody saw her. I keep calling her phone but she's not answering," Eric said nervously.

"What!" Stori yelled as she bolted out of the front door.

Nas and Eric were right behind her as they ran across the street to the corner store. The store wasn't huge but Stori still yelled Toi's name as she looked around for her. Nas went straight to the cash register to talk to the Korean store owner.

"I saw her but she didn't buy anything. She was with a man," he said in broken English.

"What man?" Stori asked.

"I don't know," the man said as he held his hands up.

"Oh, my God! No, please," Stori said as she collapsed to the floor.

"Come on baby. She hasn't even been gone that long. She can't be too far," Nas said as he picked her up and carried her out of the store.

"I need to call the police," Stori said as she sobbed uncontrollably.

"I can track her phone. We share our locations with each other," Eric spoke up.

"Where is she now? Let me see your phone," Stori demanded as she jumped out of Nas' arms.

Eric's hands were shaking as he put in his password to unlock his phone. Once he got to what he needed, he handed Stori the phone for her and Nas to see.

"Fuck the police. I'm calling Remo. We can handle this shit ourselves. Ain't nobody walking up out of that bitch alive," Nas barked angrily.

"I'm coming too," Stori said as she pulled her hair back into ponytail.

"No baby. Stay here until I come back," Nas demanded.

"Fuck that Naseem. That's my baby and I'm going to get her. You already know I ain't scared," Stori replied.

"Stay here and watch the shop Eric," Nas ordered.

"I can't Nas. I have to make sure that she's okay," Eric said, looking as if he wanted to cry.

"Fuck it, let him come too. I got enough guns in my car for everybody," Stori said as they all piled into her car. Nas called Remo to tell him what was up, as Eric tracked Toi's phone and told them where to go. Stori was serious as hell about having a few guns in her car. Nas drove as she grabbed two from her glovebox and made sure that they were loaded. If Nas never knew it before, he knew without a doubt that he was in love. Unfortunately, it wasn't the right time for him to express that to anyone.

"I'm so proud of you, baby." Kalani smiled as she and Remo walked into the restaurant. Remo had gone back to cosmetology school to get his barber's license and Kalani was so happy for him. Nas had been showing him the basics and he was a fast learner. The twins were still up to their usual mischief and that would probably never change. Nas had gone to the school a few days ago and took a test on Remo's behalf. Remo was celebrating when he made a perfect score like he had really done something. Kalani celebrated with him, although she couldn't stop herself from laughing.

"If you're so proud of me, how come you're not pregnant yet?" Remo questioned.

"Maybe it's not time for me to get pregnant Kareem," Kalani replied.

"The fuck is that supposed to mean? You popping pills behind my back?" Remo questioned as he looked at her skeptically.

"Can we not do this right now Kareem? We're supposed to be enjoying our date night. Stop focusing so much on me getting pregnant. Besides, I know you enjoy trying." Kalani smiled.

"Hell yeah. Why do you think I told you to wear a dress tonight?" Remo winked.

"Table for two?" the hostess asked with a bright smile.

"Yes, please," Kalani replied.

They kept it simple and decided to eat Chinese at P.F. Chang's that night. Kalani always tried to pick a different place because Remo really didn't care. He would have been okay with a pizza or chicken spot but she wasn't having it. Remo liked their food, so he was good with her choice.

"Follow me," the hostess said as she grabbed the menus and led the way to the dining area.

"Aww, somebody got our favorite table," Kalani pouted as she looked to the rear of the restaurant.

The place was always dimly illuminated and she loved the table in the back that was near the window. A woman and man were already seated there and they seemed to be engrossed in conversation.

"You wanna sit there baby?" Remo asked as he looked at her.

"No boo, it's fine," Kalani said as she continued to look in the direction of her favorite area. The hostess was leading them to the other side of the room and Remo could tell that his wife wasn't happy.

"Excuse me miss, but my wife wants that table back there," he said as he pointed to the occupied table.

"Um, okay. You can wait up front for a little while and I'll make sure that you get it once they're done," the hostess replied.

"Nah, I don't have that kind of patience," Remo said as he turned around and headed to the rear of the restaurant.

"Kareem, please don't cause a scene. I'm okay with wherever she seats us," Kalani said as she grabbed his arm to stop him.

"No, you're not. That's your favorite spot and that's where we're sitting. Ole girl must not know that your husband gives you whatever you want. She's about to learn today though," Remo said as he approached the table.

"Just let it go Kareem," Kalani begged.

"Good evening. I hope y'all are having a good night," Remo said as he smiled at the couple who were at the table.

"Hello," the woman replied politely.

"I hate to interrupt your meals but the hostess needs to move y'all to another table," Remo said.

"Why? Is something wrong?" the woman asked.

"Not really but this is my wife's favorite table and she wants to sit here. I apologize for the inconvenience and your food is on me," Remo said as he reached into his pocket and pulled out two crisps hundred dollar bills.

"Get the plates and let's move baby," the woman said as she gladly took the money that Remo was offering. Their food didn't even total half of that and she didn't see the problem. If all she had to do was move to another spot, then she was winning.

"Man, I'm not doing shit. Give that nigga his money back and sit your ass down. The fuck he think he is," the man spat angrily.

"We're almost done eating anyway," the woman pointed out.

"I don't give a fuck. I might want dessert," the man frowned defiantly.

"I get it bruh. You don't want to make it seem like you're a bitch in front of your girl. I understand and I respect that. But, ask yourself if it's really worth it. We don't know each other and I promise that you want to keep it that way. All I want to do is enjoy a date night with my wife. I'm not trying to be shooting up in this nice ass restaurant," Remo said with a smile that was anything but friendly.

"Get your ass up and let's go Milton. I'm not about to get killed over no damn table. Where do you want us to sit at miss?" the woman asked as she grabbed her plate and looked at the hostess.

"Follow me ma'am," the hostess replied nervously as she walked away. Remo looked at the man who was at the table and he looked scared to death. He grabbed his plate and hurriedly followed his girl to the other side of the restaurant.

"Aye, come clean this table so me and my wife can sit down!" Remo yelled to one of the waiters.

"This is so damn embarrassing," Kalani said as she lowered her head in shame.

"Fuck these people. Your man got you your table," Remo said as he led her to her chair.

A waiter came over and cleaned the table and gave them some new silverware. He took Remo and Kalani's drink orders and came back with them a few minutes later. Once they ordered their food, Remo looked over at his wife and smiled.

"See, this is what I be talking about all the time Kareem. Fathers don't behave the way you do. You can't be trying to bring a baby into this kind of madness," Kalani fussed.

"What madness? I was polite and I paid for their food. That nigga was just in his feelings but fuck him. And stop trying to tell me what kind of father I'm going to be Kalani. Me and Nas might do shit differently but we were raised right. You married me, so what does that say about you?" Remo asked.

"That I'm just as fucked up in the head as you are," Kalani laughed.

"See, that's why we're so good together. I had to take you from that other nigga. He didn't even know what to do with you. All that ass and you would have been married to a fucking policeman. I couldn't let that happen to you baby," Remo said as he blew her a kiss.

When their food came, he ordered another drink as he ate. Remo's life was hectic most times, so he was happy when he got to relax and spend time with his wife. Other women didn't even matter to him anymore. He'd had enough of them to last a lifetime. He wanted to be a good husband to Kalani and an even better father to their kids.

362

"I'm stuffed," Kalani said as she pushed her plate to the side.

"What about your dessert? You know you always get that banana shit every time we come here," Remo replied, speaking of the banana spring rolls that she loved.

"Yeah and you always eat more than me," Kalani pointed out.

"Nah, I'm good on that. I'm eating my wife for dessert," Remo said as he winked and made her blush. He wiped his mouth and pushed back from the table, making Kalani look at him strangely.

"Where are you going?" Kalani asked.

"To get my dessert," Remo replied as he got down on his knees and crawled over to her side of the table.

"Kareem! What are you doing? Get up! We're in a restaurant full of people," Kalani whispered as she looked around frantically.

Nobody seemed to be paying them any mind but she could never be too sure. She was happy that the place was dimly lit and a long tablecloth made it easy for Remo to remain unseen. Still, Kalani was usually loud and vocal in the bedroom. She didn't trust herself to be quiet once her husband started touching her.

"Relax baby," Remo whispered as his hands moved up her thighs and underneath her dress. He pulled Kalani's underwear off and pried her legs open wide.

Kalani gasped when she felt the first flick of his tongue at her opening. She grabbed Remo's head and opened her legs wider to give him better access. At that point, she didn't care who was watching. He was doing his thing and Kalani had tuned everything else out. Remo wrapped his soft lips around her clit and Kalani almost jumped out of her seat. She bit her bottom lip to keep from crying out but it was becoming harder to do. Kalani wanted to scream but she had to keep reminding herself of where she was. Remo locked her in place with his strong arms as he worked his tongue in and out of her.

"Don't stop baby," Kalani begged as she closed her eyes and focused on trying to breathe.

She was losing it and she changed her mind. She wanted him to stop before she embarrassed herself in a restaurant full of people. She couldn't keep quiet and she was unable to keep still. She used her hands and pressed it against Remo's forehead forcefully. She wanted him to back away from her but that only seemed to make him go harder. Kalani's eyes filled with tears and, before long, they were spilling down her cheeks. Remo had her cumming and crying as he ate her like the dessert that they declined to order.

"Wow, Kalani. Is this what it's come down to? You could have had a good man but you chose a street thug instead. Now look at you. Sitting in a restaurant alone, crying," someone said, prompting Kalani to open her eyes.

She frowned when she saw Omar standing there with a judgmental look on his face. He seemed to be enjoying taunting her as two other men stood there with amused smirks on their faces.

"Get the fuck away from my table Omar. You better not talk about nobody crying how my husband had you bawling like a bitch in your own house," Kalani snapped angrily.

"Husband? Please tell me that you didn't really marry that psychopath," Omar said as he scanned her hand for a ring. When he saw it, he shook his head in pity.

"Walk away Omar. I'm telling you this for your own good," Kalani warned.

"Or what?" Omar challenged.

"Or I'm about to knock your pussy ass the fuck out," Remo gritted as he peeked his head from underneath the table.

His face was slick with Kalani's juices but he didn't give a fuck. Omar must have had a death wish to even approach his wife on some bullshit. All the color drained from Omar's face as he locked eyes with the man who still had him looking over his shoulder. He had his home secured like Fort Knox and the cameras recorded whatever he missed. Remo and Nas had him scared to sleep home for a while and he didn't want trouble with them again. Instead of replying, Omar and his friends damn near ran to the exit

364

and out to their cars. Remo was ready to finish what he started but the ringing of his phone stopped him from doing so. If it were anybody else, he would have let it ring. Since it was Nas calling, he picked up on the third ring.

"I need you, bro. It's some serious shit going down. Track my phone and come to me right now," Nas said before he hung up. Remo didn't know what was up but he knew that it had to be something serious. He hurriedly stood to his feet and threw some money on the table. Kalani knew that something was wrong, so she didn't ask any questions. Remo grabbed her hand and they rushed out of the restaurant and straight to his car.

It felt like hours but only a few minutes had passed since Toi had been taken from the store. Her phone was vibrating in her pocket but she was too afraid to answer it. She thought about Stori and how she must have been feeling right now. If nobody else in the world loved her, she knew that her big sister did.

"Call and tell that nigga that we're out here," one of the men said when the car came to a stop.

Toi didn't know where they were but she heard the faint sound of music in the distance. One of the men called and told someone that they were outside waiting on him. Toi's heart started beating even faster. She just knew that she was going to be raped by three men instead of two. She remembered her and Stori watching a documentary on human trafficking and she was scared that she was about to be a victim. All kinds of crazy thoughts were running through her head as she awaited her fate.

"There he go," one of the men said, making Toi tremble with fear.

"What you niggas trying to spend?" someone walked up to the car and asked.

"We got a bill," the man who was in the back of the car with Toi answered.

"The fuck y'all got going on like that?" he asked.

"Man, you should come with us. This bitch about to break me and my bro off proper. Virgin pussy at that," the man who was driving said excitedly.

"Yeah right. I doubt if they even have virgins left around this bitch. These hoes got more bodies than the city morgue," the man outside the car laughed.

"Nah man, she really is a pure one," the driver assured him.

"Check it out for yourself. Get up lil bitch. And I dare you to try swinging again," he warned as he pulled Toi up by her hair.

"The fuck! Man, open the door! Open the muthafucking door nigga!" Eno demanded as he pulled on the door handle.

When they took too long, he reached his hand in through the window and unlocked the door himself. Eno knew Toi very well and he knew that shit was about to get real. Nas was going to be out for blood and so was Stori.

"Aye nigga. The fuck is you doing?" the man who was in the back with Toi yelled when Eno pulled her out of the car. Both men jumped out of the car but Eno was unbothered. Toi had never been so happy to see Eric's brother before in her life. Once she was out of the car, she realized that they were standing in front of Nas and Remo's strip club.

"Are you okay Toi? Did them niggas do anything to you?" Eno asked as she gripped his shirt tightly and trembled in fear.

"No, I'm okay," Toi said in a shaky voice.

"How do you know her?" one of the men asked Eno.

"Y'all niggas are in some shit that only God can get you out of," Eno said as he pulled his phone from his back pocket.

"What! We didn't even do shit. That nigga Corey put us on to her. He said that her people own him some money. He wanted us to snatch her and hold her down until they paid up!" one of the men yelled.

It was only then did Toi really get a good look at them. They were young and both of them had tattoos on their faces with gold teeth in their mouth. They looked scary and sneaky as hell. There was no doubt in her mind that they would have done a little bit of everything to her and more. She was so thankful that they decided to stop for weed first.

"What people, dumb ass? That nigga is a fucking lie. This is Nas' sister-in-law and he don't even run in the same circle as Corey," Eno said as he dialed Nas' phone number.

"Man fuck! I swear bruh, that nigga Corey put us in this bullshit!" one of them yelled in a panic.

"Tell Nas that we ain't have shit to do with all that! Corey and his bitch paid us to do it!" his brother yelled.

They didn't really know Nas but they had tried to get put on with him and his brother before. Eno was making some good money and they wanted in on it. That didn't happen but they still got their weed from him all the time. They knew Eno very well and he was who they called to serve them.

"Answer the damn phone!" Eno yelled when the voicemail picked up for the second time.

"Man Eno, put in a good word for us bruh. This shit ain't on us and we didn't even do nothing to her," one of the brothers said.

"You hit me so fuck you!" Toi yelled angrily. Eno looked at her, shocked to hear her sound so upset. He had been around Toi a few times before and she was always so nice and sweet.

"Let's go man," the brother who was driving said as he hurried back to the car. His brother had barely closed the door before he sped off and away from the club.

"What's good Eno? I'm headed that way now," Nas said when he finally answered the phone. Eric was still tracking Toi's phone and it was taking them in the direction of his club.

"Man, come to the club. I got Toi here," Eno replied.

"The fuck! How did she get there?" Nas asked.

"I'll tell you about it when you get here," Eno replied before he hung up.

It only took about five minutes before Nas was pulling up, with Remo driving up right behind him. Eric was the first one to jump out of the car and rush over to Toi.

"Are you okay Toi?" he asked as he pulled her into a tight hug.

"What happened baby?" Stori asked as she pulled her close once Eric let her go.

"We need to talk Nas," Eno said as he looked over at him.

Dame and Johnny were the two brothers who Toi was in the car with and Eno grew up with them. They used to be his neighbors for a few years before their mother got put out of her house. The brothers were always into something and the police stayed kicking down their door. The landlord got fed up and he eventually evicted them from his house. The two brothers stayed in and out of jail and their mother was always happy when they went. They gave her hell and treated her like shit. Eno remembered his grandmother having to stop them from fighting her several times before but that never stopped them from doing it. Although he was very familiar with them, his loyalty was to Nas. It was because of Nas that he wasn't out there robbing and killing to make money. Nas was the one who made sure that he and his brother ate and never wanted for anything. He would be indebted to him forever and nothing would ever change that.

"Take the car and go home baby. I'll ride back with Remo," Nas said as he looked at Stori. He looked at Toi and got pissed when he saw that her lip was busted. He didn't really want to talk in front of her but he knew that she would tell Stori what happened.

"Go back to the house with sis, Kalani. And if some shit pop off, you and Toi hide and let Stori handle it," Remo spoke up.

"Fuck you, Kareem. Come on y'all," Kalani said as she walked over to Stori's car.

Eric got into the back seat with Toi while Stori drove and Kalani rode up front. Once they were gone, Nas, Remo and Eno went into the club and straight upstairs to the office. Since they no longer managed the place full time, they didn't leave their money there anymore. Bee, Shaq and Eno shared the office now and they were the only other ones to have a key. Bee and Shaq were busy running things on the main floor, so they had the office to themselves for a while.

"What's good Eno?" Nas asked as soon as they sat down.

"I know them niggas who snatched Toi," Eno replied.

"Talk to me," Nas requested.

He and Remo listened as Eno told them everything that he knew. That nigga Corey obviously had a death wish that they were about to fulfill. Nas knew that the woman in question had to be Milan. Misty used to always say that she was crazy and had trouble letting go. She was probably used to dealing with professional men who got the police involved. Unfortunately for her, street justice was all that Nas and Remo knew.

"Damn man. Now I gotta kill four muthafuckers instead of two. They making it hard as fuck for a nigga to get into heaven," Remo sighed.

"Run them cameras back bro. I need to see something," Nas said as he sat there deep in thought. All he needed was a license plate number and his people at the DMV could do the rest. He didn't want to run up on them niggas too soon because they would probably be expecting it. Nas wanted to make them think that everything was all good before he went to pay them a visit.

"Got that ass," Remo said as soon as he saw the car come into view on the camera.

He was mad when Nas first told him how much the security system would cost them and he even tried to protest. His brother was right, as usual, and that's why he always followed his lead. The cameras showed both men's faces clearly when they got out of the car. When they pulled off, Nas got a perfect shot of their plates as well. He printed up a few things before he and Remo decided to call it a night.

"What's the plan bro? What do you wanna do?" Remo asked as he drove towards his brother's house.

"Nothing. My head ain't on straight and I got something that's much more important to think about right now," Nas replied.

"I feel you bro. Let's get through this next month before we do anything else." Remo nodded.

"These niggas getting fat as fuck," Remo said as he and Nas held and fed the babies.

"Stori be putting food in their bottles and shit. These niggas greedy as fuck. We'll be up every hour feeding them if she don't," Nas replied as he put Nakeem on his shoulder to burp him.

"Which one am I holding?" Remo asked as he looked down at his nephew.

"That's Junior," Nas replied.

"Damn man. Now I see why Jarvis used to be going crazy all the time. How the fuck do you know one from the other?" Remo questioned.

"I don't even know bro. I just do." Nas shrugged.

The babies were three months old now and looked exactly like Nas and Remo. Everybody complained about not being able to tell them apart, so Stori ordered some identity bracelets from their pediatrician. Nas couldn't wait for the bracelets to come in because he was tired of people playing the guessing game. His boys were truly identical, just like him and Remo.

"What's good with them two fuck boys? Did Eno find out anything else on them?" Nas asked.

"Them niggas were still locked up as of two days ago. He pulled up the prison website just to be sure. They get a pass for at least another week. All bets are off after that," Nas answered.

Nas and Remo now knew where the two brothers, Dame and Johnny, lived, thanks to his connect at the DMV. They waited an entire week before they got on their bikes and decided to go take a ride in the area. Nas wasn't trying to do anything. He just wanted to see what the area looked like. It was purely coincidental that the brothers got locked up the very same day and were still in jail now. As bad as he wanted them, he wanted Corey and Milan even more. His contact at the DMV couldn't find anything on either one of them and that pissed Nas off even more. The address that Corey had on his license was of an old abandoned house. Milan had never updated her info and she still had the apartment that she shared with Nas listed as her address. It was all good though. Nas had his ways of finding out whatever he needed to know. He and Stori were just happy that things turned out the way they did. Had them niggas not stopped by Eno for weed, there was no telling what they would have done to Toi. Stori was happy that her sister was safe and Toi seemed to be okay after the initial fear wore off. Stori fussed at her for leaving by herself while it was dark outside and Toi swore that she had learned her lesson. She had been scared straight and promised to never do it again.

"Where you want me to lay him at bro?" Remo asked as he stood up with his now sleeping nephew in his arms.

"His name is on the blanket in his crib. Lay him on his back," Nas instructed.

"I need all the practice I can get before I get me some little ones. I just hope mine come one at a time though," Remo laughed.

"Come on baby. We need to go home and get dressed," Kalani said as she and Stori walked into the babies room. Stori had just done her hair and makeup and Nas gave Remo a fresh cut.

"I still feel weird about bringing them to this party. I wish Jarvis and Latrice were available to babysit," Stori spoke up.

They were all going to Lady's house for her and Richard's all-white party and Stori didn't have a babysitter. Jarvis and Latrice had plans and everybody else that she trusted to watch them would be at the party too. She knew that her grandmother wouldn't mind but she would never want her to watch two babies all by herself.

"You know it's not gon' even be that kind of party baby. Richard don't look like the type to have no trap music playing and shit. We might be sitting around eating cucumber sandwiches while somebody plays the piano in the background," Nas said, making them all laugh.

"Nah, Lady said that she hired a soul food caterer. She got everything at her house for the boys that we have here, so it might not be too bad." Stori shrugged.

"My lil niggas gon' be fresh to death in their all white gear," Remo said as he watched Nas lay the other sleeping baby in his crib. Remo smiled when Nas grabbed the baby monitor before they all walked out of the room. His brother was a natural when it came to fatherhood and he was confident that he would be too.

"What time are you picking Eric up Nas?" Toi asked as she held the phone up to her ear.

"You and Eric are getting on people's nerves," Stori fussed.

"Tell that nigga to relax. The party don't start for another four hours," Nas replied.

"He said can you pay for him a cab?" Toi asked, repeating what Eric had just said to her.

"Yeah man, tell his disgusting ass to come on," Nas said while shaking his head.

Eric and Toi were both annoying as hell. Nas understood puppy love, so he didn't fuss about it as much as Stori did. She liked the way that Eric respected her sister and she was cool with him coming over too. Once they saw Remo and Kalani off, Nas and Stori got their clothes together and made sure that they had everything for the babies. Stori and Toi's hair were in pin curls, so there was nothing left for them to do. Eric had arrived but he wasn't dressed. Nas had purchased him an outfit but it was still on the hanger.

"What are y'all in here cooking?" Stori asked when she walked into the kitchen.

"Pancakes," Toi replied as she put another one on the plate that Eric was holding in his hand. She fixed one for Stori and they all sat around eating and talking.

A few hours later, Lady showed up to get the babies while Nas and Stori got dressed. Since Toi and Eric were ready, they helped her bring the babies to her house.

"Let me get some right quick," Nas said as he walked up to Stori and hugged her from behind.

"Hell no, Naseem. Your idea of a quickie is not quick," Stori laughed.

"Ten minutes baby, please," Nas begged.

"No Naseem. You told me that this morning and had me in the bathroom for over an hour," Stori said as she continued to apply her makeup.

"Alright, I want you to remember that shit too," Nas said as he slapped her on the ass.

"I got you when we come home baby. I don't want to mess up my hair and makeup," Stori promised.

"Don't try to go to sleep on me either," Nas warned.

"I'm not," Stori said as she put some nude lipstick on her lips.

Nas smiled as he openly admired the woman he loved. Stori's makeup was flawless and the white Chanel dress that she wore hugged her new curves perfectly. She had a fresh sew-in and the curls cascaded down her back flawlessly. Stori claimed that she was five pounds away from where she needed to be, but Nas disagreed. She was perfect to him and he didn't want her to change a thing.

"My boys got that body looking right," Nas said as he palmed her ass and looked at their reflection in the mirror.

"Smile baby," Stori said as she took a few pictures of them to post on Instagram.

Nas was never the type to pose for pictures with a female, but Stori had him doing everything differently. He used to only post for his businesses but Stori and his boys were all over his Facebook and Instagram pages. For the first time ever, he was happy being with only one woman and he wanted everybody to know it. Women came at him all the time but he was good.

"Let's go," he said once Stori was done with the impromptu photo shoot. Since they lived so close, they locked up their house and walked over to Lady and Richard's place.

"Where is Kalani and Remo? She's not even answering her phone," Stori said as she tried to call her best friend again.

"You know they're always late for everything. The damn party might be over by the time they show up," Nas replied.

"Where is my mama? How the hell can they have a party and lock the door? They probably can't even hear us knocking with that loud ass boring music on," Stori fussed as she rang the bell at Lady's house.

They had some kind of jazz music playing and it was loud as hell. The catering truck was parked out front, along with lots of other cars. They obviously had a lot of people there but it was crazy for them not to be out front to greet their guests. Stori was ready to go back home and get back in her bed. She was just about to call Toi's phone when Nas stopped her.

"Let's go around the back," Nas suggested as he grabbed her hand.

"This is crazy," Stori fussed as she followed her man.

She had a frown etched on her face as they walked around the massive house to enter through the rear. As soon as Nas opened the gate, Stori stopped walking to take in the scenery.

"You gon' stop playing with me so much. I wish I would wait all that time for you to marry me. We're about to do this shit today," Nas laughed as he took in the shocked expression on Stori's face.

They had a huge tent set up with a bunch of white chairs underneath it. Remo and Jarvis stood up front holding the twins, as Kalani and Toi stood next to them. Latrice walked over to Stori and took her purse. She handed her a beautiful bouquet of flowers before she rushed off to take her seat at the front of the yard. Stori didn't want to ruin her makeup but she couldn't help it. Everything was beautiful and she couldn't stop the tears from cascading down her cheeks. Her entire family was there, as well as all the employees from the shop. She couldn't believe that Nas had put an entire wedding together without her knowing about it. Everyone there was dressed in all white and it was amazing to see.

"I love you so much Naseem. I can't believe that you did all of this without me," Stori said as she wiped her eyes.

"Come on baby. Let's go make this shit official," Nas said as he grabbed her hand and walked her over to the pastor who was standing near the decorated altar.

"Baby, wait! I don't even have your ring," Stori whispered.

"I got my own shit. I was tired of waiting on you," Nas said, making her laugh.

Stori hadn't been that happy in a long time and she couldn't stop smiling. Apparently, everybody knew that she was getting married that day except for her. Nas had been planning it since she was pregnant and everyone helped him. He originally planned to rent out a hall but Lady and Richard offered to do it at their house. Their yard looked like a football field and that was even better. They rented a dance floor and had all the food catered. There was an open bar and servers were there to keep everyone full and happy.

Once the ceremony was over with, Nas and Stori took pictures and mingled with their friends and family. Everybody wanted to hold the babies and they were being passed around from one person to the next. The food and drinks were in abundance and everyone partied until late that night. Stori was happy that her family and Lady got along, at least for a little while. Once she saw her grandmother and aunties off, she sat under the tent with Nas and his family.

"Were you surprised Stori?" Toi asked when she and Eric walked over to them.

"Hell yeah I was. I can't believe that y'all did all this without me knowing." Stori smiled as she continued to stare at her ring.

"I'm just happy that the shit is over with. Me and Toi had to go through all your paperwork just to help Nas get the marriage license. I really thought you were going to figure something out. This was the hardest secret that I ever had to keep," Kalani laughed.

"We gotta get packed up baby. We're leaving day after tomorrow," Nas said as he pulled Stori onto his lap and kissed her cheek.

"Leaving to go where?" Stori asked him.

"On our honeymoon. We're going to Fiji for a whole week." Nas smiled excitedly.

Besides when he traveled from one prison to another, Nas had never really been out of town. Latrice was helping him step his game up in a major way. It was her idea for him to rent the yacht for Stori's birthday and that was the kind of boss shit that he liked. It was crazy that he was nearing thirty years old and had just gotten a passport for the first time. A lot of stuff was new to him, including having a wife. Although he was married to Milan before, it wasn't the same. They didn't have a ceremony or a honeymoon. He didn't take his vows or his marriage seriously at the time. He wanted to do everything right with Stori and he promised himself that he would. Milan was his mistake, but Stori was his destiny. From the first day he laid eyes on her, he knew that she would one day be his. Gavin was in his way at the time but Nas still got what he wanted.

"What's wrong friend?" Kalani asked as she took in the somber expression on Stori's face.

"I don't know if I want to be away from my babies that long. Who's gonna watch them for an entire week?" Stori questioned.

"Stop playing with me girl. You know I wasn't leaving my kids with just anybody," Nas replied.

"We'll have the boys, sis. Me and Latrice took a week off to stay at y'all house with them and Toi. Our oldest girl will get her sisters to school for us," Jarvis spoke up.

"And me and Remo will be there every day to help too," Kalani noted.

"Aww, y'all are so sweet. At least I'll be able to enjoy myself without worrying so much," Stori smiled. She was just as excited as Nas was now that she knew that Toi and her boys were in good hands.

"And don't be trying to sit there and hold them all day Jarvis. Nigga be at home sleeping good while me and my wife have to deal with two spoiled ass babies," Nas fussed.

"Fuck you, boy. That's my only two nephews. I'm spoiling all of my nieces and nephews the same way I spoiled my own," Jarvis replied.

"I'm trying to make you some more bro but I don't know what's up with that. This sneaky heifer must be on a plan b diet or something. I've been putting in too much work for her not to be pregnant yet," Remo said as he looked over at Kalani and frowned.

"Divorce him friend. That nigga play with you too much," Stori laughed as she looked at the serious expression on Remo's face.

"Let him keep acting crazy if he wants to," Kalani said as she gave him a warning glare.

"Don't let Stori get you fucked up out here. Remember your vows sweetheart," Remo replied.

"Ain't no divorce. This shit is until death," Nas said while looking at his new bride.

He didn't have to throw hints at her because they were good. Unlike her first time with Gavin, Stori's marriage to Nas felt right. It felt good to actually love and be in love with her husband. That was something that she couldn't say before. She was also happy to be married to the father of her kids. That was something else that she'd always wanted. It didn't happen the way she wanted it to but she was satisfied with the end result.

"Let's go baby. Congrats again guys. We'll be here and ready to work day after tomorrow," Latrice said as he gave Nas and Stori a hug.

"Yeah, we're about to go too. We need to get started on baby number three," Nas said as he winked at Stori.

"Boy, if Stori gets pregnant again before my wife, I'm going to jail. I put that shit on mama and daddy's grave," Remo swore as they all walked out of the yard together.

"Bye y'all," Kalani said as she gave her friend and brother-in-law a hug.

"I'll call you tomorrow friend. We might need to hit up the mall before I go," Stori said as she saw them off.

Remo and Kalani gave Eric a ride home while Toi, Nas and Stori got the twins and went inside. Once they gave the babies a bath and put them to sleep, Nas and Stori took a shower and opened up a bottle of wine. They discussed their upcoming honeymoon, as well as their future together. After they were done talking, they made love for the first time as husband and wife before they both drifted off to sleep.

Milan wiped her teary eyes as she continued to look at the pictures that Nas and Stori had posted. She couldn't believe that they were really married. The ink had barely dried on their divorce decree and he had remarried already. Having a husband was something that Milan always wanted. Being married and having kids was always a dream that seemed to elude her. Her ex back in Texas had her believing that he wanted the same thing but he was a lying womanizer who couldn't stay faithful for more than a week. When he broke up with Milan, she felt like she was losing her mind. She terrorized him and his new girlfriend and they didn't have a moment's peace. It wasn't until he got the police involved that Milan got her mind right. She lost her job and that was one of the reasons that she decided to move to New Orleans.

Meeting and marrying Nas was one of the best things to ever happen to her. Granted, Milan wasn't the best wife but she was trying to do better. Nas never even gave her a chance before he up and left. Then, to make matters worse, he married and started a family with a bitch that she knew. Stori had been her stylist for a little over a year. That was unacceptable and Milan just couldn't seem to let it go.

"You need me to do anything else before I leave?" Brandon, Milan's male companion, asked when he walked out of the kitchen.

He had moved the last of Milan's boxes into her new house and put them where she needed them to go. Milan had moved yet again but she was in a two bedroom house instead of an apartment. Brandon had paid her deposit and her first three months of rent. Milan could finesse her way in and out of any situation and men did whatever she wanted them to. Well, most men did. The man who she had given her heart to was in Fiji celebrating his union to another bitch.

"No boo but thanks for everything. As soon as I get settled in, I want to prepare you a romantic dinner to show my appreciation. Call me when you get off from work. Maybe you can swing by later tonight," Milan cooed seductively as she massaged his manhood through his jeans.

"Damn. Yeah, I got you, baby. I'll call you when I get off," Brandon said as he kissed her cheek and walked away.

Milan rolled her eyes when his back was turned. She walked him to the door and locked it when he left. Brandon was cool for money but the dick was trash. He worked and sold dope, so he didn't mind breaking her off whenever she needed something. Thanks to Corey's incompetent ass, Milan ended up moving again. The two dummies who they paid to snatch Toi fucked up just like his cousins did before. It was even worse that time because those assholes went to Nas and Remo's club with Toi in the car. Granted, they didn't know of Toi's relationship to Nas but that was besides the point. They weren't supposed to stop anywhere. The plan was for them to take her to the spot that Corey had provided. Because they knew where she lived, Milan didn't trust staying in her old place anymore. She knew how much niggas talked when their backs were against the wall. They were young and dumb and she was sure that they would sell her out like it was nothing.

"The fuck is he calling me for?" Milan questioned out loud when she saw Corey's number pop up on her phone screen.

She should have kept it all business with him but she just had to let shit get personal. Corey was a fuck up and Milan saw exactly why he never got ahead in the dope game. He was useless and the niggas that he ran with were even worse.

"What do you want Corey?" Milan snapped when she answered her phone.

"What kind of games are you out here playing? How the fuck you move and don't tell a nigga?" Corey asked.

"I don't have to tell you shit. You ain't my man. Besides, I don't want them grimy ass lil niggas that you be running with nowhere around me," Milan replied.

"Them niggas are locked up. The fuck is you scared for? Them dudes ain't trying to do nothing to you," Corey barked.

"I don't give a fuck about them doing nothing to me but I know how it is. The minute Nas and Remo roll up on them, they'll be selling me out to save their own asses," Milan replied.

"You act like them niggas are God or some shit," Corey argued.

"The grim reaper is more like it," Milan pointed out.

"Why do you keep trying to fuck with them if you feel like that then? I only wanted to rob the niggas. You were the one on that murder and kidnapping shit. I'm just out here trying to get this money," Corey pointed out.

"Well, you ain't trying very hard," Milan said sarcastically.

She honestly didn't know why she kept going at Nas but her wounded pride wouldn't let her give in. She was hurt and she wanted to hurt him too. There was no way that she could let him and Stori live happily ever after. Seeing their sons was a constant reminder of all the unfulfilled promises that he made to her. Nas and Stori's sons looked exactly like him and Remo and that made her sick to her stomach. She was supposed to be the one carrying his babies and living in the big house. The wedding that he gave Stori was the same one that he promised her when he was released from prison. No, Milan couldn't let go when she had so much that she was trying to hold on to. Nobody in her family was speaking to her and Nas was all that she had left.

"Where you posted up at now? Let a nigga come see you," Corey requested.

"Fuck no! I don't want you and none of them incompetent lil niggas nowhere around me," Milan snapped.

"I'm riding solo. Stop acting like that girl," Corey replied.

"I'm good on you, Corey. Thanks to you, I had to spend money that I don't even have. I'm out of almost nine hundred dollars since I had to move," Milan said, lying effortlessly.

"I got you, baby girl. I'm trying to hit this lick and I should be straight for a while," Corey replied as he drove to his destination.

"Boy bye," Milan said as she laughed at what he'd said. She'd never seen a nigga hit so many licks and walk away empty handed.

"Nah baby girl. This is some real shit," Corey swore.

"Yeah okay, just like always," Milan said as she rolled her eyes up to the sky.

"Give me about an hour and I got you," Corey swore.

"Bye," Milan said as she hung up the phone in his face.

Corey put the phone on the seat next to him and pulled out his burner phone. He parked his car on the side of the building and kept it running so that he could make a quick getaway. He didn't need his car stalling when he was trying to make a move. Once he was out of the car, Corey pulled out his gun and made a call on the phone that he'd just purchased.

"Yeah!" a man yelled when he picked up the phone. The music was loud and Corey could barely hear him.

"I'm outside fam. I got a hundred to spend," Corey replied in a tone that was deeper than his own.

"Come inside then nigga," the man barked angrily.

"I don't have my ID on me and you know security ain't having it," Corey noted.

"Who the fuck is this?" the man yelled over the music.

"This is G," Corey said as he called out a random but common name. He knew at least four dudes in the hood who they called G and he was sure that the other man did too.

"I'm on my way nigga," the man said before he hung up. Corey slipped the phone in his pocket and got in position. As soon the door to the club opened, he rushed over and put the gun up to Eno's head.

"You already know what it is nigga. Give it up or lose your life," Corey gritted.

"Relax fam. You got that," Eno chuckled.

"You find something funny nigga?" Corey questioned angrily.

Eno was taking him for a joke and he was ready to make an example out of him. Before he could do anything, the door to the club flew open and a big dude came out with a gun aimed at Corey's head. Eno ducked and the other man started shooting. Corey dropped down to the ground and started returning fire.

"Fuck!" Corey yelped when he caught a bullet to the arm.

He was happy that he kept his car running because he jumped inside and hurriedly sped away. He ducked as he drove when his back window was shot out. He didn't know why he listened to Dame and his brother. They told him that robbing Eno would be an easy lick but they obviously didn't know what they were talking about. They grew up with Eno and they claimed that he always had money and weed since he worked for Nas. The brothers had planned to rob him themselves but they got locked up before they could. As soon as they got released, they put Corey down and he was ready to take Eno for whatever he had.

Now, instead of walking away a little richer, Corey had a bullet in his arm. He needed to get to the hospital but he couldn't tell them what happened. Thinking fast, Corey called one of his baby mamas from the burner phone and told her what happened. She agreed to take him to the hospital, so he headed straight to her house. All he had to do now was come up with a believable story as to why he got shot.

"I guess the honeymoon is officially over," Nas said as he sat in the office at the club and looked at the camera footage.

He and Stori had only been back home from Fiji for two days when Eno and Bee hit him and Remo with some bullshit. Remo voiced his anger but Nas was calm as they watched it all unfold on the monitor. Eno used his head when he went to look at the camera before going outside to serve Corey. He knew that something wasn't right and he had Bee on standby. They were thankful that no one heard the gunshots because the loud music in the club drowned out the sounds. Once Bee and Eno left the office, Nas sat there deep in thought.

"I'm tired of dealing with all this bullshit bro. It's like a nigga can't catch a break. All I wanna do is enjoy life with my wife and make some babies. Is that too fucking much to ask for?" Remo questioned as he paced the floor angrily.

He was trying to do better but niggas just wouldn't let him be great. He left all the hoes alone and was a faithful husband but that obviously wasn't good enough. Niggas didn't like it when he was Kareem. They wanted to awaken the beast known as Remo but he was ready for whatever.

"What's pissing me off is the stupid shit that these dummies are doing. How the fuck you try to rob somebody but you call them outside to you? Just like them other lil niggas who snatched Toi. What kind of niggas kidnap somebody and ride with them inside the car? That's what the trunk is for," Nas said while shaking his head.

"These niggas are lame as fuck and trying to come at us on some hoe shit. Lil ass boys trying to play a grown man's game. I'm done with this cat and mouse bullshit bro. I want these niggas dead and that bitch Milan too. At least the lil niggas that shot you had enough sense to skate out of town. These lil bold bitches must be on some other shit," Remo fumed.

"Let's go take a ride," Nas said as he got up and walked out of the office.

Remo followed behind him, never bothering to ask where they were going. Nas always had a plan that he never had a problem following. When they got into the car, they were quiet as Nas drove to their destination. Remo had been to Dame and Johnny's house before, so he knew exactly where they were headed.

"Look bro, follow them niggas," Remo said when they turned on their street and saw the car that the two brothers were in pulling away from the house.

Nas followed right behind the car but not too close. They couldn't tell who was driving because the windows were tinted. He drove for less than ten minutes before the car came to a stop in the parking lot of a strip mall. Remo had his gun out, making sure that it had enough bullets to get the job done. He would never start shooting in such a crowded area but he didn't mind following them until the opportunity presented itself. Nas parked a few cars over and waited for someone to exit the car. When the doors opened, the occupants of the car were not who he expected them to be.

"Look at this shit bro. Them niggas are dumb as fuck. They out here doing dirt in their mama's car like it ain't nothing. They better be lucky that we're not some grimy ass niggas. Anybody else would have knocked their mama's head off just to send a message to them," Nas fussed. They watched as two older ladies exited the car and walked into one of the stores in the strip mall. Nas remembered Eno telling him how dirty the brothers did their mother and he felt pity for a woman that he didn't even know. He loved his mother unconditionally up until the day she died. He couldn't see himself putting his hands on her in any way other than to hug her. He and Remo wished that their mother was still alive while other niggas were out there taking theirs for granted.

"That's fucked up. A lot of innocent people lose their lives like that," Remo spoke up.

"It's all good though. Them niggas are living on borrowed time and I put that on mama's grave," Nas fumed.

"I want that nigga Corey too," Remo said as his brother pulled off.

"No worries bro. Them lil niggas gon' tell us everything that we want to know," Nas assured him. He drove Remo back to the club to get his car. Nas had to get his head on straight and he wasn't quite there yet. He hadn't even been able to really enjoy being married because bullshit just kept getting thrown at him. Nas understood where Remo was coming from and he felt the exact same way. All he wanted to do was live a normal life with his wife and kids and nobody was going to change that.

"Where did Bee get this piece of shit from? This bitch looks like it's on its way to car heaven," Remo said as he and Nas sat in the raggedy car that their cousin had loaned them.

"I don't know but I've been itching since I got up in this bitch," Nas replied while scratching at his arm.

An entire week had passed before they decided to go pay the brothers another visit. Nas had learned a few things during that time and he was ready to put in some work. Stori was still on edge about what happened to Toi and she refused to let her leave the shop if someone wasn't with her. She didn't care if it was daylight outside. Toi never went anywhere alone.

"Look bro," Remo said when the door opened and Dame came walking out of the house.

Their mother ran out behind him, followed by his brother. The older woman was yelling but they couldn't make out what she was saying. Nas was parked too far away but Remo rolled down the window to listen. Apparently, the woman didn't want them to take her car but they weren't trying to hear that. They were cursing her out like she was a bitch on the street and they didn't even feel bad about it.

"Damn! That's fucked up!" Nas yelled when he saw one of the brothers push their mother, almost making her fall.

"Them niggas are going straight to hell and we're the niggas that's about to send them," Remo said as he cocked his gun.

Nas' heart dropped when he saw the way they were handling their mother. He would knock his sons on their asses if they even looked at Stori wrong. Eno and Eric's mother was a crackhead and they still treated her with respect.

"I'm mad as fuck right now," Nas said as he watched one of them grab their mother by her shirt and push her back inside.

They were cursing her out and laughing like the shit was funny. She was obviously afraid of them because she never came back out. When the brothers pulled off, Nas was right behind them. He watched as they stopped for gas and to another store for liquor. When they pulled up to the projects, they pulled into an area that was too well lit for Nas and Remo's liking.

"Fuck! Them street lights are bright as fuck. Nobody is out here but that's still not a good look," Remo said as he looked around the area. He screwed the silencers on his and Nas' guns, ready to shoot without being heard.

"Relax bro. Just be patient," Nas said as he watched the two men exit the car.

Remo's leg bounced impatiently as he and Nas played the waiting game. Almost another hour passed before the brothers walked out of the house laughing as if they weren't about to die soon. Nas started following them again until they pulled up to a rundown apartment complex. The entire area looked abandoned and there was not a working light in sight.

"Let's do this," Nas said as he put the car in park and left it running. He and Remo didn't even bother to mask up because they didn't plan to leave any witnesses.

The brothers got out of the car, not even paying attention to their surroundings. Nas let off a silent shot, hitting one of them right in the head. His body hit the ground before he even realized what had happened. Remo hit his brother in the leg, temporarily disabling him for a minute.

"Ahh!" the man yelled out as he fell to the ground. He looked over and saw his brother's lifeless body on the ground and his eyes filled with tears. Nas and Remo kneeled close to him, so that he could see exactly who they were.

"Don't cry now nigga. You weren't crying when you snatched up my sister-in-law," Nas gritted.

"I know you ain't crying over your bitch ass brother. Save your tears lil nigga. You'll be reunited with him again real soon," Remo fumed.

"One chance and one chance only. Where is Corey?" Nas asked.

"Milan's house in Harvey," the man cried as he rattled off the address like the hoe he was.

"You done talking to this nigga bro? We gotta get a move on," Remo said.

"Finish him," Nas replied as he stood up to his full height and walked back to the car. Remo let off two shots to his head and one more to his brother's head before he got back into the car.

"That nigga dumb as fuck. He knew he was about to die and he still gave up the info," Remo said while shaking his head.

"They need to stay in their lanes. Lil niggas don't even be built for the life that they're trying to live. You can see that by how sloppy they move. Corey been doing the same shit for all these years and ain't get ahead yet. Backwards hustling and robbing niggas is not where it's at. Milan got herself in some shit that only death can get her out of," Nas replied.

"Damn man. Ole girl gotta bury two of her kids now," Remo said as he thought about Dame and Johnny's mother.

"It might sound fucked up but we probably did her a favor. Them niggas did that lady dirty," Nas replied.

"Where to now?" Remo asked.

"Home to my wife and kids. I think we've shed enough blood for the night," Nas answered.

"Two down and two to go," Remo noted.

"I thought this part of our life was over with," Nas sighed.

"It'll never be over with as long as niggas think they can try you. I told you from day one that I didn't trust that bitch Milan. She was trying too hard to take you from Alissa. That bitch is unstable," Remo argued.

"So am I," Nas replied as they pulled up to the club.

Bee came out and got his keys from them before Nas and Remo left to go their separate ways. When Nas got home, Stori was just putting one of the babies in his crib. She grabbed the monitor and followed him down the hall to their bedroom.

"You good baby?" Stori asked as she pulled his shirt over his head for him.

"Yeah, for now," Nas replied.

"What do you mean?" Stori questioned.

"Grab the monitor and let's take a shower," he replied as he walked into the bathroom.

He and Stori didn't keep secrets from each other and that was the part of their relationship that he loved the most. She knew everything, even the shit that could get him sent away for life. Stori was on the same shit that he was on and she showed him just how much she had his back. She was pissed to know that Corey was behind everything that was going on and she was baffled as to why. They had a relationship years ago but it had been over for a long time. If he was salty about that, he had years to retaliate if that's what he wanted to do. Corey was grimy so nothing that he did surprised her. Milan had more motive than he did and she proved that by her actions.

As they showered, Nas told her everything that went down. She was pissed that Milan hadn't been dealt with yet but Nas promised her that she would be. He didn't have no kind of compassion towards her being his ex-wife. She was coming after his queen and, for that, she had to die.

"Bitch, remind me again of why we came to this location," Stori said as she looked over at Kalani.

"Because it's closer to my house and the other location be too damn crowded," Kalani noted as she did a slow jog on the treadmill.

She and Stori were at the gym and her girl had been complaining since they got there. The men were relentless and they flirted like it was a sport. Stori got tired of telling them that she was married and Kalani did too. They flashed their wedding rings a million times but that was a waste. None of the men seemed to care and they were still trying to flirt. They had been there for over an hour and nothing had changed.

"I hate coming to the gym at night. You should go early in the morning before work like I do. Nobody be in there and it's peaceful. These niggas are thirsty as fuck up in here," Stori frowned.

"Don't even talk to me about work. I hope Nas tell them to hurry up and finish the renovations on the shop. I hate working in the store by myself," Kalani frowned.

"You're not by yourself. You got the two security guards in there with you," Stori laughed.

"That's not funny bitch. I don't know them niggas and Remo got them scared to even talk to me," Kalani fussed.

"Nas said that it shouldn't be too much longer. They're doing a good job," Stori replied.

The workers had to knock down a wall in the shop to make the property next door a part of it. They replaced the floors and built in some shelves for the hair and hair supplies to go on. Everything was coming along but Kalani was tired of waiting. She couldn't wait for the day when she would be working alongside her husband and best friend. Things couldn't get any better than that.

"I hope they speed it up," Kalani said as a man walked over to them. She laughed when Stori rolled her eyes because she already knew what was up.

"How you doing beautiful? You got a man?" He asked while looking at Stori lustfully.

"No, I don't have a man but I used to be one," Stori replied.

"Huh?" the man asked with a puzzled look on his face.

"I'm transgendered but I hope that's not a problem. What's your name handsome?" Stori asked as she walked closer to him. She tried to touch his chest but he backed up.

"Uh... I'm good. I got a girl," the man said as he tripped over his feet trying to get away from them.

"Bitch! Did you just tell that man that you were transgendered?" Kalani asked as she stopped the treadmill and fell out laughing.

"I sure did. Fuck him. I got a dick too," Stori said, making her friend laugh harder.

"You and Nas are definitely made for each other," Kalani said as she wiped her face with her towel.

"I'm ready whenever you are. I'm starving," Stori replied.

"Me too but Kareem wants to go out and eat," Kalani said as they walked towards the exit.

"Tell that nigga to eat only what's on the menu this time," Stori joked. She was weak when Kalani told her about them running into Omar at the restaurant. It was even funnier when Stori learned what Remo was doing at the time.

"You want to stop to grab you something to eat before I bring you back to your car?" Kalani asked. Stori had parked by her house and Kalani drove them to the gym.

"No, I cooked before I left," Stori replied. Nas and Toi were home with the babies and she made sure to feed them all before she left.

She and Kalani made small talk as she drove. Stori was trying to find something to listen to on the radio when her friend stopped at a red light. She looked up towards a strip mall that they were passing and had to do a double take.

"Pull up over there!" Stori yelled, scaring Kalani.

"For what?" Kalani questioned as she switched lanes.

"I want a smoothie," Stori replied.

"I thought your hungry ass said that you had food at home," Kalani reminded her.

As soon as she pulled up to the strip mall, Stori jumped out of the car. Kalani hadn't even made it to Smoothie King yet, so she didn't know what her friend was doing. It wasn't until she saw Stori run up to a car and pull a woman out of it did she realize what was going on. Milan was in line at a fast food restaurant next door and Stori spotted her when they were at the red light. She didn't even see Stori coming and she didn't have time to get right and fight back.

"Bitch! You got the right one hoe!" Stori fumed as she repeatedly punched Milan in the face and head. She was hanging halfway out of the car and Stori was trying to pull her all the way out.

"Stori! Get your crazy ass back in this car!" Kalani yelled.

"Bring me my purse friend. I'm about to shoot this bitch," Stori fumed as she finally succeeded in pulling Milan out of the car. She had her on the ground stomping her in the face and body when Kalani made it over to them.

"Get your crazy ass back in the car. Are you trying to go to jail?" Kalani asked as she pulled her friend away from her opponent.

Milan hurriedly hopped into her car as people watched and recorded. Kalani thought that she was going to drive away but she drove straight towards them instead. She tried to use her car as a weapon and run them over. Thankfully, they jumped back just in time before she could hit them. When she backed up, Stori grabbed her gun from her purse, ready to fill Milan with some hot lead.

"Come on bitch! Come get this work!" Stori yelled as she aimed the gun right at her. When she saw that Stori was holding a weapon, Milan's common sense kicked in. She was fuming as she sped away in the opposite direction.

"You are the female version of your husband. I don't see how it took y'all so long to get together," Kalani said as she shook her head.

"Stupid bitch better be happy that you pulled me off of her," Stori fussed.

She was pissed that Nas and Remo hadn't caught up to Milan and Corey yet. They went to her last known address but the bitch had already moved. Stori wished that she would have let Kalani follow her to see where she lived but it was too late for that now. Her anger got the best of her and she beat Milan's ass instead. Knowing that she was partially responsible for what happened to Toi had Stori on another level of anger.

"Your crazy ass is probably on WorldStar by now," Kalani laughed.

"Good. I'm happy I wore my cute gym clothes today," Stori replied.

They laughed about the incident but Kalani was happy that a fight was all that took place. Stori was trigger happy and she learned that about her friend a long time ago. She didn't mind pulling a gun out on somebody and she wasn't afraid to really use it. Kalani couldn't wait to tell Remo what happened. Stori was on the same tip as him and Nas and he loved the crazy side of her. Kalani could fight with the best of them but that was as far as she would go. She left the shootouts to her husband, best friend and brother-in-law.

"**M**an, I love my sister-in-law. Stori be bout that gun play," Remo said to Nas as he drove the rental car to their destination.

"Yeah but I don't want her on that dumb shit no more. She can't be out here fighting and shooting at people like that all the time. We got kids that we have to think about now. My baby temper is bad as fuck," Nas laughed as he thought about his wife.

No one was shocked to hear about Stori beating Milan's ass the week before. Milan was being an internet thug again and was sending all kinds of threatening messages to Stori and Nas. They ignored her, just like always, but Nas was ready to put that problem behind them. He hated unfinished business and that's exactly what Milan and Corey were. He had been going crazy trying to find out their whereabouts but he hadn't had any luck yet. There was only one person who he knew that could possibly help and they had just pulled up to the house a minute ago. They were just in time because a car had just pulled into the driveway. They waited until they saw someone get out and go inside before they made a move.

"You ready to do this bro?" Remo asked as he looked over at him.

"Always." Nas nodded as they both exited the car.

Although it was dark outside, he and Remo weren't trying to be discreet. Nas was tired of the back and forth and he just wanted it all to be over and done with. They had their guns in hand as they walked up to the front door. They didn't even think about knocking. Nas lifted his foot and kicked the door in, making it slam against the wall.

"Ahhh!" Drina yelled when both men rushed into the house.

"Where is your punk ass husband?" Remo asked as he aimed the gun right at her head.

Drina had a bottle of apple juice in her hand that fell to the floor and shattered. She was terrified and she had every reason to be. This was the second time that the two men had entered her house and she was afraid that they weren't going to leave her alive again.

"He's not here. We're separated," Drina replied in a shaky voice.

All she and Carlton did was argue and she was over all the cheating and lies. The last time the twins were there, they put her on to her husband's cheating ways and they weren't lying. Drina had followed him a few times and saw everything that she needed to see. She was in the process of moving out and she had already filed for divorce. Carlton had cheated in the past and she forgave him. She wasn't willing to keep doing the same thing though.

"I need you to understand a few things before you lie to me. My patience are nonexistent at this point and I won't feel bad if I had to do you dirty. We lost our mother at a young age and I would hate to take you away from your kids," Nas warned.

"I swear that I'm telling you the truth but my husband wasn't. He knew that Corey was involved in what happened to you. That's another reason why we're not together. He tried to protect his cousin and put our lives in jeopardy in the process," Drina said as her hand continued to shake nervously.

"Come sit down and let's chat," Nas said as he motioned towards the sofa.

He had to put fear in Drina in order for her to fully cooperate but Nas would never do anything to her. She was innocent and so was her husband. She was also one of the only people who could get them exactly what they needed in order to make something happen.

"Tell us everything that you know," Remo requested as he sat on the arm of the sofa that Drina was seated on.

"I really don't know anything," Drina replied honestly.

"I have a few questions that I need answers to. Now, you might not have the answers but I'm giving you a week to get some. And please, do us both a favor and don't try to play no games. I've had enough of that to last me a lifetime," Nas sighed in frustration.

"I'll tell you whatever you want to know. Fuck Corey! If leading you to him means keeping me and my family safe, then it's done. Carlton and I are separated but he's still the father of my kids. I don't want anything to happen to him," Drina said as tears burned her eyes.

"You and your husband are not on my radar and you never were. If he wasn't related to the nigga who I really want, you probably would have never even seen me again," Nas assured her.

"Your husband is a fuck boy for even trying to protect his no good ass," Remo chimed in.

"I agree. Corey doesn't have a good bone in his body and we all know that. He's stolen from everybody in their family and nobody can trust him. Hell, I don't even think anybody will shed tears when he dies. We've all been expecting it to happen for years," Drina replied.

As crazy as it seemed, she felt very comfortable around the two of them. She knew that if they wanted her dead, she wouldn't have been sitting on the sofa talking with them right now. She was no fool though and she would take whatever happened to her grave. They could put a bullet in Corey's head right there in her face and she would get on the witness stand and lie on their behalf. Some people were just rotten to the core and Corey was one of them.

"Here's my number. Make sure you use it," Nas said as he handed her a business card.

"Okay," Drina replied while nodding her head.

"Sorry about your door. Here, get that fixed," Nas said as he handed her a stack of money. He and Remo walked out of her house and back to their car. They were silent until they drove away.

"I don't know about ole girl bro. You're better at reading people than I am. Do you think she's gonna come through?" Remo questioned.

"Absolutely. She hates that nigga Corey more than we do. Shit, if you ask me, she hates her husband too. Her kids are the only thing that's saving his ass. She probably would have asked us to kill him too," Nas laughed.

"So, now what?" Remo wanted to know.

"Now, we wait," Nas replied as he pulled a rolled blunt from his pocket and lit it.

If nothing else, he was patient. Remo wanted microwave results but that wasn't always possible. Nas didn't mind waiting for something that he really wanted. After all, that was how he got Stori too.

Milan looked at herself in the full length mirror and smiled at what she saw. She had on a short silk nightie and her hair was pulled up into a messy bun. She had a light coating of makeup on her face to cover the fading bruises that she'd received two weeks ago. Physically, she was just about completely healed. Emotionally, she wanted Stori's head on a silver platter for what she had done. Milan wasn't a slacker when it came to fighting but she was caught off guard that time. As small as Stori was, her licks felt like they came from a grown ass man. Milan was laying low for a while but it was far from being over.

She had told Corey what happened and he assured her that he had her back. Milan had finally let him come over to her house a few days ago and that was only because he gave her some weed and money. Now, she was expecting a visit from Brandon. He worked a lot, so Milan didn't see him as much as she wanted to. She got excited when he called and told her that he had something for her. Milan was hoping that it was dick or money because she was in need of both at the moment. When her doorbell rang, Milan sprayed on some perfume and rushed to go let him in.

"Hey handsome." Milan smiled when she opened the door. Her smiled faded a little when she saw that he was standing there with his cable company uniform on. She was hoping that he'd just come from work and wasn't about to go.

"What's up beautiful?" Brandon smiled. He handed Milan a colorful arrangement of flowers before giving her a soft kiss on the lips.

"Aww, thanks boo. That was so sweet of you. Come in," Milan said as she moved to the side for him to enter.

"I can't baby. I've been called in to work to do some overtime," Brandon replied.

"This late?" Milan asked skeptically.

"Yeah, that means more money," he replied with a shrug.

It was only a little after eight but that was still too late for the kind of work that he did. That was exactly why Milan preferred to date street niggas. They didn't have a clock to punch and they made their own schedule. She had to get her shit together and find her a few more sponsors. Brandon was okay but she needed a few more players on her team.

"I guess I'll be spending another night alone," Milan pouted.

"Not necessarily. Close your eyes," Brandon demanded.

"Why? What do you have for me?" Milan asked excitedly.

"Just close your eyes like I told you to." Brandon smiled.

"Okay, they're closed," Milan said as she shut her eyes tight. Brandon reached under the chair that was on Milan's porch and grabbed the bag that he kept out of view.

"You can open them now," he said as he held the bag up for her to see.

"Oh, my God! A toy poodle! She's beautiful!" Milan squealed excitedly. She'd always wanted a tiny toy Poodle but she was never home enough to take care of a dog. Now that she had lots of free time on her hands, she was happy to finally have what she'd always desired.

"Her name is Fendi, just like you wanted. The breeder said that she's paper trained and she responds to her name." Brandon smiled. Milan was overcome with emotion when he said that. To know that Brandon actually listened to her was worth more than any gift that he could ever give her. He would never be her one and only but he would definitely rank higher than all the rest. After Naseem, she swore to never fall in love with anyone else ever again.

"I love her already. Thank you so much boo. I wish you didn't have to work. I'd been in here swallowing your babies all night," Milan flirted as she planted a juicy kiss on his lips.

"I'm off for the next two days. I'd be happy to let you," Brandon smirked.

"Well, it's a date." Milan smiled as she pulled him closer and stuck her tongue in his mouth. She kissed him long and hard while massaging his erection through his slacks. Milan was horny as hell and he was going to get the royal treatment the next time he came over. He wasn't all that good in the bedroom but she knew what to do to get herself off. Besides some head action from Corey a few days ago, Milan had been in a sexual drought.

"Damn baby. Let me get going before I don't make it to work at all," Brandon said when they finally pulled away.

Milan watched him lustfully until he pulled off and out of view. Once he was gone, she took the dog out of the carrier and cradled her in her arms. Her fur was snow white and she had a pink bow at the top of her head. The carrier had the dog's name engraved on it and so did the blanket and brush that were inside. Milan was in love already. She grabbed her phone and posted a picture of her new best friend on Instagram. After that, she made a list of things that she would need to get from the pet store. The dog had gone to sleep, so Milan ate and took a shower. Once she was done, she saw the puppy peek her head up from the blanket that she was napping on.

"Hey Fendi. I'm your new mommy. I'm gonna spoil your pretty ass to death," Milan said, right as her doorbell rang. It was after eleven that night and she didn't know who could be coming to her house so late. Only a handful of people knew where she lived, so she was baffled as to who was there at all. When her phone rang, she picked up when she saw that it was Corey calling.

"Open the door scary," Corey laughed once she answered for him. Milan was livid as she hung up the phone and stomped to her front door. She frowned when she opened it and saw Corey's smiling face standing there like he had an invite.

"How many times do I have to tell you not to pop up at my damn house? You are not my man. You don't know if I have company here or not," Milan fumed.

"Man, I'm not trying to hear all that bullshit. If a nigga was in here, you wouldn't have answered the phone or opened the door," Corey pointed out as he strolled in without being invited. The bottle of Hennessey that he was clutching was the only thing that got him in. Milan was in need of a stiff drink and all she had was wine. She closed and locked her door before joining him in her bedroom.

"I hope you got something to smoke," Milan said as she flopped down on the bed.

"Always. Where did this ugly ass dog come from?" Corey asked as he pulled a rolled blunt from his pocket and handed it to her.

"Fuck you, nigga. My baby is not ugly. And what the hell are you doing here anyway?" Milan questioned as she lit the blunt and took a long pull.

"I'm making my rounds to see all my hoes before I go," Corey laughed.

"You must have me confused with the next bitch. If I am a hoe, I'm not one of yours. Besides good weed and head, you can't do shit else for me," Milan replied, making him angry.

Corey felt played by how she always tried to handle him. Milan made him feel like a joke and no other woman had ever made him feel that way before. Truthfully, Stori was on a higher level than Milan and she was Corey's girl for over a year. Milan always had her hand out but she never wanted to put out.

"It's all good. I'm leaving New Orleans and all these hoes behind. I'll send for my kids once I get settled," Corey replied as he opened his bottle of liquor and took a huge gulp.

He was going to Dallas by his aunt and hopefully get a fresh start. His cousin, who had a hand in trying to rob Nas, was there and he seemed to be doing good. He had a job and was taking welding classes at night. Corey was ready for a change of scenery. He laid low after being shot outside of Nas and Remo's club but he knew that he couldn't hide forever. Corey's car was a piece of shit but he sold it to a chop shop just to put some money in his pockets. He was using that money to take a bus to Dallas the following morning and hopefully start a new life. He wanted to be able to help with his kids when he needed to. Besides being their father, he had never really done anything else for them. He was happy that their mothers handled business because he never did.

"Damn, I'm gonna miss that mouth more than anything," Milan said as she laughed and choked on the weed.

She grabbed Corey's bottle and took a few big sips before sitting the blunt in the astray. After a while, the weed and liquor had her feeling good but she needed Corey to make her feel better. He obviously felt the same way and she was happy that she didn't have to ask. He took the initiative and walked over to her before she could ask. He removed Milan's clothes and spread her legs wide. She was still puffing on the weed when Corey buried his entire face between her legs. Milan arched her back and moaned as she grabbed the back of his head. She wanted him to make her cum and she didn't want to wait. Milan held on tight to the back of his neck as she gyrated her hips and humped his face. She needed a release and Corey wasn't disappointing.

He kept up with her wild movements as he sucked her clit up into his mouth. Milan's head was spinning and she knew that the weed and alcohol were the reason behind it. Corey was devouring her and she held on tight for the ride. When she felt her body start to shake and twitch, Milan grabbed on to the sheets and cried out as she came long and hard. She was still as she laid in bed but the entire room seemed to be rotating. She was sorry that Corey was leaving but that was the best going away present ever.

"Damn girl. When was the last time you had some dick?" Corey asked as he got up and wiped his mouth.

"Too damn long," Milan said as her chest heaved up and down rapidly.

"Let me help you out with that. No need to go without when I'm right here," he replied while licking his lips.

"I'll pass. You just got me right so I'm good for a while," Milan replied as she tried to get out of the bed.

"Nah, see, I wasn't asking," Corey said as he pushed her back down. Milan cringed when she saw him pull down his pants and boxers.

"Move Corey! Are you out of your mind nigga?" Milan yelled.

"Yeah, I really must be to let you play me for so long. I've been giving your hoe ass money, weed and more head than all my baby mamas combined. You owe me bitch and it's time to pay up," Corey hissed. Milan tried to get up again but he grabbed her by her neck and held her down.

"Corey stop. Please don't do this," Milan said as tears fell from her eyes.

"Don't cry now bitch. You didn't cry when you were taking my money and weed. You never cried when I was eating your pussy two and three times a day like you begged me to. Fuck that. It's time to pay up," Corey gritted as he rammed his dick inside of her. He wasn't trying to be gentle. He didn't want to make love to her ass. He was trying to fuck.

"No! Stop!" Milan screamed and cried. She had her radio playing softly on her nightstand but Corey reached over and turned it up louder. Milan lived in a house now but he still didn't want anyone to hear her screaming.

"I knew this pussy was gon' be good. Stop fighting me and take it," Corey said as he pumped in and out of her vigorously.

"Please stop. You're hurting me," Milan whimpered.

"Shut the fuck up bitch! I'm surprised that your hoe ass even got walls left," Corey grunted.

There was no need for Milan to fight any longer. Corey had her hands pinned above her head as he fucked her with no remorse. She cringed when she felt his hot tongue gliding along her exposed breasts. That was her spot but she was not aroused. When he stopped and pulled out of her, Milan released a breath of gratitude. When he entered her anally, warm tears spilled from her eyes as the searing pain enveloped her entire body. She'd been anally penetrated several times before but she always used some kind of lubricant. She was too dry but Corey didn't seem to care.

"Corey stop, please," Milan cried and begged. Her cries of discomfort seemed to make him go even harder. He grunted and moaned as he picked up the pace and fucked her harder. Milan wanted it all to be over with. She had never felt so violated in her life. Even when she danced, she had never done anything that she didn't want to do. She was never forced.

"Ahh!" Corey yelled suddenly as he pulled out of her.

Milan's eyes popped open to see what was going on. She was terrified when she saw two masked men with guns standing at the foot of her bed. One of them had obviously hit Corey in the head with the gun because he was holding the wound that was leaking blood all over her comforter. Milan hurriedly covered her naked body with a sheet before scurrying to the top part of her bed. She rested her back against the headboard as her heart beat rapidly in her chest. When the two men took their masks off, she trembled in fear at the sight of Nas and Remo standing there.

"This nigga was straight up taking the pussy. Where they do that at?" Nas questioned with a smirk.

He was shaking his head at how pathetic Corey was. He and Remo heard Milan's screams before they entered the house but they didn't know what was going on. When the music was turned up, Nas used his gun to shoot the lock off the door for them to enter. Since the silencer was attached, no one ever heard when they walked in. They didn't bust up in the room right away. They listened for voices to see how many people were in the house. What they didn't expect to hear was Corey's sad ass raping someone. As grimy as Milan was, Nas didn't approve of that at all. Pussy was everywhere and it wasn't hard to get. It wasn't even that serious for him to be taking it.

"That's good for her stupid ass. You got this fuck boy coming at my brother on some bullshit and look at how dirty he did you." Remo frowned.

"Fuck both of you niggas. I'm too real to beg anybody for anything, including my life. Do what the fuck you came here to do," Corey barked angrily.

"With pleasure my nigga," Nas replied as he aimed the gun at his head and let off two shots. The first shot probably killed him but Nas wasn't taking any chances. Corey talked all that shit but his eyes told the real story. He was afraid and he had every reason to be.

"Ahhh!" Milan screamed, as Corey's lifeless body slumped across her bed.

"The fuck you making all that noise for dummy? You should be happy that the nigga is dead after what he was in here doing to you," Remo snapped.

"Why didn't you just leave like your sister did Milan? I gave you more than one chance to back off but you just couldn't let the shit go," Nas said while shaking his head.

"I'm so sorry Naseem. I'll leave tonight, I swear. You'll never see or hear from me again. Just... please. Please don't kill me," Milan cried as she begged for her life.

"I'm a savage but I do have a heart. You were my wife at one time Milan. I would never take your life and that's a promise," Nas assured her as he lowered his gun. Milan visibly relaxed as she watched him put the weapon in the waistband of his jeans. Nas made some kind of hand motions to Remo and he raised his gun and aimed it right at her head.

"Noooo!" Milan screamed, right before a single shot entered her head and silenced her cries.

"Stupid ass bitch must be on dope if she thought she was walking up out of here alive," Remo spat angrily.

"Well, I kept my promise. I didn't tell her that she wasn't going to die. I just told her that I wouldn't kill her." Nas shrugged as he looked around the house.

Remo grabbed the gun that they'd used on Dame and Johnny and wrapped Corey's hand around it. He knew exactly how the law worked. If they ran ballistics on it, Corey would be identified as the shooter. His prints would be the only ones on the weapon. But, just in case they didn't, he threw a few bags of coke next to his body and a few on the floor. He was an expert at staging a crime scene, thanks to being a criminal all his life.

"Let's roll bro," Remo said once he was done.

He and Nas headed for the door until something else got their attention. When a small dog came from up until the table, Nas bent down and picked it up.

"Grab all that shit for me bro," Nas said as he motioned to all the dog's accessories that were on the floor.

"The fuck is you doing bruh?" Remo asked.

"Bringing home a surprise for Toi," Nas replied.

Remo gathered all the dog's belongings before he and Nas headed around the corner to the car that they had arrived in. For the moment, their problems were solved and they could breathe a little easier. Nas was over all the drama and so was Remo. They were married now and they were trying to be done with all that street shit. Nas had two kids to think about and he wanted to be there to see them grow up.

"Kalani missed her period," Remo said out of the blue as Nas drove.

"Yeah! Congrats bro!" Nas replied excitedly with a big smile covering his face.

"Thanks bro but I hope it's good news. I don't want to get my hopes up and be disappointed," Remo sighed.

"Nah bro. It's good news, I can feel it," Nas said.

"My nerves are bad as fuck too. We got like three tests but I'm too scared for her to take the shit. I'm never scared of nothing but finding out the results of my wife's pregnancy test terrifies the hell out of me," Remo rambled.

"Do it bro. We've solved the last of our problems for now and it's time for a nigga to be happy. My boys are getting bigger and I don't have time for the dumb shit no more. We're finally seeing the kind of money that we want to see and life is lovely. Kalani being pregnant is just the final piece of the puzzle," Nas said as they pulled up to the club.

"Alright bro. Keep your phone close by. I'm telling her to take the test as soon as I get home. Love you bruh," Remo said as he leaned over the seat and gave his brother a hug.

"Love you too bro," Nas replied before they got out of Bee's car and got into their own.

It was late and Nas just wanted to cuddle up with his wife and relax. When he pulled up to the house, he saw that the light was on in their bedroom. Nas looked in on his boys and smiled at them sleeping peacefully. It still amazed him how much they looked like him and Remo. Stori carried them but that was all that she did. When Nas went down the hall to their bedroom, Stori jumped up from the bed and rushed over to him.

"Are you okay baby? Why did you leave your phone here? I was trying to call you," Stori rambled as she walked over to him.

Nas smiled when she started undressing him like she always did. It was crazy that he was a grown ass man who was spoiled by his wife. Stori did everything that a wife was supposed to do and more. All Nas had to do was pay the bills because she did a great job of running the house.

"I'm good love," Nas assured her with a kiss to the lips.

"What the hell is that?" Stori asked as she pointed to the dog and carrier that he had sat down on the floor.

"A gift for Toi. I guess her name is Fendi. That's what all her stuff says." Nas shrugged.

"Okay Naseem but where did it come from?" Stori questioned.

"Grab the baby monitor and let's take a shower," Nas requested.

Although Stori had already taken a shower, she followed her husband into the bathroom and prepared to take another one. Nas replayed the events of the night to her but Stori wasn't surprised. Carlton's wife had come through for them like she promised and got Milan's address. Nas didn't know how she did it and he really didn't care.

"I know that it had to be done but I just want you and Remo to be safe," Stori said once she and Nas were done showering. She dried Nas off before doing the same to herself.

"We're good baby, I promise," Nas assured her right as his phone started to ring.

"That's Remo," Stori said as she handed it to him. Nas was hoping for good news but not more than Remo. When he answered the phone, he already knew what was up.

"It's positive nigga! I'm about to be a muthafucking daddy!" Remo yelled excitedly as Nas smiled.

"Congrats bro. I'm happy for you, nigga." Nas said. Becoming a father was one of the best things that could have ever happened to him. He was happy that his brother was about to experience it too.

"I'll call you tomorrow bro. I'm about to celebrate and get pissy drunk up in this bitch," Remo said before he hung up the phone.

"What happened?" Stori asked.

"Kalani is pregnant," Nas replied with a smile.

"I know. She took a test earlier because Remo kept stalling," Stori laughed.

"I'm happy as fuck for that nigga. My bro is finally getting him a lil one," Nas replied.

"Are you hungry baby? You want me to fix you something to eat?" Stori asked.

"No but you can come hop in the bed and make another baby with me," Nas winked.

"We can do what it takes to make one but I pop my pills faithfully," Stori replied.

She squealed when Nas picked her up and threw her in the bed. She tried not to think about what he told her in the shower but it was hard not to. She hated what happened to Milan and Corey but it had to be done. Stori knew that they would never have a moment's peace as long as they were around. They were the ones who started the war. It was their own faults that they became casualties of it.

WOR$T CA$E $CENARIO

38

E31119560F

ONE DOLLAR

&&I hope you feel better boo," Stori said as she talked on the phone with Kalani.

She and Remo were supposed to be meeting Stori and Nas at the restaurant but they cancelled at the last minute. Kalani was three months pregnant and morning sickness was kicking her ass.

"Thanks friend. Bring the babies over here before y'all go home. Me and Remo want to see them. I'm going lay down for a little while," Kalani replied before she hung up.

"That baby is fucking over sis," Nas said as he grabbed a napkin from the table to wipe Nakeem's face.

"I know the feeling," Stori replied.

"Your fat ass know you be full and still be trying to eat," Nas laughed as he fed Nakeem some more mashed potatoes.

The twins were seven months old now and their

appetites were something serious. Stori gave up on breast feeding and the bottles didn't even fill them up like they did before. When their doctor said that they could start eating some soft solid foods, that was the best news ever.

"Don't feed his greedy ass no more. He should have had enough by now," Stori fussed.

"I'm not starving my baby Stori. He'll let me know when he's had enough," Nas replied.

"You know he's only gonna start throwing up. They never get full and be throwing up when they get too stuffed," Stori pointed out. Junior had stopped eating and was just sitting in the high chair looking around.

"That nigga better not throw up on me again," Nas said as he stopped feeding him.

Stori wasn't surprised when her son started kicking his little fat legs. At only seven months old, the twins were known to catch temper tantrums. Stori was shocked when it first happened but Nas thought it was funny. He would always tell them to calm down, as if they understood what he was saying. He didn't like it when people did the baby talk thing and he was the only one who never did. He talked to them like he talked to anyone else and he swore that they understood him.

"Aww shit," Stori said when her son started to have a fit.

"That's enough Nakeem. Come on bruh. I know you should be full by now," Nas said as he picked him up from the high chair.

When Junior started crying, Stori knew that it was time for them to go. She was happy that they had already eaten because she wouldn't have been able to enjoy her food if they hadn't.

"I hate when they do us dirty like that. It's like one can't even cry without the other one joining in," Stori fussed.

"They got that twin shit down packed," Nas laughed.

"Call for the bill and let's go," Stori said as she took Junior from his high chair. People were looking at them smiling but there was nothing cute about it. Two crying ass babies in a restaurant was not something to smile about.

"Aww man, this lil nigga got me again," Nas said as Nakeem threw up on his hand and pants. Nakeem had on a bib that was now soaked with his vomit.

"I told you," Stori laughed. She was happy that both babies had calmed down and wasn't crying anymore.

"Why you do your daddy like that bruh?" Nas asked, making Nakeem laugh.

"Go clean him up. I'll take care of the bill and meet you at the car," Stori said as she handed her husband the baby's bag.

Stori reached into her purse and pulled out enough money to cover the bill and tip. She grabbed Junior's bag and headed out of the restaurant to her brand new Mercedes truck that Nas had just purchased for her. She was about to strap her son in his car seat when someone called her name. Stori was shocked when she turned around and saw Gavin standing there smiling at her.

"Damn, those babies really did your body good." Gavin smiled as he licked his lips lustfully.

Gavin hadn't seen Stori in a while but she looked good as hell. She seemed to have more curves than she did before and her ass was sitting up perfectly in her romper. She had her hair pulled back from her beautiful face with a pair of Gucci shades on top of her head. Gavin looked at her son and had to do a double take. He looked like a pint sized version of Nas with the same completion and curly hair. Jealousy consumed him as he continued to eye the baby's features in awe. It was as if he was seeing Nas and Remo in the form of an infant.

It was Gavin's first time being back in New Orleans since he first left. His parents had visited him and Summer a few times but he wanted to bring his girlfriend to his city since she'd never been before. Gavin was doing okay for himself in Texas but he wanted to be doing better. He found a job and was making decent money but it was nothing compared to what he used to make. He was stacking his money in hopes of having his own shop soon. He really didn't want to work in a shop with anyone else. Unlike in

New Orleans, Gavin wasn't trying to make friends in Texas. He was cool with a few people but he never talked his business or hung out with anyone. After losing his wife and almost losing his life, he had definitely learned his lesson. Besides Summer, he spent most of his free time with his girlfriend.

New Orleans would always be home to him but not to live. He would never be safe there and he had good reason to feel that way. Nas and Remo were a different kind of crazy and he learned that the hard way. He was thankful to be alive but not everyone could say that.

Misty and her mother had to come down to identify Milan's body but they had her remains shipped back to Texas and held her services there. Gavin wasn't surprised to learn that Corey had been killed but he was shocked to know that they had been murdered together. He didn't even have to wonder about who did it because he already knew. The police were calling it a drug deal gone wrong but he knew better. They were saying that Corey had a gun on him that was used in two recent murders but Gavin didn't know if that was true or not. Because of that, he seriously doubted if the police were even looking for the murderers. Misty and her mother took it hard, even though they didn't have the best relationship with Milan lately.

"Fuck off Gavin," Stori snapped angrily, pulling him away from his thoughts.

"What's with all the hostility? I was just coming to say hello," Gavin said.

"If I were you, I'd be saying goodbye instead. I guess those bullets made you dumber than you were before," Stori replied.

"It's all good love. Your nigga and his punk ass brother ain't the only ones with guns," Gavin pointed out. He'd never shot a gun before in his life and he prayed that he never had to.

"Maybe not but, unlike you, they're not afraid to use them. And get it right boo. He's not my nigga, he's my husband," Stori corrected as she flashed her huge wedding ring.

Gavin already knew that they were married but that didn't stop him from getting angry. Had anyone told him that Stori and Nas would be married with kids one day, he probably would have laughed in their face. Gavin didn't foresee that outcome and he was blindsided by their relationship. He still had a hard time getting the image of them having sex out of his head. They were too comfortable with each other and that was what had him so baffled.

"I just need to know one thing Stori. The shit has been bothering me for a long time. No matter how many times I've tried to let it go, I just can't," Gavin rambled.

"What the hell are you talking about Gavin?" Stori asked as her face twisted in frustration.

"Were you dealing with Nas while the two of us were together? I know that it's irrelevant now but I just need to know," Gavin said.

"Although I didn't love you like a wife was supposed to love her husband, I honored my vows. I was attracted to Nas the first day I saw him but I never once acted on those feelings until I knew for sure that I was done with you," Stori replied.

Gavin's feelings were hurt but he appreciated her honest reply. Had he known that his wife was attracted to the man that he'd once considered a friend, he would have never welcomed him into their home. He felt sick to his stomach as he thought back to some of the things that he'd told Nas in the past. Gavin basically opened Stori's legs and invited Nas to come fuck her. He now knew better and he swore that he was going to do better. Still, he wasn't about to give the woman that he still loved his blessing to be with a nigga who he now despised. Gavin didn't want them to be happy and he wasn't about to pretend that he did.

"What's up lil man? Looking like your fake ass daddy," Gavin said as he touched Junior's tiny hand.

"Five bullets later and you still don't get it. I guess you want me to commit a murder in the presence of my sons, huh?" Nas questioned as he walked over to his wife's truck. He strapped Nakeem in his car seat before he walked closer to Gavin. Nas was tall, so he folded his arms and looked down on the other man menacingly.

417

"Damn bruh, I never took you for the insecure type," Gavin replied with a smirk.

"And I've never met a nigga who was begging to die. You can't keep dancing with the devil and wonder why you're still in hell. Don't make your mama buy that black dress fam. You're her only child and she doesn't deserve that," Nas threatened with a calm but deadly tone.

"Let it go baby. It's not even worth it," Stori said, as Gavin tried to swallow past the lump in his throat. It wasn't Nas' threat that had him shook. It was the fact that he knew he'd make good on it that had Gavin nervous.

"Dismiss your bitch sweetheart. I don't want my sons exposed to fuck boys. That shit is contagious." Nas frowned as he took Junior out of her arms and put him in the car.

"Get the fuck on somewhere Gavin. If you wanna commit suicide, just put a bullet in your own head. You of all people should know that stepping to my husband is punishable by death," Stori snapped as a woman came walking over to them. She smiled at Stori before she turned her attention to Gavin.

"Hey baby. Are you ready to go?" Gavin's girlfriend asked him. She was in the nail salon with his mother next door to the restaurant that Stori and Nas were in. Gavin had just stepped outside for a minute when he saw Stori walking to her car.

"Yeah, let's go," Gavin replied as he grabbed her hand and hurriedly walked away.

He'd had enough trouble with Nas in the past and he didn't need any more. He should have known that Stori wasn't by herself. According to their Instagram posts, she and Nas rarely did anything separately. They even worked together and had expanded the shop. They were making power couple moves and doing a damn good job.

"Do I need to dust off my guns Stori? I don't have a problem making your ex-husband join my ex-wife," Nas warned.

"Really Naseem? I didn't even want the nigga when I had him. I damn sure don't want his ass now." Stori frowned.

418

"Play dumb if you want to. That nigga is on some obsession shit," Nas fumed as he pulled out of their parking space.

"What!?" Stori yelled as she fell out laughing.

"That shit ain't funny Stori. Stop acting like you ain't peep ole girl out. It ain't no coincidence that you and the bitch kind of look alike," Nas pointed out.

"I know you ain't jealous," Stori said as she looked over at him.

"I don't have a reason to be. He got the Great Value version but I'm rocking with the original." Nas smiled.

"Act like you know then nigga. Gavin ain't no competition for nobody," Stori said.

"Come on now baby. You know a nigga like me don't do no competing. I would have been on my Malcom X shit if I had to. I was getting you by any means necessary," Nas replied.

"How, when I was already married?" Stori noted.

"That nigga was just a placeholder. I had too much hoe in my blood back then to commit to anybody. He just held you down until I was ready for you," Nas said like he was so sure of himself.

"Boy bye. I'm not a cheater. If Gavin wouldn't have fucked up, I would have probably still been in that miserable ass marriage," Stori replied.

"Keep believing that shit if you want to," Nas said.

"It's the truth. We probably wouldn't even be together right now if Gavin wasn't trying to be a hoe," Stori noted.

"Picture your husband getting killed and I'm the nigga who gives you a shoulder to cry on. I'm telling you baby, this shit was happening by force or by choice," Nas assured her.

"It wasn't even that serious," Stori laughed.

"You see them two lil niggas back there?" Nas asked, referring to their sons.

"What about them?" Stori countered.

"It was very serious to me. Shit happened exactly the way it was supposed to. You spent months trying to have a baby for that nigga and it never happened. I came through there and shut shit down on the first night. Nigga gave you a two for one special," Nas bragged.

"Shut up Naseem. I did not get pregnant the first time we had sex," Stori laughed.

"You probably did but all of that is irrelevant right now. I got you and I didn't have to knock a nigga's head off to do it. I always have to be prepared for the worst case scenario though," Nas replied.

"Go to Remo and Kalani's house before we go home. They wanna see the babies," Stori noted.

"We have to get Toi too," Nas reminded her.

"Yeah, I know," Stori replied.

She felt better about letting Toi out of her sight since Corey and Milan were no longer a threat. Toi wanted to go by Maddie and Hannah for a little while, so they dropped her off first. She didn't go anywhere without her dog, so she took Fendi with her. Their old house had sold the month before and an older woman now did hair in the salon. Stori got a nice lump sum of money from it that she added to her savings account. She and Nas had a joint account but he always wanted her to have a backup plan.

They were making good money with the shop and even more now that they sold hair and other hair care products. Stori's clients loved the convenience of it all. They got their bundles from the same place where they got their hair done. Kalani was happy because she no longer worked in the store alone. Even Remo had been doing good in cosmetology school. Nas was teaching him the basics, just as Jaden had done for him, and Remo caught on quick. They were looking forward to the day when they both worked in the shop and got money together.

The strip club was still making nice money and Nas hired Eno on as an assistant manager. Bee didn't have a title and he didn't care, as long as he got paid. Eno still sold pills and weed for them and Stori was trying to teach Nas how to make edibles. He was trying to make sure that he and his family never went broke and he loved having different streams of legal and illegal income. He and Remo were looking to buy a few more houses to renovate and rent out as well. For the first time ever, Jarvis didn't have to worry about his little brothers running wild out there in the streets. He had Stori and Kalani to thank for that and he loved them both.

"Damn baby. We got five more months to plan for their first birthday. That time passed fast as hell," Nas said as he drove to his brother's house.

"I know. I haven't even played around with any party ideas yet," Stori replied.

"I really don't want them to have a party right now. They're too young to really understand all that shit. Let's go on a cruise or some shit," Nas suggested.

"They're too young for that too," Stori pointed out.

"Yeah but I'd rather spend money traveling than on a party that other people will enjoy more than they will. The only time I ever travelled was when I was in jail. That shit don't even count because I was still in Louisiana. I want my boys to have it all," Nas said.

"Okay baby. We can go somewhere for their birthday," Stori said as they pulled up to Remo's house. They weren't surprised to see that Jarvis was already there. He made it a point to see his nephews every day and he didn't care where they were. When Nas parked, he turned to Stori and grabbed her hand.

"I love you baby. Never in a million years did I picture my life being as good as it is now. I was content with cutting hair and selling dope for the rest of my life. Being with you made me want to be a better man. I can honestly say that this is the first time that I've ever loved somebody with my whole heart. Other women don't even exist to me because I'm so happy with you. My only regret is that we didn't do this sooner and have more years together," Nas said as tears spilled from Stori's eyes.

Nas told her that he loved her all the time but he never got that deep. Not only was his words heartfelt and genuine but his facial expression was too. Everybody was always saying that he was mean but Stori didn't see him in that light. She saw the softer side of him as a husband and father. He was an alpha male in every way and he liked to be in control. Stori had to learn how to be submissive because he wouldn't have it any other way.

"That was so sweet Naseem. I love you too, baby," Stori said as she climbed into his lap and gave him a kiss.

Her feelings mirrored his and she was the happiest that she'd ever been too. She remembered being so unhappy at one point in her life that she used to cry every time she took a shower. That was her alone time and her thoughts always came to her then. Now, the only tears she cried were those of joy. Gavin fathering a child out of wedlock was a blessing in disguise. He got out of the way for her real husband to enter the picture. They had two happy, healthy babies and life for them couldn't get any better than that.

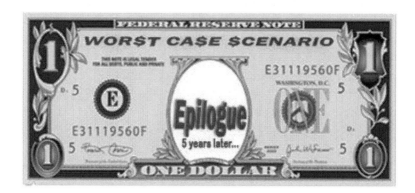

"Aww, he's so cute. He looks just like Keem and Junior," Stori said as she held Kalani and Remo's third child and first son.

Kalani's two daughters, Karly and Kyla, were three and four years old and were a mixture of her and Remo. Kalani had just come home from the hospital the day before with their newest addition. Remo was so excited to finally have a son and he was already asking for another one. Nas and Stori's twins were about to be six and Karly would be five soon after.

"I just hope he don't be bad like their little asses," Kalani laughed.

"I don't know why not. You and Stori kill me with that shit. They're boys and they're supposed to be bad. Y'all want my nephews to be on that feminine shit," Remo spoke up.

"Shut up Kareem. Junior and Keem don't do no

wrong in the eyes of you and Jarvis. I hate to say it but Nassir is starting to act just like them," Kalani said, speaking of Stori and Nas' three year old son.

They now had four kids and their daughter, Nashya, was the baby of the bunch. She was only a year old and Stori felt bad for her already. She had three big brothers and a crazy daddy that would probably make her life a living hell. Nas had her so spoiled that he could hardly take a shower without her. The twins and Nassir were in school, but Nashya went to the shop with them every single day. Nas had a section in the shop set up just for her. She was a crybaby and nobody wanted to keep her. Nas had to put her to sleep just so that Toi would be able to watch her. Lady and Jarvis were the only two who could watch her if Nas and Stori wanted to go somewhere. That was only because they had spoiled her too.

"Bitch, you know it's bad when an ass whipping don't even do the trick," Stori said while shaking her head.

"Come on baby. We need to get going. I don't want my baby waking up and I'm not there," Nas said as he stood to his feet.

"That's a damn shame how you spoiled that baby," Kalani laughed.

"Just wait because my boy is about to be the same way," Remo said as he smiled at his son. His daughters were spoiled too but not more than Shy. Nas wanted a girl too bad, so no one was surprised by that.

"What time is the meeting?" Kalani asked.

"In twenty minutes but I don't care if we're late. I'm so tired of going to this damn school for these lil boys." Stori frowned.

"Man, fuck them people sis. They be calling y'all down there like Junior and Keem are so bad. You want me to go up there again bro?" Remo asked while looking at Nas.

"Hell no Kareem! I don't want you and Jarvis to do nothing else," Stori yelled.

The last time the school called about the twins, Nas and Stori were busy at work. Remo took off that day because Kalani had a clinic appointment, so he and Jarvis volunteered to go. Stori and Nas never got the entire story but they did know that the police had to be called. The twins were angels in the eyes of their uncles but Stori knew that she had given birth to devils in disguise. They acted like younger versions of Nas and Remo and that wasn't a compliment.

"We got it bro. I'll call you later," Nas said as he gave his brother dap and left his house. As soon as he and Stori got into the car, his phone rang, displaying Jarvis' number. He never did give Nas a chance to say anything before he started going off.

"What are them bitches complaining about this time?" Jarvis asked angrily.

"We never got there yet bruh. We're on our way now," Nas replied.

"I want my nephews the fuck up out of there bro. This shit is starting to get ridiculous. They did the same thing last year when they were in Pre-K. All the money y'all pay them and all they do is complain," Jarvis fussed.

"They're not complaining for nothing though Jarvis. Stop acting like Keem and Junior are so innocent. Nobody ever complains on Kalani's girls and Nassir. It's always the twins who keep getting into shit. They're bad as fuck and you and Remo act like y'all are blind," Stori replied.

"Being active is not the same as being bad. They're boys and they have a lot of energy," Jarvis noted.

"So, filling our pool with two containers of red Kool-Aid to dye Fendi's fur is not being bad? It took forever for the dog's fur to grow back after Toi had to get it all cut off. It took a month to get our pool right again," Stori said.

"They were just curious," Jarvis replied like that was normal.

"Oh, my God," Stori said as she sighed in disgust. Jarvis defended everything the twins did and that drove Stori crazy. He went through the same thing when Nas and Remo were younger but he made excuses for his nephews.

The last few years had been very interesting to say the least. Between having four babies, working and running the house, Stori welcomed every vacation that Nas took her on. Her twins were like two living Chucky dolls and her only daughter was a crybaby. Nassir seemed to be the only one who didn't drive her crazy, but the twins were starting to corrupt him too. Her sons had no fear and that's what scared Stori the most. Nas taught them to be tough but they took it to the extreme. They didn't even talk like other kids their age. Nas was saying that he wanted another daughter but he had Stori fucked up.

"You want me to meet y'all over there bro?" Jarvis asked.

"No!" Stori yelled.

"We're good bro. I'll let them call you later," Nas laughed.

"Don't whip my nephews Stori. At least hear their side of everything first," Jarvis said.

"Bye Jarvis," Stori sighed before Nas disconnected the call.

"This shit is starting to get on my nerves man. I feel like we come here every other week," Nas said when he pulled up to the school.

Stori didn't even reply. She just got out of the car and headed for the front entrance. Once they checked in, she and Nas took a seat until the principal called them into the room. When they walked in, Stori was shocked to see that the assistant principal, disciplinarian and the teachers were in there waiting for them as well. That was a little extreme for two five year olds, but it was obviously necessary.

"Mr. and Mrs. Donaldson, thank you so much for coming," the principle smiled.

"You act like we had a choice," Nas snapped in response.

"Baby," Stori said as she grabbed his hand and squeezed it.

"I'm good love," Nas assured her while kissing her hand.

"What seems to be the problem?" Stori asked politely.

"Well, there are several issues that we need to address. The first thing is our inability to tell the boys apart. Naseem sat in the class on his brother's behalf while Nakeem went to fight another student in the bathroom," the principle said.

"That's what the identity bracelets are for," Stori replied.

"Yes but they never keep the bracelets on," one of the teachers chimed in.

"That's all on y'all though. My wife asked y'all to let them wear different shoes but everybody said no. Y'all were too busy worried about all the kids being in uniform, so that's a problem that y'all will have to solve!" Nas barked.

"Naseem, please don't," Stori whispered.

"I'm good baby. I'm not on no bullshit right now," Nas said.

"Oh God," Stori groaned. She already knew what that meant and bullshit was exactly what he was about to be on.

"Y'all call me and my wife every other week complaining about something different. Nobody was complaining when we wrote that fat ass check to help renovate the gym though. Y'all got us at a round table meeting with all these people for two five year olds. The fuck are we paying y'all for if y'all can't even handle them," Nas argued.

The principal's face turned a bright shade of red as everyone else shifted nervously in their seats. Stori wanted to disappear but she held her head high and had her husband's back. Nas could be intimidating at times and no one knew that better than she did.

"Your boys are very smart Mr. Donaldson. Truthfully, they're the smartest two in the kindergarten class but their behavior is not always the best," one of the teachers spoke up.

"Maybe my brother is right. I might need to get my boys the fuck up out of here. I can save money on this high ass tuition and find a school that can get the job done. Go get my kids man. They're leaving early today," Nas ordered.

"That's not why we asked you to come here Mr. Donaldson. Your boys are getting a very good education right here with us. We just want you and your wife to have a talk with them about their behavior. I'm told that Nassir is doing very well in our Pre-K 3 program. Your nieces are doing great here as well." The principle smiled.

"We'll have a talk with the boys tonight. Since it's so close to school being out, we'll take them all home and bring them back in the morning," Stori replied politely.

Kalani's mother usually got her girls from school, so Stori didn't want to take them. She kept them for a few hours every day to give her daughter and son-in-law a little break.

"Of course," the principal smiled as she instructed the secretary to call for all three of the boys.

Nassir was the first to be escorted in. He smiled when he saw his parents standing there and he ran and jumped into Nas' arms.

"What's up bruh?" Nas smiled as he hugged him.

"I want ice cream daddy," Nassir said, just like always. If he could live on ice cream, he would damn sure try. Stori kissed his cheek and he smiled and blushed.

"I got you, lil man," Nas promised right as the twins walked into the office.

They had their curly hair cut into a mohawk just like he used to wear his. They saw an old picture of their father's hair and they wanted the same cut. They asked to get it colored too but Stori wasn't having it. If Nassir wasn't so small, the three of them could have passed for triplets.

"Where are y'all identity bracelets?" Stori asked as soon as they walked over to them.

"Right here," both boys replied simultaneously while holding up their wrists for their mother to see. Stori was no fool and she already knew what was up. Knowing them, they probably put them back on right before they walked into the office.

"Let's go," Stori said as she walked out of the office with Nas and their sons following behind her.

"I'm getting real tired of coming to this damn school for y'all," Nas fussed once they got into the car.

"We didn't even do nothing," Keem said as he looked over at his brother. Junior made a motion with his hands and Keem responded with a hand gesture of his own.

"Stop! Stop it right now! Don't even start that shit!" Stori fussed. She hated that Nas and Remo taught her sons sign language and the school taught it too. She had never taken the time to learn and she was sorry that she hadn't.

"Y'all chill out bruh," Nas warned sternly while giving them a look in the rearview mirror.

"I want ice cream daddy," Nassir chanted.

"I got you, bruh," Nas promised, right as Stori's phone rang.

Toi was calling to tell her that Shy was up and they were at Lady's house. She probably woke up crying and Toi had to bring her to Lady to calm her down. Toi was almost twenty-one years old now and she and Eric had their own apartment. She was in nursing school and he was a welder at a power plant. He was back in school for his business degree and they were doing good for themselves.

"Can we go to the white house to see Mimi and Pops?" Keem asked, referring to Lady and Richard. They had been calling their huge home the white house since they were old enough to talk.

"Hell no. Y'all are punished," Stori replied.

"For what?" Junior asked.

"Man, them people be lying on us," Keem pouted.

"Somebody is always lying on y'all," Nas said as he looked back at both of them.

"Dad, I promise, them people are lying on us. Our uncles said the same thing," Junior swore, referring to Remo and Jarvis.

"You need to stop giving them your money," Keem said as Stori shook her head.

The duration of the ride was quiet but Nas could see that Stori was aggravated. Admittedly, the twins were a handful but he wasn't going to let them stress his wife out. Stori's greatest fear had come true and their sons were an identical version of him and Remo.

"Can we just go speak to Mimi and Pops?" Keem asked.

"Yeah and bring y'all bad asses right back," Nas replied.

"Okay," Junior said as he and his twin hopped out of the car. Nassir had fallen asleep, so he didn't budge. Once the twins were gone, Nas grabbed Stori's hand and turned to face her.

"Talk to me baby. What's wrong?" Nas asked.

"Nothing," Stori replied.

"Don't let them lil niggas stress you out, baby. Just let me handle it. Shit, if Jarvis survived raising us, I know damn well I can survive them," Nas said.

"That's not how this works Naseem. Jarvis raised y'all because your parents passed away. You're not a single father. We're supposed to be in this together. I'm telling you right now Naseem, if we don't get a grip on this shit now, it's only gonna get worse later," Stori replied.

Nas hated to admit it but his wife was right. He saw Keem and Junior headed down the same path that he and Remo were once on. Thankfully, they turned out okay but he wanted better than that for his sons. He didn't want them in and out of jail with bad or no credit. Nassir was paying attention to them and he wanted them to be a good example for him to follow.

"You're right baby. These lil niggas got me out here on daddy mode and I got soft. They must not know that we're the black Bonnie and Clyde around this bitch. We bust our guns together and these niggas come along and want try to run shit," Nas said, making her laugh.

"They're still my babies but they need to know that there are consequences for their actions," Stori replied, right as Lady walked out of the house holding Shy. When she saw Nas, she started screaming for him to hold her.

"Aww, my baby is sleeping. I got him some ice cream," Lady said as she handed Stori a bag with some ice cream cups inside for Nassir.

"Was she crying?" Nas asked as he kissed Shy's chubby cheeks.

"She was when Toi first came over. She calmed down once she saw me though," Lady replied.

"Alright ma, I'll call you later. Tell Toi to come to the house before she goes home," Stori said once the kids got back into the car.

None of the kids had homework, so Stori fed them and Nas made sure they took a bath. Toi and Eric came over for a while to eat and talk. As soon as they left, Nas put Shy and Nassir to bed while Stori cleaned the kitchen. Junior and Keem were always in each other's rooms playing the game, but Nas and Stori had something for their asses.

"You ready to do this baby?" Nas asked as he held his fist out to her.

"Yep," Stori replied as he bumped her fist with his.

Nas had an empty laundry basket in his hand as they walked down the hall to Junior's room. He wasn't in there but that didn't matter. They unhooked all of his electronics and placed them in the basket. Once they were done, they went into Keem's room and found them playing the video game.

"What are you doing ma?" Keem asked when Stori turned off the game and Nas started unplugging stuff.

"Y'all are punished. No game, no tv and nothing else until y'all get it right," Stori replied.

"Dad," Junior said as he looked at his father for some help.

"You heard what she said nigga. And you can go to your own room because you're not sleeping in here. I don't want to hear that people are lying on y'all bullshit. We're tired of coming to that school and y'all are punished until we get a better report," Nas replied.

"We didn't even do nothing!" Junior yelled.

"Who you getting loud with lil nigga?" Nas snapped as he walked up to him.

"Sorry," Junior said in a lower tone.

"Get your ass in that room and go to bed. You too Keem. Go to sleep and I don't want to hear shit else from y'all tonight," Nas barked angrily.

He didn't have to tell them twice. Junior rushed across the hall to his bedroom and Keem pulled the covers over his head. Nas rarely raised his voice and they knew that he wasn't playing.

"Look at you sounding all sexy and shit," Stori said once they walked out of Keem's room.

"You like that baby?" Nas asked her.

"Hell yeah and I got something for you," Stori said as she gave him a kiss.

"Take all that shit off. I'm going put Shy in her crib," Nas said as he slapped her ass.

He picked his baby girl up and prepared to bring her to her nursery that was right next to their room. Once he laid Shy down, he grabbed her monitor and walked out of the room. If Nas would have blinked, he would have missed Keem sneaking out of his room and going into Junior's. That was how fast his son was moving. He could have gone in there and put him out but that would have been useless. The minute he would have gone back to his room, they would have done it all over again. His sons were tight just like he was with his twin. Stori didn't understand that kind of bond and he didn't expect her to. Nas remembered something that his brother said when Stori was pregnant and he was right. Their bond started in the womb and they were close. The twins were definitely Nas and Remo reincarnated just like his brother said. And just like always, Nas was always prepared and ready for the worst case scenario.